INSTINCT

Ike Hamill

INSTINCT

www.ikehamill.com

Cover design by BelleDesign [BelleDesign.org]

ISBN: 0692283838
ISBN-13: 978-0692283837 (Misdirected Books)

Dedicated to
Bruno & Finn

Thanks to Emilio Millán,
who gave me this laptop
so I could write.
Bruno tried to
eat the laptop, but it
survived.

Note to readers:
This is the second book of a pair. If you haven't read *Extinct*, please turn back now. If you choose to press on, I'm not sure any of the following will make sense. You can find *Extinct* at most major retailers, or contact me at ikehamill@gmail.com and I'll help you get a copy. Enjoy!

CHAPTER 1: NEW HAMPSHIRE

"You ready?" Pete asked. His voice was just a whisper.

Brad held up a finger. He pushed aside the curtain and looked across the yard. There was just enough starlight for him to see the minivan parked at the curb. He was more concerned with the concrete walkway that led from the front door to the sidewalk.

Brad turned and pointed to his eyes. He then motioned for Pete.

Pete crawled over to the window and looked. When he drew close, Brad could smell the fear on Pete. It was the same scent he smelled on himself whenever he took off his jacket.

"That was there," Pete whispered, motioning out the window. "It's runoff."

"Don't step on it. Just in case," Brad said. The last three words brought back a memory of his grandfather.

Pete moved back around to the boy's feet and Brad took the shoulders. They exchanged a glance and lifted. The boy wasn't heavy, but when they moved through doors or had to make a dash across a lawn, it was easier for two people to carry him. Pete backed up to the door and held the boy's ankles with one hand while he opened it.

After looking back and forth, Pete moved. They barely slowed for the steps down to the walk. The only time Pete hesitated was when he reached the thin stream of water that ran across the concrete walk. It was a thin dark streak in the starlight. He took a giant step over, moved a little, and then waited for Brad to do the same. The door of the minivan slid open as they arrived. Pete and Brad handed the boy through to the hands that came out from the darkness and then climbed in behind him.

Brad slid the door closed most of the way. He waited for Romie to start the wheels turning before he latched it.

"I need light," Romie said.

"Keep moving," Pete said. "I'm on it."

He ducked down under her legs before he turned on his little flashlight.

Brad helped Lisa lift the boy into place so she could snap a seatbelt over him. Lisa put her hands on his young cheeks and lifted his head up. She looked into his blank eyes and held his head for a second, like she was trying to balance it on his neck. After she was satisfied that it would stay up, she let go and moved into her own seat. Brad sat in the third row.

"Got it," Pete said. When he popped the fuse back into the socket, the headlights came on.

"That's better," Romie said.

✪ ✪ ✪ ✪ ✪

Brad looked out his window at the passing houses. They were all dark. Some of the front doors were open, inviting him into their blackness. He tried to imagine someone asleep in one of the houses. It was impossible. It felt like these houses had been empty forever, and would always be empty. They had a derelict, abandoned look, like empty skulls. There was no life inside.

They rarely talked when they traveled. Romie would slow whenever she saw a streak of liquid across the pavement. Pete would either motion for her to drive through, or signal that they should find another way around. They made terrible progress. Sometimes they would have to backtrack a mile or two just to find another path. Pete always navigated, and he always found another route when their road was blocked by the killer liquid, but sometimes the diversion would add hours to the trip.

Brad tried to sleep. It was impossible. Every time his eyes

drifted shut, an alarm would go off in his brain. He felt like he was falling and he would shoot his legs out to catch himself. His eyes would fly back open and his body would pulse with electricity.

"Stop kicking my seat," Lisa whispered.

"Sorry," Brad said.

When the horizon started to glow orange, Pete directed them uphill. It always felt safest at the higher elevations. They had to get in a building before the liquid started to move again. It moved more in the daylight.

Romie pulled up in front of a tall three-story house. Brick stairs were cut into the hill. The door that led out the side porch was wide open.

Lisa unbuckled the boy.

"I got him," Brad said.

"Are you sure?"

Brad nodded.

Pete, Romie, and Lisa went around back for the bags and Brad pulled on the boy's armpits as he backed out of the van. He crouched on the curb and pulled the boy closer until his waist was on Brad's shoulder. He pulled at the side of the van to stand up with the load.

Brad was panting by the time he got to the top of the stairs. Lisa came out of the house after dropping off their bags. She helped Brad carry the boy into the house. They laid him out on a day bed in the den.

Lisa pulled a bottle of eyedrops from her pocket and squeezed two drops into each of the boy's eyes. She closed his lids and pulled a blanket over him.

"He needs a bath," Lisa said.

Brad nodded. "We all do, I think."

"Good point," she said. She walked out and left him there. Brad sat down in the chair behind the desk. He didn't mean to fall asleep. He was looking through the window at the brightening sky when he drifted off.

"You want some soup?"

Brad opened his eyes to bright sun. His eyes went first to the boy, who was in the same spot where they'd left him. He blinked and saw Lisa standing in the doorway. She was holding out a steaming bowl.

"We should get him on the toilet," Brad said.

"He can wait a few minutes," Lisa said. "He's not squirming yet."

Brad nodded. He stood and propped himself up on the desk until his legs would support him. They were nearly numb from the chair. He took the soup and thanked Lisa.

"What day is it?" Brad asked. He lifted a spoon. It was the vegetable soup with the little letters in it. His mouth already anticipated the salty taste.

"Six," she said.

"I can't do it," Brad said.

"It will be tough," Lisa said. She looked over to the boy. She walked alongside his daybed and laid a hand on his forehead. She pulled back the blankets to expose his upper body before she left.

✪ ✪ ✪ ✪ ✪

The kitchen table was covered with Pete's maps.

There was no reason to keep their voices down, but Brad couldn't help it.

"I know we said one more week," Brad said. "I can't do it."

"I feel the same way," Pete said, "but we have to. Robby would be the first person to say it."

"It's the same as Ted," Romie said. "It's the same as with you."

"No," Brad said. He shook his head. "It's not the same. He's right in there, and he's still alive. If we put food in his mouth, he swallows. If we sit him on the toilet, he goes."

"Take a closer look at him, Brad," Romie said. "Even if he woke up, I doubt he'd be able to walk. He's wasting away."

"You carried him up the stairs on your shoulder. Do you think you'd have been able to do that two weeks ago?" Pete asked.

"Maybe I'm getting stronger," Brad said.

They sat in silence for a minute. Lisa stood and went back to the cabinets. She sorted through the contents again, looking for anything else they should take with them.

"I'll stay here with him. This place is up on a hill. I don't see any damp pavement around. When Robby wakes up, we'll come track you down," Brad said.

"How do you think you're going to find us?" Pete asked.

"Forget about Robby waking up," Romie said. "Who's going to stop you if you try to walk out into the daylight? You think just because we've traveled a few miles, those things aren't around to snatch you up into the air? How long ago was it that Pete tried to walk away? Three days ago?"

"Four," Lisa said.

"Just because nobody has tried to walk off in four days, you think it's safe?" Romie asked.

Brad waited to see if anyone else would try to convince him. He gave his final argument. "I saw Robby do this before. Granted, it was only for a few minutes, but I saw this exact behavior. Judy called it his 'deep cycles'. When Robby is considering a really complex problem, he sometimes disappears into himself. The good news is that when he wakes up, he has the solution to the problem. Don't you want to know what the solution is?"

Nobody answered. Brad tried to look in their eyes, but they all looked away.

Pete was looking down at his maps when he answered. "I guess I'm not confident that our current problems have solutions, Brad."

✪ ✪ ✪ ✪ ✪

When they began to pack up the van, Brad pulled Robby's body from the bed. He lifted him to his shoulder and maneuvered through the door. His hamstrings ached from the morning's exertion, but he had to admit that the others were right—Robby was only a fraction of his former weight. He would chew and swallow when food was presented, but his body burned right through the energy. Brad could feel the heat radiating off of the boy's head. His brain was like a furnace inside there.

Romie slid open the door when Brad came across the walk.

"I thought you were staying," Romie said.

"He has until tomorrow," Brad said. "I'll wait and see the next place."

Lisa was driving. She waited for Brad to buckle Robby in before she pulled away from the curb.

With each mile west, they found more hills. As long as Pete could keep them out of the valleys, they seemed to find less killer liquid that they had to avoid.

Brad decided to break the silence. "Pete, you need to tell me how you can see the difference between normal water and the killer stuff," Brad said.

"It's not hard," Pete said. "The killer stuff looks alive. It pulses. It has a heartbeat."

Thirty minutes passed before Pete was able to show him an example. Brad moved forward and squatted between the front seats. Pete pointed through the windshield at a dark streak across the road. At first, Brad thought Pete was making it up. There was a hill on the right side of the road, and it looked like rain or snowmelt had run down the hill to cross the road. Lisa turned and looked behind them. She was nervous to back the vehicle away from the dark patch of asphalt, but Pete told her to stay put.

"We'll go if it comes at us, but Brad needs to be able to see this," Pete said.

"I'm more worried that we'll get boxed in," Lisa said.

Pete ignored her. "There! Do you see it? It's easy with the headlights."

Brad shook his head. He didn't see anything unusual about the dark spot at all. It just looked like a dark patch of road where water was flowing. There could be a thousand reasons why it was there—spring runoff and blocked drainage was the most likely suspect.

He narrowed his eyes and let the world blur. There was something there. It was really subtle, but there was something there.

"Do you see it?" Pete asked.

"I don't know," Brad said. "Maybe. I guess I need to see regular water now, so I can be sure."

Lisa backed away. Brad went back to his seat.

Brad was trying to keep himself awake when he saw Pete motion for Lisa to stop again.

"What about this one?" Pete asked.

Brad moved forward again. He did the same trick. He let his eyes blur and waited. He couldn't see anything. "I don't know. I don't see anything. I think the other one had a shimmer to it. I don't see it with this one."

"Neither do I," Pete said. He motioned for Lisa to pull forward. They'd all grown accustomed to taking Pete's word for it. He had a perfect track record for spotting the killer liquid. This time, he didn't sound completely confident. Lisa's knuckles went white on the steering wheel as they crossed through the puddle.

Nothing happened.

"See?" Pete asked.

"I think so," Brad said.

"You just have to be extra careful about wishful thinking," Pete said.

"What do you mean?"

Pete leaned over with a folded map. He triggered his headlamp and Brad blinked until his eyes came into focus on what Pete pointed to.

"You see this bridge?" Pete asked. "We would have to go all the way up here if there wasn't a way to get to this bridge. And we're on the only road that goes down into this part of the valley. So that line of water we just crossed was pretty important."

"Why?"

"Because if it hadn't been crossable there, we'd have to go all the way up here to get around," Pete said.

"Oh, I see," Brad said. "You really didn't want to have to sidetrack like that."

"It would have taken hours," Pete said. "So I have to be extra careful. Maybe I thought I saw something, but I just hoped I didn't. You'd do best to err on the side of caution."

"Got it," Brad said.

They were rolling down into a small town. Out here, a lot of the towns were just collections of buildings that surrounded a convenient place to put a mill on the river. Brad had seen a dozen of them—they all looked the same. The road widened with slanted parking spots on each side. They passed under a dark traffic signal.

Lisa slowed at the train tracks. Where the rails cut through the road surface, it was difficult to tell if the dark area was just a shadow, or maybe a thin line of water. Pete examined it through the windshield and declared it safe. They pushed on towards the bridge.

Pete turned around in his seat. "I don't want to get too comfy, but it almost seems like there's pattern to that killer liquid. I'm going to start marking it on the map. It might be a regular grid."

Brad looked out the side window. The river was running fast and high. All the snow melting in the northern part of the state was finding its way down to the ocean. The dam near the brick mill was overrun. The bridge sat high enough over the water that it seemed like it should be safe.

"Guys?" Lisa asked.

Pete turned around.

"Does that strike you as odd?" Lisa asked. She was pointing off to the side. She stopped the van about a third of the way across the bridge.

"What?" Pete asked. He peered into the darkness.

Lisa turned the wheel and gave the van some gas. The headlights swept to the right until they lit up the bridge's railing.

"I don't see anything," Brad said.

"Those cans," Lisa said. She pointed again.

It still took Brad a few seconds to see it. Where the railing met the bridge surface, there was a grate to let rain wash down into the river below. Clustered there, Brad saw four or five soda cans. They would have rolled away except the uneven surface of the grate held them in place.

"Wrappers, too," Pete said.

Pinned into crevices around the cans, Brad saw candy wrappers.

"Litter?" Brad asked. "I don't know..."

He was cut off by a sound from behind him. Brad was s kneeling just behind the front seats of the minivan and he spun c his feet. The sound was coming from Robby's mouth, which hun; open. Romie was sitting behind him. She leaned forward.

"What the hell?" Pete asked.

Robby's moan coalesced into a word. "Noooooo," Robby said.

"Robby? Can you hear me?" Brad asked. He reached out and touched the boy's hand.

Robby's eyes were still dead. They stared forward, focused on nothing at all. "Back up," Robby said. His lips barely moved.

"What?" Pete asked.

The world fell away from Brad. He braced himself on the seats as he dropped. With a bang, the van came to stop and he crashed into the floor.

He spun to see what was happening.

Lisa pushed the shift lever into reverse and gunned the engine. She wasn't looking backwards. Her eyes were locked straight ahead at the bridge that was tearing itself apart in front of them. A crack split through the center of the bridge, separating them from the other bank. The half they were on had fallen several feet.

The structure of the bridge groaned. Brad realized that it sounded just like Robby's moan.

With a thunk, the world dropped another half of a foot. The van's tires squealed on the pavement. It couldn't get traction on the sloped pavement. Just as they began to creep backwards, the bridge dropped again and the tires lost the ground they had gained.

Pete pushed open his door and twisted in his seat to poke his head out.

"We have to get out!" Pete yelled over the noise.

Lisa turned the wheel and the tires caught. They jerked backwards and Brad fell to his ass. He grabbed for Robby's seatbelt and used it to pull himself upwards. The boy's mouth was still open and his eyes stared at nothing. The van hit something behind them and Brad fell into Robby. He grabbed Robby's seatbelt buckle and tried to release the belt.

Lisa revved the engine even higher. The tires screamed and

ething. She thrashed against the wheel, like she
e van to move.

on," Pete said. "We have to get out."

reached for the van door and pulled up on the latch. The vas heavy and he was trying to push it uphill. He got his lder into it and raised it a couple of feet. He reached for bby and pulled at the boy's shirt. Even in his unconscious state, Robby was bracing his legs against falling. He resisted Brad's pull.

"Help me," Brad said to Romie. She was working at her own seatbelt.

"I can't get it undone," Romie said.

Brad heard the rushing water as Pete's door fell all the way open. He heard the engine wind down as Lisa gave up and threw it into park. When she took her foot off the brake, the van slumped forward. The door crunched into Brad's shoulder. By tugging on Robby's arm, he managed to pull him to the side a bit. Robby slid towards Brad.

Pete rolled the door open and Brad pulled Robby around.

Through the window he saw Lisa tugging at the other sliding door. She couldn't open it.

The bridge dropped again with the sound of tortured metal.

Brad pulled Robby from the van and nearly tumbled backwards down the slope of the bridge span. He held Robby with one arm and caught himself on the passenger's door that Pete had left open. He heard the muffled crunch of glass as Lisa used a tool to smash through the van's window.

"Robby!" Brad yelled. "I know you're in there. You have to help me if you want to live."

His voice was almost lost in the sound of the rushing water below.

Pete was holding the sliding door open and reaching his other hand out to help Brad climb the slope of the bridge.

With a loud "tock" the van dropped away a few inches. Brad crashed backwards into the passenger's door again. Pete couldn't help and hold the door open at the same time. He let the door slide shut and reached for Brad's hand.

They locked arms and pulled. Brad got Robby going up the

slope as the van made the "tock" noise again. Brad understood what was happening—the mechanism that was supposed to stop the van from rolling when in park was giving way. The weight on Brad's arm decreased. Robby was moving on his own.

Linked together, the three climbed.

The van slipped again and Pete fell to his knees. He began to slide towards the widening gap behind them. The bridge surface began to vibrate as the rushing water tugged at the collapsing structure. Brad took the lead and pulled at both Robby and Pete. They climbed as the bridge wilted beneath them. Pete got back to his feet and let go of Brad's arm. They threw themselves forward to grab at the crack that opened where the bridge met the bank.

Behind them, the van picked up speed and skidded down into the water. Brad couldn't look back. He knew that if he lost concentration on pulling himself forward, he would be the next to slip back into the water.

He dragged Robby forward until the boy's hands found the crack. With both arms unburdened, Brad was able to climb the steep surface. He reached forward and his hand couldn't get enough friction on the horizontal road. He tried to dig his fingernails into the asphalt. Beside him, he sensed that Robby and Pete were doing little more than hanging on.

An arm shot out of the darkness and grabbed his hand.

Brad looked up to see Romie.

✪ ✪ ✪ ✪ ✪

They climbed up onto the road and crawled away from the edge. Lisa helped Robby, and Romie gave a hand to Brad and Pete. When they got to safety, they all collapsed to the pavement. When a piece of the bridge groaned and tore away, Brad scrambled back another couple of feet.

"Flood damage?" Romie asked.

"Maybe," Pete said.

"Maybe not," Lisa said.

"Why do you say that?" Brad asked.

"There were cans and soda wrappers," Lisa said. "It looked to me that someone had waited up there for a while. Maybe they were standing guard while someone sabotaged the bridge."

"Why would someone do that?" Brad asked.

"Maybe the killer liquid, and fire monsters, and snatchers aren't the only things to be afraid of around here," Pete said.

"How did you get out?" Brad asked, turning to Romie.

Lisa held up something in the darkness. Brad didn't have to see it to understand. Lisa had given them all the same tool. It was something she had found in a convenience store. One end had a plastic cap protecting a sharp point for smashing car windows. The other end had a recessed blade you could use for cutting through a seatbelt.

"How did he get out?" Romie asked. She pointed to Robby.

The boy still had the same empty look on his face. He was staring straight forward and sitting next to Brad.

Brad reached out and shook the boy's shoulder. He didn't respond.

"I don't know," Brad said. "But he definitely moved on his own when his life was threatened."

"Speaking of which," Pete said. "We can't stay here. It's too dangerous to be outdoors like this."

They began to push to their feet.

"I need more maps. We have to get all new gear. All our traveling food was in there," Pete said.

Lisa put her hand on his elbow and Pete trailed off. She was staring off into the night.

"What?" Pete whispered. His voice was carried away by the sound of the river.

"I saw something," Lisa said. She pointed up the street.

All Brad could see was the dark traffic signal. It was bobbing and swaying in the wind. The buildings were dark. The windows were black rectangles cut into the sides. On the left, the big windows looked like they belonged to a general store. On the right, Brad saw a place he imagined had sold appliances or furniture. There were one or two cars parked in the spaces. Brad wondered how far up the hill they'd have to walk to find another suitable vehicle. It wouldn't be comfortable to pack all five of them into one of the little cars he saw. Plus, they would need to find a set of keys.

"Where?" Pete asked.

"Up there," Lisa said. "On the left. Second floor, fourth window down."

The windows above the stores could have belonged to offices or maybe even apartments for the owners. Brad counted out the windows, but he didn't see anything there.

"What did you see?" Pete asked.

"I don't know," she said. "It might have been a candle, or a flashlight."

"Maybe it was just a shooting star reflecting off the glass," Pete said.

She didn't say anything. Brad saw her head shaking in the dark.

"Let's go find a car," Pete said. He started to walk.

Brad turned to Robby, who was still sitting on the pavement. He reached down under the boy's shoulders to lift him. At Brad's touch, Robby rose on his own. Brad found that he could just tug on Robby's arm and the boy would walk. Brad kept his eyes on the window as they walked by the building.

CHAPTER 2: NEW YORK

JUDY THOUGHT: *THEY HAVE no idea how dangerous he is.*

Luke was a chameleon as he moved through the group. He swaggered over to a group of bearded men. These were the type of men who always seemed to have a rifle slung over their shoulder. To them, Luke projected a brash confidence that resonated with their rebel spirit. When Luke moved on to talk to the two family-types—people who had clumped together into more or less nuclear families—he dropped the swagger and adopted a thoughtful, mellow demeanor. With the cynical young people, he had an acerbic wit. With the older group, Luke appeared both proud of and offended by the state of the world around him.

"Well?" a voice asked from behind her.

Judy jumped. She fumbled her hands to her shirt pocket to reach for a pack of cigarettes that wasn't there. She had quit days before, but her hands hadn't gotten the message yet.

"Well, what?" she asked. She turned to look at Ron.

"Do you think there's any chance we'll get there today?" Ron asked. "Or are we going to spend another night under the stars?"

"Either way we'll be under the stars. You don't think there will be housing for everyone, do you?" she asked. She folded her arms to keep her hands from searching for another pack.

Ron shook his head and swept his eyes through the parking lot. They were waiting for the raiding party to come out of the grocery store. Judy hated this part of the day. It was always miserable.

Waiting was terrible—after what had happened in New Hampshire, she felt on edge all the time. The only thing worse than waiting was when she was picked for the raiding team. Going into a dark store, full of rotting smells and a shifting shadows, felt like robbing a grave.

"Look at him," Ron said as Luke moved on to the next faction of their group. "It's like he's running for office."

"I can't tell if you're attracted to him, or just afraid," Judy said.

"Both," Ron said. "Why wouldn't it be both? Try to act normal. Here he comes."

"Hey, Luke," Ron said. There was just a tiny bit of flare at the end of his greeting. Judy heard just the tiniest hint of flirtation there.

"Ron," Luke said. He put his hand on Ron's shoulder and steered him away from Judy. She heard Luke conveying some contrived task to Ron as they walked away. This was Luke's process—he wouldn't say, "I need to talk to Judy." He would come up with some reason to pull Ron away and double back. Judy was tempted to walk away before Luke could return. She wasn't interested in dealing with a chameleon at the moment. She stuffed her hands into her pockets—still no cigarettes there—and turned towards the bushes.

"Judy," Luke called. When they'd first met, Luke had poured on his southern accent. Back then her name sounded more like "Jew-uh-dee," coming from his mouth. Judy had a low opinion of southern drawls, and somewhere along the way Luke had figured that out and adjusted accordingly. Now he hardly sounded southern at all when they chatted.

"I was just..." she said. "Bathroom, you know?"

"Sure," Luke said. "Just give me a second, would ya?"

"Sure," she said. She tried to swallow her sigh and make it sound like a normal exhale. She was somewhat successful.

"I wanna get your opinion on morale. How do you think everyone is doing with this whole trip thing?" Luke asked.

"The whole 'trip thing'?" Judy asked.

"Yeah," Luke said. He lowered his voice. "People trust you. What can we do to keep them moving for another few days?"

"Few days?" Judy asked. "I thought we were going to get to your ranch today or tomorrow? Why would it be another few days?"

"You know how people are," he said. "We have to under promise and over deliver at this point in time. I'll say a few days and then ev'ryone will be excited when we show up."

"Just be honest, Luke," she said. "You need to be honest."

"Oh sure, sure," Luke said. "I'm an open book."

"Really?" Judy asked. "Let me ask you something—why have you had guys with guns around the camp every night? What happens if I decide I want to leave? Would they shoot me?"

"What?" Luke asked. He looked sincerely shocked by the concept. She wondered if swaggering Luke—the one who had been talking to the bearded rednecks—would also be shocked. "Those men were doing everything they could to keep everyone safe. If we have to post a thousand guns around this group to keep us safe, that's what we'll do."

"Have you seen anything out here that could be stopped with a gun?" Judy asked.

"I don't pretend to know all the dangers we face, Judy," Luke said. He was in full politician mode now. "If you get a chance, could you maybe chat up some of the others? Maybe give them some more hope to cling to? I know a little change in morale would carry us a long way."

"Sure, Luke," she said. She wondered how many other people he'd tasked with the same mission. By nightfall they would all be trying to convince each other of the same thing.

Luke left her and walked off towards the front of the store. He passed by the bearded men again and that swagger came back, if only for a few seconds. He patted one of the men on the back and they shared a laugh. Judy reached for her cigarettes again.

Ron jogged up and pulled in a big lungful of air to catch his breath.

"What did I miss?" Ron asked.

"Nothing," Judy said. "He's running for president again. What did he have you do?"

"I was scouting the road to make sure our escape route is

clear."

Judy nodded.

"He pretty much admitted that we aren't going to get there for a few days," Judy said.

"What?" Ron asked. "Two days ago, it was supposed to be yesterday. Then yesterday he said today. Are we getting farther away from this place?"

"What makes you think there's a place?" Judy asked.

"He wouldn't drag us across four states to some made up Eden, would he?" Ron asked. "Tell me we haven't been hunting snipe."

"I don't know what he's doing," Judy said.

"I'm going to go ask him. This is absurd. Why can't he just show us on a map where he's taking us to? He can't keep it secret forever. We're going to live there, right? I'm going to go ask him."

Judy put a hand on his arm before Ron could walk away.

"Don't do that," Judy said.

The raiding party burst from the doors of the store with shopping bags loaded down. It was the same thing they always got: dry goods, bottled drinks, and cans. The people carrying the bags looked like a strange collection of train robbers. They had bandanas pulled up over their noses to help filter out the smell and mold. Judy went to help load the food into the vehicles.

✪ ✪ ✪ ✪ ✪

Judy woke to a single shot. She knew the sound. The people who carried guns always seemed to find some excuse to fire the weapons. They claimed that they had to adjust the sights, mostly. But it was dark out. She raised a hand to block out the light from the overhead lamp. The Land Rover bonged a tiny chime to alert everyone that the driver's door was open.

"What are we doing?" Judy asked the woman in the passenger's seat. Her name was Erika, and Judy had only talked to her a few times.

"There was a fire up ahead," Erika said. "I think someone shot at it."

"Shot at a fire?" Judy asked. She didn't wait for an answer. She spilled out into the night and moved away from the line of vehicles to get a better perspective. She saw a line of Land Rovers with their doors open and people walking towards the front of the line. This wasn't protocol. At the sign of a threat they were supposed to disperse and collect again at the last rally point. Judy glanced behind herself. There was a thin strip of woods and then a neighborhood. It would be easy to hide in one of those houses until the group gave up on her. She wouldn't be the first person to try to desert the group. She took a step backwards.

Ron appeared at her side.

"What are they doing?" he asked.

"I have no idea," Judy said.

"We shouldn't all be wandering around. It could be dangerous."

Judy nodded.

"Come on," she said. "Let's go find out why everyone is crazy."

✪ ✪ ✪ ✪ ✪

Luke had climbed atop the horse trailer and someone handed up a pair of binoculars to him.

"I see six. Maybe seven. Listen," he said. He took the binoculars away from his face and looked down at everyone. "These things go after anything mechanical as far as I figure. We go down there on foot and I think we can skirt right around them."

Judy bit her lip. The group was silent. She looked around at her fellow travelers and wondered why they weren't all grumbling at the thought. They'd been on the road a long time in those same vehicles. They had a process.

"Don't you think we should find a way around them, Luke?" Frank asked. If Luke was the president, Frank was the VP in charge of asking obvious questions. When Frank expressed a dissenting opinion, it was always so Luke could argue it down and shut the book on the opposition. This, on the other hand, sounded like an honest question.

"No," Luke said. "We're too close, Frank."

Luke began to slide backwards to the ladder bolted to the side of the trailer. He lowered himself down.

"I'll take Cincinnati and scout it out. The rest of you start putting supplies into bags so we can carry them. Wake everyone up and get ready to travel on foot," Luke said.

He opened the side door of the trailer and started talking low to the horse inside. Judy chewed on her thumbnail and looked at the group. Nobody was following orders. Luke emerged from the trailer and moved around back to open the doors and lower the ramp.

"Get moving," Luke said. "If those things spotted the vehicles, they'll be on their way. It's mechanical stuff they like. Houston, why don't you take one of the Rovers in back and drive it away from the group. Leave it runnin' and shut th'others down." Amongst the bearded men, Frank and Luke were the only ones who went by their real names. All the rest of the bearded guys were nicknamed for the town or city where they'd been born.

Judy began to move back towards the vehicle she'd been riding in. She'd left her bag on the seat. It only had a few things in it, but they were the things she counted as her own.

"Hey!" Ron called. "Judy, wait."

"What?" she asked, turning.

Ron got close and talked low.

"Are you thinking about bailing out?"

"No, of course not," she said. There was no version of her plan that worked better with Ron in tow.

"Because if you were, I think we could follow Frank back to that vehicle and wait for him to leave it running," Ron said.

"Don't be crazy."

Judy walked fast, hoping to leave him behind. The Cruiser she'd been riding in was empty. Erika and Mike, or Matt, or whatever his name was, had already grabbed their stuff. Judy snatched her bag and moved out of the way as people arrived to pull the storage bins down from the roof. Some of the Cruisers were packed full of people. They liked to clump together with friends and turned the act of travel into social bonding. Judy always migrated to a Cruiser that carried supplies. With only one or two people inside, they were quiet and Judy could read. She wasn't close with any of these people. She spent more time with Ron than anyone else, and she merely tolerated him.

Judy put her bag over her shoulder and inched backwards out of the light from the vehicles. The woods, and their complete darkness, were only a few paces away. If she could cover that distance, she could slip away while everyone was busy.

"Can you grab the other end?" a man asked.

Judy looked around. Everyone else had their hands full. He was talking to her.

"Sure," she said.

The man was Brighton. He had a big frame that looked like it was built to carry a lot more bodyweight than he had. She picked up the other end of the storage bin and gripped under the plastic lip. It wasn't too heavy, but it was bulky. It was about the right size to be a child's coffin. Judy shook her head to clear the image. Brighton turned and held the thing behind him so he could walk forward.

They started walking towards the front of the line. Ron fell in behind her. He was carrying a bag over each shoulder. They swung and banged on his thighs as he walked.

Their group was clustered at the front of the line of vehicles. One of the bearded men, Chester, was on top of the trailer with the binoculars.

"He's getting close to the first one," Chester said. "It's not moving."

"Can we set this down?" Judy asked Brighton.

"Sure," Brighton said. He lowered his end and Judy dropped hers. Ron was right behind her, so she moved to the side, like she was trying to get a better look down the hill. Frank jogged up out of the dark. All the lights and engines were off now, except the one vehicle that Frank had moved away from the others. It looked like a lonely island of light off in the distance. In the other direction, the fires burned like little candles.

"Get down from there, Chester," Frank said.

He climbed up to replace the man, and then ended up doing the same thing Chester had been doing. He took the binoculars and said, "I think he's looking at the fire. He's coming back."

Frank didn't give any more progress reports, but he stayed up there. After a second, they could all hear the sound of Cincinnati's hooves beating their way up the hill. Luke arrived at a trot and came to a stop. He stayed up on his horse to issue his commands.

"Okay," Luke said. "Let me get Viv, Bill, Daniel, and Judy. Can you guys come forward. Not you, Bill, I mean Bill Cody."

Judy looked around and tried to gauge her odds of escape. If she dropped her bag, she might be able to sprint towards the woods and get away. It was hopeless and she knew it. There were two members of Luke's militia just a few paces away. They had flashlights and guns. She couldn't come up with a reason why they would shoot her, but she had no doubt that they would.

"Where's Judy at?" Luke said.

Eyes turned towards her and she started to move forward.

"The rest of y'all are gonna disperse into these woods. Just stay low and stay put until I come back for you. It won't be long," Luke said.

Judy frowned. Everyone else was now being ordered to do the thing she had planned.

She arrived next to Viv and Daniel. Bill Cody was still fumbling with something from a bag that his girlfriend was holding. He hugged her tight before he came to join them.

Frank's bearded militia organized the others into groups to go hide by the roadside. Luke circled back to his hand-picked four and looked down at them from atop Cincinnati.

"What are we doing?" Bill asked.

"I want you guys to act as representatives," Luke said. "You're going to introduce us to the locals."

"Locals?" Viv asked. "There are locals?"

"So it seems," Luke said.

✪ ✪ ✪ ✪ ✪

Daniel walked in front and Bill Cody brought up the rear. Viv and Judy walked side by side. They walked down the middle of the dark road, staying on the double yellow line. They passed by an abandoned car on the side of the road. Judy had seen plenty of these. She knew what would be inside. The keys would be in the ignition, the battery would be dead, and there would be no gas in the tank. They were beyond the eye-popper zone. Around here, the residents had simply disappeared. The world was a ghost town. Dinners were still set on tables, faucets still open in shower stalls, and keys still in the ignition.

Judy didn't like the way their footsteps seemed to die around them. There was no echo in the night. She glanced back at the distant light of the Land Cruiser up on the hill. Right when she looked, someone shut the lights off. Their beacon was gone. Now they just had the seven flames they were approaching.

"Why us?" Viv asked.

"Hush," Bill whispered. "Don't give away our position."

Judy had a pretty good idea of why they'd been chosen. With the exception of Bill Cody, they were singles. And Bill just had a girlfriend. He hadn't really linked up into a whole family unit yet. The four of them looked normal, kept themselves clean, and weren't entrenched in Luke's little society. They were decent ambassadors, and they were completely expendable.

They were close enough to see the first flame. It wasn't some mysterious column of fire, like Luke had described seeing down south. This was just a torch, stuck into the ground by the side of the road. Judy couldn't even tell why it was there at first. There was a gentle bend in the road, but it didn't seem significant enough to mark with a torch.

"Oh," Daniel said.

"What?" Bill asked.

Daniel came to a stop. Judy walked up next to him. The torch was still a ways off, but she understood it significance. The torch marked a spot where the road was washed out. Because of the slope and the bend, you couldn't really see it. If not for the torch, the washout might look like a shadow on the pavement until you crashed down into the gully.

Judy moved forward alone. She got closer and verified her assessment. The seven torches simply marked the spot where the road was impassable. On the other side of the pavement, she saw black skid marks. Apparently, someone else had seen the washout just in time.

Judy turned back to the other three.

“Look, we don’t have to do this,” Judy said.

“What do you mean?” Bill asked. He glanced back up the hill, where his girlfriend was hiding back there in the darkness.

“Whoever put these up might be friendly, or they might be dangerous. We don’t know. There’s no reason why we have to risk our necks.”

Bill didn’t hesitate to argue. “We all sacrifice for each other. It’s our turn.”

“We do things as a group,” Judy said. “Since when are people expected to stick their necks out alone? We’re being used as pawns here.”

“We’re here voluntarily,” Bill said.

“No, she’s right,” Daniel said. “The question is, what other choice do we have?”

“We could run,” Judy said.

“Leave the group?” Bill asked.

“Could we make it on our own?” Vivian asked.

“Or whatever,” Judy said. “All I’m saying is that we don’t have to walk right into danger just because Luke told us to.”

“I’m going,” Bill said. “It might be dangerous, but everything is dangerous. Just waking up is dangerous. I’m going to do my part for the good of the group.”

He started to walk around Judy. With that action, the debate was over. Viv and Daniel followed Bill. Judy stood there for a second and then followed as well.

By the light of the torches, they climbed through the washout and walked around the bend in the road. On their left, the trees thinned out and were replaced with a single line of tall trees, bordered with a three-rail fence. An open field swept up to a set of buildings outlined against the sky. The driveway was farther up the road, but there was a footpath trampled through the grass near the washout. Bill followed that.

Judy arrived at the fence as Bill was climbing over it.

“Watch out,” Bill said. “That wire is live.”

“What?” Viv asked. “Ouch!” she said.

"Hush," Bill said.

Next to her, Daniel extended a finger towards the fence. On the inside of the rails, there was a bare wire strung. When his finger got close enough, a blue spark jumped out to his finger. Daniel jerked his hand back.

"It's not bad," he said.

Judy watched the way he climbed over and then reproduced his actions.

"They have electricity. That's encouraging," Daniel said.

Bill started up the hill. The grass was short and tidy in the field, but was dotted with the occasional weed. Bill veered around something and when Judy reached the spot she saw that it was manure. Farther up the hill, a cluster of big animals bolted off into the night. The four of them stopped. When the animals crested the hill and disappeared, they began walking towards the house again.

As they neared, Judy saw that the first building was a big white estate. Behind it, several barns or outbuildings stood. All the windows were dark in the house.

"What do we do?" Viv asked. "Go up and knock?"

"I suppose," Daniel said.

Bill apparently had another idea. He climbed over the fence that separated the pasture from the lawn. When he landed on the other side, he broke into a trot. Judy was just climbing down the other side when Bill was already looking into one of the dark windows.

"What's he doing?" Viv asked.

Nobody answered. Daniel, Viv, and Judy, stood there on the lawn. The grass was ankle high and damp with dew. Bill rounded the side of the house and they couldn't see him anymore.

They turned when the animals in the pasture thundered by again. She couldn't really see them, but Judy assumed they were horses. She couldn't imagine what else would run that fast. As if to confirm her speculation, one of the animals let out a questioning whinny. After a few seconds, it was answered by an animal from much farther away. Judy wondered if maybe Cincinnati was on the other side of that call.

Finally, Bill came around the other side of the house. He ran back over to them.

"I don't think there's anyone inside," Bill whispered.

"What about that person?" Viv asked. She was pointing towards the house. Judy looked up as the front door opened. In the darkness, they saw a candle appear.

✪ ✪ ✪ ✪ ✪

Viv approached first, She paused at the steps and waited for the others to catch up.

"Hello?" she asked.

The candle wavered and then the door opened wider. Judy saw the shape of the person holding the candle. She couldn't see the face.

"Sorry to show up in the middle of the night," Viv said. "Can we talk to you?"

"Please," a woman's voice said from the darkness. "Come in."

CHAPTER 3: PENNSYLVANIA

"THERE'S A BIG ONE," Tim said. "Do you see a spot to land?"

He glanced at his companion. The Golden Retriever probably couldn't hear him. Tim wore his headphones out of habit and because the airplane was too loud without them. His voice was picked up by his microphone and echoed back into his own ears, so he didn't talk all that loud. He circled the stretch of highway three times to make sure it looked okay for a landing. Everything looked clear, but he still felt nervous as he executed his landing checklist. He had one added item on the bottom of his list: check Cedric's harness. He reached over and made sure the dog was strapped in. Cedric seemed to have a pretty good understanding of landing at this point, but safety was paramount.

They touched down on the dashed white line and rolled to a stop.

Tim looked through every window before he cut the engine. He kept his hand on the throttle, ready to run it back up. There was nothing out there—just a stretch of highway with suburbs on one side and a junky field on the other.

Tim spoke again as the engine wound down.

"Power lines, streetlights, overhead signs," he said to the dog. Cedric looked over at him. "If a crosswind comes up, we have to get out of here fast. I should have picked a wider chunk of road."

Cedric fidgeted in his seat. The dog knew from experience that he had to wait for Tim to release him from the harness, but he was itching to get out of the plane.

"Hold on," Tim said. "Let me chock the wheels first."

Cedric let out a tiny sound.

"Hold on," Tim said again.

He opened his door and jumped out quick. The brake would hold the plane as long as the road wasn't sloped too much. It was hard to tell. He kicked the wooden blocks under the wheel and climbed back in. When he unbuckled the harness, Cedric squeezed by Tim and bolted through the door.

Tim shoved his map into a bag and followed the dog out.

✪ ✪ ✪ ✪ ✪

"It seems pretty nice so far," Tim said.

Cedric was peeing on the side of a concrete barrier. He finished and began sniffing at some trash by the side of the road.

"Come here, Cedric," Tim said. He pulled a leash from his bag. Tim unbuckled his belt, threaded the end through the handle of the leash, and then buckled his belt again. He clipped the other end of the leash to Cedric's harness.

Cedric stayed at his side as Tim walked the length of the retaining wall. The top of the wall sloped down towards the road, as did the hill it held back. On the other side of the bank was the entrance to the highway. Just beyond that, a tall concrete barrier rose at least twenty feet. This is what Tim came to see.

He kept his eyes pointed at the ground. Tim blocked out most of his vision with a hand. He saw the corner of red graffiti on the wall. It was about twenty yards away, but that was close enough.

"If I screw up, you know what to do," Tim said to Cedric. He pulled his camera from his pocket and got it ready before he raised it.

✪ ✪ ✪ ✪ ✪

Tim's eyelids fluttered. He heard the dog panting and the scraping of a body against sandy pavement. He felt the grinding on the back of his head. The scraping sound was him.

"Okay, okay," he said. His voice was slurred. He was stretched out on the side of the highway. From his belt, the leash was stretched tight over to Cedric's harness. The dog was still pulling, dragging him down the road. "That's enough. I'm awake."

Tim was careful to close his eyes as he rolled over to his stomach. Cedric ran over to him. His legs were tangled in his leash and his tail was wagging so hard that it created a breeze.

"Thank you," Tim said. He pushed up to his hands and knees and then touched the back of his head. It was sore, but not bleeding. Tim unclipped the leash and then removed it from his own belt. He crawled down the length of the retaining wall until he was sure it would block out the far wall with the graffiti.

The camera dangled from the strap around his neck. Tim covered half of the display with his hand and powered the camera on. The first thing he checked was the clock. It read 11:50am. It wasn't accurate, but it would tell him how much time had elapsed. He checked the time on the first picture. It read 11:25am.

"That was twenty-five minutes," he said to Cedric. The dog was digging in the sand at the side of the road. "That's the longest yet. That thing must be huge."

He scrolled through the first few pictures. They wouldn't have an effect as long as he kept his hand over half of the image, but he didn't want to take a chance. He only looked at half of them before he shut the camera off.

Cedric unearthed a tennis ball from the sand. He squeezed it in his jaw with his tongue hanging out to the side.

"That's disgusting," Tim said. He pulled his bag from his shoulder and tucked the camera inside. He dug around until he found a new tennis ball. "You want this one? It's clean at least."

Cedric dropped the ball he'd found and looked off into the distance. Tim turned slowly to see what the dog was looking at.

"Shit," Tim said. He dropped the ball he held and ran.

✪ ✪ ✪ ✪ ✪

Tim tried to focus on the preflight checklist, but his breath was coming fast and his eyes wanted to glance back over his shoulder.

Cedric emitted a low and steady whine.

"I know, I know, I know," Tim mumbled as he worked his way down the list. "Fuck it." He tossed the book over his shoulder and ran up the throttle. The plane didn't move.

"Chocks!" he yelled. Tim reached for the door handle. His eyes locked on the sky and he froze. Each funnel cloud was spinning clockwise, but the whole circle of them revolved counter-clockwise. They rose up and down like needles on a destructive sewing machine.

Tim licked his lips. They were numb.

Behind him, Cedric barked. Tim whipped around and in the corner of his eye he saw the wheel chocks on the back seat. He had remembered to remove them after all. Tim looked down and saw that the brake was still engaged. When he released it, the plane began to roll.

Tim fumbled through a hasty takeoff. As soon as he cleared the power lines, he turned east to put the tornadoes at his back. The plane bounced through choppy air. Tim fumbled his headphones on as soon as he could. Blocking out the sounds of the plane brought him more focus. He retrieved the laminated book with the checklist and worked his way through. Even in a panic, he'd managed to do most of the items. Flying the little plane was starting to become instinct, but he knew he needed to maintain his diligence.

When he'd been through the list twice, and was sure that the plane would stay in the air, Tim worked on Cedric's harness. He got the dog clipped in and comfortable. Tim finally took a deep breath. He used the bodies of water and highways to place himself on the map and set the plane on the proper heading to get him home. It wouldn't be difficult once he got within a hundred miles. He'd flown enough to recognize a ton of landmarks around his house, especially on such a clear day.

"I think we should head north tomorrow," Tim yelled to Cedric. The dog turned towards him.

The ground marched by steadily below them. Hills transitioned to a valley, where roads branched out to service a community. Tim let his eyes wander to the south. Somewhere below that haze, where the land met the sky, was the end of the intact world. He'd flown that way a few times, but promised himself he'd never go back. It was too depressing to see all that black earth, ravaged by fire and patrolled by columns of multicolored flame.

Cedric didn't like going south either. It was probably something in the air. Some smell made the dog whine whenever they got within ten miles of the scorched land.

Tim let himself zone out while the plane floated along. The air was smooth here and the sun heated up the interior of the plane. It was peaceful and relaxing to listen to the drone of the engine. Even Cedric's head was beginning to droop when Tim spotted the familiar ridge. He sat up straight and Cedric woke up too.

"There we go," Tim said. "Better alert the tower."

His thumb strayed to the radio's trigger, but he didn't press it. At night, he could trigger the runway lights with that switch, but there was no need in the middle of the afternoon. Tim executed his checklist and brought the plane down gracefully.

When the engine was off, Tim released the harness. Cedric bounded off towards the house.

Tim dragged the hose over to the tank's inlet and walked back to the hand pump. He had an electric pump hooked up to a generator, but it seemed silly to waste gas to pump gas. It was just as easy to pump by hand. Before he put the plane to bed he ran through a list of his own. He had a number of chores that other pilots might consider superstition. Tim liked a routine. He liked superstition.

When Tim walked across the lawn, Cedric dropped his bone and picked up a frisbee. He dropped it at Tim's feet.

"Not right now," Tim said. "I want to copy these pictures and start dinner first."

There was plenty of time for play. It was a beautiful evening and the sun would be out until at least eight.

Tim compromised. He started some rice cooking on the propane burner and set a timer. Then, he took his computer out to the back deck. Cedric brought him a ball and he tossed it into the tall grass. He settled back into his chair and put his feet up on the picnic table.

He opened his images.

The window that showed the images was placed carefully so that he could only see half of a photo at once. All he really cared about was the edges anyway.

The latest images were the most powerful he'd seen. Even looking at only half of it could make him feel dizzy. As he knew from earlier that day, if he looked at the whole thing, he might be unconscious for twenty-five minutes. The laptop monitor was set to shut itself down after one minute, but he still wanted to be careful. The rice would be done in twenty.

The image showed the big concrete wall next to the highway. Along the bottom, someone had used black spray paint to write, "BRO," down the length. That paint was faded compared to what Tim cared about. Tim was interested in the big red symbols. They probably stretched down fifty yards of the wall and some of them were fifteen feet in the air.

Cedric dropped the ball at the side of Tim's chair. He reached down and picked it up. He held it while he spoke.

"They must have used a ladder, or maybe one of the those bucket trucks," he said.

Cedric sat and panted, waiting for Tim to throw the ball. Tim stared at one of the big red symbols painted on the wall. It must have been four feet high. On his screen it was only a couple of inches. It looked like a spiral made of right angles. The line went up, took a right, went across, took a right. The lines weren't exactly parallel as they spiraled in though. They were off by a few degrees so the thing looked like it twisted clockwise as the segments got smaller and smaller. The lines were thinner too, almost like they were getting farther away. The twisting lines could have been painted on a tunnel that went right into the wall. It was a place you could walk into and explore...

Cedric barked.

Tim shook his head and covered the symbol with his hand. He tossed the ball for the dog and scrolled the image so the spiral would move off the screen.

"Powerful," he muttered.

At the edge of the mural, he saw something familiar. The red symbol almost looked like a rough representation of a person sitting in a chair. He'd seen it before. Tim had the other images named for the places where he'd found them. He pulled up an image he'd catalogued as "Roanoke: Edges." This would be just the edges of a mural he'd photographed down in Virginia. There it was —on the right side of this image, a symbol matched the one he saw on the left side of his Dayton picture. A couple of smaller glyphs were a match as well.

Cedric dropped the ball. He had mud on his front feet.

"You're filthy," Tim said. "What do we do about your hair in the summer? Did they used to shave you or something? Does it need brushing?"

The timer went off in the kitchen. Tim threw the ball again and closed his laptop.

After dinner, Tim confirmed his find and verified the other edge of the photograph. He had his laptop on the round kitchen table.

"That's it," he said to Cedric. The dog looked up and tilted his head. He was sitting on the braided rug in front of the stove—his favorite place. Tim noticed that the dog had brought his muddy tennis ball inside. "We've got pictures of the whole thing, I think."

On one of his maps, he had made notes of all the locations. Tim unfolded the map and spread it out.

"The closer the mural is to the burn zone, the bigger it is, generally. They make a semicircle that ends down in Wilmington. I wonder if there are any under the ocean."

Tim smiled at the idea of an underwater society with big red murals painted on coral reefs. His smile faded fast.

"What do you think would be at the center of the circle if we were to follow it inward?" he asked Cedric. The dog lowered his head back to the rug. "I bet there's something. It's either in the ocean, or it's in Canada, or Maine, or maybe New Hampshire." He ran his finger over the map.

"What do you think?" he asked the dog. "Now that we've finished the mural project, it seems like we should come up with something to do. Should we explore towards the center of the circle?"

CHAPTER 4: NEW HAMPSHIRE

THEY PASSED BETWEEN THE dark buildings and began to climb the hill on foot. They didn't use either sidewalk, but walked right up the middle of the road. Brad glanced up at the dark windows on either side of them. The rows of two-story buildings on either side of him reminded him of the old west. They were walking up the middle of the street like gunfighters. But it wasn't high noon, and they had no guns.

At least Robby was walking on his own. Brad was happy he didn't have to carry him.

Romie touched Pete's shoulder.

She leaned in and talked low. They were all a bit spooked.

"There's a parking lot behind the buildings over there. Do you think you could hot wire one of the cars?" Romie asked.

"Of course not," Pete said.

About a block up, a residential street led off to the left. The five of them stopped in the intersection. The tall trees on either side of the street were just starting to get their leaves.

"I imagine we could find something up that way," Pete said.

Nobody moved.

"Come on," Romie said. She led the way.

They walked in a line except for Brad and Robby. Brad kept his hand on Robby's elbow, guiding him forward.

"That one?" Romie asked. She was pointing towards a house.

"No," Lisa said. "The door's open. More likely to find keys

inside if the door is closed."

"If you say so," Romie said.

"She's right," Pete said. "Think about it. In a lot of cases, the person who had the house keys also has their car keys on the same ring. If they left..."

He stopped talking when Romie put a hand on his shoulder. She was looking back towards the intersection.

"I saw something back there," she whispered.

"What?" Pete asked.

"I don't know, that's why I said 'something' instead of what the thing was."

"That house. Let's go," Pete said. He pointed up the street. They broke into a trot. Brad pulled on Robby's hand and he adopted a shuffling gait, just fast enough so that Brad didn't pull him off his feet. As they crossed the yard, Brad got a look at the tiny car in the driveway. It would never hold the five of them. Pete got to the front door first and threw it open. He waved everyone inside and locked the door behind them. Romie and Pete fanned out and spied through front windows at the dark yard.

"Anything?" Brad asked.

"Who knows," Romie said. "I can barely see."

"I don't see anything," Pete said. "You guys look for keys. We'll keep watch."

Brad left Robby in the living room with Pete and Romie. He dug through his pocket and pulled out the tiny light he carried. He turned it on as he moved down the hall. He saw Lisa's light come on at nearly the same time. Brad headed for the kitchen. The back door was open a few inches. The screen door was closed, but not latched. Brad pushed the back door shut and set the deadbolt.

He turned back to the kitchen. He imagined it would be a cozy spot in the daylight, but by flashlight it held too many shadows. He pushed aside the mail on the counter, and dumped out a basket that held pens and a notepad. He spun slowly, looking for a bowl, or pegboard, or anywhere you might keep a set of car keys.

A pair of black bananas had turned to liquid near the microwave. Near the toaster, a plastic bag looked like it contained more mold than bread. He pulled open a few drawers and finally found the one that contained random screws, tools, and junk. That's where he would keep his spare set, if he lived there. Nothing.

Brad backed out of the kitchen and scanned the dining room quickly. That room looked barely used.

He returned to the living room.

"Nothing in the den, or hall, or laundry room," Lisa said. She came into the living room from the other entrance.

"Nothing in the kitchen or dining," Brad said.

Robby was still standing there, like he was supervising Pete and Romie. They practically had their faces pressed to panes of the front windows.

Lisa turned her light towards the stairs and Brad followed her.

They split at the top of the staircase and Brad found himself in the master bedroom.

He still found no signs of the occupants. From the pictures and the dressers, it looked like an old couple shared the room. One bureau had spare glasses, a brush, and a couple of watches. The other had jewelry boxes and perfume. It reminded Brad of his grandfather's bedroom. He crossed quickly to the nightstand. His grandfather kept keys in that drawer.

Brad pulled it open. He shone his light inside and frowned at a jar of Vaseline, and a wallet.

Brad jumped when Lisa's voice came from the doorway.

"Anything?" she asked.

"Nothing. You?"

"Just a bathroom and guest room. I think they took the keys with them."

"Maybe," Brad said. "But grandpa's wallet is here."

He picked it up. It was too light. He opened it and found nothing inside.

"Oh," he said, holding it open to Lisa. He dropped it on the floor.

She turned away and opened the closet. On a hook on the inside of the closet door, a pair of pants were hanging from the belt still looped through the belt loops. She put her light in her mouth and pointed it forward as she dug her hands into the pockets.

"Gum," she said through her teeth. She pulled a pack from the pocket and flipped it to Brad. "Wallet," she said. Brad caught that as it sailed over to him. "And keys."

She turned with the ring dangling from her finger. She wore a big smile.

"Well done," Brad said.

"My dad used to do the same thing," she said. Brad followed her out of the room. "He wore the same pants every time he left the house. Didn't wash them until the end of the week."

At the bottom of the stairs, Lisa paused.

Romie and Pete were now looking out the same window and Robby had moved too. He was standing just behind the pair, like he was looking over their shoulders.

Brad was about to ask what they saw when Robby started to make noise.

✪ ✪ ✪ ✪ ✪

The sound began as a low groan, but it formed itself into a name as it progressed.

"Lyle," Robby said.

"What?" Brad asked.

"Quiet," Pete said.

Brad moved over to where Robby was standing. He put his hand on Robby's shoulder as the boy said "Lyle" again. This time the name was more clear.

"Robby," Brad whispered. He shook Robby's shoulders. Even with the trace amount of light coming in through the windows, Brad saw consciousness return to Robby's face. It was like a spark animated his features all at once. The boy turned to Brad. "What is it, Robby?"

"Lyle," Robby whispered back.

"There," Romie said. Lisa joined them at the window.

"Who's Lyle?" Brad asked.

"Bad," Robby said. "Very bad."

At the window, Lisa hunched forward. "What is it?" she asked.

Pete shook his head.

"We don't know," Romie said.

"Why is he bad?" Brad asked.

Robby pointed to his mouth and showed his teeth, as if that was an answer. He looked up and away, like he was lost in a memory.

"Robby? What are you saying? Robby?"

Robby clapped his teeth together. Brad shrank back. The boy fixed him with a stare that clamped an icy hand around Brad's heart.

"He eats people," Robby said. "He knows you. He knows Romie, too."

"What?" Brad asked. He saw Romie's head twitch at the mention of her name. She kept her eyes on the shadows outside.

"From the Chinese buffet," Robby said. "You stole his food."

"I don't know..." Brad began. He trailed off as an image floated forward from the back of his mind.

From the back of the house they heard glass crack and then fall to the floor.

✪ ✪ ✪ ✪ ✪

"Could be two of them," Pete said. "Maybe more."

"Upstairs," Lisa said.

"No," Romie said. "They could burn the place down. We have to get out."

"Through the side porch," Pete said.

He led the way and crashed his shin into the coffee table. Romie and Lisa moved around him as he threw it to the side.

On the far end of the living room, glass doors led out to a screened-in porch. Romie and Lisa threw the doors open and the others followed them out. Lisa had a knife. She slit a hole through the screen, cutting from the bottom up, and slipped through. On the other side, she tumbled into a bush.

Brad was the next through. He pushed slashed screen apart and stepped through. After helping Lisa to her feet, Brad turned and tugged on Robby's hand, to lead him. They found their way to the other side of the bushes while Pete and Romie followed.

"I've got keys to the Ford," Lisa whispered to Pete and Romie.

Brad moved to the corner of the house. They were on the opposite side of the house from the driveway. The car was partially hidden by the house and another set of bushes. There could be anything hiding in those deep shadows. Someone approached Brad from behind. He turned, expecting to see Romie or Lisa. It was Robby.

"Lyle," Robby said.

"It's too risky," Pete said, moving up behind Robby. "We don't want to cross out in the open in case they have guns."

Pete pulled at his sleeve and Brad let the man direct him away from the house, deeper into the shadows. They ducked under low branches of some fir tree and wound single-file to the yard of the neighbor's house. They stayed close to the back of the house, crossing the back deck and hunching down as they swerved around the shed.

Brad brought up the rear, pushing Robby out in front of himself.

The next yard was surrounded by a tall stockade fence. Romie found the gate, and Brad closed it behind himself. They spotted a back gate and stayed low as they walked to it, so the fence would hide them. Brad took deep breaths to stay on top of his fatigue. Robby's breathing came in shallow pants. To Brad, the boy sounded like a wounded animal in the dark.

The other side of the back gate was a sea of black. Their faces were assaulted with branches of the packed trees. Brad lifted his feet high but still stumbled on roots and rocks. He crashed into Robby's back several times before they stopped.

"I can't see," Romie said.

"I can," Robby said.

The boy moved away and Brad found himself alone in the dark. He heard the boy's footsteps, but that was his only connection to the world. A hand reached out of the dark and found his arm. He was guided forward by the insistent tug.

They walked through the dark, stumbling down a bank and

then back up an even steeper one. Sometimes the hand propped him up, and sometimes Brad had to help the owner back to their feet after a stumble. He caught the occasional spot of light, but it was soon cancelled out by a branch. He felt his sense of direction evaporate in the dark.

When he caught a glimpse of something white through the trees, his eyes locked on it and drank it in. The shape was blocked out and Brad shifted his head frantically to try to get it back. With a few more steps, it was back. He saw the sharp, orderly lines, and as they moved through the patch of woods, he understood them. It was a big white house across a shaggy lawn. They didn't have any cover, so they ran as fast as they could. Robby reached the building first and he disappeared around the side.

Brad stayed behind Romie. Her pace was slow, but Brad didn't want to run by her and leave her behind. When they finally got around the side of the house, Pete was standing on a porch, holding open a storm door. He waved them inside. Brad found himself in a dark mudroom. A bench sat over a row of shoes and below a set of windows. Brad knelt on the bench and looked out into the dark as Pete pulled the door shut behind them.

Lisa joined Brad in the watch.

"Robby, who is Lyle?" Brad asked over his shoulder.

The boy was still panting. Brad heard the boy's throat click as he swallowed.

"Lyle?" Pete asked. Brad glanced back. Pete was shutting the door to the rest of the house.

"He's very bad," Robby said.

"Who is?" Pete asked.

"Lyle," Robby said.

Pete abandoned the questioning and turned his attention to talking through a plan.

"I don't think they could have tracked us through the dark. I say we lock this place up, tuck ourselves away in a dark corner, and wait for daylight," Pete said.

"That sounds like a good plan," Romie said. "But we need to maintain two escape routes. There's a porch roof over the far side. In a pinch, we could bail out through a window. Let's plan at least two escape routes, name them, and then we can hide."

"Good," Pete said.

"Should we at least hear what Robby knows about this guy first?" Brad asked.

"No offense, but he's been conscious for what? Five minutes? Let's do Pete's plan and we can listen to Robby's thoughts when we're safely hidden," Romie said.

"Guys," Lisa said. Brad turned around. His attention had strayed from looking out into the night. Fortunately, Lisa had stayed vigilant.

"Lyle sees everything," Robby said.

Pete and Romie moved to the windows.

"What did you see?" Pete asked.

"Right there, just beyond the swing set. Do you see?"

"No," Romie said. "What is it?"

"There," Lisa said.

Brad saw it. He was pretty sure they all did. One of the shadows withdrew until it was once again a part of the dark woods.

"He knows we're here," Robby said.

"Just hush," Romie said. "What should we do?"

"We don't know what we're up against," Pete said. "We don't know how many of them there are, or what kind of weapons they might have. I wish we had that van. At least on the road we could draw them out into the open."

"What if we loop back around to that house?" Lisa asked. "I have that key for the Ford. It will be tight, but we can all pack in there."

"We don't even know if it will run. It's been sitting for months," Pete said. "What if the battery is shot? How long until daylight?"

"About five hours until dawn," Brad said after consulting his watch.

"We have to keep running until we lose them," Pete said. "Let's go out through the front, cross the street, and make our way from block to block. We'll turn uphill to keep away from the river. We don't want..."

Pete stopped talking when they heard the groan of the door. The four of them all turned at once. The door to the outside was open and the storm door was swinging shut. Robby was gone.

CHAPTER 5: NEW YORK

"ARE YOU ALONE HERE?" Judy asked.

Daniel, Bill, and Viv had already walked through the door. The older woman with the candle still held the door open, but Judy paused on the porch.

"I suppose I should say I'm not alone," the woman said. "I should tell you that there are half a dozen strong men asleep upstairs. Yes, I'm alone."

The flickering candlelight made the woman's face seem fluid and malleable. It almost looked like there could be a smile twitching at the corner of the woman's mouth, but that could have just been a trick of the light.

"Come on," Viv said.

A flashlight came on inside and then another. Bill and Viv were lighting up the place. Judy's fear waned with the addition of more light.

She walked by the woman and saw a genuine smile cross the woman's face. When Judy stepped through, she closed the door behind them.

"We can talk in the kitchen," the woman said. "It's right down the hall."

Viv and Bill were investigating the rooms they passed with their probing flashlights. The woman didn't pay them any mind. She kept shuffling down the hall. She wore a modest nightgown that hung all the way down to her slippers. Her long gray hair was tied in back. Judy followed, but left plenty of room between herself and the woman, just in case. She remembered her own flashlight and began to pull it out from her back pocket as they reached the kitchen.

There was no need for it. As soon as she reached the table, the older woman touched her flame to the many wicks of candles that decorated the center of the table. Judy glanced around at the kitchen. It was modern and practical, but trimmed in wood and stone, which gave it the feel of a country house. After the older woman took a chair, Judy took a seat.

In the center wall, she saw a fireplace under a brick arch. It held an iron pot suspended from a hook. Judy wondered if it contained soup made from the bones of earlier visitors. She looked back to the older woman's smile. Shadows danced up her face.

"I'm Viv. This is Judy, Daniel, and Bill."

"So nice to meet you. I'll need to hear those names a few more times before I get them. I used to be one of those people who would hear a name once and then remember it forever. I guess my brain is getting tired. Oh, and everyone calls me Woolly."

"Nice to meet you," Viv said.

Daniel and Viv sat down, but Bill was still wandering around the kitchen.

"Does this work?" Bill asked. He turned his body so they could see that he was pointing at a hand pump, mounted to the counter over a sink.

"It does," Woolly said. "It's one of the best parts about this kitchen. I don't think it had been used in years. They probably kept it just for the ambience, but it's been a lifesaver."

"Woolly is an interesting name," Viv said.

"My parents called me Mildred, after my mother's grandmother. I hated it. There's no good nickname for Mildred. I hate Milly. It sounds like the name of an old cocker spaniel. My nephew called me Woolly because I always used to knit with wool. I took the name as my own. I even insisted that they call me Woolly at work."

"When did you come to this place?" Daniel said.

"I lived a few towns over," Woolly said. "When everyone

disappeared, I wandered around. I didn't know what to do. When I found the horses here, I decided that someone had better take care of them. I tried to let them out, but they kept coming back. There are still some loose around here, but I keep most of them in the paddock just so they won't get into trouble."

"And you said you live here alone?" Bill asked.

Woolly frowned. "I've answered one of yours already. How about we go back and forth? How exactly did you come to my door this evening?"

"We came down from up north," Viv said. "There was a tremendous amount of snow up there, and there was a stretch where instead of disappearing, people just died. We decided to see if it was safe to come back into the area where there were no dead bodies, and where there wasn't so much cold and snow."

Woolly nodded.

"Yes, I live here alone with the horses. It's my turn. How did you manage to travel without vanishing, like everyone else?"

Nobody said anything for a minute. Daniel was the one who finally ventured an answer. "We don't know for sure. After the big day where everyone disappeared, a few people were taken here and there. For the most part, it seems like the mass disappearance is over. Why is it the horses here survived? Do you have any idea?"

"I have a theory," Woolly said. "It seems there's something different about this hill somehow. If you stay up here, it seems you have some sort of immunity to disappearing. I haven't seen anyone taken since I've been here."

Bill looked like he was going to come over to the table to take a seat, but something caught his eye. He moved to the glass that made the upper half of the back door. Bill flipped up the back of his shirt and suddenly his hand was filled with a gun.

"Who's out there? What are those lights?" Bill asked. He wasn't pointing the gun at anyone yet. He held it towards the floor.

"I told you," Woolly said, "I live alone. I burn torches down at the road. I'm terrified that one of the horses will fall in the ditch." Bill wasn't meeting her eyes. He was turned so everyone at the table was in his peripheral vision, but his attention was focused out the window.

"You said you live alone and then you said you haven't seen anyone taken since you've been here. Who are you referring too?"

"Bill, put that away, would you?" Viv asked.

"Answer the question, Mildred," Bill said.

Woolly's eyes jumped between the other three, begging them for help.

"She probably just meant..." Viv began.

"Don't answer for her," Bill said. "Who hasn't been taken, Mildred?"

"Just the horses, I suppose," Woolly said. Her voice started to falter and she swallowed hard. "I've been living here alone. I've come to think of them as people."

"I don't buy it," Bill said. He backed away from the door. When he was halfway across the kitchen, he swung the gun towards Woolly. "How many, and where are they?"

"There's nobody," Woolly said. "I live here alone."

They all heard the creak from down the hall as the front door swung open. Bill darted towards Woolly and positioned his gun just inches from Woolly's temple. Her hands came up defensively, and she froze with them raised to her shoulders. Viv, Daniel, and Judy all slid back from the table to put some distance between themselves and the firearm.

"Who's there?" Bill asked.

"Bill, calm down," Viv said.

"I'm perfectly calm," Bill said. His gun hand, trembling, and his darting eyes told a different story.

"I'll go see who it is," Judy said. She would have done almost anything to extract herself from the kitchen at that moment. The potential danger down the hall seemed trivial compared to the scene unfolding at the table.

"No," Bill said. "Let them come to us. They won't do anything if they value Mildred's life."

Judy didn't listen. She rose slowly and backed towards the hall.

"Judy?" Bill asked. His hand was shaking now. He grabbed the gun with both hands. That seemed to steady it.

Judy took the final two steps and was free of the kitchen. She turned and looked down the hall. There was a man pushing his head through the doorway at the end of the hall. He had a beard. Judy's heart raced for a second before she realized that she recognized him. The man looked up at her and she saw the recognition in his eyes as well.

"Bill," she called over her shoulder. "It's just..."

The gunshot drowned her out. The man coming through the door immediately dropped into a low crouch and slinked through the doorway into the living room. Judy turned towards the kitchen, and then turned back to the front door when another bearded man came through and ran upstairs. She didn't know where to turn.

From the kitchen, Viv cried out.

✪ ✪ ✪ ✪ ✪

Judy lowered herself to the front stairs and put the cigarette between her lips. She couldn't get her numb hands to operate the lighter. The end of the cigarette bounced and swayed. When she finally got a flame, she couldn't get it focused on the end of the cigarette for long enough to take a puff. She threw both to the side and put her head in her hands.

She felt a weight settle on the stair next to her.

Through her fingers, she recognized Ron's pants.

"She attacked you guys?" Ron asked.

"I don't want to talk about it, Ron."

The headlights from the Land Cruisers were bathing them with light. Judy didn't want to be in the dark anymore. She wanted them to leave the lights of the vehicles on all night and she would just stay out on the porch until dawn.

"The others must have run off," Ron said. "We've had people all over this place and all through the barns. Nobody has found them yet. You want to come inside? Bill, and Viv, and that other guy, are in the living room. What's his name? Daniel?"

Judy took a deep breath and let it out slowly.

"I didn't think this place existed," Ron said. "I thought that Luke was making it up this whole time. I can't wait to see it in the daylight."

"Cars," Judy said.

"What's that?"

"How did you get the cars here?" she asked.

"Oh, it's funny," Ron said, "after you guys walked down the hill, someone found this place on a map. We saw there was a parallel road. That road had a bridge, so we were able to drive right around the washout and come in from the other side. It was quick and easy."

Judy sat there with her hands covering her face. The lights from the vehicles sparkled between her fingers. She wished Ron would go away, but she didn't want to speak.

"I think they've cleaned up the kitchen, if you want to go inside. Bethany was making a fire in the brick oven. She said she was going to bake some bread. Did you see any of the other guys who were living here? I wonder where they went. Do you think they have some secret hiding place around here? I guess it would make sense. I hope they're not dangerous."

Judy didn't say anything.

"Here comes Luke. Do you want to be alone?"

Judy nodded.

Ron stood. "Luke, do you mind giving her a few minutes? She really wants to be alone right now." Ron walked towards Luke as he spoke. Judy lowered her head to her knees and pressed her face into her legs. She wanted to curl into a ball so tight that she disappeared.

Footsteps approached across the dooryard.

"Judy?" It was Luke's voice. She didn't answer.

"Judy, I need to ask you about what happened in there," Luke said.

She curled tighter, still hoping to disappear.

"Bill says he was attacked. The story from Viv and Daniel sounds a bit different. I want to know what you think."

Judy didn't respond. She wished for the cigarette she'd tossed aside. One of the bearded men had pressed it into her hand after they'd cleared out the house. It was the only one she had, and now it was laying in the dirt, probably soaking up the dew. If she had it back, she would find a way to get it lit. She shouldn't have given up on it just because her hand had been trembling. Her hand had trembled like Bill's had, as he held the gun up to Woolly's head.

"Hayden said you were in the hall when Bill shot, but I need to know what you saw when you were still in the kitchen. Can you tell me that?"

Judy wished for Luke to go away. Once he did, she would track down that cigarette.

"I don't blame Bill for acting to defend himself. I just want to make sure that's what happened," Luke said. "Your perspective is important to me."

Judy stayed silent and kept her face hidden. She knew Luke was still there, waiting for an answer.

"Judy," he said.

She jerked up her head and opened her eyes. She immediately regretted the action. The headlights stabbed bright daggers into her head. Luke was lit from behind and looked like a floating god, outlined in white light.

"You made your human sacrifice, and you got your blood. What more do you want?" Judy asked.

"Nobody wanted an old woman to die, Judy," Luke said. "If I shouldn't trust Bill with a gun, I need to know. We have women and children around. Do you think we can accept the risk of having an unstable person in our midst? If he's going to panic and shoot someone every time something goes bump, people have a right to know the exact details of what happened, don't you think?"

"You got your details from Viv and Daniel, I'm sure. I wasn't even there. I can't tell you anything."

"So be it," Luke said. He raised his hands to his shoulders, just like Woolly had. "So be it."

He gave her a second. He stood still while she dragged in a ragged breath and let it out.

"Listen—there are some beds upstairs if you want a chance to get a good night's sleep. We're going to set up a camp here in the yard, but you can sleep inside tonight if you'd be more comfortable there. Bethany is baking some bread. I'll make sure they save you some for breakfast."

Luke backed away before lowering his hands. His deference

brought her more anger. When he'd left, she walked to one of the Land Cruisers and looked for one with an empty back seat. They were parked in a semicircle, all pointing with their headlights towards the house. Half of them were running, the other half were burning the headlights from the battery. Judy crawled inside a vehicle and curled up on the seat. She slept.

CHAPTER 6: PENNSYLVANIA

TIM WEIGHED EVERYTHING BEFORE he loaded it into the plane. He wanted to balance the load and he wanted to know exactly what to expect. He ran through all his periodic maintenance, even items that weren't yet due. He brought enough rations, for both himself and Cedric, to last a week—ten days if he remained thrifty.

"What am I forgetting?" he asked.

Cedric sat on the tarmac. He knew he was supposed to wait until Tim told him to jump up onto the wing.

"It's not like we're going to be flying around for a week. We'll have to land and find more fuel. I'm not even going to let it get below half a tank, in case we can't find a hand pump. I should bring that siphon."

Cedric wagged his tail and it swished back and forth on the ground.

"Yeah, okay, get in," he said.

Cedric sprang up onto the wing and then nosed open the door. He was in his seat with a flash of auburn fur.

Tim could barely resist the urge to go back in the little house and wander around again. He'd already made several passes through the place. Anything he needed was already packed. It was an adorable airstrip. Tim was sad to leave it behind. When he'd discovered it, he thought he might never leave. Now, he was about to depart just because he couldn't think of a reason to stay. There might be more people out there somewhere, and it was more important to find them than to stay at his perfect airstrip.

He climbed into his seat and buckled Cedric into his. The dog closed his mouth and let out a low whine.

"I brought your ball. It's in the back. I can't have it rolling around on the floor while we're in the air."

Cedric didn't cock his head at the word "ball" like he usually did. His eyes were fixed on the little pond next to the house. It was his favorite place to get muddy. Cedric let out another tiny whine.

"I know," Tim said. "If we don't find anything, we can come back. I promise."

He pulled out his preflight checklist.

✪ ✪ ✪ ✪ ✪

Tim headed north and west until he found the shore of Lake Erie. He flew low and slow up the shore, looking for any signs of life. He was looking for movement or smoke. Cedric looked through the window for a while and then settled against his harness. The dog's head bobbed as he slept.

This lake seemed very democratic. Sure, there were golf courses and plenty of big, stately houses, but there were also a ton of little camps and farms along the shore. This wasn't just a playground for the rich. This was everyone's lake. Tim thought about finding a manual on water landing and looking for a plane with pontoons on the bottom. Maybe he could live right on the shore. Fuel would be a problem. At least with wheels on his landing gear he could always find a stretch of highway and steal some gas from an abandoned car.

Up ahead, a spit of land extended into the lake. The shore was stacked with big gray stones that looked out of place. The whole extension looked like maybe it was man made. That was one way to get more shore property—you just created it. The stones caught his eye at first, but what kept his attention was the white fluttering in the lawn. Near a long building, strung between two trees, someone had hung sheets. They blew in a strong breeze. Tim scanned the building and lawn, looking for any other movement.

Little wind-driven waves lapped at the rocks. The branches of the trees swayed gently. Tim couldn't find the owner of the sheets anywhere.

"Wake up," Tim said to Cedric. He nudged the dog's shoulder. "There might be someone down there."

The dog seemed to wake up with his nose first. It began twitching and then his eyes opened. He looked at Tim.

"Wouldn't you come outside if you heard an airplane for the first time in months? Those sheets can't have been hanging there since last Thanksgiving, could they?"

Tim banked the plane so he could get a better look at the house. He descended and circled. There was nowhere to land. The road that led along the shore was too narrow and was lined with trees and power lines. Tim brought up his altitude to look for a highway or at least a road big enough to safely land on. It looked like the nearest road was miles away.

He pulled out his map and marked the location.

"We'll keep going and see if there's anything else to investigate," he said. His heart was beating fast. Leaving behind the fluttering sheets was torture. He wanted nothing more than to take to ground and find his way back to that point, but it wasn't logical. If he intended to land, he needed a plan. Every time he brought the plane down he was taking a risk, and a set of hanging sheets wasn't enough reward.

✪ ✪ ✪ ✪ ✪

Tim flew all the way to Buffalo before he turned the plane around. His mind wandered back to the sheets. He imagined people living in that long house. In his thoughts, they were probably out gathering supplies when he flew by. They'd heard his engine and rushed back to see him disappearing on the horizon.

He felt a hard, hot lump in his chest when he saw that point of land again. It was harder to see the sheets from this direction, but when he circled back around, he was certain. He struck off east, to find a good place to land.

The nearest open space was a field. It might be fine, but it was impossible to know for sure from the air. There could be holes, or other pitfalls hidden below the growth.

He went farther and found a long parking lot next to a strip mall. It didn't have any dividers or curbs that he could see, and if he headed into the wind, he should be able to take off again. He shook his head and changed his mind. His plane was heavy with gear, and the day was warming up. It wasn't worth the risk.

Tim had to travel several more miles before he finally found a big open stretch of road with no hazards. He circled several times before he brought the plane down without issue.

Cedric wiggled in his seat, eager to explore the smells of this area.

"Okay," Tim said. He unbuckled the dog and opened the door so Cedric could bound out into the afternoon. "Don't go far. We have a way to travel."

He tried to find his location on the map. He had to approximate. Some of the roads he'd seen weren't on his map. They looked black and fresh. They might be recent construction.

Tim brought a small bag with a map and essentials. He climbed out.

The first few cars he found were all in the same condition. They had keys in the ignition, no fuel, and dead batteries. The people who'd abandoned the cars were simply gone and it seemed like they'd taken the vitality of their vehicles with them. This was familiar territory for Tim. Serviceable cars were getting harder and harder to find as the world aged. Back when the whole world had been alive, Tim had thought of cars as dependable, permanent machines. Now he saw them as spoiled fruit. They were beyond ripe and no longer fit for consumption.

"You ready?" he asked Cedric. The dog was sniffing around the tire of a dead car. He tilted up his leg and peed on the tire while Tim tightened the straps on his pack. Tim bent to stretch his legs and retie his laces.

When he was ready, he struck off in a casual jog. It took about a mile for him to really hit his groove, and then his feet moved automatically. He wasn't fast, but he could jog for miles. Cedric moved in spurts at first. He would run ahead, investigate something until Tim passed, and then catch up. Eventually, the dog moved to his side and kept time with Tim's jog.

They only stopped to consult the map.

✪ ✪ ✪ ✪ ✪

"Stay right with me," Tim said to the dog as they turned down Sunset Point Road. It was a wide expanse of asphalt that was in better shape than the main road. Cedric stuck very close to Tim's thigh.

The grass was high, but he saw no weeds in the lawn. Tim and Cedric walked down the middle of the road. They were flanked by two perfect rows of maple trees. One tree had a sign that read, "Private Drive."

Their footsteps flushed some birds from the grass. Cedric turned his head and perked his ears, but he didn't leave Tim.

The road ended in a circular drive at the entrance of the long building. A nice breeze blew across the narrow peninsula. They stood for several seconds, regarding the house from the circular drive. Tim tried to imagine someone looking out from those tall windows.

He approached as the hot lump of anticipation returned to his chest. His leg muscles were still twitching from his run, and it felt like he was walking on springs. He climbed the stairs and the shadow from the porch roof covered him and the dog. The porch ran the length of the house and the breeze swept through the space. It would be a great place to cool off on a hot day.

Tim walked to the front door.

The big black door was hidden behind a thin wooden frame that held a screen. Tim opened the screen and knocked. He waited and then knocked again. The sound was swept away by the wind.

His imagination took over. He pictured a dim, dusty room where a lifeless woman was laying on a bare mattress. He imagined her eyes flying open at the sound of his knock.

Tim shook away the vision.

"Let's walk around back," he said to Cedric.

They followed the south side of the house and walked down the length of the building. A row of tall lilac bushes flanked the building. The white paint was peeling away where the leaves were closest to the building's siding.

They passed a picnic table and a swing suspended from the branch of another maple. They finally came around the final corner and saw the clothesline. The sheets were nearly horizontal in the breeze.

Hanging from the line was a homemade bucket. It was the bottom half of a bleach container. A clothes hangar was hooked through each side and served as the handle. Tim took it down and saw it contained clothespins. There were no old leaves in the bucket. It didn't have rainwater in the bottom. It hadn't been there long. Tim hung it back up and spun around in a slow circle.

"Hello?" he yelled. Cedric turned with him and barked once, like he was trying to help call.

Tim looked up at the sky. It was still pretty clear, but there were thick clouds hanging on the western horizon.

"I thought we'd find out the sheets had been here forever," Tim said. "I figured there was about a ten percent chance that we'd find someone here. I never considered that the sheets would be recent, but the place would be empty."

He looked out over the water. The wind kicked up little ripples on the surface. It was a beautiful day on this private point. Tim looked at the grass. It wasn't long here. Someone was keeping this lawn mowed. It was yet more proof that someone should be here.

"We have to go inside," he said.

They walked over to a side door on the back part of the house. Tim looked through the window and saw a big room with a bar at one end and chairs along the wall. He knocked on the glass and waited. Cedric was right at his side.

He reached for the handle.

The voice called out as soon as his hand touched the brass knob.

"Can we help you?"

Tim turned around. Cedric, who had been panting with his tongue to the side, in his carefree way, closed his mouth. The young couple was standing about a dozen paces away with the water at their backs.

"Sorry," Tim said. He felt the blood rising to his face. "We were just looking to see if anyone was here."

Cedric sat down at Tim's side.

"This is our house," the young woman said. Tim guessed that they were, at the most, twenty years old. The girl was plain, but pretty in her summer dress and bare feet. The boy looked like he spent most of his time trying to look menacing. He wore dirty jeans and a white t-shirt that was smudged with grease. It looked like some of that grease might have made it into his hair. It was slicked back and shiny.

"I'm sure," Tim said. "We saw the sheets from the air. That was us flying overhead earlier, if you heard the plane."

"We didn't," the boy said.

Tim nodded. "Anyway, we saw the sheets and came down to see if anyone was here. I knocked several times. We were just looking for whomever hung up the sheets."

"Those are our sheets," the girl said.

"Of course," Tim said. He took a step down the porch stairs. "My name is Tim, and this is Cedric. We've just been flying around, looking to see if anyone else was still in the area."

The young couple exchanged a glance with each other, but they didn't respond.

"Anyway," Tim said, "I'm thrilled to find more people alive. It has been months since Cedric and I have seen anyone. We spotted a small group in Columbus, but by the time we landed, we couldn't find them."

"What's in your bag?" the young man asked.

"Nothing, really," Tim said. He began to take the bag off. The boy stiffened and a hard look crossed the girl's face. Tim slowed his movement and removed the bag slowly. He held the strap delicately between two fingers and set the bag down on the steps next to Cedric.

They were still looking at the bag.

"I've got mostly maps and a few snacks. I wasn't sure I'd be able to find your place, so I thought I might have to camp out somewhere tonight." Tim clamped his lips together to stop any more words from spilling out.

The girl came forward. She swung her hips for the first couple of steps, like she was trying to hypnotize him, but then she lunged and snatched the backpack. Cedric stood up. She smiled as she backed away. She pulled at the zipper and dumped the contents of the bag in the grass. The young man knelt down and pawed through the maps and food.

The young man raised up the book of laminated maps.

"You marked our house," the young man said, while he traced his fingers over the map.

"I saw it from the air," Tim said. "What's your name?"

The young woman opened a bag of cashews and dumped them into her mouth. She moved on to some dried fruit. Watching these kids help themselves to the contents of his pack, Tim decided he was no longer interested in making their acquaintance.

"Listen, I'll just take my map and we'll go," Tim said. "You can keep the food."

The young man found one of Cedric's tennis balls in the pack. The dog's full attention was on the ball. The young man smiled and waved it back and forth. The dog's head snapped left and right.

"You want to fetch? You want to go get it?" the young man asked. He turned and hurled the ball towards the lake. Cedric tore across the yard, passing within arm's length of the girl. She paused with a piece of fruit halfway to her mouth and watched the dog run. She laughed.

The ball splashed in the water about ten feet out. Cedric barely slowed when he hit the water. He swam out with a few quick strokes, snatched the ball between his teeth, and turned. When he climbed back onto the shore, he dropped the ball and shook from head to toe. He grabbed the ball and jogged back towards Tim.

The young man caught Cedric by the collar and jerked him to the side before he could run by.

"Give me that," he said pulling the ball from the dog's mouth. "Give it."

"Hey," Tim said. "Be gentle."

"He's fine," the young man said.

Tim wasn't talking to Cedric, but he kept that information to himself. Tim took a couple of steps forward. He had his hands turned open, showing they contained no threat. The boy's attention was towards the lake. He threw the ball again and watched Cedric run. The girl was watching Tim. She stopped chewing when he began to walk forward. She elbowed her friend.

"Stop right there, asshole," the boy said.

"Hey, I just want my map. You can keep the bag and the food. We'll leave you alone. I can tell you want your privacy," Tim said.

"I've killed bigger guys than you," the boy said. His tone didn't sound boastful or threatening. It sounded more like he was just stating a fact that had just occurred to him. The tone sent a chill down Tim's spine. A cold weight settled into Tim's stomach as the boy reached down to the grass. His hand came up with Cedric's red leash. The boy clipped the leash to the collar. Cedric looked up at the boy. The dog grabbed the ball from the ground when the boy stood.

"We're keeping the map. It has the location of our house, so it's ours now," the boy said. "You can go."

"If we see you again," the girl said, "we'll kill you." She had found one of the little bags of salty crackers that Tim carried. She was chewing them on one side of her mouth. The other side hung open with a sneer.

Tim shook his head. "You know what? Fine. At some point you're going to need people again. You might break an arm and need a doctor. At that point, this anti-social behavior is going to come back and bite you in the ass."

"Shut the fuck up," the girl said. "You don't know our business."

Tim inched his way to the side. He had given up on the bag, and food, and the maps. Those things were all replaceable. With each step he assessed his legs and their ability to run. He had run all the way over here and then stood around for a while. That was a bad combination. He could feel the hot acid deep in his muscles. He would have to pick up his feet carefully with each stride. It would be easy to trip and fall with his worn out legs.

The collar around Cedric's neck would never hold. He only kept it on the dog so that he had a place to clip the harness. It prevented the harness from slipping down around the dog's shoulders, but it was easily big enough to slip over Cedric's ears. Tim was paranoid about choking the dog, so he kept it loose. It was also one of those breakaway collars that would snap if Cedric got tangled up in something. With one good jerk from the boy, the collar should give up.

Still, Tim waited until he had put some more distance between himself and the rude youngsters. He turned as he walked, keeping his shoulders square to the young couple. Cedric watched him carefully. The dog seemed to understand the game.

"If we even see you," the girl called, "we'll kill you. Remember that."

"No problem," Tim said. "I wouldn't dream of coming back here."

"What's my new dog's name?" the young man asked?

"He said Cedric or something," the young woman said to her friend. "Don't worry. We'll change it. I know where we can find some dog food."

Tim was taking big strides at this point. He wanted a good lead. Cedric looked like he was gathering his legs beneath him—practically wiggling with anticipation. Tim was almost to corner of the long building. He glanced over his shoulder at his escape route. He had the whole access road to cover before he would get to some woods. It was chilly for a swim, but he might have to take to the water to get away. The young man was distracted by his conversation about dog food, so Tim took the chance. He let out a quick, shrill whistle. Cedric broke into a sprint.

✪ ✪ ✪ ✪ ✪

He didn't need to pull off or break the collar. The young man was so distracted that the leash pulled right from his hand. Tim hadn't counted on how quick the young man would be. In an instant, he turned and dove after the dog, catching both of his back legs. If the dog hadn't been wet, he would have been ensnared by the young man's grip. Because of the lake water, the dog's legs slipped between the young man's fingers and the young man collapsed to the grass, empty-handed.

Cedric reached full speed in two strides.

Tim turned to run. The dog caught up with him by the first maple tree. Tim turned to look back. The young man was just getting off the ground. The woman held his elbow and helped him to his feet. Tim smiled. The couple wasn't even giving chase.

His legs burned by the time he reached the end of Sunset Point Road. He slowed his sprint as they rounded the corner. The dangling leash caught Tim's eye. He slowed to a stop, letting his feet slap against the pavement.

"Give me that," he panted. He removed the leash and the collar. He stuffed the collar in his back pocket and tied the leash around his waist. Cedric looked up at him with his tongue lolling. He looked eager to move on. Tim nodded at him. They ran down the road.

Before they reached the first turn, Tim heard the distant whine of an engine. The way it revved and shifted, he knew it was a motorcycle. It sounded like something with a small engine—maybe a dirt bike.

Tim threw his arms out to the sides for balance and launched over the little gully next to the road. He climbed into the scrubby bushes and whistled for Cedric. A low fence separated them from a big lot filled with parked boats. They were covered in shrink-wrapped plastic for the winter and left there by owners who wouldn't be returning. Tim and Cedric ran along the fence until they found a spot where the sections of chain-link weren't joined particularly well. Tim dropped down to squeeze through the gap. He held it open for Cedric.

When he heard the approaching motorcycle, he said, "Down!" Cedric dropped to the ground and looked at Tim with wide eyes, rimmed with white. "Hush," Tim whispered. He crouched low, holding the dog's head down as the motorcycle zipped by on the road. He stayed low for several more seconds before he edged away from the fence and the road. They moved between the rows of parked boats to the other end of the lot. They left through the gate and found their way to a side road.

Tim relied on his memory and sense of direction to navigate.

The sound of the motorcycle disappeared in the distance.

Tim ran when he could, but they spent a lot of time ducking and hiding every time Tim thought he heard a noise. It took hours to finish the trek back to airplane. When he figured they were within a hundred yards, Tim moved off the road and guided Cedric on a slow trip through the woods. His navigation was accurate. They saw the plane through the scraggly weeds.

Tim watched the plane for several minutes and then began to slowly creep towards it. He didn't see any movement. The sun was starting to go down. If he was going to get in the air—and he really wanted to put some distance between himself and Sunset Point—he would have to do it soon. Tim broke from cover and ran towards the plane.

He didn't make it far before he slowed and stopped. The tires were flat. There was a spiderweb of cracks across the windshield. Sooty black marks stained the fuselage just above the door. Tim crawled up on the wing to look inside. It was worse than he imagined. The interior had been splashed with gas and burned. He could smell it. The limited air inside the cabin had put the fire out, but everything was destroyed.

Tim looked around. He wondered if they were watching him right now.

Cedric seemed to sense something was wrong. He didn't even jump up on the wing to get inside. He stayed on the pavement. Tim joined him.

"Let's get out of here," he said. They ran.

CHAPTER 7: NEW HAMPSHIRE

BRAD RAN FOR THE door and pushed through it. He reached the corner of the house as Robby got to the center of the yard and stopped.

"Robby!" Brad whispered. He started towards the boy.

"Stop!" a voice yelled from the trees. "Come any closer and we will kill him."

Brad stopped. He backed up and put the corner of the building between himself and the voice. A dark shape began to emerge from the dark tree line. Robby stood in the middle of the yard. Inside the house, Brad heard an interior door swing open. He looked through the window, but couldn't see anything except Lisa and Romie pressed against the windows from the inside.

"Why did you leave me?" the voice called from the darkness.

If Robby answered, Brad couldn't hear it.

"We could have been such good friends." The owner of the voice took another step forward. Brad's eyes tried to make sense of the shadows. They didn't look right. "I followed that other group for a while, thinking you were with them. When I realized you weren't, I decided to stay here to wait for you. I had the feeling you would be along eventually. I'm so glad you came." The man's voice got softer as he talked.

Robby took a step closer to the woods.

Brad clenched his teeth, wondering if the threat was real. Did they really have a weapon pointed at Robby, or was there a chance to dart out and save him? He hoped Pete was moving through the house to circle around on the dark man's position. He hoped Pete had a plan.

✪ ✪ ✪ ✪ ✪

Robby smoothed his hands down the pockets of his pants. It took him a second to realize what he was looking for. The last time he had confronted Lyle, he had been in a dark rest stop by the side of the highway. That night, his salvation had depended on a can of pepper spray. His hands were looking for that can once more. Of course it wasn't there. Robby could barely remember how he had gotten to this suburban back yard. He had no idea who had dressed him in the stiff jeans that he wore. Of course there was no pepper spray.

"I've thought about you," Lyle whispered from the dark.

Robby's brain ticked through the possible outcomes to this confrontation. He was pretty sure that Lyle was alone, but that didn't mean that he wasn't dangerous. Robby was close enough to see the faint glow coming from Lyle's head. He was likely wearing some kind of night vision apparatus. That's how he was able to track them so easily. He likely carried multiple weapons. Even with superior numbers, Robby's group could be eliminated, one at a time. That's why he had come forward to confront Lyle.

Robby needed to engage Lyle and lure him out into the open. He hoped that Brad and Romie, or maybe even Pete, were working to circle around Lyle while Robby distracted him.

"I know what you like to do to bodies," Robby said. "I've seen it."

"You never told me your name," Lyle whispered. "I told you mine. That hardly seems fair."

"Robby. I want people to call me Rob, but they still call me Robby."

"I know," Lyle whispered. Robby's nerves jangled when Lyle suddenly yelled. "I know what you're doing over there. I told you—if you come any closer, we'll kill Robby."

"They won't come," Robby said. He glanced over his shoulder

and was disappointed to see Brad's face near the corner of the house. "They're afraid of you."

"They should be," Lyle said.

"I'm not afraid of you," Robby said. In the black shadows under the trees, he couldn't see any distinct shapes. Still, he sensed some movement there. Robby took a step back.

Lyle emitted a low chuckle.

"You know nothing of yourself. How could you know anything about me?"

"You can't become them, Lyle," Robby said. "You can try to do the things they do, but it won't make you immune to them."

"I have no idea what you're talking about." Lyle forgot to whisper. That was good. Robby needed Lyle to forget himself.

"You were making bodies disappear, just like the invaders. You thought that if you could reproduce what they did, it would make you as powerful as them."

"That's silly."

"Then why did you do it?"

"Do what?" Lyle asked.

Robby turned his body. When he turned back, he had moved back another half step. He spoke quietly, so Lyle would move closer.

"Why did you eat people?"

"I choose the best atoms the world has to offer," Lyle said. "I choose the most powerful materials to construct my body."

"Maybe you should eat diamonds instead of dead people."

"You're playing a game with me. I offered you my friendship once, and you lashed out at me and fled. I've already shown you more courtesy than you deserve."

"Do you know why I'm not afraid of you?"

Lyle didn't respond. Robby sensed movement to his right. He didn't look. Lyle's attention was focused on him, and he didn't want to disturb that trance.

"I'm not afraid of you because I'm not dead. You're clearly a menace to corpses, but you haven't displayed any ability to take a life."

"You haven't been watching me, Robby. You have no idea what

I'm capable of."

"Show me. Last time you shot at me, I only ran away. What kind of coward has to use a gun against a boy? Why don't you come over here and show me what you're capable of with your bare hands?"

"You wouldn't last a minute. I have a hundred times your strength."

"I don't believe you."

Lyle forgot himself. He stalked forward, coming at Robby with his hands up. He was reaching forward. His hands clearly wanted to wrap themselves around Robby's throat. When Lyle stepped from beneath the trees, into the starlight, Robby's eyes jumped to the man's head. He wore some kind of goggles with big, circular lenses. He had the eyes of an owl. His hands were empty, but on each hip, he had a gun holstered.

Robby charged.

✪ ✪ ✪ ✪ ✪

Brad caught bits of the conversation from his position near the corner of the house. He focused on the woods and the neighboring yards. He was watching for movement or any sign of the man's accomplices. While he watched, he kept his hand busy. Near the corner of the building, there was a steel pole hammered into the ground. Brad worked it back and forth and tugged. It was slow work, but he was gradually liberating the pole from the ground.

Robby appeared to be taunting the man, and it was working. The man was leaving the overhanging branches and moving out into the light. He barely looked like a man. His shape bulged with odd curves. Brad scanned the area again to see if the man's movement would flush any more attackers.

The man said something and Robby launched at him. Brad jerked on the pole. It was almost free. Robby hit the man in the midsection, and the man's hands immediately went to Robby's neck. Brad abandoned the pole and ran.

Robby and the man hit the ground with Robby on top. Brad experienced an instant of hope before it was dashed. The man's hand went to his waist and came up holding a gun. He was swinging it around to point it directly at Robby. In the second piece of bad news, Brad saw another figure streaking towards Robby and the man. This person was coming from a neighbor's yard. It appeared that the man had an accomplice after all.

Brad considered veering towards the other attacker, but changed his mind. The man under Robby was holding a gun. Robby grabbed the man's wrist, diverting his aim for the moment. It was a short-lived victory. The man was stronger than Robby and he pushed the gun back towards Robby's head.

The gun went off.

The flash and sound hit Brad like a slap to his senses. The light blinded him and he heard nothing but a soft ringing and his own breathing. Brad's vision began to return as his feet slowed. He accelerated once more and threw himself at the man's gun hand. Robby slumped to the side.

The man was still on the ground.

Brad caught his wrist in both hands. He drove the wrist back, above the man's shoulder. He felt popping and tearing conveyed up through the man's arm into his own hands. The gun went off again.

The other figure arrived and Brad braced himself for impact. Instead of hitting him, the other figure landed on the man. Brad turned his attention to the gun. He pulled at the man's fingers and twisted the metal to break his grip. It worked. The gun fell to the side.

"Get his other gun!" Pete shouted.

Brad finally recognized his friend as the other shadowy shape. Brad did as he was told. He climbed over Pete, found the holstered gun, and threw it into the night. As it left his hand, he regretted the throw. He could have kept the gun and pointed it at the man.

Pete tore the goggles from the man's face. The man thrashed under Pete's weight.

Brad found Robby's limp body. He had rolled off to the side.

"Did you get hit, Robby? Robby?" Brad ran his hands over the boy's head, expecting to find a big wet hole where a bullet had torn away a section of skull.

"Brad!" Pete yelled.

He turned to see the man escaping Pete's grip. Brad's eyes were drawn to the black spot on the grass. The edges of the black metal caught the starlight. It was the gun. The man was going straight for it. Brad left Robby and ran towards the man. He wasn't going to make it on time. Pete was still on his knees and the man was bending over to pick up the gun.

A huffing shape blew by Brad and plowed into the man.

Pete and Brad arrived to find Romie pinning the man to the ground.

"Get the damn gun," Romie said.

Pete bent for the weapon. Brad jogged in the other direction and found the gun that he'd thrown into the night. It was sitting right next to a birdbath.

Lisa arrived.

Romie and Pete were holding the man to the ground, but he was thrashing wildly.

"Help!" the man yelled. Brad looked towards the dark line of woods. He didn't see anything. Romie clamped her hand to the man's mouth, but then pulled back with a yelp. She glanced at her hand for a split second and then formed a fist. She plowed it down at the man's head until he went limp.

"What did you do?" Lisa asked.

"He bit me."

Brad returned to Robby. Lisa joined him. They knelt on either side of the boy. Lisa pulled out a flashlight and cupped it in her hand so it wouldn't blind them. They searched his body and rolled him halfway over, looking for any injury or blood.

"I don't see any holes," Lisa said.

Robby emitted a low moan and raised a hand to his head.

Brad tried to help him up, but Lisa shook her head. "Keep him on the ground." Brad shrugged.

"Are you okay?" Brad asked. "Where does it hurt?"

Robby sat up. Lisa didn't stop him. Robby looked over to where Romie and Pete were still sitting on top of the man.

"He's alone," Robby said. "He's dangerous though. Kill him."

"What?" Lisa asked. "We can't do that."

"I think we have to," Romie said. "What are we going to do, put him in jail? He wants to kill us."

"We don't know that for sure," Brad said.

"So what do you propose?" Romie asked.

"Brad," Robby said. The boy was holding his hand to his temple. "Do you remember that body you found in the Chinese restaurant?"

"Of course," Brad said. He and Romie had found it together. There were pieces missing from it. "I'm surprised you remember."

"It was Lyle," Robby said. "He was the one who did that. I suspect he did it a lot. He's mentally ill."

"You can't just kill people," Lisa said. "We have his guns. Why don't we just scare him away? If he comes back, then you can shoot him."

"We don't know how many guns he has," Pete said. Beneath him, Lyle began to stir. Without notice, Romie hit him again in the head. Lyle was still again.

"He's probably half-dead already, the way you've been hitting him," Lisa said. "Could you please stop doing that until we come to a decision."

"Why don't we tie him up, and then a couple of people can guard him with guns until we find a car? When we're ready to go, we cut his ropes and leave him here," Brad said.

"I like Brad's idea," Lisa said immediately.

The others didn't say anything. Robby shook his head.

"Fine," Romie said.

"I'll go find some rope," Lisa said. "Brad, don't let them kill him, please?"

"I'll try," Brad said.

Lisa walked back towards the house. Brad looked away when she pulled her hand from her flashlight and let the full beam light up the yard.

"Are you sure he's alone, Robby?" Pete asked.

"Pretty sure. Sure enough."

"How do you know this guy?" Brad asked.

"I ran into him my first night alone," Robby said. "He was at a rest stop near the highway."

"You never mentioned that," Pete said. "What happened?"

"It's a long story. I think we should figure out a plan first."

✪ ✪ ✪ ✪ ✪

They had three flashlights on the floor of the garage, pointing up towards the ceiling. The man strapped to the step stool looked like he'd been in battle. Brad looked over at Robby. The boy didn't look much better. Robby wasn't bleeding, but a big lump stood out on his temple.

Now that the adrenaline was wearing off, Brad found his eyes sliding closed. He had to stay awake. There was still a chance that Lyle had accomplices in the area.

"What happened to you?" Brad asked.

"When?" Robby asked. Robby got up and walked over to the workbench. The person who had owned this place spent a lot of time in this garage. All the tools were put away and clean. There was a squat white refrigerator next to a tall red tool chest. Robby didn't open the fridge, but ripped open a box that sat on top. He came back with a couple of cans of warm soda. He handed one to Brad.

"When we were back in Maine," Brad said. "That bird disappeared, we all decided we should go to New York, and then you just collapsed. You were catatonic for weeks. What happened?"

Robby shrugged.

"Come on. I'm guessing this isn't the first time this has happened to you."

Robby looked up at him and frowned.

"Judy told me that you would go into a trance when you had a hard problem to figure out. Is that what you were doing? Figuring out a problem?"

"Not exactly," Robby said. "I was back with my grandmother."

"What does that mean?"

"When I was a kid, my mom and I would go out to my grandmother's house a few times a year. My dad always had to work, and he didn't like my grandmother much anyway, so he usually didn't come. I missed my dad, but it was fun. My grandmother always let me do more than my parents would."

"Grandparents love to spoil."

Robby nodded. "It was more than that though. She trusted me more than my parents did. She trusted that I knew the right thing to do."

Robby took a big sip of his soda and didn't continue.

Lyle had begun to snore. His head was slumped to the side. He had woken up while they were strapping him to the stool and Romie had smacked him on the head again. It wasn't even a hard smack, but Lyle had gone unconscious immediately. Brad was starting to wonder if Lyle would live to see the morning. Romie apparently packed quite a punch.

"So you went back to where you used to feel safe?" Brad asked. "Somehow you slipped into a trance and you were at your grandmother's?"

"No," Robby said. He coughed and gingerly touched the lump on his temple. "There's a time when I was a kid that I remember, but I picture it like someone else told me."

"I think that happens to everyone."

"Maybe," Robby said. "But I think it's different for me, and there's a reason. I guess I used to be really smart."

Brad laughed. "I'm pretty sure you still are."

Robby shook his head. "No. I don't mean to sound conceited, but I think I was *really* smart. One day my grandmother sent me up a ladder to get something from on top of the cabinets and I fell. I hit my head. After that, I wasn't so smart."

"Did you have a concussion?"

"I was in the hospital for a long time. I remember hearing people murmur about me, about whether I would make it, but I was asleep the whole time. After that, I could tell that people didn't think I was as smart anymore. Sometimes I think I remember what it was like to be able to figure everything out, but it doesn't last. It's impossible to understand. The ideas just don't fit inside my head anymore."

"It could just be your imagination. Maybe some side effect of the trauma."

"Maybe," Robby said. "Anyway, sometimes when I'm trying to figure out a really hard problem, it's almost like my brain overheats or something. I end up right back there in the hospital. I can't do anything until I figure out the answer."

"So that's what happened after the bird disappeared? You went into a trance to figure out a problem?"

Robby nodded.

"What did you come up with? You woke up—do you have an answer?"

"Not really," Robby said. "It was Lyle that woke me up. I'm afraid of him."

"But he's neutralized and you're still awake. Are you afraid of him right now?"

Robby nodded.

"Wait, you said 'not really.' Did you come up with some kind of answer?"

"Yes. I think so," Robby said.

Brad sat up straighter. He set his soda down. He no longer felt the need for the caffeine to keep himself awake.

"Well?"

"I haven't figured out exactly what to do, but I figured out why the problem isn't solved yet."

"The problem?"

"We didn't get rid of all organisms that came to prepare the planet. They're still working to sterilize and get the environment ready."

"They haven't gotten the message yet, you mean?"

"Yes. And it's possible that another embryo might come, too. Maybe they're keeping the nest warm for the next egg you know?"

"I suppose," Brad said. "Is it also possible that none of our previous ideas were true, and now we're just scrambling to try to fit the new evidence into our debunked model?"

"Of course," Robby said. "That's one of the reasons why the problem isn't yet solvable. We need more data to fit into the theory to decide if the theory is relevant. There's always a chance that we're off-track until we get more information."

"More data," Brad said. He sighed. "We lost a lot of people

chasing after theories. If we had gone along with Luke before, we might be a much bigger and stronger group."

"I know."

Brad and Robby both jumped when the side door of the garage opened. Lisa stepped inside.

"We're getting closer," she said. "We found a decent car, a battery charger, and plenty of gas." She ticked the items off on her fingers. "Romie and Pete are trying to get a generator started so we can charge the battery enough to start the car."

"It's not standard?" Brad asked.

"It is, but there are no hills nearby, and the thing is really heavy. I don't think we'd want to push it far. How's he doing?" she asked, pointing at Lyle.

"Same," Brad said.

Lyle was clamped to the step stool by ratcheting straps. Brad stood when Lisa approached Lyle, but he wasn't too concerned. She raised his eyelids one at a time and flashed her light in his eyes.

"He has a concussion for sure. He might have internal bleeding or brain damage. I think we should stay here until he stabilizes. He's not a threat to us in this condition, and he'll die if we leave him."

Brad took Lisa's arm and guided her away from Lyle.

He spoke softly to spare Robby from hearing. "I don't know what he did to Robby, but the boy is still pretty traumatized. Maybe we should just let nature take its course with this guy. We have no reason to be kind to him."

She pulled away from his hand. "Brad, this is a person. If you haven't noticed, there aren't very many of us left. I refuse to abandon my humanity."

Brad was about to argue, but they both turned towards the door when they heard the engine.

"Is that the generator?" Lisa asked.

"No. That's a car."

Headlights swept through the garage windows. Robby moved over to the door.

CHAPTER 8: NEW YORK

JUDY WOKE WHEN THE sunlight hit her face. The inside of the vehicle was stuffy and warm. The windows were closed, but she could hear the bustling activity going on outside her little coffin. She pushed up from the seat and blinked to clear her eyes.

It looked like there were people everywhere. When she focused, she realized she recognized them. It was their walk that made them look different from before. Instead of hunching, like they were expecting hail, everyone stood upright and walked tall. She couldn't believe this was the same group of people. She let herself out and took a deep breath of fresh air. It smelled different here. Everything seemed clean.

Judy walked by a fence, where a bunch of people were lined up. They watched three women out in the field. They were trying to round up a bunch of horses. The animals paced away from the women. They held their heads and tails high as they ran. Judy kept moving.

A big patch of dirt next to the house was the focus of another group. Some stood and pointed while others were on their knees, pulling weeds.

Still more people were taking bags of supplies in through the front door and walking them down the hall. Judy moved through the scenes, not addressing anyone. She walked around the house and followed a shed to a big barn. The doors were wide open. Judy walked down the concrete floor of the aisle. All the stalls were empty except one, which held Cincinnati. Judy grabbed a handful of hay from a bale. She gave it to the horse through bars of the stall.

"How come you're in here while everyone else gets to play outside?" she asked him. "That doesn't seem fair."

"They think he'll get sick," a voice said. Judy spun around to find Ron. He was coming out of one of the other stalls. He set a big rake down and leaned it against the wall. Ron wasn't the type of person she expected to see in a barn. He usually kept himself away from manual labor and things that might dirty his clothes. He wore boots that were laced over the cuffs of his jeans.

"Why would he get sick? Are the other horses sick?"

"No. It's something to do with the grass. I guess he hasn't been able to graze or something. Too much grass all at once will make him sick. I heard he's going to go out for a couple of hours this afternoon."

"That sucks. He's been carted around in a tiny metal box for all this time. Now he's boarded up into a wooden one. He's destined to be a prisoner, I guess."

"Luke rescued him from starvation, so I guess he's lucky to be alive at all. But I guess we all are."

"Luck? You call this luck? I call it being too stupid to get the hint. We're clearly not supposed to still be alive."

"I guess," Ron said. "I signed you up for one of the bedrooms tonight. Luke said you should get first pick because you were in the party that made first contact and you didn't take a room last night. Everyone else who wants to stay inside is on a waiting list. Everyone else is in a tent."

"I don't want a room. I'm not sure I want to go back in that house again."

Ron frowned. "You're going to have to eventually. You'll be on kitchen duty before too long."

"We'll see," Judy said. She had no intention of setting foot in that kitchen again. "Is this the chore you drew? Are you the stable boy now?"

"No," Ron said. "I actually pulled gardening, but I traded with one of those prissy kids. He didn't want to clean horse shit and I didn't want to get dirt under my nails. This isn't so bad. I get to wear gloves and use a long rake."

"Perfect," Judy said. She looked out the back door of the barn. A little road, that was little more than two ruts in the lawn, ran between the fences and curved off into the woods. "What are the other chores they're doling out?"

"I don't know. I saw water hauling. Some people were setting up a laundry at the creek. Some of Luke's militia are setting up a perimeter, so there must be some guard duty."

"Hunting?"

"Not that I know of. There was some talk about heading into town to raid the grocery store. I haven't heard about any hunting trips though."

Judy nodded.

"Have fun with your horse shit," she said. She wandered back towards the house.

She stopped when she got to the fence where a group was watching the women try to round up the horses. They weren't even getting close to the animals. As soon as they swept them into a corner, the horses would break through the gap and run to the opposite end of the pasture. People next to Judy shouted encouragement and suggestions. Nothing was helping. Judy wasn't watching the horses. She was scanning the other side of the fence, where the woods began. She saw him eventually. One of Luke's bearded men was leaning against a tree.

They'd dealt with defectors before. Luke's group didn't take rejection well. At the beginning of their trip, Luke had lectured about the importance of forming a cohesive unit. He had warned them that if even one person decided to go their own way, the group would fall apart. He didn't have to convince everyone. He only needed to convince enough people to enforce his plan.

A young man named Harrison had been the first to try to leave. Harrison was seventeen, and he'd joined up with Luke's group in western Maine. Living alone had made Harrison quiet, impulsive, and independent, but he was drawn to the traveling group and came alone willingly. By the time they got to Vermont, the kid was miserable. He couldn't submit to Luke's authority.

When Harrison tried to leave, he had the sense to do it quietly. The boy waited until midnight and then snuck off. Luke's militia caught him a few hours later and dragged him back. People were just waking up when the bearded men marched Harrison back to the convoy of vehicles. Judy had expected that everyone would feel the same way she did—let the boy go if he wanted to leave. If he wanted to go out on his own, that was his decision.

The group voted on Harrison's fate. The ballots were numbered. Although not every ballot was cast, the ones turned in were unanimous. Harrison was forced to stay with the group. He was escorted at all times and his hands were cuffed while he slept. The next time he tried to leave the group, he was shot. The injury wasn't fatal, but the resulting infection turned out to be. Harrison was the first and last person to attempt to leave the group.

He was not, however, the only person they'd lost. The snatchers—things that made a person disappear into the sky—had taken a couple, and they'd lost several to what the kids called "water monsters."

Judy watched the guard on the other side of the fence until she saw him signal down the way. She followed the direction of his signal and found the next guard. They likely formed a perimeter around the farm.

Judy walked back to the house.

On the back porch, the lists were posted. She found her own name on a list entitled, "Garbage Detail." She scanned the "Supply Run" list until she found the right name. Judy asked around until she found the woman setting up a tent in the side yard.

"Vera!" Judy called. The woman was connecting poles and trying to feed them through a slot in the tent.

"Hi, Judy," Vera said. She wore an exasperated smile and frowned at her own hands.

"Let me help," Judy said. She straightened the nylon so Vera could feet the pole through the slot. "I saw you were on the supply run. When is that, tonight?"

"Yeah," Vera said. "They're waiting until sunset in case there are any water monsters in town."

"Creepy," Judy said.

"Yeah. I'm not looking forward to it. I'd be okay if it were like the third or fourth run, but it sucks to draw the very first supply run into a new town. It doesn't even seem like we need to go. There's a full pantry in there. Seems like we could live for a while on that."

"There's a lot of us now," Judy said. She looked around at the other tents in the yard. As they'd moved from Maine to New York, they'd picked up new recruits every day. They were all volunteers. Nobody was forced to come along if they didn't want to, but most did. And—as Harrison's story had reinforced—once you joined, you were in for life.

"I was just thinking that last night. It was different when we were on the road. You didn't know how far the column of vehicles stretched. Once we all collected here, I couldn't believe how many people we had."

"How do you feel about garbage?"

Vera laughed. "How do you mean?"

"I'm supposed to be on garbage duty. It's not that tough. According to the sheet you just have to take garbage from the bins there and drag it off to a big pit they found over there in the woods. There are guards, so it doesn't seem risky at all. I just have a thing about garbage. It's not my favorite."

"I guess I don't mind it," Vera said.

"Trade?" Judy asked. "I'll go on the supply run if you take my garbage duty."

"I don't know. Are we allowed to trade?"

"Ron said he traded stables for gardening. I saw some other names exchanged on the lists. I think it's okay."

"I'd feel better if we cleared it with Wallingford, or one of the others."

Judy knew what Vera meant by "others." Nobody ever said it aloud, but people cleared things with the bearded men.

"I'll clear it," Judy said. "If you don't mind, that is."

Vera thought about it for a minute. She finished feeding the pole through the slot.

"Deal. *If* you help me finish setting up this tent."

"No problem," Judy said.

✪ ✪ ✪ ✪ ✪

She rode in the passenger's seat and watched the two tiny red lights. Richmond, the bearded man behind the wheel, kept their vehicle glued to the rear bumper of the car in front of them. They had replaced the brake lights with two pinpricks of light, and drove in a tight column.

Richmond wasn't the man's real name. Most of the militia men had taken to calling each other by the name of the town where they were born. He reached for his mug and Judy tensed. All the interior lights were off, so she couldn't tell how fast they were going. Every time he took his hand off the wheel, she felt like they were going to crash.

She cracked open her window. Richmond spit into his mug. He was chewing tobacco, and using the mug as a receptacle for his spit. The spearmint smell made Judy's stomach turn.

The column of vehicles swept around a bend and Judy saw the headlights of the lead vehicle. They were passing between a narrow gap of abandoned cars.

"How far is this place?" she asked. She was wondering if it might be wise to look around for something to vomit into.

"Don't know," Richmond said. He spat again.

The red dots of light flashed and they began to slow. Judy's stomach clenched and rolled.

The radio crackled and a voice came through the speaker. "Parking. Escape formation."

Richmond slowed and the tiny lights swept off to the right. Judy saw the lights of the other vehicles. Richmond spun the wheel and then backed into his spot. They fanned the vehicles so they were pointing in different directions, in case one or more should be blocked in by something. The backs of the vehicles pointed at the store.

Judy waited and turned on her headlamp when Richmond turned his on. They gave off a dim red light. It was just enough to see by. Judy grabbed her bag.

Inside the store, they split up and headed down the aisles.

Judy had her list memorized. She was looking for canned fruit, olives, and pickles. Once she had those items, she was allowed to grab anything else that looked good. The store was still pretty clean. Someone had been through already, but they hadn't made a mess of the place. It always amazed Judy when they'd find a store with broken glass and food scattered all over the floor.

She set down her bag and started to pile in cans of fruit salad and pineapple. Most of the good stuff—peaches, and pears—was already gone. She packed in two layers of cans and tested the bag. It wouldn't do any good to pack more than she could carry. They never used carts anymore. It was a superstition they all shared. One man had broken an ankle when he was accidentally rammed with a cart. Since then, they always used bags to collect their groceries.

Judy moved her bag down to the savory end of the aisle. She grabbed some jars and then some more cans. She tested the bag again. She could probably carry more, but her goal wasn't to get as much as possible. Judy turned for the front of the store.

She slowed on her way between the registers. The candy was all gone. There was never any candy. She waited for the pair of headlamps to move through the door. They would be the cereal and dry-goods people. Those things were so light and bulky that they would be the first out. She wanted them to be loading the vehicles when she exited.

Judy moved the strap of her bag to the edge of her shoulder as she slipped through the door. She dropped the bag at the exit, moved out from under the roof's overhang and dropped her headlamp. She turned and ran into the night.

✪ ✪ ✪ ✪ ✪

When people were snatched up into the sky, it almost always happened during the day. Sometimes, in the middle of the night, a person would get up from their bed and walk outside. If you could stop them from getting to the door, their trance would break in a few minutes. But, if you let them get outside, one of the invisible forces would pull the sleeping person into the sky and you'd never see them again. You might find a sock or a glove on the ground, but the person would be gone forever. Judy hoped that Richmond and the other people in the supply run would assume that she had suffered that fate.

She waited until the building was far behind her before she dug the other headlamp out of her pocket. Her lungs burned. Too many cigarettes had ruined them. She held the light in both hands and ducked behind a car. Down the hill and across the parking lot, she saw a cluster of red headlamps. She was still too close to risk using her own light. She stayed low and crept farther away.

Judy stumbled over train tracks and crept through gravel. She had to cross an open lot to get around a tall fence. There was a cluster of shops across the street. Judy moved behind them so the buildings would block the sight of her from the grocery store. She decided to risk the headlamp. It was too slow to move without light. Down another side street and up a hill, she found a neighborhood.

She took rapid, shallow breaths. Pulling air in too deep just hurt. She felt a sharp pain just below her ribs on her right side. She held her hand to the spot as she ran. Pressing made it hurt less. Judy slipped between two houses that were separated only by a narrow driveway. She opened a low gate and rounded the corner. She rested with her back against the brick wall of a house. Judy shut off her headlamp while she waited in the dark. She tried to take deeper breaths, hoping the pain would subside.

There was a sound from the darkness. Judy held her breath.

Judy thought about the house she'd grown up in. It was a tall house. In the landing at the bottom of the stairs, a grandfather clock sat. Judy's dad had hated the chimes, so he'd disconnected them, but every time the clock got to the top of an hour, it would give an extra loud TOCK as the mechanism wanted to start banging the chimes. Judy loved that tock. It sounded like the clock was angry that it had been neutered.

She remembered sitting down in the living room, looking at the sunrise light up the blue landscape of winter. She was waiting for six o'clock, when the alarms upstairs would ring and people would come down to open presents.

Their tree had two stars on top. It always had two stars. They always got what her father called a "binary" tree. They would search lot after lot, looking at Douglas firs and Scotch pines. They rejected dozens of trees that any other family would be thrilled to take home. What they were looking for was special. They were looking for a tree with two tops. People always assumed that the tree with two tops was a nod to the twins, Jon and Wes. Judy's mom always told people it wasn't.

In her memory, Judy folded her legs beneath herself and tucked in her nightgown. It was cold in the living room. When her dad came down he would wait for a few presents to be opened and then use the paper to start the fire. By the time breakfast was ready, the living room would be toasty warm. While she waited on the couch, mesmerized by the sunrise illuminating the frost on the storm windows, Judy waited for the grandfather clock to...

TOCK.

She heard the sound, but it wasn't followed by the distant bell of her father's alarm clock. Her father kept a windup clock on his nightstand that said "Baby Ben" in black letters on its glow-in-the-dark face. It was normally in perfect sync with the grandfather clock.

Judy sighed and looked at the picture on the mantle. It was her brothers, Jon and Wes, in their matching sweaters. Most of their outfits were matched. Even if one of them got a ketchup stain on a shirt, it seemed that the other would have a matching stain before the end of the day.

One of Judy's friends had brand new twin baby brothers. Judy had stood at the end of the crib, looking at the two perfect little faces, and she'd wanted to warn her friend. "They'll take over everything. Your whole family will revolve around them," she had wanted to say. She hadn't said anything, of course. After all, Jon and Wes were older than Judy. As far as she knew, they only monopolized the house because they'd come first. Maybe the same fate wouldn't befall her friend.

Judy had been fascinated by the baby twins because of one thing: she could tell them apart. They were clearly identical, but something about their personalities showed through when you looked at their faces. You could immediately discern one from the other. That wasn't the case with Jon and Wes. Judy had spent her entire life looking from one to the other, and she never caught the knack of which was Jon and which was Wes. Her mother claimed to know the difference, but Judy had seen her slip up as well. The strangest part was that sometimes it seemed that the twins themselves didn't know. She caught them one time in their room, pointing at each other, and deciding which one was Jon and which was Wes.

The whole thing was creepy.

TOCK.

Judy looked around at the clock. It read six. Alarms should be sounding. People should be coming down soon to open the presents. Most of the gifts under the tree were in identical twin boxes. The gifts were side by side, waiting for Jon or Wes to pluck them with identical hands.

Later, after all the presents were open and Judy was upstairs washing for dinner, her grandmother would come. Judy loved her grandmother. She was the one who'd say, "Can't you twins go play in another room? You're so loud."

Judy's mom would protest. The twins didn't actually speak that much. They seemed to communicate with each other by a series of subtle glances and narrowed eyes. "Why do you insist the twins are loud, Mother? They haven't said a word."

"They don't have to," Judy's grandmother would say.

Judy refused to use the nickname for her grandmother. The twins called her "Wooly." They were forever inventing nicknames for people, as if they couldn't remember the proper thing to say. It was bad enough they called her Wooly, but when they wrote it on cards, they even spelled it wrong. They used only one L, and Judy's pocket reference said that it definitely should have two. Judy's mom said that it didn't matter—nicknames didn't have to be spelled correctly.

Judy took a deep breath and felt the pain in her side. Her brain wouldn't let go of the name Wooly. It should have two L's. It should be Woolly, but it wasn't. Even when she'd met another woman named Woolly, she hadn't connected the two people.

Where had that been? She couldn't remember and it seemed important. Suddenly Judy wasn't on the couch anymore. She wasn't in her childhood home, waiting for Christmas. She was standing in the dark with her back pressed against a brick wall and waiting to catch...

TOCK.

"Hey, Jude," her father said as he came down the stairs.

"I didn't hear your alarm," Judy said.

"You better go get washed up. You can't sit around in your pajamas all day," he said.

Judy looked down. She was still wearing her nightgown. There were no more boxes under the tree. Everything had been opened. The twins had already run off with their loot. Judy's gifts were in a pile on the coffee table. The paper was in the tinderbox. A fire raged in the fireplace, and it was about ninety degrees where Judy sat.

"Where's Wooly?" Judy asked.

"Your grandmother?" her father asked. "I haven't picked her up yet. I'm going to leave in a few minutes." He made his way around the couch and attended to the fire. For some reason, he added another log to the center of the blaze. Judy could feel beads of sweat starting to form on her forehead. She wouldn't be able to wear her new sweater if the house was going to be this hot.

"I thought Woolly got shot," Judy said.

Her father laughed. "What a crazy dream."

"Bill shot her. He thought she was hiding something."

"Who's Bill?" her father asked.

Judy didn't know what to say. The ideas of Bill, and Luke, and the horses, didn't fit in this setting. They didn't match her childhood home. She couldn't figure out how to express the concepts in words her father would understand.

"Why am I here?" Judy asked.

TOCK.

"You'd better get dressed if you want to come with me to pick up your grandmother."

"I can't," Judy said. Her father didn't respond. He just looked at her until she was sure he'd turned to wax. Nobody could stand that still.

TOCK.

“Let’s go, Judy. You’ve got so much to do,” her father said.

Judy looked down. She was wearing clothes. Her hair was pulled back. She had on her new sweater. It wasn’t too hot after all, but it was itchy. She stared at the pattern of green and white yarn. Pretty snowflakes made of little white V’s decorated the front. She could get lost in the pattern.

TOCK.

Judy shook her head. She pushed away from the wall and pulled at the bricks to get around the corner. She gained speed as she ran between the houses. When her feet got to the street, she nearly tripped on the little lip there. She flailed her arms as she slapped her feet against the dark pavement. In the distance, she saw bobbing red lights. Judy ran for them. She stumbled over a curb and then nearly lost her footing as she ran over the roots of a huge tree. She ran downhill, throwing her feet out into the dark and trusting that they would land on solid ground.

The lights grew closer.

She heard and felt another TOCK.

Judy pressed her hands to the side of her head to block out the sound. She started to scream. When she reached the red lights, their hands encompassed her.

CHAPTER 9: LAKE ERIE, NEW YORK

TIM AND CEDRIC SPENT the night in a shed between a lawnmower and a tiller. The door to the house was open, but it didn't look right. After all the running and walking they'd done that day, Tim was too tired to take a risk on a house that didn't look right. They'd curled up in the shed and slept on the concrete floor. Tim woke at dawn. He had to pee so bad that his legs felt numb. He burst out of the shed and barely got his zipper down in time.

There was a low mist on the lawn. It seemed to flow in and out of the back door to the house, like the building was breathing. The dark windows looked like eyes. Tim was glad he hadn't ventured inside. Cedric approached the house slowly, almost like he was stalking it. When he got to the side of the house, he cocked his leg and relieved himself on the siding. Mist flowed out of the back door. Tim imagined the house was hissing at the dog.

They walked back out to the road.

His stomach gurgled and he patted his pockets, hoping that somehow he'd forgotten about a reserve of food. He found nothing. Cedric lapped muddy water from a puddle.

The road they followed was a state highway. The interstate was nearby, and might have better opportunities to find an airfield, but Tim wanted to stay off the big road. Somehow he thought that the young man and woman from Sunset Point might look for him there.

Tim and Cedric raided a country store and found breakfast.

There was even a dusty box of dog biscuits. Even offered a nice piece of jerky, Cedric preferred nothing over a dog biscuit. He would sit at perfect attention, lay his ears back, and drool from the corners of his mouth, as he waited for a treat. Tim found a bag and packed what he thought might be useful. They stepped out over the broken glass and stood on the store's porch to look at the morning. It was going to be a beautiful day. There were just a few clouds at the horizon, and the mist had already burned off. It would be hot by noon.

Tim thought about running, but decided that walking was a better plan. His muscles were still sore from the day before, and he didn't want to risk injury. A pulled hamstring might take a week to heal, and he didn't even have a place to stay. The houses on either side of the road were old and quaint. On another day, they might even look inviting. Today, they looked like hungry mouths waiting to swallow him whole.

Tim was waiting for Cedric when he looked up and saw the sign.

It read, "Westfield Aviation Flight School." He'd been heading towards Buffalo, thinking that the closer they got to the city, the more likely they would find an airfield. Private would be best, but public might do. A flight school was more than he could have hoped for. He imagined a big hanger, filled with bulletproof, simple-to-fly machines, all meticulously maintained. To get insurance on a flight-school plane, you needed to demonstrate maximum attention to detail.

Tim couldn't help himself. He broke into a jog as he started the two miles to the school.

✪ ✪ ✪ ✪ ✪

Tim loved the transition. There was a moment when exertion transitioned to floating. For the first half mile or so of running, more if his course started uphill, Tim tore ragged breaths from the air. His throat felt like it might close as he wheezed in and out. Then, as his pace settled into an easy rhythm, his breathing slowed and became part of the forward momentum. He would take three strides on each inhale, and three on each exhale. It was Tim's meditation. It was his way to turn over the compost that cluttered his mind and reveal fresh, fertile soil.

Everything he cared about had been in that bag or in that plane. Everything except Cedric, of course. He looked down at the pretty Golden Retriever and smiled at the way the dog's tongue slipped out of the side of his mouth as he ran. He would gladly trade all those possessions for the dog. Now, he didn't need to make the choice. The possessions were gone. He had considered the maps his key to survival. They were annotated with all the knowledge he'd accumulated about this new world, and now they were gone. The next few weeks would prove to him, one way or the other, just how crucial those maps had been.

Cedric looked up at him and seemed to smile with his eyes.

Tim hadn't been a dog person before. He hadn't understood the logic of pets at all. Petting them supposedly decreased your blood pressure, but it was a lousy tradeoff. Couldn't you take the time that you would spend feeding, caring, and cleaning up, and find a more efficient way to decrease your blood pressure? Pets were nothing but a constant drain on money and time. When he'd heard the barking coming from the little blue house on Thanksgiving, Tim had almost kept walking.

✪ ✪ ✪ ✪ ✪

Back in real life, Tim had lived in a tidy little apartment overlooking the park. He treated his home like a puzzle—he only placed something in there when it would be a perfect fit. He researched every appliance, and every stick of furniture. He made a list of each activity he expected to do in each room, and had furnished and decorated accordingly. The apartment had operated like a precision timepiece. A sloppy, hairy, drooling dog would have never fit that lifestyle.

On Thanksgiving morning, everything was going according to plan. He had deconstructed the idea of Thanksgiving into seven components: fowl, starch, starch, vegetable, booze, indulgence, and gratitude. His bird was in the oven, packed with one of the starches, and he was dicing potatoes when the power went off. At first, he thought it was just the lights in the kitchen. Then he noticed that the sound of the parade on TV had shut off in the living room. Tim had stared at the oven for a minute. Some part of him thought that if he held still, everything might just come back to life and there would be no crisis to deal with. The oven was electric. Gas cost more, and meant a separate bill each month, so he'd gone with electric. In his years of living in the little apartment, the power had never gone off before.

After a minute, Tim washed his hands and retrieved his phone. He still had the number for the power company in his address book. He dialed. Using the automated system, he reported his power outage and hung up. Regarding dinner, there was nothing to do but wait. The bird needed at least another hour to cook. He wondered how long the oven would stay hot if he didn't open it. It was just him for dinner. He was lucky the guy from accounting had turned down his invitation. At least he wouldn't need to make any excuses.

Tim moved to the living room and fiddled with his phone. Perhaps if he got a feel for the scope of the outage, he could guess at how long the power might be out. If it was just his block, or just his building, maybe it would come back quick. If it was the whole neighborhood, he could see if the Chinese place down the street was open. They were always open on Christmas. Maybe Thanksgiving was another trend they bucked.

He couldn't connect with the website. Tim fiddled with the settings for a minute, thinking that his phone might be trying to connect with his home network. The network was up—his battery backup would last about an hour—but, of course, anything it normally connected to would be down. After a couple of minutes, he gave up. If there was a way to fix the issue, he wasn't savvy enough to figure it out. He tried the phone number again, hoping that he could get an estimate if he could just talk to a person.

The phone rang a few times and then a busy signal buzzed in his ear. He pulled the phone from his face and looked at it. He couldn't remember the last time he'd heard that ugly sound. Tim tried again and his phone wouldn't even place the call.

He began to feel unsettled. When he looked through the window, the feeling got worse. The family who had been playing football in the park had gone inside. The park was empty. Their football was still sitting there, unattended in the withering grass. Out on the street, nothing was moving. There was a car double-parked over on Chatham Street. Its blinker flashed, but it didn't move. Tim couldn't even see anyone behind the wheel.

Tim grabbed his keys from the ring, and put on a light jacket. He shut his door quietly and walked up the hall to the elevators. He actually stood there, pressing the button, for several seconds before he remembered the power outage. Tim walked to the stairs.

He kept his arms to his sides rather than touch the railing. At one time, he loved taking the stairs. Then, some homeless person had found a way to get into the stairwell, and had been peeing into the drain. The smell had been disgusting. The building manager had replaced the locks and poured bleach down the drain, but Tim had given up on the stairs. He would rather add another mile to his run than potentially walk through urine. Now he had no choice. His nose was on high alert as he walked down the last flight. He pulled his sleeves up over his hands as he pushed open the door and let himself outside.

It was a beautiful fall day. A lot of people hated the Pittsburgh winter, but Tim suffered it gladly as long as it was preceded by a crisp autumn. Down in South Carolina, fall was a soggy, moldy affair. In Pittsburgh, the air had a nice round bite to it. Tim took a deep breath and smiled. His concern about the power was, for the moment, distant. He decided to walk around the block and see how far the outage stretched.

Tim walked down the sidewalk and glanced over at the football. He considered picking it up and setting it on a bench, but decided against it. The people were probably looking through their window, waiting for someone to steal their ball. His path took him close to the double-parked car. He frowned. The engine was running. The door was even open to traffic. It was like the driver had just gotten out and walked away. Tim shook his head and wondered if he should call the police.

Around the corner, he didn't see any lights on in the

businesses. The Chinese restaurant had a plastic sign in the window. It was flipped to "Open." Tim walked in and a bell over the door rang. He walked up to the little counter where the register sat. There was usually a tiny little woman sitting on the stool. She didn't seem to do anything. In fact, her eyes were so squinted and wrinkled that Tim often wondered if she could even see the customers. Today, the question was academic. She wasn't there.

"Hello?" he called.

Their power was obviously out too, but they probably had gas stoves out back. As long as they could make change, maybe he could get a hot lunch to take home.

"Hello?"

Still no answer.

Tim walked back to the fish tank. They'd recently won their case to keep the giant koi fish. Some regulation made them illegal, but the restaurant had fought the state and managed to keep the tank. With the power out, there were no bubbles in the back of the tank. The treasure chest lid didn't rise and fall. Tim looked closer. Maybe they'd lost the case after all—there were no fish in the tank. He glanced around the dark restaurant and wondered if the sign had been lying. Maybe this place was closed and they'd just forgotten to lock the door. There was certainly nothing going inside that made it appear open.

"Hello?" he called once more.

Tim walked towards the back. There was a bit of light showing through the porthole window to the kitchen. He tentatively pushed open the swinging door. The back room was lit from windows high on the walls. Blue flames danced under big pots on the stove. There were heads of cabbage on the cutting board in the process of being chopped. Nobody was home.

Tim backed out of the kitchen and then turned to make his way out of the empty restaurant. It was suddenly creepy in there.

He walked three more blocks, looking for any signs of life. As soon as he tuned his senses to the silence, it was obvious. There were no kids, no radios, no birds, and no moving cars. He found a couple more cars running, but they were abandoned, like the double-parked car near his apartment. Tim turned for home, not knowing what else to do.

He walked back along Spencer Street. It was a good street for walking, but it was usually lousy for jogging. The road was usually lined with parked cars and the sidewalk clogged with strollers. He thought that if there was anywhere he might find signs of life, it would be here. These people seemed to live to be out in their front yards, or cluttering the sidewalks. He found nothing.

About halfway up the block, a sharp sound startled him.

From a tiny blue house, he heard a barking dog.

Tim stopped and looked at the house. The door was open a few inches. He glanced around at the other houses on the block and saw a few more open doors. The dog barked again. Tim took one hesitant step up the walk. He didn't know how, but he knew that it wasn't an aggressive bark. The thought made him consider his co-worker, Meredith. She had a new baby boy and enjoyed telling Tim about all the wonderful instincts she was discovering. Tim thought it was a load of garbage. People were learners. Instinct was for wild animals. She had told him that child-rearing was ninety-percent instinct, and he had told her that she was crazy. She had told him that she could instinctively tell what the baby needed just by the sound of his voice. She had said that she could tell the difference between hungry, wet, teething, and hurt. He had dismissed it all as wishful thinking.

Listening to the dog, he distinctly heard dismay and excitement. He heard no aggression. He almost kept walking.

Tim had walked up to the door, tried to push it open, and frowned when it stopped short. The door was chained. He heard the barking again—pure excitement this time—and saw the shiny black nose appear in the gap. The dog licked its nose and sniffed the air.

"Hello?" Tim called. He knocked on the door.

The dog barked once in response.

Tim stopped halfway down the walk. He glanced back over his shoulder when the dog barked once more. He heard frustration in that bark—lonely, hurt, frustration. Tim turned back and returned to the front door of the little blue house.

"Are you alone in there?" he asked. He blushed. It was stupid to talk to a dog. It was worse to ask a question. Tim pushed on the door and it banged against the chain. How much pressure would it take to break a chain like that? His father had told him, "Locks only keep the honest people out." He pushed slightly harder on the door when it bounced back. The chain held. He heard a thumping from the other side of the door and guessed that the dog's tail was beating against a wall or something.

Tim looked up the street. What was he doing? There had to be an explanation for why everyone had disappeared. Maybe there was a street fair or a parade he didn't know about. Maybe there was a gas leak or a bomb scare. He should be evacuating the area. He should be headed to the court house, or the hospital, or the high school. Someone would tell him what to do. What he should *not* be doing was messing with someone else's dog, legitimately locked in their own house.

"Who locked this door?" he asked. He didn't blush this time. He wasn't asking the dog. He was asking himself. If the door was chained, then someone must still be inside. That person might need help.

Tim ran across the lawn, stepped over a low hedge, and found his way to the neighbor's door. He tried the doorbell and then remembered the power outage. He banged on the door. It swung open. There was no chain holding this one back.

"Hello?" he called. Next door, he heard the dog bark a response. "Hello? Is your phone working?"

He heard no response and saw no life inside the messy living room. Whoever lived here was the kind of person who felt comfortable leaving plates of half-eaten food on the end table. They felt fine walking away from a scatter of newspapers on the couch next to a pair of tube socks. Tim saw the phone sitting on the side table. It was cordless. There would be no power for the base station.

The dog began barking again.

Tim exhaled. The festival or parade idea didn't seem very

likely. When everyone headed off to a big gathering, they didn't often abandon their houses with the doors wide open. This was starting to feel like a place that Tim shouldn't stay. He couldn't just leave that dog in a locked house though. He would try one more thing.

Tim glanced around as he rushed between the houses. The back yard was fenced. Tim let himself in through the gate. He climbed the back porch and cupped his hands to the glass of the storm door. He knocked. When he heard no response, he tried the latch. The storm door opened, but the back door was locked. Through the glass he saw a yellow kitchen with dark, looming cabinetry. The appliances were old, but clean. At least this wasn't the house of another slob, like the neighbor. Past a china cabinet, he saw into the hall. Bright red streaks caught his eye. Something was scrawled on the wall. At first he thought it was a child's handwriting. The letters were impossible to read. But they were too tall. No child could reach that high to make that symbol that looked like a lopsided smiley-face.

On the floor, just poking around the corner, Tim saw the edge of a shoe. He leaned to side and saw that the shoe was connected to an ankle. Tim pushed away from the house and ran to the gate.

✪ ✪ ✪ ✪ ✪

Around the front of the house, he didn't slow as he leaped up onto the porch. He hit the door with his shoulder and regretted his momentum. The chain gave way much easier than he expected and Tim spilled into the house. The dog barked. He was big. Not super tall, like one of those comical Great Danes, standing on stilts for legs, but the dog was barrel-chested and solid. His ears were folded back and he barked again.

Tim saw the body.

The woman was laying in the hall. One hand was resting near her head, as if she'd pressed the back of her hand to her forehead before she'd fainted. Her other hand was in her stomach. Tim recoiled and then looked at the dog.

The dog couldn't have done the damage he saw. If the dog had done that, his mouth and chest would have been covered in blood. This dog's long, auburn hair looked clean and brushed. Tim glanced back at the woman, keeping his eyes to the periphery of the gore. He didn't even see any paw prints in the blood.

Tim exhaled slowly and forced himself to look.

He saw the knife. It was red up to the hilt and leaning against the wall.

He saw the ropes of intestines. They spilled from the woman's abdomen. Her left hand was reaching inside her ruined stomach, like she was looking for something in there. Her face was ageless in its agony. Based on her short hair, the pleats in her jeans, and her pink walking shoes, Tim guessed that the woman was at least forty, but the terror on her face made her look like a frightened child.

When he couldn't stand to look at the gore for another second, Tim turned his eyes to the wall. Someone had used the woman's blood to paint a mural of symbols there. They were nonsense characters of a foreign alphabet. Each was a different size. They extended down the hall towards the yellow kitchen that Tim had seen from the back porch. Based on the bloody footprints on the floor, Tim was ready to identify the artist. The woman must have made the mural herself. There were no other prints leading away from the scene.

Tim backed towards the door.

Out on the porch, Tim glanced at the house number. He whispered, "4508 Spencer. 4508 Spencer. 4508 Spencer."

The dog pushed his way through the door and looked at Tim.

"You're on your own, dog," he said. I'm going to go find help.

Tim broke into a run when he got to the sidewalk. There were no pesky strollers today. Maybe the stroller people had all spilled their guts in their hallways, like the pleated-jeans woman. The thought made Tim's stomach flip.

He looked down as the dog pulled alongside him. Tim ran faster, hoping to leave the dog behind, but the dog accelerated too. At the end of the block, Tim turned towards his own building. He ran down the middle of the street and veered around the double-parked car. It was still running.

At the front door of his apartment, Tim used his lobby key and squeezed through a narrow gap, to keep the dog outside. The dog barked once and then sat down. Tim waved through the glass and turned towards the stairs.

He forgot about his prohibition on using the railing as he climbed. He found his apartment as he'd left it. It was stuffy, and smelled of roasting bird. Aside from that, everything was normal in there. The digital clock next to the window was dark, but that was the only signal that anything was out of the ordinary. Tim went to the keyring for his car keys and saw the potatoes on the cutting board. They were already turning brown. He could deal with them later. He had a suicide to report, and he had yet to find a single living person to report it to.

Tim locked his apartment behind him and ran down the stairs.

He had his wallet, his keys, and his jacket. He couldn't think of anything else he absolutely needed. It occurred to him for the first time that he had never checked the pulse of the woman on the floor. He'd just assumed that she was dead. How could someone live with an injury like that, or with all that blood spilled on the walls and floor? He couldn't even imagine how she'd stayed upright long enough to scrawl the symbols. She had sliced right through all that muscle—what had kept her standing?

Tim shook his head to clear the image as he pushed through the back door for the second time that day. He jogged to the parking area and hit the button on his keyring to unlock his doors. The lights of his Volkswagen flashed and Tim slipped inside. Everything was perfect inside the tight little car. He kept it neat as a pin inside.

Tim started to back up and then stabbed the brakes. The dog was back there. He backed up slowly and the dog graciously moved to the side to let him turn into the aisle. Tim rolled forward and realized he wasn't going to make it far. There was a long, blue sedan blocking the end of the row. He turned in his seat. Behind the dog, at the other end of the lot, a concrete wall held back a grassy hill. He was boxed in.

Tim pulled the brake and left the car running as he got out.

The sedan's door was open. There were no keys in the ignitio and it was in park. Tim cocked his head and tried to understand. Somehow the driver had backed up out of their spot, blocked the row, and then decided to shut off the car and leave? It didn't make sense.

He sighed as he looked up at the sky.

The dog appeared at his side.

"Plan B," Tim said.

He took the time to pull his car back into its spot. He didn't want to be the next person blocking the aisle when the sedan was finally moved or towed. He locked it up and flipped his keys over to his bike lock. The bikes were parked in a room next to the building's utility room. The door was always open. That's why Tim kept his bike locked to the rack. The room was dark. Tim propped open the door with a rock and found his bike. It took him several minutes to puzzle out the lock in the dark. He rolled the bike outside on its back tire and carried the front. He assembled it out in the light and kicked the rock away.

"Stay here," he said to the dog. "Or go home. I don't want you to get caught up in my spokes or something."

The dog didn't obey. As Tim jumped the curb to get out to Chatham Street, the dog was right there, bounding down the pavement. He was headed for the hospital when he saw the answer he didn't know he was looking for. The police station was an enormous building made of gray stone. It sat on the corner, with a parking garage around the other side and a church next door. Tim rolled to a stop in front of the steps. There was nothing to lock his bike to except a "No Parking" sign. He didn't bother to remove the front wheel. He just looped the lock around the frame and called it good.

"No dogs allowed, sorry," he said. The dog was panting from the run. With his mouth open like that, he looked like he was smiling. Tim shook his head and climbed the steps. There were eleven stone steps leading up to the arched doors. The building almost looked like a church. It had a lot in common with the building next door.

The big blue and white letters reading, "POLICE," over the door were unambiguous. Tim pushed open the door.

The lobby had a mellow glow from the high windows that ran down the side wall. Tim stood, listening, while the door closed slowly on its pneumatic hinge behind him. The door creaked and Tim spun to see the door opening again. He saw the dog's face press through gap, forcing the door open with his shoulder.

"You're going to be in trouble," he whispered.

Tim advanced to the front desk. It ran the length of the lobby and had one of those flip-up portions of counter to let an officer come around. It didn't look like this lobby did much business. Tim figured they must lead the criminals in through another door, or maybe they had a handicap entrance around the side where most people came in. There was a tall chair behind the center of the desk. That would be where an officer should sit, to answer questions like the ones Tim had. This would be the officer in charge of keeping the peace and settling jangled nerves, like the ones Tim had.

The place was empty except for Tim and the dog. There wasn't even a pile of woman guts to welcome him to the station.

The dog whined. Tim turned to look at him. The whine turned into a growl. Tim followed the dog's eyes to the windows that ran along the ceiling. The ones on the left showed a taller building across the street—it was a bank, if Tim remembered correctly—but the ones on the right showed nothing but blue sky.

"What are you...?" Tim started to ask. He stopped his question when the shadow passed over the window. The dog stopped growling at the same time. The next sound Tim heard was the scrabble of the dog's toenails as it tried to run on the tile floor. The dog finally got traction and took off like a shot for the gap in the counter where the folded-down door separated the lobby from the official police area. The dog disappeared around the counter.

Tim's eyes returned to the window when the shadow passed again. He saw nothing but blue, but something had blocked the light. He saw one of the dog's eyes appear around the corner of the counter, and saw the way the dog's ear was cocked.

Tim stopped trying to figure out the dog's motivation and decided to follow his lead. Tim ran for the gap in the counter. Behind him, he heard the door creak once more as something pushed its way inside the police station lobby.

CHAPTER 10: NEW HAMPSHIRE

WITH THE GARAGE DOOR open, the headlights of the van lit up the interior. The bright lights seemed to insist on immediate action. Everyone was impatient to act.

"No," Pete said. "I'm not going anywhere with him. He was armed and hunting us. He can rot here."

"He never even shot at us," Lisa said. "You're sentencing him to death because he was carrying guns? We had a gun in the old van."

"He said he was going to kill Robby," Pete said.

"He said if we came closer, he would kill Robby. He might have just been frightened," Lisa said.

"Are you serious?" Romie asked. "You're defending this guy? Robby—did he intend to kill you?"

Robby nodded. "Yes. He has wanted to kill me for a long time."

"Case closed," Romie said. "We'll leave him here." She turned towards their new van.

"I think we should bring him with us," Robby said.

"You too?" Romie asked. "You're both crazy. Just because life is scarce, doesn't mean that it's all worth defending. This guy is crazy and wanted to attack us. We have enough things in our lives that are trying to kill us. The last thing we need is one more threat that we're dragging along with us. Not to mention, he's seriously injured." Romie moved to within striking distance of Lyle as she talked. She looked like she might be in the mood to injure him some more.

"He might know something that we don't," Robby said. "He might have seen something or experienced something that can inform us."

"And he's incapacitated," Lisa said. "He's no threat to us now."

"And when he wakes up, we could get him talking and find out what he knows," Robby said.

Robby and Lisa moved closer together as they defended Lyle. Pete approached them with his hands turned up. He beseeched them. "Can't you see what a terrible idea this is?"

"I think I have to agree with them, Robby," Brad said. "We have to be able to..."

His sentence was finished for him by the loud pop. They all turned to Romie. She was standing with her arm extended towards Lyle. When she turned away, Lyle slumped and they saw the gun in her hand. It was one of Lyle's own.

Lisa didn't say anything. She turned and walked to the van. She got in the back seat and closed the door.

Brad could barely hear Pete from the ringing in his ears.

Pete was looking around the garage. "Okay. What do we need from here?"

Romie tossed the gun towards the workbench. Brad flinched as it landed. He was convinced it would go off and send a stray bullet in a random direction. It didn't. Romie headed for the driver's door.

Pete didn't find anything to take from the garage. Maybe he didn't want to disturb any of the orderly tools. Robby grabbed the box with the remaining warm soda. They all walked towards the van. As Romie backed away, the headlights of the van encircled Lyle in cold light. His head was slumped to the side. His chest was a shiny red hole. His crotch was darkened from the urine that had released when he died.

Pete had an old folded map that he had found somewhere. He bent over it, using the light from the glove box to decipher the symbols.

"Take a right," Pete said.

He guided them north, over a twisty country road, so they could get to the nearest bridge. Nobody talked.

"Left up here."

Romie let out an exasperated sigh as she slowed for a patch of water across the road. Brad leaned forward to see if he could tell if it was the dangerous kind of liquid.

"Go ahead. It's nothing," Pete said.

Romie accelerated. She normally hit wet patches at a cautious speed, regardless of Pete's confidence. This time she threw the vehicle at the streak of liquid on the road. Brad fastened his seat belt. They crossed the bridge over the rushing water. Somewhere downstream of their position, their last minivan had drowned in this same river. Brad pressed his face against the window as Romie rolled over the bridge. This one sat higher and didn't look like it had any intention of collapsing. When Brad looked back up, the headlights lit up a sign that read, "Welcome to Vermont. The Green Mountain State."

A hundred yards beyond the sign, Romie stopped for another patch of liquid.

"Okay," Pete said.

Romie stomped the gas pedal and the minivan lurched forward.

"WAIT!" Pete shouted. She slowed to a stop. For a second, Brad wondered if she was going to just barrel through. They were so close to the patch of wet pavement that Pete had to push himself higher and stretch his neck to see.

"Back up," Pete whispered.

Romie pushed the transmission to reverse and let the van idle backwards. Brad leaned forward.

"It's happening again," Robby said from the back seat.

"What's happening?" Lisa asked.

"The liquid is collecting again for..." Robby started to say.

"No!" Romie said. "I've heard enough speculation. I only want to hear facts. Which way do we go, Pete?"

"I don't know," Pete said. He was flipping the map over. The river and the bridge were located right on a fold in the map.

Romie was still rolling the van backwards and Brad suddenly had a better view of the liquid. He saw what had made Pete yell. On the right side, near where the liquid came over the side of the road, it glistened. It was strange enough that there would be a stream of liquid across this patch of road. The road was crowned in the center and had drainage ditches on either side. With no standing water in the ditch, Brad couldn't imagine how runoff could get to the point where it would crest the road. That wasn't the only clue. The liquid also glistened in the headlights. Over near the side he could see it ebbing and flowing, like it was getting ready for something. After that back and forth movement, a wave pulsed and flowed down the wet patch. The wave flowed across the road.

"Which way, Pete?"

"I don't know. I guess we have to go back across the bridge. We haven't passed any other roads on this side of the river. We're going to have to go..." He flipped the map and unfolded another section. The interior of the van was filled with the sound of crinkling paper. "I think we have to go twenty miles north. Wait. Thirty miles."

"I wouldn't," Robby said.

Romie practically growled at him. "Is this more speculation? Are you about to make another guess at something?"

"I wouldn't keep backing up," Robby said.

Brad looked at the boy. Robby sat in the seat behind Brad and didn't appear to be looking anywhere but forward. Romie tapped the brake pedal, for whatever reason, and when the red lights joined the white reverse light, Brad saw something terrible.

"STOP!" Brad yelled.

They jerked to a stop.

"Will you people quit yelling?" Romie asked. "I can follow orders that aren't screamed."

Brad was tugging at his door. "We have to get out of here."

Behind the van, the liquid was moving much faster than the gentle wave that had flowed across the road in front of them. Behind them, lit up by the brake lights, the liquid was pulsing and flowing like a flood. Two runners of fluid led the way, seeming to mark where their tires had rolled. Farther back, lines of liquid zigged and zagged back and forth, covering the road in a spiderweb.

Romie threw the vehicle into park and took her foot off the brake. Brad's view of the liquid was gone. His fingers finally found the secret to the door. He had to pull it back while he tugged the handle. The door rolled open.

Pete flipped the map. "There is a..."

"We have to get out of here," Brad said. Nobody seemed to understand.

Brad jumped out into the night. He pulled out his flashlight and swept it to the pavement behind the van. The liquid was coming fast. It would be to the van at any second.

"Get out!" he yelled. "Come on. Come on."

Lisa and Robby began to follow through Brad's door. Romie swung her door open and Pete looked up from his map. Through the back window, Pete must have seen what Brad's light showed, but he just sat there. Romie got a clue and pulled his sleeve. Pete crawled over the center console and followed her out into the night.

"This way," Brad said. He pointed his light in the same direction as the headlights. The liquid was still pulsing across the road in that direction, but the flow wasn't wide. "We can jump it."

"Take big strides," Robby said. He almost sounded bored.

"What? Why?" Romie asked.

"Just do it," Lisa said.

They all ran towards where the liquid formed a line across the road. They all hopped from foot to foot, taking big strides. When they got to the edge, Brad's flashlight beam swept across the sky as he leapt across the liquid to the other side. Robby and Lisa followed. Romie backed up and took a running start. Pete jumped and windmilled his arms to catch his balance. Lisa grabbed him and pulled him forward.

Brad led the way up the road.

"Wait," Romie said after a few paces.

Brad turned around. She was looking back the way they'd come. The headlights shining in their eyes made it difficult to see.

The beams jerked when the liquid reached the vehicle. They heard the rear tires of the van explode and the headlights pointed up, over their heads for a second. Then, when the liquid exploded the front tires, the headlights came back down again. They didn't last long. Something shorted in the vehicle as the liquid consumed it. The headlights flickered and then went out, leaving a glow on Brad's retinas.

"We should head uphill," Lisa said.

"We won't be able to see the liquid in the grass," Pete said. "We have to stay on pavement."

Brad turned his flashlight forward again and it was joined by Lisa's. They moved at a fast walk. Lisa turned her beam around periodically to look in the direction they'd come from.

"Will it follow us?" Lisa asked.

"Yes," Robby said.

They hadn't gone far when they saw the next line of liquid. It was wider than the last. Brad jumped over it before anyone could debate what to do. Only Romie had trouble with the jump. She ran to the edge and leaped, but she didn't get much height. Her foot came down very close to the edge of the liquid. Lisa's light was pointed to the ground where Romie had landed.

"It senses us," Lisa said.

Brad joined his light to hers and saw. The edge of the flow broke open and Romie's footprint filled with the stuff. They all backed away as they watched it. A pencil-thin bead of liquid reached out in their direction. It moved slow.

They ran.

Brad counted his paces and got to eighty before they found the next line. The road was flat ahead of them and there was nothing but Vermont forest on either side. He wasn't absolutely sure, but it seemed like this flow was closer than the last had been. He wondered if they were just getting closer and closer to a place where the liquid covered the entire road.

The only good news he saw was that this flow wasn't as wide across. They all jumped easily and settled into a slow jog. After seventy-two paces, they found the next one.

"The gap between them is getting smaller," Pete said. Brad had been just about to make the same comment. "We have to figure out a different plan. What if we head into the woods between the flows and maybe climb a tree? Do you think the liquid will go away?"

"What if it's a grid? Didn't someone say it was a grid?" Lisa asked.

"Speculation," Romie said.

"We keep going forward until we're forced into something different," Pete said. "We know what's behind us."

"Yeah," Lisa said.

The rest agreed silently.

✪ ✪ ✪ ✪ ✪

Over the course of the next fifty paces, the road crested a small hill. When their lights swept over the pavement on the other side, they saw a strange pattern of wet asphalt. A couple of bands of pulsing liquid ran perpendicular to the direction of the road, but down its length, they saw intricate trails of the stuff. In some places, big patches swelled and flowed. In others, it was like a fine network of threads.

"What the hell is it doing?" Romie whispered.

"Can I borrow your light?" Pete asked Lisa.

She handed it to him. Pete headed off to the side of the road. The rest watched as Brad's beam explored the surface. The liquid seemed oblivious to them. It was busy creating its patterns. Brad found a spot a few yards away where the liquid moved through a few gentle turns. Dotted down the length, the liquid swelled into shapes that looked like footprints.

"Someone was here," Romie said.

"This is where they camped," Robby said.

Brad kept his light on the road, but turned to look at the boy. His blank eyes were staring up at the sky.

"Hey," Pete said, as he jogged back up to them. "We might be able to go this way."

Pete led them over to the side of the road. He pointed Lisa's flashlight into the tall grass. The ground fell away into a ditch and then quickly climbed up a small hill where the tall grass ended and the trees began.

"What makes you think it's safe?" Romie asked.

"You can see the liquid there," Pete said. He pointed the light more to the west. He was right. The liquid coated the stalks of grass up to the tops, making each one droop a little. The top of each stalk glittered in the light. The pulsing moisture caught the light and sparkled.

"So we get into the woods—then what?" Lisa asked.

"Look at this wall," Pete said. He focused the light on an old rock wall, under the canopy of trees. Some of the rocks had tumbled away, but it looked pretty good for an ancient wall that might have once demarcated the edge of a cow field. They could see where the liquid passed near the rock wall. It made a clear path on either side of the rocks, but it must have flowed under, rather than over, them. They were dry on top.

"This seems like a bad idea," Romie said.

"Do you have a better one?" Lisa asked.

✪ ✪ ✪ ✪ ✪

It would have been impossible, if not for the trees. They grew close enough to the wall so the group could lean on the trunks when the footing was bad. It was bad most of the time. As they walked down the length of the wall, Brad wondered about its origin. Some of these rocks were so big he wouldn't have been able to get his arms around one. They were big round monstrosities that someone had pulled free from the soil and moved into this straight line.

Back when the world made sense, Brad had owned property with rock walls. But those walls were made from jagged pieces of ledge, that you could imagine two people might carry.

Ahead, Romie slipped and her leg shot out to the side. With lightning-fast reflexes, Pete caught her arm. Her foot stopped an inch from the wet leaves.

Brad turned around. Behind him, Robby had his arms out to the sides. He looked like a kid practicing his balance on a curb. The experience didn't seem to bother him in the slightest.

"Pete?" Lisa called back, from the front of the line. Brad swept his light in her direction. "There's a gap in the wall."

She moved off to one of the out-of-place stones and the rest gathered the best they could at the edge of the gap. Robby pulled himself up into a maple tree while Romie watched nervously.

Ahead, the rocks were little islands in the forest. Someone had knocked a hole in the wall, about the right size for a vehicle to pass through. It was overgrown, but Brad thought he could see the remnants of a road. Pete took Lisa's flashlight again and used it to identify the places where the liquid pulsed over the forest carpet.

"What do we do?" Lisa asked. "We can't jump that, and the liquid is everywhere. We have to go back."

"Back where?" Romie asked. "We're boxed in. We should have turned around when we had the chance."

"We tried, remember?" Pete asked. "We were doomed as soon as we came across that bridge. Maybe that's why that other bridge was booby trapped. Maybe someone was trying to keep us from running into trouble."

His logic seemed flawed, but Brad didn't bother to argue. They had bigger problems to worry about than incorrect conclusions.

"It doesn't seem to flow up these rocks," Lisa said.

Brad looked down and saw a fairly small rock near his foot. He carefully crouched, using a tree next to him to keep his balance, and lifted the thing. It was heavy for one hand, but he managed to get his fingers under it and brought it up to waist-level as he stood. The others saw what he was doing, and nobody objected. Brad cast the stone out into the gap in the wall. It landed with a hollow thump and rolled over before it came to a stop. It was right in the middle of a pulsing patch of wet leaves. The top of his rock remained dry.

"Are there enough rocks though?" Pete asked.

"There was a clump of pretty small rocks farther back," Brad said. "I think we could lift most of them."

Brad walked backwards down the wall, leaving the others where they stood. He found what he was looking for. One section of the wall had been created with a few big rocks and then chinked with dozens of liftable stones. He grabbed one and turned.

With the extra weight in his hand and the flashlight in the other, Brad lost his balance. His foot slipped on a mossy patch and shot out the side. Brad clutched the rock to his chest as his light swept up towards the sky. His right foot came crunching down in the leaves. When he tried to pull back, he only slipped more. His leg buckled and his knee slammed into a rock. He pointed his light down. His foot was a hair away from a pulsing tendril of liquid that flowed through the leaves.

Brad dropped the rock and threw his torso down on the wall to pull his leg up from the leaves.

He looked back. He had somehow managed to avoid touching the liquid. Brad carefully got his feet underneath him again and lifted the rock.

It was too difficult to walk the wall and carry the rock. Pete appeared in the faint glow of Lisa's light, and put his hands out. Brad handed him the rock.

They formed a chain of hands. Brad propped his light in the crook of a branch and he found the stones. He handed them to Pete, who turned and handed them to Romie. Behind them, they were creating a nearly impassable gap.

"We think that's enough," he heard Romie say to Pete.

Pete waved Brad forward. He grabbed his light and followed.

On their side of the gap, Lisa had placed a few stones side by side. On the other side, it was just a line of small rocks. Some looked uncomfortably far apart.

"We need more rocks," Brad said.

Lisa shook her head. "It's too dangerous. It's getting harder and harder to place them. I think we should just try it."

"No," Brad said. "It's impossible."

Robby ducked under Lisa's arm and stepped out onto the stones. At the beginning, he was able to step back and forth, straddling two stones at once. About halfway across, he had to move in a straight line. The rocks were just big enough for his feet. The second one rolled as Robby stepped on it. He sprang forward, and ran the last few steps before leaping up to the wall on the other side.

Brad was focused on the rock that rolled over. The side that turned up was wet. As he watched, the liquid parted in the center and flowed down the sides of the rock. Another rock fell out of the dark and landed next to the rock that had rolled. Brad raised his light and saw Robby. He turned, crouched, and came back up with another rock. Robby added a few more stones to the sparsest part of the path.

"We need more rocks," Brad said.

"No," Romie said. "We'll make do." She took Lisa's hand and lowered herself down to the rocks. Brad held his breath. He wanted to tell her to stop. She would never make it across. He couldn't. They had to move forward. It was their only option.

Worse than watching Romie move across the rocks was listening to Lisa suck in a startled breath each time Romie faltered. More than once, Brad wanted to go out after Romie, so he could perhaps reach out and stabilize her. But she needed plenty of room. Romie would lose her balance and have to retreat several stones before she could move forward again. Robby reached out from the other side and Lisa exhaled her relief when Romie's hand finally made the connection with the boy.

He helped her up to the other side and Pete stepped down on the rocks.

"Throw the light," Romie said from the other side. "Half the problem is the damn shadows."

Brad realized she was right. They had both of the flashlights on one side of the gap. He looked at Lisa and motioned for her to throw. Brad would go last across the gap.

They made it without incident, but not without stress. Brad's heart pounded by the time the hands pulled him up on the other side. He looked back across the gap. At this pace it would take them until dawn to move a mile. Dawn was when it became dangerous to be outside. Dawn was when you had a stronger possibility of being plucked backwards into oblivion by unknown forces. They had to find shelter. They had to find somewhere to hide from the sky.

A while later, Pete must have been thinking the same thing.

"We have to start moving faster," Pete said.

"I'm exhausted," Romie said. "If I try to move any faster, I'm going to fall off this damn wall."

"I think maybe that's okay," Pete said.

Brad looked up from his feet and saw that Pete was looking off to the side. He trained his light on the leaves where Pete was staring. The leaves looked dry.

"Do you think we've gone past it?"

"Looks like it," Lisa said. She was shining her light up the hill on the other side of the wall. She moved her light from spot to spot. There was no glistening liquid under her beam either.

"What do you think?" Brad asked. "Should we risk it?"

They heard the leaves crunch and Brad and Lisa turned their lights forward. Robby was walking off through the woods.

"Robby!" Lisa called.

"It's fine," the boy said over his shoulder. "There's a thing over here."

Brad couldn't tell what he was talking about. Lisa took the plunge next. She stepped down off the wall and followed the trail of rustled leaves that Robby left behind. The others went as well. Romie was the last to trust herself to step off the wall, but as soon as both the lights started to move into the forest, she didn't have much choice. Brad heard her pulling up the rear. She made a relieved sound when her feet hit the forest floor. Brad knew the feeling. After walking on the uneven rocks for as long as they had, his ankles were fatigued to their limit. Walking across the leaves felt like a vacation.

✪ ✪ ✪ ✪ ✪

Robby was standing with his face pressed to the window when Lisa and Brad arrived. Pete stood off to the side, unwilling to commit to a course of action.

"What is this place?" Lisa asked.

"Ranger station," Pete said. "According to the sign."

"What's a ranger station?" she asked. She swept her light across the face of the building. It was a two-story log cabin, but Brad doubted if there was anything behind those upper windows. They looked like they were only for show. The logs that made up the siding were stained dark and blended well into the surrounding woods. The porch roof was shingled with cedar shakes. Except for the glass windows and the green metal door, the place looked like it could have been two-hundred years old.

"Great," Romie said as she walked up. "Now we're in Little House on the Prairie."

"It's shelter," Lisa said. "We might need it." She walked up the steps and pointed her light through the window. She and Robbie examined the interior of the place as the others stood well back. They watched as Robby walked over to the door and tried to turn the handle. Robby turned and thrust his elbow into one of the panes of glass in the upper half of the metal door. He made a face and hit it harder.

"Wait," Pete said. "You're going to cut yourself." Pete went to the side of the porch where he found a stove-length piece of wood. He handed it over the porch railing to Robby. The boy rammed the end of the wood into the glass several times before it cracked. Romie looked into the dark woods to see if the noise was drawing any attention.

Brad came forward to add his light to the door. The glass broke with a crunch and Robby knocked out the stray pieces with the log. Robby reached in carefully to unlock the door. When he swung it inwards, the glass scraped on the floor.

Robby stepped through first. Brad trotted up the porch stairs and followed him in. Lisa's light angled through the window as she moved down the porch to follow them inside.

The air smelled like it held colonies of dry spores. Brad imagined that with each inhale, raiding parties of harmful organisms were settling into his lungs. Their virulence would be awakened by the moist environment of his body. Brad pulled his shirt up over his nose. Brad's flashlight found only a few furnishings in the room. He saw two desks along the back wall. A bookshelf held a small library of field guides and picture books. A rack held a bunch of information pamphlets. On the right side of the room, a small table sat between the wood stove and a small refrigerator.

"What died in here?" Romie asked from the doorway.

"Over here," Robby said. Brad pointed his flashlight to the table where Robby stood. The boy used the light to find a pack of matches. While Robby lit a candle, Brad turned his attention to the rack of pamphlets. Most were just glossy advertisements of local attractions, but one of them had a map of trails. Brad pulled it out and took it to the desk to unfold it.

Robby lit his candle and then found a few more in holders mounted to the wall. It looked like a major fire hazard with the flames so close to the unfinished walls, but Brad figured they could get out quickly enough if they had to.

Romie finally came in and Pete took up her spot in the doorway. He left them to the investigation while he looked off into the night.

"You guys never answered me—what's a ranger station?" Lisa asked. She was pointing her flashlight up a steep set of stairs that led up through a hole in the ceiling. It was so steep that Brad thought it might be better described as a ladder, although it did have little treads instead of rungs.

"This is probably a National Forest," Pete said from the doorway. "The rangers stay here to answer questions and help people out if they get stuck in the woods."

"It's like a field office," Romie said.

"Oh," Lisa said.

"Pete, this map might be helpful," Brad said. He carried the paper over to the door and held a flashlight on it. Pete unfolded it the rest of the way and snapped the folds from the paper.

"It's more of a trail map, but it does show the local roads," Pete said. "Maybe we can hike over this way."

Brad kept his light trained on the map. His eyes wandered. Romie was pulling open desk drawers. Lisa was climbing up the ladder. Robby had found a lantern on a shelf and was trying to unscrew the top of the thing. His face was twisted with effort as he tried to get a grip on the rusted cap nut.

All eyes turned to Lisa as she crashed down the steep steps. She didn't yell once as she landed on her butt. Robby was the first one over to her.

They all took Lisa's cue and stayed very quiet.

"What happened?" Romie whispered.

Lisa pointed up. "Someone's up there."

"Are you okay?" Pete asked. Lisa nodded.

Robby was on his toes, trying to see up through the hole without touching the ladder. Romie took the flashlight from Lisa's hand and moved around the boy. She didn't hesitate. Romie climbed. When her head breached the hole in the ceiling, Romie stopped. She angled her flashlight around and got a good look before she began climbing again. She waved a silent hand down, beckoning them to follow.

Pete went up next.

Brad looked over to the door of the cabin. He crossed to it and tried to close the door. He had to kick some of the broken glass away to get the thing to close. He re-locked the door and pulled the little green curtain across the broken glass. Before returning to the stairs, he double-checked Robby's candles to be sure that they weren't about to catch the walls on fire. Robby's feet were just disappearing through the hatch in the ceiling as Brad got to the bottom of the ladder. He heard their whispers up there.

He remembered the little dog house dormers and thought again that the space up there must be small. For a second, he considered waiting at the bottom. They would come down and tell him what was up there. Was there really a need for all five of them to go up?

Brad held his light out with one hand and climbed.

The second floor of the cabin was bigger than he thought. There was enough room to stand and there two full beds in the attic bedroom. The dog house dormers cut out little sections of the sloped ceiling and made the room feel less oppressive. The window at the far wall showed the woods below. The trees looked like apparitions in the dancing candlelight leaking from the first floor windows.

Brad's group was clustered around one of the beds. Brad couldn't tell what they were looking at until he got closer and could see between Romie and Lisa. There was a body there.

The way the hands were positioned around the hole in the chest, it looked like something had exploded out. Then he saw the gun. This person—a man, as far as Brad could tell—must have shot himself in the chest and then tried to close his hands over the gaping wound. His face was too far gone to reveal anything. Time had reduced his skin to a taut black webbing, connecting the peaks of his face bones.

Lisa turned to the other bed. She pulled the blanket and brought it over. Pete helped her stretch it out to cover the man.

"Wait," Robby said. Before they had settled the blanket down, Robby reached out for the little book that sat on the bed next to the body.

Brad sucked in a breath. He was sure somehow that one of the mummy's brittle hands would shoot out and grab Robby's wrist as soon as he touched the book. Maybe the boy felt the same thing, because he paused right before he touched it. Then, when his fingers took possession of the little book, he snatched it back. Brad exhaled.

Lisa and Pete settled the blanket down. The smell of moldy garbage puffed out from the body and Brad pulled his shirt up over his nose again.

"I wonder if he did it before or after," Romie said.

"After," Pete said. "He must have done it after. Maybe he knew everyone else disappeared, he got depressed, and he decided to check out. It's understandable."

"Did you ever think about it?" Romie asked. She still held Lisa's flashlight. She still pointed it where the blanket was propped up by the mummy's head.

"No," Pete said.

"Do we have to talk about this here?" Lisa asked.

Brad swept his light around the living quarters once more. He didn't see anything more interesting than a chest of drawers. He couldn't imaging anything in there that he would need. He headed back for the stairs.

When they were all back on the first floor, Lisa kept glancing up towards the hole. Robby took the little book over to the table and sat down. He dragged a candle close to the pages. Robby closed one eye as he flipped through the book.

Pete moved to the window near the door. He looked out into the night before unlocking and opening it. He didn't keep it open long. He leaned through the window. When he pulled back inside, he closed the shutters and latched them. He locked the window and moved to the next one.

"So we're staying here during the day?" Romie asked. "Move out when it gets dark again?"

"I guess," Pete said.

"The liquid is extra aggressive on this side of the river. What makes you think the snatchers won't be too?" Romie asked.

"I don't know," Pete said.

"We need sleep, either way," Lisa said. "Might as well be here." Her voice trailed off as her eyes darted back to the upstairs hatch again.

"I haven't seen a single spider since last year, but somehow I'm guessing this place is full of them," Romie said.

Everyone turned to Robby when he spoke. His head was hunched over the little book and his voice sounded strange. The angle of his neck gave his tone a strained and strangled quality. He had his left eye squinted shut as he read.

"I saw the claws of the one that took Ursula. They were clear as glass and must have been just as sharp. Blood shot out from her shoulders and then she disappeared into the sky," Robby said.

"What is that?" Lisa asked.

"His journal," Robby said. "It ends with his suicide note, but before that he describes seeing a bunch of people get snatched. He talks about the snow, too. I think he was up north of here when it happened."

"Suicide note?" Lisa asked. She moved away from the stairs, as if she suddenly thought the condition might be contagious.

"He was convinced that there was nobody still alive," Robby said. He flipped through the pages of the journal.

"What was his name?" Lisa asked.

"He doesn't say," Robby said.

Pete finished shuttering the windows and he was back at the

door. He pulled aside the curtain, looked through the broken glass and then closed it again. "Help me with this," he said to Brad. He was pointing at the bookshelf.

Brad set his light down on one of the desks and moved to the other side of the bookshelf. The books swayed as they lifted. They shuffled the bookcase over in front of the door. It only rose to about halfway up the glass part of the door, but it covered the hole.

"What's the point?" Romie asked. "They'll put us in a trance and draw us outside if they want to take us."

"If you're in a trance and you try to move this bookcase, I'll wake up and stop you," Pete said.

Romie shrugged.

Pete went to the table and picked up the lantern that Robby had been fiddling with. He used a corner of his shirt to get a grip on the rusted nut. He had the cover off after a few seconds.

"Needs a new mantle," Robby said without looking up from the book. He pointed off to the side. Pete followed the direction of his finger and saw a trunk next to the desk. Brad watched him walk over and flip up the lid. He pulled out a metal can of fuel and a package of wicks. Pete looked over at the boy. Robby hadn't looked in the trunk before—there hadn't been time. Pete didn't ask how he knew where to find the supplies. He just took the things back to the table and set to work.

The ranger station only contained four chairs, so Brad pulled up the trunk. Even flipping it up sideways, he was shorter than everyone else at the table. Lisa divided up the food. They'd found a sealed container with some snacks and dark green bags labeled "MRE."

"It means meals ready to eat," Pete said.

As Brad opened his bag, his wrists were level with the surface of the table.

"It comes with chores," Brad said. He pulled the white sheet of instructions from the bag. He was instructed to pour water from his canteen into the little envelope and set that under his propped up tray.

"I don't get it," Romie said.

"Yours has a chemical heater," Pete said. "It's to warm up your beef teriyaki."

"Gross," Romie said.

The lantern started to sputter and all eyes turned to it. It threw off way more light than the candles, but the noises it made were somehow disquieting.

Robby was already spooning cold rations into his mouth and chewing happily. Brad set aside the pouch of chemicals and decided to follow Robby's lead. They didn't have a whole lot of water to waste on warming up a meal anyway.

The dawn light was starting to show through the shutters and curtains. They rushed through their meal. It was easier to make it through the day asleep, and they were all exhausted.

"It's nice to have you back, Robby," Lisa said.

"It's nice that we don't have to drag you around like a mannequin," Romie said.

From upstairs, they heard a thump followed by a creak. All eyes turned to the steep stairs.

"I'm sure it's just the wind or something," Brad said.

"It's the building settling," Pete said.

"That's what you said last time," Lisa said. "How comes it only happens when we're all down here?"

"There's nothing up there to make any noise," Pete said. "We've checked three times."

Brad wiped his hands on the little napkin as he chewed and swallowed. "I'll go," he said. "I want to steal the blankets and pillows from the spare bed anyway. At least we can make the floor more comfortable."

"Throw down the whole bed," Romie said.

"If it will fit," Brad said.

He grunted when he stood. He walked over to the staircase—so steep it was more like a ladder—and then remembered his flashlight. His knees ached, right near the dimples on the inside of his kneecaps. It was probably from all the twisting. Walking on rocks was hard on old knees.

Brad put the end of the flashlight in his mouth so he could grab the rails on either side. He used his arms to help pull himself up. He barely needed the light upstairs. The sky outside was beginning to brighten, and the shutters up here didn't cover the entire windows. Light was leaking in from the windows on the ends of the room and through the dormers.

Pete and Romie had been upstairs three times, but this was only Brad's second trip. His attention immediately went to the tented figure on the bed. He remembered how the corpse looked, with his hands framing the giant hole in his chest. He remembered how the gray skin was stretched across the bones of the man's skull.

The other bed had one folded blanket and two sheets. He took that and the two pillows and dropped them through the hatch. With his outstretched arms, he gauged the width of the mattress. It was thin and might fold, but he didn't think it would fit through the hatch to get it downstairs. He wondered how it had made it up here. Most of the furniture up here looked too big to fit.

Brad opened a couple of drawers and found two more blankets. He turned to...

THUNK.

Brad spun just his head. His hands still held the blankets in the direction of the hatch.

On the bed with the corpse tent, the blanket fluttered where it hung down over the sides of the bed. Brad stared at it. He was frozen in place. He heard the creak of springs. Brad spun on his heels and backed towards the hatch. He was unwilling to take his eyes off the blanket that was tented over the corpse.

Brad's foot floated over the hatch and he nearly fell backwards. He regained his balance and dropped the blankets behind him.

"Hey!" Romie called from below. "Watch where you're..."

"Shhh!" Brad said. It sounded strange. He still had the flashlight in his mouth.

As he watched, the angles of the corpse tent changed. The shadows on the right deepened and one of the peaks moved closer to the left edge. Brad wondered if he could get down the stairs fast enough so he wouldn't have to witness what was going to emerge from under there.

His escape was cut off as he heard someone climbing behind him. Brad's eyes darted to the hatch and then returned to the corpse tent. It was Romie coming up. That was good. She was pragmatic and strong. No matter what was under that blanket, she would be an asset.

"What are you shushing me about?" she asked. "What's going on up here?"

Brad reached up and pulled the flashlight from his mouth. He kept the beam trained on the bed. He laid a finger across his lips and then pointed.

"Him? I don't think he has bothered anyone in quite..."

Romie stopped as she saw what Brad saw. Something was sliding under that blanket. The edge of the blanket rippled a bit. Just when he thought something would pop out from the edge, the shape reversed direction.

"He can't be moving," Romie said.

"This wouldn't be the first moving corpse we've seen," Brad whispered.

"Those were different," Romie said.

She didn't hesitate any longer. She strode over to the bed. For a moment, she blocked Brad's view of the corpse tent, and that was okay with him. She reached the side of the bed, rubbed her fingers together and then snatched up the edge of the blanket. She pulled it off and sent it back and to the side.

CHAPTER 11: NEW YORK

JUDY PRESSED THE TEARS from her eyes with trembling hands. She looked down and realized that she was sitting in the same chair that the old woman had been sitting in when she died. The part of her that should have been horrified was numb.

"Do you want a cigarette?" a man asked.

She looked at his hands. They were empty. Maybe if she had seen one, ready to light, she would have caved. She shook her head.

A rush of people came in through the side door. They wore beards. Luke was in the lead. He crouched down next to her chair and kept his hands a respectful distance as he looked up into her bleary eyes.

"Judy, what happened?" Luke asked.

"I... I don't know," she said, stammering.

Luke turned to his right and addressed one of the bearded men standing against the wall. "Get Winslow in here, will you?"

"Judy, they said you were attacked. What attacked you?"

"I don't know," she said.

The kitchen shadows danced with candlelight. The candles were everywhere—on the table, on the windowsills, and down the counter. The flames didn't seem to send out enough light somehow. The kitchen still seemed like it was drowning in soft shadows.

Judy flinched when Luke's hand came forward. He was

reaching for her ankle.

"May I?" he asked, pausing his hand.

She closed her mouth on her lips and nodded.

He gently pushed her jeans up from her ankles. Judy was wearing sneakers and ankle socks. Luke's fingers touched her bare skin. He was gentle and quick.

"You're okay. You're okay," he said. He seemed to be talking to himself.

A pair of bearded men came through the door. Judy barely looked at them. She was concerned whether Luke's hands might want to touch her again. She hadn't been repulsed by his touch, but that's what concerned her.

"I thought you said she was hurt?" Luke asked one of the men.

"I didn't say that. Richmond is the one who said that."

"Well, goddammit, get Richmond in here. What the fuck is wrong with you people?"

Another man pressed through the door and took Winslow's place. Judy recognized this one.

"I'm right here, boss," Richmond said.

"I thought you said she was injured."

"Nossir," Richmond said, in one slurred word. "I said she was attacked. Helen was the one that got snared by the vines. They're working on her up in the bathroom. They got about half of the thorns out, but she's bleeding all over the place."

"Okay, okay," Luke said. "Shut the fuck up." When he turned back to Judy, his face had reverted back to gentle condescension. "You didn't see what attacked you?"

"It wasn't," Judy began. She swallowed hard. Luke motioned to one of the bearded men and he somehow knew to fetch a glass of water. "It wasn't a physical attack," she said. Her mind raced. She realized quickly that she had to embellish the truth or she would reveal her own escape attempt. "I was drawn up into the neighborhood. It was like my body was taken over."

Luke's eyes narrowed a tiny bit, so she veered back to the truth, the whole truth, so-help-her-God.

"I heard a loud noise. It sounded like two big wooden blocks clapping together. You know those wood blocks they used to use for percussion in grade school?"

Luke nodded. She wondered if he knew, or if he was just nodding to keep her talking.

"It sounded like those. It was a hollow sound and it made me remember."

The room was dead quiet when she paused. One of the bearded men set a glass of water on the table and the sound of it seemed to echo in the room. She picked it up and took a silent sip. Judy was careful to set it down carefully so it didn't make a sound.

"It seemed like the sound drove me into the past. I wasn't just remembering—I was there. I was back on Christmas Day, waiting for everyone to come downstairs so we could open presents."

"Was that a happy memory?"

"Yes, mostly. There were sad things around the edges. I felt excluded and ignored. But I was also excited. You know. I was a kid at Christmas. I had that anxious feeling."

"And you associate these memories with the sound you heard?" Luke asked.

Judy nodded. "Absolutely. I could tell that it was what drove me into the past, but I couldn't ignore it or break the trance."

"So you knew, while it was happening?"

"Yes. Well... In a way. It was like when you get caught up in a movie. You know you shouldn't be frightened because it's just a movie, but it's still scary. That's a bad example. I wasn't all that scared because I was home."

"Luke?" a man asked from the door. It might have been Winslow. Judy had a hard time telling the bearded men apart.

"Yeah?"

"You might want to come talk to Helen. She's talking about Dayton."

"I'll be right there. Hold tight and have someone write down everything she says." Luke turned back to Judy. "Can you do that too? Can you write down everything you remember from tonight. Start right at the beginning, when you left here. I want to know mostly about the sound and the dream, but I'd like to have a full text. Understand?"

"Sure," Judy said. She reached for the glass again and her hand was trembling even worse. She paused until she could get it under control.

"You know what? Let me find someone who can write for you. That way you can just dictate, okay?"

"I'd..." Judy began. She stopped herself. She wasn't quite sure what she had been about to say.

"What?" Luke asked.

She glanced up at Winslow, who was still waiting to take Luke upstairs. She wished Luke would just go, but he was waiting to hear the rest of her thought.

"I'd prefer to go outside, if I could," she said. She felt herself blushing and hoped it wouldn't show up in the candlelight.

"No problem."

Luke pointed to one of the men and gave him quick instructions.

✪ ✪ ✪ ✪ ✪

As Judy recounted her story to a bearded man named Norway, she developed a fresh perspective on the situation. Her story wasn't very remarkable on its own. Something else must have happened for them to want so many details from her.

She got near the end and then paused. Norway wanted her to continue. She wanted information.

"What happened to Helen?" she asked.

"I don't know," Norway said.

"You must know something."

He shook his head and looked down at the pad he was writing on. Judy felt that she was terrible at reading people, but Norway was clearly trying to hide something.

"I was there," she said. "I was attacked. I deserve to know what happened to the others. Did something happen with..." She struggled to remember the other name she'd heard. "Dayton? Wasn't she partnered with a man named Dayton?"

Norway let out a surprised gust of air, like he'd been hit in the stomach.

"What happened?" Judy whispered her question and leaned

close.

Norway looked up from his pad. He glanced around to make sure there was nobody else around before he decided to talk.

"I don't know for sure, but I heard that they were almost eaten by some kind of monster."

"What? Are you serious?"

He nodded and put the tip of his pencil down in the margin of the paper. He made a dot there and then looked back up.

"A couple people said it was a plant. Yonkers said it had poison flowers that would shoot out spores or something."

"And thorns, right? They said they were pulling thorns from Helen?"

Norway nodded.

"Yeah, they cut her free from the vines and got them off. She was lucky. I heard Dayton was torn in half."

"That's terrible," Judy said. She shuddered.

"But you didn't see any plants like that?"

"No," Judy said. She finished her story. Norway wrote for several minutes after she finished talking. He asked a few questions so he could accurately record the story, and then wrote some more. When everything was written, he closed his book, thanked her, and left.

Judy picked at one of her cuticles and glanced at the kitchen window. They must have put out some of the candles. There was barely a glow coming from in there. She tried to remember the features of each of the bearded men. How many had been with their group since the very beginning? How many had been at that Denny's meeting where she'd first met Luke? Frank was the only one she knew for sure. Maybe some of the other bearded men had been there. She couldn't say. Certainly this Norway guy had joined on the trip. She would have remembered him. He seemed more likable than the others.

Judy recognized that her memory was terrible, just as she admitted that Luke's memory was awesome. He knew the names and stories of every single person in their group. It was probably why he remained so popular. He could greet each person, remember their hometown, who they missed, what kind of food they liked, or anything else he'd heard. Luke would definitely remember Brad's story about the killer vines, and rock monster, and weird memories. Judy was struggling to recall the details. She'd heard Brad's story twice, but she'd heard a lot of things back then and retained only a few.

"Hey," a voice called from the dark.

Judy watched until the face materialized from the night. It was Ron.

"Hi," she said.

"I heard you had an adventure," Ron said.

"Yeah, I guess."

"You lost four people? Must have been quite an ambush."

"I guess it was," Judy said, with a sigh. She'd only known for sure that they'd lost Dayton. Was it possible they'd lost four? She wanted to find out for sure. Ron's gossip was never accurate.

"I had an adventure of my own while you were gone," Ron said.

"Yeah?"

"I haven't told anyone yet. I'll wait until daylight. They're going to shit."

"What are you talking about, Ron?"

Ron looked her in the eyes for several seconds. She was impressed. This was easily the longest amount of time he'd ever held onto a secret, as far as she knew. He caved. He came forward with a pleased smile and lowered his voice.

"I found a secret place," he said.

"What are you talking about?"

"You know that little grain shed behind the barn?"

Judy shrugged. The farm was littered with little sheds and buildings, not to mention at least three barns. He could have been talking about anywhere.

"I finished my chores early, so I decided to clean it out. One of the metal bins had a rusted corner and the mice got into the grain. Looks like it happened years ago. I decided to take out the old bins so we could use the space to store something more important."

"Does this story have a point, Ron?"

"I'm getting to it. Anyway, I took out the old metal and was going to keep the wooden framing there, but then I saw something. I almost yelled for everyone right then, but then I figured it might be interesting to just see for myself before I got anyone else involved. Some of it is uncovered now, but I'm going to need help to do the rest. That's why I'm going to wait until daylight and then I'll have my big reveal. That way everyone will know at once."

"What are you talking about?"

"It's like a bomb shelter or something. There's a door built right into the floor underneath where the grain bins were. They must have decided it wasn't useful anymore and then covered it over or something. Who knows what's down there? We could find supplies and stuff."

Judy nodded. His enthusiasm was not contagious.

"Do you want to come see it?"

Judy picked at her cuticle some more. "I should get some sleep. It's been a long day." She yawned, only to drive home her statement, and then she really did feel tired.

"Come on. Just come see it. It's going to be like opening presents on Christmas morning."

Suddenly, she was fully awake.

"Fine."

Ron made her go all the way inside the little shack before he would turn on his headlamp. It was about the size of a big walk-in closet, but she would never want to put clothes in here. The place was filled with dust and spiderwebs. The room served one purpose—it housed three big bins. They were framed in wood, but lined with metal. Judy could see the details of their construction because Ron had torn one of the bins out. Under the neighboring bin, she saw shredded paper and dried grass stuffed under there. It was probably the remnants of an old mouse nest.

"Look," Ron whispered.

She couldn't see anything. His headlamp was directed up towards the ceiling and the shadows were deep.

"Give me that," she said. She grabbed the lamp from his head and knelt down. He had bent up the floor of the left bin. She saw the corner where the metal was rusted through. She imagined mice chewing through the red metal. The idea made her teeth hurt. She had to get low to see under the bent metal. Ron usually hated getting dirty. She couldn't imagine how he'd come upon this discovery.

She saw it.

The bent metal was sitting atop a wooden frame. Through the gaps in that frame, she saw underneath to where the door sat. It was big, round, and gray. The top was arched and the back had two giant hinges. It looked like the exhaust cap of the old tractor, although a much larger version. Judy was about to get up off the dusty floor when she saw something else. There was another set of hinges, but these were attached to the wooden frame.

"It's cool, right?" Ron asked. His voice was still low, but his excitement was evident. "We'll have to tear out this whole bin and the one in the middle. That's why I need more help. I won't be able to get these things out on my own."

"Hold on," Judy said. She was trying to piece together what she was looking at, and Ron's constant babbling was interrupting her thoughts. There was a gap between the bins and the back wall. It was bridged by shelves, but why would you put bins in and not set them against the back wall? "Help me," she said.

It wasn't difficult since the shelves were empty. All they held was dust and spiderwebs. The air became cloudy in the enclosed space as she handed the shelves to Ron and he stacked them against the side wall. When the boards were moved, she removed the metal supports that were hanging from the rails. Judy nodded when she took down the supports. There were scrapes on the rails. These supports had been inserted and removed many times before, from the look of it.

"What are you doing?" Ron asked.

"Shhh!" Judy said. She wanted to figure out the next part. With the shelves out of the way, there was enough space above the bins. And the hinges would allow the bins to tip back towards the wall, but there would have to be some other type of mechanism somewhere. It would make sense to put it somewhere convenient.

Judy spun around, looking at the walls of the shack. They were unfinished. A randomly-spaced set of studs were the scaffolding for the horizontal planks. They were rough-cut. She could still see a cross-section of bark along the edges. Between the planks, she saw the tarpaper that sat between the planks and the outer clapboards. She couldn't imagine how any mechanism would be hidden there.

"It must be down here," she said, kneeling in front of the bins.

"What are you talking about?"

She reached under the front lip at the bottom of the middle bin and felt around. Her fingers found the cottony balls of old spider eggs and she frowned. She wanted to wipe her hands off. She expected to be stung or bitten at any moment. Her finger found a metal ring and her eyebrows shot up. She pulled on the loop and it made a satisfying thunk.

"What is it?" Ron asked.

Judy didn't have to answer. The bins answered for her. When she released the ring, the entire rack of bins began to raise up on springs. They creaked and then stopped. Judy pushed up to her feet and then pressed on the front of the bin, giving it a push upwards.

Surprise spread across Ron's face. His mouth made an O. When the bin had risen about two feet, the front of it began to tip back. It was rotating on the hinges Judy had seen earlier. It tilted back until the bins came to a soft landing on the back wall. The bins now occupied the space where the shelves had been.

When Judy pointed the light down, they saw that the bins had lifted away to reveal the metal door.

"Wow," Ron said. "Let's go get the others. They'll want to see this."

"Wait," Judy said. She laid a hand on Ron's arm. "Maybe we should just check it out ourselves first. Then we'll know what to tell everyone. We don't want to get them excited if it's nothing."

Ron nodded. He had a flare for the dramatic, and this idea resonated strongly with him. When she saw that he was on board, Judy knelt and pointed her light at the metal door.

"Go ahead," she said. "You found it. You should get to try it first."

Ron nodded again. His tongue darted out and wet his lips as he knelt down. He brushed the dust from the patch of floor where his knees would land and then he reached forward under the bins. There was a metal latch on their side of the door. He squeezed the latch and smiled when it popped in his grip. The door began to rise slowly. It's pneumatic mechanism brought the door up about a foot. Ron coaxed it up another foot so they could see down inside. They didn't see anything except a ladder. It descended into the darkness.

"Well?" Judy asked.

Ron held out his hand and motioned for the light. Judy took off the headlamp and gave it to him. He glanced up at the frame holding the grain bins and then slowly stuck his head under them. He pointed the light down into the hole. Judy stood back, watching. She bit at her cuticle.

"What is it?" she asked.

"I don't know," he said. His voice had a hollow echo to it. "It goes too far down. I can't see"

"Weird."

✪ ✪ ✪ ✪ ✪

She climbed down with no light except the dim blue circle overhead. From below, she heard Ron's feet clanging on the metal rails of the ladder. It was her own fault that she didn't have a light. Ron had wanted to take a minute so they could go find more lights, but she knew what that might lead to. If they had delayed, Ron would have found someone else to tell of the discovery. If there was an advantage to keeping the secret, Ron would have squandered it.

"Oh!" she heard him say below. Judy stopped and looked down. His light quickly moved away from the bottom of the ladder. At least she had a sense of how much farther she had to descend.

"What is it?" she asked.

"I can't tell."

In the darkness, Judy rolled her eyes and sighed.

She reached the bottom. The tube they'd climbed down opened up into a small room of gray metal. It was small enough that Ron's headlamp was able to illuminate the whole space. The room was a cylinder, like the tube they'd come down to gain access, but it was at least four or five times wider than the ladder tube.

"This is no bomb shelter," he said.

He was right. On one side, a panel was built into the curved wall. A rolling black chair sat in front of the panel. The surface of the chair was covered with splotches of white mold.

Judy walked over to it. She didn't want to touch the chair. The mold looked like it was dying to release its spores. The panel was formed in the shape of a sloped desk. Little TV sets were mounted across the wall, and the flat surface was covered in buttons and levers. Nothing was labeled.

"Swing your light over here, will you?" Judy asked.

Ron was investigating something on the opposite wall. She heard a deep metal clang and spun around Ron was standing in front of a black rectangle that had appeared in the wall.

"I found a door," he said.

She approached slowly, expecting something to reach out of the darkness and snatch Ron to unknown depths. Judy was ready to leap for the ladder if that happened. He spun and pointed the light in her eyes.

"It's stairs," he said.

Judy glanced at the ladder. Exploring was her idea, but she was beginning to think that they'd gone far enough.

"You want to go back?" he asked.

Judy surprised herself. "No."

The stairs spiraled down through another tight cylinder. Their footsteps echoed with a metallic ring. Judy stopped on the second-to-last stair and watched as Ron reached for the latch of the big metal door. This door looked like it was meant to keep out, or maybe keep in, something serious. It was studded with big metal rivets and it looked like it weighed as much as a car.

When Ron pulled up on the latch, the mechanism sounded like a block of metal dropped to a concrete floor. Ron pushed. The door squeaked inwards. Cool, damp air washed over them.

Judy stayed on the stairs as Ron walked through the door. She saw his headlamp sweep over a big space.

"Wow," she heard him say. "You could fit a..."

His voice was lost to the echoes.

"Hey, Ron?"

His light disappeared around a corner. She was alone in the dark.

She raised her voice. "Ron?"

Judy gripped the railing. She could find her way up the stairs and then feel around until she found the ladder. It shouldn't be too difficult. But would the hatch under the grain bins still be open? Somehow she thought it wouldn't. Somehow, when they'd opened the door to the spiral stairs, the hatch would have closed. Somewhere, on that dark, unlabeled panel, there was a dead button that was designed to open that hatch. It had probably been broken since before she was born. She would be trapped down here until someone else from their group just happened to stumble into the grain shack, and happened to find the mechanism to raise the bins.

She would starve, clinging to the ladder until her strength dropped her next to that moldy chair. She would hit every dead button on that dead panel, fruitlessly trying to find a way...

"Are you coming?"

His light was back in her eyes.

"Where did you go?"

"In this room. You have to see it."

She followed close this time, staying in the protective bubble of the glow of his light. He led her into the big room. She didn't get much of a look at it, because he immediately turned to the right and then turned again. She followed him into a smaller room with desks down opposite walls. Cork boards on rolling stands divided the room. Pinned to either side were maps, memos, and photos.

Ron moved to the first one and pointed his light at the center.

"Here," he said.

He handed her a heavy metal object. She found the switch and a dim yellow light came from the end. It was her very own antique flashlight. It barely produced any light, but it was her new favorite thing in the whole world.

She joined her beam to the board where Ron was looking.

"This place was some kind of monitoring center," Ron said. "All these surveys and photos show changes in the landscape over the years."

Judy scanned the photos. They were mostly of trees and streams. They looked like the album of an amateur nature photographer. The composition was terrible. There was no art to the photos. In more than one, she saw men who wore shorts and Hawaiian shirts. They looked funny with their shaved heads, grim expressions, and cheerful shirts.

"Binaural beats induce theta rhythms in ninety-three percent of subjects," Ron read from the other side of the board.

Judy was looking at a map of the farm. It showed all the buildings, fields, and the road. There were several stars affixed in a circle around house. She used her fingers to gauge the scale and figured that the radius of the circle was about five miles. Only one of the stars was annotated. A line led to a note that read, "Alpha Site: infestation eradicated with +47089 protocol 0-21-7."

The star was pretty close to a big rectangle of a building. Judy traced the lines. It was only a guess, but she was pretty sure that the star marked the location of the grocery store she'd visited earlier that evening.

"Why would they put this place here?" Ron asked from the other side of the board. He came around to Judy's side. "We're not close to anything. There's nothing strategic to protect out here, right?"

"I think maybe this place is in the middle of something," Judy said. She traced her finger over the ring of stars on the map.

"Ugh. Like what? Nothing but trees, if you ask me. The only thing good about this place is that it's supposed to be safe from the air monsters. And we haven't seen any water..."

"Shhh!" Judy said, cutting him off.

"What?" he whispered.

She took a deep breath and shut off her light. Ron reached up and shut off his headlamp, too. As the darkness settled around them, the sounds of the place came to life. It was mostly themselves that they heard. Judy recognized her own breathing and heartbeat as the majority of what met her ears. She could hear Ron's breathing too. It amazed her how quickly her ears became tuned to their surroundings.

She heard it again. It was a loud, "THUNK," from the big room. Judy extended a hand and moved towards her memory of the doorway.

"I heard something," Ron whispered.

"Shhh!"

Judy's hand found the doorway and she grasped the cold metal. As she leaned forward, she could tell the difference when her head moved into the big room. It sounded more open. She resisted the urge to turn on her flashlight. She wanted to hear everything, and using the light would only dull her attention.

Click, click, click, click.

It could have been footsteps across a metal floor, or some clockwork mechanism in a machine. She sensed Ron approach her from behind.

BANG!

The sound reverberated in the room for what felt like an entire minute.

"We should get out of here," Ron whispered.

Judy agreed.

She turned on her weak yellow light and Ron lit the place with his headlamp. They moved towards the doorway to the spiral steps. They were almost there when Judy heard the clicking again. This time, it was five clicks. They definitely came from the spiral staircase.

Ron tapped her on her shoulder and she almost screamed.

She looked back. He was pointing to another doorway, across the room. It took her a second. She was about to ask him why he was pointing to the other door when she saw why. Above the door was a red and white sign, that clearly read, "EXIT."

She nodded. Another exit seemed like a great idea.

Before they reached the other exit, they heard another, CHUNK.

Judy only hesitated for a moment, and then they both hurried for the other door. It wasn't another staircase, as she'd hoped. This was a straight hallway that stretched so far that her light couldn't find the end. They began to run slowly down the length.

Judy turned off her light. She could see fine with the glow from Ron's headlamp, and she wanted to conserve the batteries, just in case.

At the other end of the hall, they were both panting for air. Judy hoped it was just her smoker's lungs, and not a lack of oxygen that caused her lightheadedness. Ron tried the door. He was careful, but the latch still made a racket when he turned it. It sounded like some ancient mechanism slammed into place when he dragged the handle downwards. He pulled on the door and the old hinges squealed. Judy looked back the way they'd come. She expected to see some black shape following them. There was nothing but darkness behind them.

"You first," Ron said, pointing at the door.

"Fine," Judy said. She stepped through the door and smelled the musty air. It was even cooler and damper than the air they were already breathing. Through the door, they found a landing. Another set of spiral stairs led down into the dark.

"I thought this was an exit?"

"It must go back up later," Ron said.

Judy gripped the handrail and started down. Behind her, she heard Ron move in intervals. He ran down a few steps until he was caught up, and then he shined his light towards the top. He looked between the stair risers, watching for pursuit.

Judy stopped.

"What?"

"We can't go this way, unless you have SCUBA equipment on you."

"What?"

Ron turned to look over Judy's shoulder. The cylinder was flooded. The water was perfectly clear, but even so, they couldn't see more than three turns of the spiral stairs before the light wouldn't penetrate any farther.

"So much for this exit," Judy said.

"We have to go back," Ron said.

"You think?"

They climbed. They didn't make it far before a noise from below stopped Judy again. It was a wet, bubbling sound, followed by what sounded like a heavy piece of meat slapping against a cutting board.

"Faster," she whispered.

They ran up the steps.

With all their clanging on the spiral stairs, it was hard to hear anything from below, but Judy thought she did. She thought she heard the noise of something enormous crawling out from the water. They'd woken something with their stupid lights and now it was gaining on them as they wound up and up, around the tight spiral of the stairs. When Ron slowed, Judy pressed on his lower back with her free hand. Her flashlight was tipped straight up.

They reached the top of the stairs, pulled themselves through the door and slammed it behind them. Ron wrestled the handle until the door was latched once again. They didn't have anywhere else to go. The hallway ended at the door.

Ron spun towards the other end of the hall when they heard the noise. Right on cue, Judy's light flickered and then went out. At the far end of the hall, from where they'd come, the door opened and revealed a white rectangle of light.

CHAPTER 12: LAKE ERIE, NEW YORK

TIM SMILED AT CEDRIC and turned his attention back to his stride. He had a habit of scraping his right foot when he wasn't putting his full energy into his running. That scraping would trip him up when he got tired enough. It would also eat up his right shoe.

After another ten minutes of easy jogging, Tim pulled up and stopped. Cedric looked up at him.

"I think we've gone more than two miles. Did I miss a sign while I was thinking about Thanksgiving?" he asked the dog. Tim spun slowly and looked around. They were on a country road with widely-spaced houses and a faded double-yellow line down the center.

Cedric sat down on the pavement.

"You look thirsty," Tim said. "I'm thirsty."

Tim lifted his heel to his butt, stretching his thigh. He repeated with the other foot. He headed towards the only house that was close. Cedric bounded ahead.

The door was closed, but unlocked. After testing the handle, Tim knocked and waited.

"I know it's silly, but after those crazy people on Sunset Point, I don't want to take any chances."

He knocked one more time and then opened the door. The house was stuffy and warm. It smelled of baked dust. Tim knew what to do. He started with the kitchen. Their best bet was a well-stocked pantry. He threw open a few cabinets. He found some cat food, some crackers, and a sealed bag of chips. Anything non-perishable, he moved to the table. He swept aside a stack of junk mail.

"No bottled water," he said, as he dumped some cat food into a small bowl. Cedric waited for him to place the bowl on the floor before he dove in.

Tim found a couple of big pots in a lower cabinet. He whistled as he glanced around for the basement steps. For an old place, the basement was in good shape. It was a poured foundation, with little windows on two sides that let in plenty enough light to see. Cedric came down the stairs as Tim squatted in front of the well's pressure tank. He positioned a pot in front of the drain spigot and turned the handle. Clear, cold water flooded into the pot. Tim switched it out when it was full.

"Don't drink it yet. Better safe than sorry."

Tim took the pots up one at a time and set them on the gas stove. He lit the burners to boil the pots of water. He dumped another can of cat food in Cedric's bowl and then sat at the table.

"When we were running, I kept thinking about the day we met," he said to the dog. "I swear, you saved my life in that police station."

Tim couldn't sit still. His legs still wanted to run. He pushed up to explore the rest of the house.

The first floor had one bedroom and another tiny room that served as an office. The desk took up most the room. Tim sat down in the office chair and opened the laptop sitting there. The battery was dead. He pulled open the drawers and glanced at the contents.

He heard a noise behind him and spun to see the dog.

"You scared me."

Cedric wagged his tail.

Tim turned back to close the drawers. As papers slid, he spotted something silver. It was a spare battery for the laptop. Tim pressed the little button. He was surprised when three green lights appeared.

"Half charge!" He turned and gave a thumbs-up to Cedric.

Tim plugged the battery in and turned on the laptop. It booted while he walked back to the kitchen. There were still several things that could go wrong. The machine could be broken, or locked by a password. He went to the stove and watched the water heating up. The machine made a welcoming sound and Tim looked over to see that it was up and running.

"Surprise, surprise."

Tim patted his pockets until he found what he was looking for. He pulled out a USB drive and turned over the laptop until he found where to plug it in. When he did, a window popped open with the contents of his drive. He scrolled through until he found what he was looking for.

"You know what? Better safe than sorry."

He copied all his images to the machine and then removed the USB drive and put it back into his pocket. With the images duplicated to the machine, he began to review them once more. He slid the window to the side so he wouldn't see the preview. Most of the pictures he had were of the hypnotic murals. He didn't want to collapse in this strange house with water boiling on the stove.

"Here it is," he said. He opened an image of a map he'd scanned. The edge of the map ended just south of his location. "Damn," he whispered.

The water boiled. He turned off the burners and shutdown the laptop. He added the computer to the stack of useful things he'd found.

"It's still hot. You can't have it until it cools down. You should know that by now. How long do dogs remember things? Do you remember your old house? That little blue place with the suicide? That's the first place I saw one of those murals. I don't have a picture of it. I didn't start taking pictures until after the police station. I don't think I've ever been more scared than that day."

Tim remembered.

He slid to a stop under the counter and pulled his legs around the corner. He heard the door creaking as its spring slowly dragged it closed. He looked at the dog. Its amber eyes were wide and its ears twitched at each sound. The dog's nostrils flared as it sniffed the air.

Tim couldn't see much but the floor under the desks. Another shadow passed across the windows and he watched it make it a quick pass, back and forth, over the floor. From the lobby, he didn't hear a thing. He didn't hear footsteps, or breathing. Tim waited. He forced himself to breathe slowly, in and out. His instinct was to hold his breath, but he knew if he did, he would eventually have to suck in noisy air.

That's when Tim's memory of the day had a strange gap. He knew he had been hiding, trying to not make a sound. He had been huddled under the counter, with his legs pulled to his chest. The next thing he knew, he had a strange pain in his arm.

Tim looked down, surprised to see that he was on his knees and his head was about to move around the corner, in full view of the lobby. His arm was clamped between the jaws of the dog he'd rescued from the locked house. The dog wasn't squeezing or tearing at his arm. In fact, although it was painful, he doubted if the bite had even broken his skin. But the dog was persistent. It didn't let go, even when Tim tugged.

He pushed his arm towards the dog and caught the dog's eyes in a stare. After a second, the dog's jaws opened and let go of Tim's arm.

Tim actually opened his mouth to thank the dog, when a jar of pencils fell to the floor a couple of desks away. Tim closed his mouth again and looked under the desk. The jar was still rolling back and forth. He saw another shadow pass between the desks.

A low hum seemed to vibrate the air around him. It sounded like a machine, very far away, but the vibration was close. He could feel it making his hair dance and making his knees itch where they touched the floor.

Tim looked to the dog again.The dog was squinting its eyes, like it was expecting to be hit. While he watched, the dog closed its eyes entirely and rested its head on its paws. Tim didn't know why, but this suddenly seemed like a good idea. He closed his own eyes and rested back on his heels.

This time he did hold his breath. He focused all his attention on what he could hear, which was just the humming sound and the rocking sound of the pencil jar, which refused to sit still.

Something brushed by Tim's face, but he kept his eyes shut. The feeling was cold and prickly on his skin. The thing brushed the back of his hand, and then his ear. Tim kept his eyes shut. Whatever it was, he didn't want to see it.

He waited there until his shoulders began to cramp and his knees ached from the hard floor. He heard the rattle of the dog's tags and finally opened his eyes. The room seemed brighter than before.

The dog had its eyes open. It sniffed at the air and then rose to its feet. It glanced back at Tim and then started to weave between the desks. Tim wasn't sure what to do. He could go back out through the heavy doors and hope that the thing was gone. If his bike was still there, he could continue on his quest to find the authorities. Perhaps the police station had some communication device that was powered by a generator. Maybe he could find a way...

The dog reappeared between the desks and looked at him.

Tim glanced around. He didn't know what the dog wanted. In fact, he had just started to think that he might be free of the dog.

The dog didn't make a sound, but somehow communicated to Tim with only its eyes. Tim crawled after the dog.

They went through the back door of the station and found stairs that led to the parking garage. Tim stayed low and followed the dog behind a short concrete wall. The dog used its nose to choose their path. It looked around often to make sure Tim was following—at least that's how Tim interpreted the dog's actions.

Through a gate, they found a path that ran alongside a tiny graveyard. The space was bounded by the garage on one side and buildings on the others. The dog moved quickly between the old headstones and waited at the backdoor of the church. Tim followed. He was sure the church would be locked. It was Thanksgiving—most everything was probably locked. He tugged on the door and was surprised to find it swing out. The dog slipped inside.

Tim continued to follow. The dog seemed to have a purpose.

They ducked into a few rooms that were dead ends.

Apparently, the dog's navigation wasn't perfect. These would look like normal offices and classrooms if it weren't for the religious paintings and statues everywhere. Tim avoided the icons with a deep superstition.

They eventually found their way to a side exit. The dog sniffed at the gap under the door and Tim looked through the window. He didn't see anything in the sky, and didn't see any unexplained shadows passing overhead.

He waited until the dog scratched at the door and then he pushed it open a few inches. They both seemed to have the same concern. Both Tim and the dog peered through the crack up to the sky. He didn't know what he was looking for, but Tim studied the sky for any threats. It seemed risky to move out to the street and he didn't even know why.

He let the door close on its own and stood back from it. Tim wiped his face and tried to think. Whatever had been in the lobby of the police station could follow them here, or it could be outside. He didn't know enough to make a decision. The windows on either side of the door had panes of frosted glass. Each pane had a painted handprint in the center. They looked like pedestrian traffic signals, telling Tim to stop.

The dog walked forward until its nose hit the door. The dog pushed forward, deflecting its own nose until its whole face pressed against the metal. Still, the dog's legs tried to propel it forward. Tim cocked his head as he watched. He heard a click within the door and then recognized it as the latch mechanism. The door was about to open by itself, allowing the dog to walk out into the sunlight.

Tim grabbed the dog's collar, hoping its head wouldn't swing around to bite him again. He knew better though. He knew the dog hadn't been biting him earlier. It had been saving him. Now he had the chance to return the favor. The dog was strong and its will increased as a sliver of light appeared in the crack of the door. Tim dragged.

He pulled the dog to the stairs that led down into the darkness. The dog's feet slid against the tile as it pushed all four legs straight out, trying to resist Tim's pull. The light from the door cast a thin band of brightness on the floor. The band was growing wider each second. Something was pulling the door open. Tim pulled the dog. Tim was four stairs down when the dog's front feet finally slipped over the edge of the top stair. The change in balance seemed to wake the dog up. Its head whipped around, it saw the door, and life returned to the dog's eyes. It shot past Tim and ran down the stairs. Tim followed.

✪ ✪ ✪ ✪ ✪

Tim eased the door shut behind him. The room wasn't entirely dark, but it was close. Only tiny pinpricks of blue light on his right gave him reference. Tim shuffled forward. The dog was somewhere up ahead, moving silently. As Tim neared the lights, he saw the dancing blue flames. They were pairs of pilot lights, burning on a long stovetop. They gave him just enough light to navigate the long kitchen. At the far end, a swinging door led to a much larger room.

It was a small gymnasium, with a basketball hoop at one end and a badminton net stretched across the center. On the far wall, high windows looked out at the sidewalk. Tim looked down. The dog poked his head through the gap in the swinging door that Tim held open. The dog looked at him. Tim shook his head. Either the dog understood, or it had the same thought. They backed up and let the door shut. They were alone in the dark kitchen with the eternal blue pilot lights.

Tim found a wall and put his back to it. The dog pressed to his side.

He worked blind, untying and then unlacing his shoes. He tied the laces together and then made a knot around his wrist. The dog didn't protest as Tim attached the other end of his laces to the ring on the dog's collar. They were tethered. Tim let his eyes shut.

The church was a noisy building. Creaks and knocks made Tim jump constantly for the first hour. The dog calmed him. The dog rested its head on Tim's leg and its breathing settled into a slow rhythm. Eventually, the dark won and Tim fell asleep.

✪ ✪ ✪ ✪ ✪

Tim woke to the dog nudging his hand with its cold nose. He blinked at the darkness and saw the top half of the room in the blue glow from the pilot lights. He crawled to the swinging door and lost one of his shoes in the process. The gym was now darker than the kitchen. The windows were like little optical illusions at the far end of the room. They let in just enough light to give Tim a reference.

Tim backed up and found his shoe. It took roughly forever to untie his makeshift rope and re-lace his shoes. Tim headed back for the door that led towards the stairs.

While he slept, it seemed that the geography of the church had changed. Nothing made sense and he had to feel along each wall to find the next doorway. His hands found wooden frames and cold glass. The dog stayed pressed to his knee and helped him find the way. When he stumbled into the stairs, he was almost ready to give up hope. The dog led the way up the stairs.

They found the door to the street still open. It was locked at the end of its hinges. The night air felt warm and potent. The dog didn't hesitate to walk out into the night. Tim followed.

The city was dark. The sky above them glowed with low clouds.

Around the corner, Tim found his bike still locked to the sign. He glanced over and saw the dog relieving himself against the corner of the police station. Tim looked around nervously before following suit.

When he swung his leg over his bike, he glanced again at the dog. Now, he hoped the dog would follow. His outlook had changed completely in just a few hours. It seemed unfair to whistle to the dog though. He didn't have any answers, and it would feel dishonest somehow—like an implicit promise—to call the dog. Instead, he pushed off and rolled away silently. When he heard the dog's running paws keeping time with him, Tim smiled.

CHAPTER 13: VERMONT

ROMIE LET THE BLANKET fall to the floor behind her. Rivers of dust swirled in Brad's flashlight beam, and the smell of moldy decay filled his nose and stung his eyes. He kept the flashlight perfectly still, like it was pinning the corpse in place. The body was complying. They saw no movement.

"It must have been a trick of the..." Romie began.

CLICK.

The noise cut her off. Brad wasn't sure, but he thought that the body's left arm had moved. Romie took a step closer.

"What are you doing?" Pete asked from the hatch. His head was poking up over the edge of the floor.

Brad and Romie didn't answer. They simply stared at the corpse.

Pete came up the stairs and stood next to Brad.

All of Brad's attention was focused on the corpse.

The creaking gave away the movement before his eyes could detect it. The fingers of its left hand were trying to move. They were fighting against dehydrated muscles and mummified skin. Brad saw little puffs of dust from the fingers with each click.

"What the hell?" Pete asked.

Romie moved forward and shot her hand out. Brad couldn't imagine what would motivate her to get that close to the corpse until he saw what she did. Romie grabbed the gun from the bed. She held it out. It wasn't exactly pointed at the body, but it could be in a fraction of a second.

Brad heard another click and this time the dust puffed out from the thing's stringy hair. Its head had turned a tiny bit towards Romie and the gun. Brad heard a series of tiny sounds, like clattering insects, and saw the fingers of the thing's other hand working against its shirt.

"We should burn it," Romie said.

"It's like the corpses we took north. It's like remote control. That's not a person, it's a puppet, and it looks like it's not in very good working order at this point."

"So it won't matter if we burn it," Romie said.

"These woods are a tinderbox," Pete said. "And who knows what kind of attention an outdoor fire will bring."

With the next click, Brad saw a tiny gap appear between the thing's teeth. The jaws were opening.

"Let's go downstairs and discuss what to do," Brad said. He didn't make a move towards the stairs.

"No way," Romie said. "I'm not taking my eyes off that thing."

With a pop, one of the legs moved.

"Maybe we could break it up and burn it in the wood stove," Pete said.

Out of the corner of his eye, Brad saw Romie shrug.

"That's a really disturbing idea," Brad said.

"I think we have to do something," Pete said.

Robby's head appeared from below.

"Throw it out the window," he said.

"Yes," Brad said. His flashlight bobbed as he nodded in agreement with himself. "We'll throw it out the window."

"You're going to touch it?" Romie asked.

Brad glanced at Pete, whose eyes were locked on the corpse.

"I guess," Brad said, but he didn't move.

Robby climbed up through the hatch and crossed behind Pete. He glanced at the dormer and then headed for the window at the end of the room. It was farther away, but there were less obstacles to deal with. Romie backed up and held the gun with both hands. It was pointed at an angle, down at the floor.

Pete moved forward, but stopped as Robby walked back to the

body. The boy didn't hesitate. He grabbed the corpse by the ankle and spun it on the bed.

Brad's flesh crawled when Robby touched the thing. It creaked again. He couldn't tell if it was trying to move, or if it was just stretching and tearing as Robby pulled it. The corpse tumbled from the bed. Romie tracked his progress by sweeping the end of the gun across the floor.

When the leg broke, Robby paused to adjust his grip. He pulled on the pants instead of the shin. Brad saw the corpse's fingers straighten with another set of audible clicks.

As Robby approached the window, Pete finally broke his stasis. He trotted after the boy. Robby pulled the leg from the pants and Brad saw that it had torn free at the hip. The empty pant leg fell to the floor as Robby tossed the naked limb out the window.

Pete stood over the thing's torso. He looked down and then looked at his own hands. He finally knelt, but didn't touch the corpse.

Robby didn't wait. He pulled on the other leg and slid the whole corpse closer to the window. Robby propped the remaining foot of the corpse up on the window sill and stepped around, next to Pete. That seemed to spur Pete to action. He grabbed the corpse under the shoulders and lifted.

"It's light," he said.

"Yeah," Robby said.

Robby grabbed the empty pant leg and lifted.

Brad moved closer to better aim his light.

The arm popped as the hand reached towards Pete. The man gave a little yell and shoved the thing away from himself. The corpse knocked into Robby and he stumbled backwards. It tilted up and hung on the upper pane of the window. Pete kicked at it. Robby fell down.

The corpse finally tumbled out the window and Pete rushed forward to slam the window shut. He backed away, wiping his hands on his pants as Robby stood up.

"Good," Pete said.

Brad walked forward and angled his light down through the window. He couldn't see the ground where the thing landed.

"What are you doing up there?" Lisa called from below.

"I don't know why that's any better," Romie said. "It's not like we don't have to worry about it just because it's outside."

"It can't get in," Pete said. "Everything is shut downstairs."

"So we're just going to assume that the thing obeys physics even though it just showed a total disregard for being dead?" Romie asked.

Pete shrugged.

"We'll be okay," Robby said. The boy moved towards the hatch. Romie looked at the blankets and pillow on the bed where the corpse had been. Everything was stained black where the thing had lain. Brad considered the blanket that Lisa had covered the thing with. He and Romie seemed to silently agree that it was soiled now too.

Brad climbed down last. He swept his light over the second floor one more time, just to be sure it didn't hold any more secrets. He reached the first floor to see Lisa trying to get a good look through the shutters.

"We should leave, right? We have to leave," Lisa said.

"It will be dawn soon. Everything's more active during the day. You want to risk that?" Pete asked.

"If it means that the thing outside might be more active, then maybe we should," Lisa said.

"We'll be fine," Robby said. He shook out one of the blankets that Brad had thrown down. He draped it over the back of a chair and picked up another blanket.

"Why exactly are you being so casual?" Romie asked him. "Why do you have to pretend that the dead rising up is such a normal thing? We've seen it exactly once, and it was a pretty goddamn dire situation."

Robby finished with the blankets and moved on to the pillows. They only had two. A couple of people would have to lay their heads on rolled up jackets, or only their arms.

"Twice," he said. "You've seen it once. I've seen it twice."

Lisa looked over from the window. Pete folded his arms.

"What?" Romie asked.

"Thanksgiving night," Robby said. "I was near a highway. The embryo was sending energy down the highway and it called the corpses to itself."

"More bullshit," Romie said. Suddenly, Brad noticed that she was still carrying the gun from upstairs. She pointed an arm in Robby's direction. The gun wasn't aimed at the boy, but it pointed in his direction.

Brad looked at the faces of his friends. Lisa and Pete seemed to be holding their breath. Romie was focused entirely on Robby, who was bending for the last pillow.

"That's where I met Lyle," Robby said. He set the pillow on the table and took a seat.

Romie gestured with the gun. "What?"

"He was at the rest stop, near the highway. I think he was mentally ill before Thanksgiving, but when everyone died and their eyes popped out, he began to think he was a god."

"What does that have to do with the one-legged corpse that's now outside the window?"

"Nothing, except I know what it looks like when an embryo calls to the dead. They're like metal filings near a magnet. That corpse upstairs has probably been putting on that same show every night for a week."

Nobody else spoke. They waited to see if Robby would offer more explanation. After a moment of silence, he did.

"There were cracks in his dried skin when we first saw him. Little cracks where the skin wasn't elastic enough. And there was no dust on the parts that moved. There was dust around him, and in his clothes, but most of him was dust-free. He's been moving for a while, and he never made any progress from that bed."

"The corpses we saw were able to move just fine. They didn't just twitch in their beds," Romie said.

"They were relatively fresh, and we were right on the highway. Here, we're away from the road, and the corpse was old."

"Another crazy theory, with no way to prove or disprove."

"The next corpse we find, assuming the person didn't commit suicide, will have no eyes. We're entering the band where the thing will be banking biological resources," Robby said.

"That's hardly a bold prediction. We've seen plenty of eye

poppers."

"Back east we did," Pete said. "It's been a long while since we've seen any."

"Because we were beyond the band," Robby said. "We're entering a new band now."

"Listen," Romie said. Brad was aware that the gun came back up. "I believed your bullshit once, and it accomplished nothing. No, wait, that's not true." She gestured crazily with the gun. Lisa began to shrink back against the wall. "Listening to you did accomplish a few things. We lost Ted, Sheila, Nate, Brynn, and that other lady."

"Christine," Pete said.

"Yeah, her too," Romie said. She swept the gun towards Pete as she acknowledge him. He flinched, but didn't duck.

"Let's calm down," Lisa said. "Why don't you have a seat, Romie?"

"He's a teenager," Romie said. "We've been listening to a teenager. Do you realize that? He wouldn't tell us what was going to happen to the thousand corpses when we took them north, and now he's claiming that he knew all along. After he screwed us and got half of us killed, did we hold him accountable? No! We dragged his ass across two states while he was unconscious. Do you think he knows how many times you wiped his ass?"

Robby had been calmly watching Romie during this rant. At the mention of his bodily functions, he blushed and glanced down at the floor. His eyes returned to Romie quickly, to hear the rest of her condemnation.

"But he's just a kid, right? Shame on us for listening to him in the first place. But I'll be damned if I'm going to listen to even more of his bullshit. He never says anything that you could use or witness. It's always this loosey-goosey bullshit."

Romie's voice got louder and louder as she got worked up. She approached Robby as she talked and soon the gun was pointed at the boy. She held it at arm's length and the barrel was no more than a foot away from his face. Brad cursed himself. Perhaps if he'd made a move for the gun earlier, when it was still aimed at the floor, he could have snatched it. Now it seemed like any move would end with Romie pulling the trigger.

Robby held his ground. He didn't back away or break eye-contact with the woman. Brad wished he would. Maybe if the boy gave in to Romie's accusations, she would take pity on him.

Robby's hand moved and Romie's finger squeezed the trigger a little. Brad could actually see it move from where he stood.

Slowly, Robby completed the action. He picked up the dead man's journal that was on the table next to him. Without looking, he flipped the thing open and held it up towards Romie.

The gun didn't waver, but Romie's curiosity got the better of her.

"What *is* that?" she whispered. Romie kept the gun trained on Robby as she leaned in. She kept getting closer and closer to the book. Brad couldn't see what she was looking at. From his angle, the page looked like it was covered with squiggles.

Romie eased forward until she was absurdly close to the book. Brad thought that Robby might have come up with a way out of his jam. All the boy had to do was reach out and he could push the gun away so it wasn't pointing at him any longer.

Robby didn't need to. Romie moved just a quarter inch closer, and she collapsed.

The gun went off when she hit the floor.

Robby turned and looked at the fresh bullet-hole in the wall. The boy reached down and picked up the gun from the floor. He fiddled with it for a second and popped out the magazine. With another motion, he emptied another round from the chamber.

Brad finally found his wits and moved forward. Lisa and Pete seemed to have the same thought. Brad knelt down next to Romie as Robby picked up the dead man's journal.

"What did you do?" Lisa asked. She and Pete rolled Romie onto her back.

Pete leaned in and put his ear close to her mouth. "She's breathing."

Brad started to figure it out as Robby spoke.

"Before he committed suicide, the guy upstairs drew some symbols. They're like the ones I recorded back home. If she hadn't been leaning forward, she would have just gone into a trance. I didn't mean for her to fall down. It affects some people more than others, but anyone who looks at the things will go into a trance."

"But you didn't go into a trance earlier," Lisa said. "And you read the book."

"It takes both eyes," Robby said. He closed an eye, so they would understand.

"Let me see that," Pete said. He took the book from Robby, who didn't object. Pete moved away from the others before he opened the journal. Pete closed his left eye and began flipping through the pages.

"How long will she be out?" Lisa asked.

"I don't know," Robby said. "It affects everyone differently. I think a mother and daughter would have a same response. I haven't tested it very thoroughly. Judy was barely responsive. Brad went under for quite a while."

"You've seen these things too?" Lisa asked.

"Yeah, I guess," Brad said. He shrugged and turned up his hands. "There were strange symbols on the wall in Robby's basement."

"You can't even read these things," Pete said. "Why the hell would they make her pass out?" He tossed the journal back towards the table. It hit with a hard slap.

✪ ✪ ✪ ✪ ✪

Brad was asleep when Romie came out of her trance. He heard her mumbling and he woke to see her sitting up with Lisa sitting by her side.

"Where's Robby?" Romie asked.

"He's upstairs," Pete said. "He went up to sleep on the mattress up there."

"No! It's not safe!" Romie tried to get to her feet, but her limbs weren't obeying her. Brad understood as he watched her try to rise. It was tough sleeping on a hard floor. His joints didn't want to cooperate either. He looked to the window. The light coming through the blinds was low and pink. It would be time to get up soon anyway. He got up and moved to the ladder.

"Robby?" Romie called.

The boy's head appeared through the hole.

"Be right down," he said.

Lisa was rubbing Romie's back with one hand and supporting her under her armpit with the other.

"I'm fine. I'll be fine," Romie muttered.

Pete was pushing aside the curtains on the door and looking out to the woods. Brad walked over to the door. He turned to see Robby coming down the stairs.

"Listen," Romie said. She was still waving off Lisa's help. "Everyone, listen. We have to get out of here. It's not safe. We've got to get closer to the center of this thing. That's the only place we'll be safe from the liquid and the snatchers."

"What are you talking about?" Lisa asked.

"I know what we have to do," Romie said.

"You've had a long night," Lisa said. "You'll feel better in a few minutes."

"No, you have to listen. I know what to do. I talked to God."

✪ ✪ ✪ ✪ ✪

"I'll tell you, but only when we're moving," Romie said. "We need to get moving."

"Did God tell you how we're supposed to get out of here with all that killer liquid on the roads?" Pete asked. He moved to one end of the bookshelf and Brad took the other. They moved it aside to unblock the door.

"Yes," Romie said. "You have a trail map, right?"

"Sure," Pete said. He pointed at the table. He grunted as he forced the door open through the broken glass.

Romie unfolded the map and held it up.

"We can follow this trail. It goes alongside a stream. The liquid doesn't like regular flowing water." Romie said.

"That makes sense," Robby said.

"Great, now we've got two of them," Pete said. He kept his voice low. Brad wasn't sure if anyone else heard the comment.

Lisa gathered up the few things they'd found in the cabin and joined Romie as she headed for the door.

"Watch out for our friend," Pete said.

They found the corpse on the side of the building, still resting below the window. As far as they could tell, it hadn't moved from when they'd pitched it out. The leg was a few feet away.

"There," Romie said. She was pointing.

Brad looked in the direction of her extended finger and saw the trailhead marked with a blue and white blaze.

"Does it go to the river?" Pete asked. He was looking around, trying to get his bearings.

"No. Away from it," Romie said. Pete joined her at the map and they consulted. "See, we're on a ridge or something. Streams go both ways. We're moving away from the river on this trail, but sticking close to this stream. It ends up at this little pond, here."

Pete nodded and mumbled as he watched her finger trace out the trail. "Okay, I get it," he said after they had conferred for a moment.

Romie led the way and Pete walked just behind her. The light was fading fast. It gave the woods a beautiful, flat look, that Brad found incredibly peaceful. Everything was perfectly still and glowed in the light from the sunset. They marched through underbrush to the trail and then followed it as it wound around and down, alongside the creek.

Before long, their path met the rock wall that they'd followed the night before. The creek and the path cut perpendicular to the wall and continued downhill. Brad knew what was next. They would find the road somewhere up ahead, and they would know if Romie's prediction was correct.

Their trail was gravel in some places, and wood chips in others. Romie strode with confidence. Pete kept his head turned towards the ground. He was on the lookout for any mysterious liquid crossing their path. Up ahead, the woods cleared out, and it looked like the trail ended at the edge of the highway. Even at a distance, Brad saw the lines of liquid that made their grid on the asphalt.

"Now what are we going to do?" Lisa asked.

The question was a couple of seconds premature. With a few more strides, they saw that their trail ducked under the road.

There was an overpass. Between the concrete sides, the stream and the trail joined together to flow beneath the highway.

"It's fine," Romie said. "I told you—the liquid doesn't like flowing water."

She kept walking. Brad paused. On road above, the liquid coursed and pulsed. If it had any opinion about the flowing water, it wasn't apparent from it's behavior on the overpass. He followed a line of the stuff as it flowed into the grass to the side of the highway and then down a ditch and up the hill. Here and there, he saw where the liquid glittered in the grass. Most of the time, it was hidden. He'd never seen anyone step in the stuff, and based on Robby's description, he was sure he never wanted to.

Romie was moving without fear.

Pete walked fast behind her to keep up.

Brad caught up as Pete grabbed Romie's shoulder and dragged her to a stop.

"Wait, would you?" Pete asked. He kept his voice low. They were nearly under the surface of the highway. Their path was totally dark where it passed under the road.

"It's fine," Romie said.

"Maybe it is," Pete said. He had a tiny flashlight that he'd found at the ranger station. He knelt and pointed his light parallel to the surface of their trail. The light picked up a few chunks of broken glass and a wet spot just a couple of paces in front of where Romie stood.

Pete shuffled closer to get a better look.

"It's fine," Romie said. She walked past him and trudged right through the wet spot. The others held their ground until she stepped back onto dry concrete, several paces later.

Pete stood up and followed. Brad brought up the rear.

The light began to fade for real as they walked into the forest on the other side of they highway.

"Guys," Brad said. He was pointing his light behind them, where they'd come from. Lisa's arm shot out when she saw. The liquid had closed on the side of their trail. It stayed off the gravel, but they could see it moving through the leaves and just next to the rocks.

Farther back, there was a clear margin between the trail and the start of the liquid. Brad saw why—it was at a spot where the trail and creek were fairly close together. The liquid wasn't respecting the path, it was keeping its distance from the running water in the creek.

"She's right," Pete said.

"No shit," Romie said. They kept walking.

The creek eventually disappeared into a culvert and their trail ended when it came to a bike path. Robby found the sign. The path was a converted railroad track.

"Which way?" Pete asked.

Romie and Robby spoke at exactly the same time. "West."

It made sense. To the east, the bike path must have headed towards the river.

"Can I see that?" Pete asked. He borrowed Brad's more powerful light and cast it down the surface of the bike trail. "It looks clear."

They headed west.

CHAPTER 14: NEW YORK

"WHO'S THERE?" RON CALLED.

Judy grabbed his arm to shut him up. He didn't get the message.

"Who's down there?" Ron asked.

The lights bobbed and swayed and began to come down the hall.

Judy thought her heart would stop. She imagined ghost soldiers of this forgotten place, rising up to capture the intruders.

"Stop!" a voice called. "Identify yourselves."

"It's us!" Judy yelled. Despite the order, she ran forward. She didn't know exactly who the voice belonged to, but she was certain that it was one of Luke's bearded men. For the first time, she was happy to have one of them near.

"Stop!" the voice yelled again.

"Relax, they're with us," another voice said.

Ron was right behind Judy as she approached. She saw the frightened faces behind the beards and she pulled to a stop.

"Thank god you guys found us. We saw this ladder and then we got lost down here. I didn't think we were ever going to get out," Judy said. She flashed a glance to Ron, warning him to keep quiet.

"You're lucky we happened to go into that shed. You could have been down here a long time."

Judy wondered exactly how much luck was involved.

"Do you know which way is out? We got all turned around and

we couldn't find anything," Judy said.

"This way," one of the bearded men said.

One of the men led the way and the other brought up the rear. Their flashlights explored the space as they moved through. They took them up the ladder. Judy took the night air deep into her lungs, happy to be aboveground once again.

"You should stay out of here. Consider this area off-limits until we figure out what's down there."

"Absolutely," Judy said. She was thankful that Ron had kept his mouth shut. She grabbed him by the arm and led him away from the shed. The men stayed there, debating which one of them should stay and which should go find the others to report their find.

"I'm the one who found it," Ron whispered. "Now they're going to take all the credit."

✪ ✪ ✪ ✪ ✪

Judy was engrossed in her book when the sides of her tent shook. It was one of the biggest problems of living in a city of tents—there was no good way to knock. People ended up thumping the side of her tent when they were looking to come in, and it always surprised the hell out of her.

"Yes?" she called. She tucked her book under her sleeping bag and pulled her knees up to her chest.

The flap zipped open and Luke's head appeared.

"You decent?"

"Come on in," she said.

It was a process. Luke opened the flap and stood while he untied his shoes. He stepped carefully out of them and left them outside when he stepped into her tent. He sat at the entrance.

She normally had a nice cross-breeze through the vents in the side of her tent. The flow was disturbed by the open flap.

Luke didn't say anything.

"What's up?" she asked.

"You had a busy day yesterday," he said.

Judy frowned and nodded.

"Kinda coincidental, yeah?"

"How do you mean?" she asked.

Luke paused, as if carefully considering her perfectly normal question.

"Well, you had the whole encounter in town and then you had the underground exploration."

"Yeah," Judy said. Nobody had talked to her about the hatch. She was beginning to think that maybe the two bearded men had left her out of the story. If they really wanted to take full credit, their account might have ignored Judy and Ron completely. Apparently, she wasn't that lucky.

"I came for two reasons," Luke said. "One, I want to make sure that you're not running around telling a lot of tales about either of those events."

Judy shook her head.

"But you're not really the type. That part of the conversation was really more for your friend." He made a motion with his hand of a flapping jaw. All things considered, it was actually a decent impression of Ron. "The second part is for you—do you suspect that the two things might be connected in some way?"

His question surprised Judy. Why would he think the two things were connected? She was pretty much a victim in both.

"You *happen* to discover a malevolent force in the town and then a couple of hours later you *happen* to discover a secret military base that seems to have been dedicated to tracking those types of forces."

"Pardon?"

"I'm just wondering if maybe one didn't lead to the other."

"I don't know what you mean."

"How did you find that underground bunker?"

"I didn't. Ron found it. I just went down there to see what it was. We thought it might be a bomb shelter or something. It didn't occur to me that there might be some big secret place under the ground of this perfectly normal farm."

"There's nothing normal about this farm. I think we all know that."

"Pardon?" She hated the way she sounded when she said that,

but it was all that she could think to say.

"This place is untouched by those things. There's something special going on here. Either the people who built that underground base figured a way to repel the monsters, or they chose this place because it naturally repels them. One way or the other, this place is unique."

"People died on that supply mission," Judy said. She hadn't witnessed it herself, but she believed the accounts. "I think there are plenty of monsters around."

"Over in the town, maybe. But this place is immune somehow. It's immune to monsters, but not to people. I left this place empty. Then, when we all came back, someone was living here. Who do you suppose she was working with?"

"I don't know. A man you hand-picked as your envoy put a bullet in her head before she could say much."

"Some circumstances are hard to plan for."

Luke seemed to be waiting for Judy to say something, but she didn't know what. He seemed to be accusing her of something, but she didn't know what that was either. She couldn't tell what he wanted from his open expression and the hint of a smile he wore on his lips.

She said the only thing she could think of. "You seem to lose your West Virginia accent when you talk all smart like that. You talk about circumstances, and I wouldn't guess you're just a simple mountain man."

His smile didn't change.

"What did you learn down there?" he asked.

"Nothing," she said. "We found out it wasn't a bomb shelter and then we got lost. I should thank the men who found us. I think I forgot to last night."

"Ron mentioned you spent quite a while in the war room, reading the documents."

Either Luke was lying or Ron had been bragging. Either thing was just as likely.

"Your men followed us down pretty quick. We didn't have time to do any more than glance around."

"What did you see?"

"Maps, mostly. I saw some photos." She held up the vintage flashlight. "I found this."

"Do they know about the bunker?" Luke asked.

"Pardon?" Judy frowned. That stupid word again.

"Did they tell you about the bunker? Is that how you knew where it was? Did they send you to collect information so you could take it back to them?" Luke asked his questions rapidly, not giving her any chance to respond.

Judy realized that he was reading responses from her face, and he was getting it wrong. He was confirming his errant suspicions somehow in the expression she wore.

"Listen," she said, "Ron happened to stumble on that place and I went down there strictly out of curiosity. I had no idea what we would find."

He frowned and narrowed his eyes. After a second, his face broke into an easy smile.

"I know you've struggled to trust me, Judy. We've all been through a lot."

With such a quick transition, she heard him slipping back into his West Virginia twang again. When he said, "to trust me," it came out more "tah truss me." He drew a hand back over his shaved head. He lowered his eyes. It was an inviting gesture. It was a gesture that said, "You don't need to be afraid of me. I'm just a simple, kind-hearted soul."

When his eyes met hers again, she saw that his smile didn't quite reach them.

"Who are you?" she asked.

"Whaddya mean? You know everything 'bout me, Tib."

He hadn't called her that in a long time. "Tib" was a generic endearment he used for any woman he was trying to charm.

"Why do I have the feeling that you knew about the bunker even before Ron found it? Did you also know what we'd find there in the town? Did you send us on that mission to collect information about the monsters there?"

"You need some more rest. Get your head together."

"Can I leave?" Judy asked. "You always said we had to keep the group together because you didn't want us to splinter apart as we traveled. Now that we're here, are we free to go if we want to?"

"Of course y'are, Tib. I suggest you travel at night and stay safe," he said. "Why don't you rest up and I'll get you taken off the rotation?"

He was gone before she could agree or object. For several minutes, Judy sat and stared at the tent flap that he'd zipped behind himself. The conversation had taken such a weird turn. She replayed it in her head over and over, trying to make sense of it.

Judy felt around under her sleeping bag and found her book. She read the same page several times before she gave up. She couldn't concentrate.

The image of Luke asking her, "Did they send you to collect information?" kept playing in her imagination. If she had to guess, that was the real Luke. That was the Luke that he never let anyone see. And that Luke had *known* things. That Luke appeared to have a sense of an us-versus-them war that was still playing out. She wondered what else he knew and how he'd come to know it.

Judy hid her book again and unzipped her tent. She intended to head for the woods where a team had dug a latrine. The bearded men changed her mind. They sat playing cards a few dozen paces away. One glanced up when Judy left her tent. He said something low to the other one. She began to walk out of the little tent city and she spotted another pair of bearded men standing under the trees at the corner of the pasture. One of the those men glanced in her direction as well.

Judy veered left and headed towards Ron's tent instead. She thumped the side.

"Hello?" she called. She thumped again.

She unzipped his door and looked inside. All of Ron's stuff was neat and orderly. Ron kept an organized tent. Nothing was out of place, except Ron. She closed his tent and spun around. It was the middle of the day. He could be anywhere.

Judy headed for the house and checked the chore lists. Luke worked fast. Her name was already scratched off of garden duty and laundry. Luke had made good on his promise to take her off the rotation. In fact, since there were already new people assigned, she guessed he'd done it before he had visited her. She scanned the lists for Ron's name. He was scratched off as well.

Judy turned for the barns.

The horses were turned out and the stalls were clean. She found a teenage boy hauling a bucket of water and trying to lift it over the wall of the stall to hang it on a hook.

"Let me give you a hand," Judy said.

"I got it." The kid almost sounded angry about it.

"Have you seen Ron?"

"He's not here. I heard that he volunteered for a special detail."

"Doing what?"

"I don't know. Something special."

"If you see him, can you tell him I'm looking for him? My name is Judy."

"I know your name," the kid said. He had a look of complete disdain that only a teenager could successfully muster. "I don't know when I'm going to see him again. Me and my sister have double shifts in the barn because he's off the rotation. Apparently, we're the only ones qualified to shovel horse shit."

"Well, if you do." Judy walked away.

She paused at the door. Two bearded men just happened to be taking a stroll over near the fence. They just happened to pause when she appeared in the doorway, and one of them just happened to look in her direction.

Judy walked back over to where the boy was pulling buckets from another stall. She grabbed the buckets from the next stall without asking. She followed him out to the place where he dumped the dirty water.

"When do you muck out the stalls again?"

"Tomorrow morning," he said.

"And where do you dump the shit?"

"There's a manure pit down that path," he said. He pointed.

"I'll do you chores for you tomorrow."

He shook his head. "We're not supposed to trade chores. They don't want just anybody doing the horse chores."

"I've got permission, and I'm not asking you to do my chores. You just sleep in and I'll take care of it."

His skepticism was quickly beaten out by his laziness. "You

won't tell anyone?"

"Not a soul."

Judy helped him fill the rest of the buckets and then found her way out the latrines. She tried to ignore the pairs of bearded men who always seemed to be hovering around her.

✪ ✪ ✪ ✪ ✪

When morning came, Judy found her way to the barn as the sun was coming up. Two men sitting on the fence watched her pass. They had cups of steaming coffee and were deep in a conversation, like hanging out on a fence at daybreak was a normal thing to do. When she had passed, Judy glanced back to see that their conversation had mysteriously come to an end as soon as she'd moved out of earshot.

The big cart was parked at the end of the aisle. Judy rolled to the first stall and grabbed the rake she'd seen Ron use. Judy opened the first stall door and wheeled the cart inside.

"You're supposed to put the horse out first," the kid said.

"Why?"

"I don't know. It's dangerous or something."

"You have a sister?" Judy asked.

"Yeah, why?"

"I don't know. I've been thinking about it since you said so yesterday. I don't think I've met anyone who had family that was still alive."

"We're twins," the kid said.

"Why does that make a difference?"

"I don't know."

"And why are you here?" Judy used the rake to scoop up some of the soiled shavings from the stall. It was a bit like cleaning an enormous litter box.

"What do you mean?"

"I said I'd do your chores. Why are you here?"

"We're not supposed to trade," the kid said.

"It's not a trade if I didn't ask you to do anything."

"Still."

While she worked on that stall, the kid began turning out the rest of the horses. She was glad he was there. She never would have been able to get the giant animals to bend to her will the way he did. He just pointed and they ran for the gate.

She moved on to the next stall and he turned out the horse that had eyed her while she cleaned.

"My cart is full," she said.

"You're picking up too much," he said.

"I'll go dump it."

She had to keep the cart right on the wheel ruts or it bogged down. Her trip was slow until she figured that out. She saw a pair of bearded men move down the fence on the other side of the pasture. They were keeping time with her. She didn't mind. There were only so many of Luke's bearded men.

Judy pushed the cart between the lines of white fence and to the edge of the forest. She saw where the grass was trampled from cartloads just like the one she pushed. It seemed like a long haul for each cartload of shavings. But, then again, it was better than polluting the area next to the barn. Down a short path, she found the pit. Grass grew at the edges, but the center was all fresh shavings and horse shit. She pushed the cart as far as she could and dumped her load.

She couldn't see the bearded men, but figured they must be keeping an eye on her.

Judy left the cart where it was and began walking. She circled the pit and stepped into the woods. The hill sloped down towards the road. She didn't make any attempt to sneak. The leaves crunched under her feet with each step. She got about a hundred paces downhill from the pit before he called out to her.

"Judy!"

She turned. Luke was up the hill. Even at a distance, she could see the gun holstered to his belt.

"This is a pretty feeble escape attempt," he said.

"Who's trying to escape? I was doing chores and I stepped away to heed nature's call."

Luke walked closer before he spoke again. He stopped about ten paces from her. Ten quick strides downhill and he would be close enough to grab her.

"We prefer that everyone use the latrine. We want to keep our area clean."

"Besides," she said, "even if I do decide to leave, you suggested I travel at night, but that's not an order, right? If I decide to leave in the morning, you wouldn't stop me, would you?"

"I'm going to escort you back to camp now so you can get some more rest. If you remember, you've been relieved of your chores for the moment. You've had a stressful couple of days."

"I certainly appreciate your concern," she said. She turned back downhill and began walking again.

"Judy," he said. "Judy!"

She heard the frustration building in his voice. It could have been a snapping stick, but that clicking sound also might have been the snap on the holster he wore. Judy didn't turn around to see. She was pretty close to her goal.

"I'm not going to ask again, Judy," he said.

"That's good," she said over her shoulder. She didn't turn to look at him. She needed him closer. "It will save us both trouble if you don't bother to ask again. The answer is the same. I don't want to be a part of your group, Tib." She could almost feel his anger building.

"That's not one of your choices," he said.

"I'm fuzzy on my choices. Could you go over them one more time for me?"

She heard him exhale. He was getting closer.

"You can return to camp, or what's left of you can end up in that manure pit."

"Why are you giving me a choice at all?"

She heard him take the final steps to close the distance between them. She turned to see that he was within arm's length. He was so focused on her, and whatever perceived threat she represented, that he had failed to fully take in his surroundings. This is what she had been counting on.

"We have a mission here, Judy. You're a smart person, and we might need a person like you."

"Smart? That's what you're looking for? Somehow I thought

you might be looking for breeding-age females. I've got some bad news for you, Luke. I'd be willing to bet that there's not a fertile person in your whole group. Think about it. You'll see the pattern."

"You're crazy," he said.

"Me? You came out here all by yourself. Who's the crazy one?"

"Judy," he said with a smile. "You're not going to make me use this, are you?" He pulled his gun halfway out of his holster and took a half-step back. She had seen him draw before. When they were on the road, he would sometimes put on quick draw demonstrations as entertainment. He could snatch that gun from the holster and shoot a tin can twenty paces away without even seeming to aim.

This wasn't a demonstration, and Judy wasn't a tin can.

"What are you smiling about?" Luke asked.

She wasn't looking at him or his gun. She was looking just to the side of him, where a small tree grew. It was no more than three inches in diameter, and it looked like it would probably be choked out by the thick vines that grew up the trunk. Luke turned to follow Judy's gaze. They both watched.

What seemed like a million years before, in a Denny's where they had held a meeting of the survivors of the apocalypse, a man named Brad had described the phenomenon they were witnessing. He said it was like the "world's slowest fireworks display," if Judy remembered correctly. That was a pretty apt description.

As they watched, pink and purple flowers opened on the vine. They started at the tip, where the flowers were small, and moved down to the base of the tree. They alternated in color: pink, purple, pink, purple. As Luke's eyes followed the opening flowers to the ground, Judy saws realization dawn on him. They were standing in a shallow river of the vines. They stretched up in a band from down the hill.

Luke tried to take a step backwards before he realized that the vines were already looped around his shoes, and tightening around his ankles. He fell on his ass and threw out his hands to catch his fall. As soon as they landed, they were tangled in the thickest vines. The coils wrapped around his wrists and began to find their way over his torso.

Just a couple of feet away, Judy stood unmolested by the plants.

Luke opened his mouth and his scream was cut off immediately by a vine that wrapped around his throat. His last expulsion of breath sounded like a faraway train whistle. Luke's eyes bulged with the effort.

Judy stepped over Luke and began to walk back up the hill.

CHAPTER 15: LAKE ERIE, NEW YORK

TIM AND CEDRIC WALKED out of the little house rehydrated and resupplied. In a bag, Tim carried some food, water, and a laptop with half a charge. In his last tour of the house, Tim had taken the computer's charger, in case they ever ran into another working generator on their travels.

Tim walked this time, and was careful to read every sign. He didn't want to zone out again and miss the turn for the airport. When he saw it, he couldn't imagine how he had ever missed it.

A giant blue sign read, "Westfield Aviation Flight School – Where Your Dreams Have Wings – .8 Miles."

"What does that mean?" Tim asked Cedric. "Your dreams have wings? Does that make any sense to you?"

They turned down the road. Tim wasn't surprised when the pavement ended and their road continued on as a combination of gravel and hard-packed dirt. Before the whole world ended, recreational aviation had already been dying. Where Tim learned to fly, a lot of the pilots who hung around were battling so many health problems that they had difficulty keeping their licenses. The glut of pilots from WWII were dying, and those were the last veterans who seemed to have nostalgia for the skies. People like Tim, who flew just because they enjoyed it, were few and far between. A modest flight school like this, in the middle of nowhere, was lucky they could afford to maintain their road at all.

Tim's step quickened when he saw the hangar. It was a nice big building. There could be any number of planes in there. Cedric ran ahead.

Tim stopped to look across the runway. He adjusted the bag on his shoulder. It wasn't as bad as he had feared. He'd seen more than one overgrown grass runway, choked with weeds. He didn't mind landing on them, but takeoffs were a tad frightening. This one had been well-maintained concrete and tarmac. Here and there, untended cracks allowed grass and weeds to poke through, but it was way better than Tim had any right to expect. He set down his bag and walked over to the door on the side of the hangar. It was locked, but the upper half was glass. He knocked it out with a rock and let himself in. It was clean, tidy, and nearly empty. Tim's hope evaporated. Over a desk, a cabinet was marked, "Keys." He swung open the door and saw hook after hook. They were empty. He saw one set of keys on the bottom row and he reached for them. They hung from a metal keyring in the shape of a peace sign.

Tim smiled. On one side, the metal was enameled with rainbow colors around the perimeter of the circle. He turned back to the hangar. It was nearly empty, but in the far corner an old parachute was draped over something. He walked halfway across to it before he allowed himself to believe his eyes. There was an airplane under that parachute.

✪ ✪ ✪ ✪ ✪

Cedric stayed on the ground and guarded the bag while Tim took the plane up for the first time. Once he had changed out the spark plugs, the plane seemed to run fine. But still, his breath had come in short gasps as he took the thing up for the first time. Once in the air, Tim settled down. He circled the airport a couple of times and brought the plane back down while Cedric was still being good. He didn't want to worry about the dog in the middle of the runway as he tried to land, so he kept his time in the air short, while the dog was still guarding the bag.

He killed the engine and got out.

"I think we're good!" he shouted. He opened his mouth wide

and popped his ears, so he could hear again. Cedric was still sitting there, right next to the bag. "You ready to go?"

Cedric eased his way down until he was laying on the tarmac.

"Come on! Let's go," Tim said. He had a tilted, half-smile on his face. The dog's behavior was confusing.

Cedric looked to the side of the hangar as the young man came around the corner. One of his arms was looped under the armpit of the young woman. It was the pair from Sunset Point. The girl wore the same dress, but it wasn't nearly as pretty now. Tim's eye was drawn down to where her right leg ended. The foot was tilted towards her other leg, at an odd angle.

Tim didn't even notice the boy's other hand until it swung upwards. The young man held a gun. He pointed it directly at Cedric.

Tim's panic immediately shut down blood flow to his extremities. His hands and feet went numb and his blood ran cold with fear. His eyes automatically measured the distance. He had about ten paces to his best friend, Cedric. There were only about two paces between the dog and the unstable young man who was pointing a gun at him.

"Take it back," the young man said.

"Whuh?" Tim tried to get enough lubrication in his mouth to make it work properly. "What?"

"You cursed Amy," he said, nodding at the woman he was propping up.

Tim glanced at her eyes. There was a glassy calm there. Perhaps it was a drug-induced calm.

"What?" Tim asked.

"Say 'what' again!" the young man yelled. His thumb pulled back on the gun's hammer. His eyes were blue steel, but the corners of the young man's mouth were turned up, as if he were amused.

Tim spoke slowly. "I don't know what you mean. Please don't shoot him."

"You cursed Amy Lynne. You said she would break her leg. When we jumped down from your airplane, she broke her leg. Take back your fucking curse."

Tim shook his head. He couldn't stop shaking his head as he replied. "Listen, I didn't... I don't have the ability to curse someone. I'm really sorry..."

The boy pulled the trigger.

Tim's hands went to his eyes. He couldn't look. He dropped to his knees. As the ringing in his ears began to fade, Tim hear the click of Cedric's toenails. He opened his eyes to see the dog slinking towards him. His ears were back and his tail was curled up under himself, but he was moving. Tim took the dog into his arms. His hands searched the dog for a wound as he looked up to see the gun pointing right at him.

"The next bullet goes in the dog instead of the ground," the young man said. "Now take back your curse."

✪ ✪ ✪ ✪ ✪

Tim could barely control the words that were coming out of his own mouth. Panic was beginning to shut down his ability to form coherent thoughts.

"Listen," he said. "Please."

"Take it back."

The girl moaned and then smiled she adjusted her leg and her foot swayed. Tim's eyes moved back and forth between the end of the gun and the unnatural leg. They were running a close race for the most disturbing thing he'd ever seen.

He wanted to go back in time. If he'd only piled Cedric into the plane and taken off instead of doing that test run, they would be safely in the sky by now. The pair, with their gun and broken leg, would be watching as Tim and Cedric flew away.

"We don't have all day," the young man said. "I don't have many more pills to give her. I think maybe I gave her too many."

The gun dipped as the young man looked down at his companion. Her head flopped down on his shoulder.

"I can't take back the curse," Tim said. The gun came back up. The round circle at the end of the barrel was impossibly black, like it was a portal to deep space. "You see her leg. It's already broken. You need to get her help."

"So get her help then." There was panic in the boy's voice too. The end of the gun shook as he adjusted his grip on the girl.

"All I can think is that you need to find a doctor. Have you seen anyone else around besides me?"

"YOU made her break her leg and YOU NEED TO MAKE IT RIGHT!" the young man shouted. "I'll just shoot you anyways. I've killed bigger people than you."

"Okay, okay," Tim said. He put up one hand defensively and kept the other wrapped around Cedric. An idea occurred to Tim. Less than twenty-four hours earlier, the very same idea had occurred to a boy several hundred miles east of him. The outcome of their ideas would draw them to the same place. "Listen. There's a laptop in my bag there. On it, I've got instructions on how to treat a broken leg, okay? If you can read those instructions to me, I'll be able to help, okay?"

The young man assessed Tim and then glanced at the bag. He seemed reticent to move.

"It's the only way I can help," Tim said.

"You read the instructions. I don't want you touching Amy Lynne."

Tim frowned and glanced at the girl. "I've got experience. I'd hate to have things come out wrong since it's your first time. Plus, you won't know if I'm telling you the right instructions if I'm reading them."

"Then I can read them myself," the young man said.

"Fair enough," Tim said. The right logic finally came to him. "But who is going to hold the gun on me if you're reading and doing the work?"

The young man considered this for a long time. Tim thought it was too long. The logic wasn't sinking in and he was going to have to try again.

"I'll read the instructions and you do it. But I'm going to keep my gun pointed at the dog."

Cold washed through Tim's veins again. He nodded.

The next few seconds were painful. He watched the young man try to help Amy Lynne to the ground while keeping the gun trained on Cedric. Tim wanted to go help, but when he made the slightest move, the gun came up again.

The kid was strong. He managed to support Amy Lynne's weight as her good foot stayed straight out and she focused on keeping her bad one from hitting the ground. Her bleary-eyed concentration was unwavering.

When she got to within six inches of the ground, they both fell backwards. For a second, the gun swung up towards the sky and Tim's muscles tensed. Some part of him wanted to rush the kid, just to have the confrontation over.

The young man and Amy Lynne hit the ground. She groaned with pain. The sound was quickly replaced by her slurred laugh. She rolled to her side and raised her leg. The way her foot turned towards the ground at the end of her straight leg made Tim's stomach turn.

The young man took a long look at her before he moved to the bag.

"What's your name?" Tim asked.

"Jackson," he said without looking up. He opened the zipper and pulled out the laptop. The way Jackson flopped the laptop on the tarmac, Tim wondered if it would still work.

Jackson looked up suspiciously, right as Tim exhaled. Tim realized that he had been holding his breath in anticipation, and he forced himself to try to act normal. What was normal when a crazy kid pointed a gun at you?

"What's it under?" Jackson asked.

"There's a bunch of photos in a folder on the desktop. I took pictures of the instructions."

"These look like outdoor stuff."

"Yeah, that's them. The instructions are written on walls." Tim once again searched for a tone that might seem normal.

"Walls?" Jackson asked. Fortunately, his fingers kept working at the laptop. With any luck, he would open the pictures and he would...

Jackson flopped backwards and the computer rolled off his lap. Tim ran forward just as Amy Lynne began to register that something was happening.

Tim pried the gun from Jackson's hand and held it out. He felt like a bank robber as he loaded the bag with one hand and held the gun straight out with the other.

"What are you doing?" Amy Lynne asked. Her voice sounded so weak and pathetic. Tim looked at her. Her eyes were confused and unfocused. She looked down at her own ankle and he had the bad judgment to follow her glance. Between her dress and her swollen foot, the skin of her ankle was torn. Amidst the clotted, black blood, white bone glistened.

"You need serious help," Tim said.

"What?"

Tim dragged the bag away from Jackson and then stood. He trotted backwards, keeping the gun roughly pointed towards the kids.

✪ ✪ ✪ ✪ ✪

He rushed his preflight and manhandled Cedric up into the cockpit. Jackson didn't move. Amy Lynne did little more than roll around. Tim was ready to go before he allowed himself to really consider the question: one, none, or both?

"Just the girl," he said to Cedric. The dog was sitting in the back seat. He didn't have a harness or even a seatbelt. Landing would be a nervous affair with a dog loose behind him. How bad would it be with an angry, drug-addled, injured girl?

"Just the girl."

Tim left the engine idling and climbed out.

She was already up to her knees, which surprised the hell out of Tim. He held the gun straight out and glanced at the side. He didn't know if the safety was on or off. Since he didn't plan on pulling the trigger, he figured it didn't really matter. Still, the idea of the thing in his hand didn't give him confidence or assurance. It felt like he was handling a stick of dynamite, and the fuse was lit.

"Come on," he said.

"What?" Amy Lynne looked at Tim like he was something brand new. No recognition registered on her face.

"I'll find you help," Tim said.

"Something's wrong with Jack," she said. Her mouth turned

down, into a pout.

"He's going to be fine in a couple of minutes. You need to come with me to find help."

"No."

Tim looked at the plane.

"You have a good point," Tim said. He started to back away.

"Wait," she called.

Tim kept backing away.

She slipped forward, like she had lost her balance, and caught herself on her palms.

"Please help me!" she yelled.

Tim paused. He didn't know handguns, and he didn't know if the thing was even still cocked. The idea of carrying the girl while holding a weapon was preposterous. He set the gun down on the runway and ran back to the girl. Jackson was still out. Tim wrapped an arm around her and dragged upwards. She yelled as her foot swung. Tim moved forward anyway.

He was more quick than gentle as he pushed her up onto the wing. She held up an arm against the air from the idling propellor. Tim climbed around her and opened the door.

"Come on," he said.

She was looking back at Jackson.

Tim's panic rose with the young man. He was pushing his way up.

"Let's go! I'll leave you here, I swear it."

Tim looked at the girl and then at the gun, which was about halfway between the plane and Jackson.

He picked Amy Lynne up beneath her armpits and dragged her backwards. He held the door open with his butt and tried to pull her inside.

"Hey!" she yelled. She was laughing again.

Jackson was gaining speed as he moved forward. Tim got the girl in her seat, although her legs were still hanging out through the door. He flopped into his own seat, released the brake, and increased the throttle. The plane began to move. With one hand steering, Tim tried to pull the girl's legs inside. He got her left in and cringed as the door closed on her right calf. The wind was making the door bounce against her leg just inches from the compound fracture.

"What are you doing? Stop it." Amy Lynne pushed at him with weak arms and flopped her head onto his shoulder.

"You have to help me get your leg in," Tim said. "That door is going to have a lot of pressure against it very soon."

He pushed against her back and she rolled forward. She actually raised her hand to the door, but she didn't move it. Tim looked back. They were moving slow and Jackson was starting to catch up. For some reason, the young man looked back and then ran the other direction. Tim was glad until he realized why—Jackson was going to for the gun.

Tim leaned over Amy Lynne, pressed open the door, and dragged her other leg inside. Her foot bashed against the door and then the frame. Amy Lynne screamed. Her voice was cut off as she flopped forward and sunk her teeth into Tim's shoulder. He filled the void with his own scream.

Tim flailed back with his arm and made contact with Amy Lynne's head. She slid backwards.

"Hey. That's not nice," she said.

Tim turned his attention back to flying. He checked on Cedric. The dog was sitting in the back seat and looking through the window at the passing terrain. Apparently, this was a normal takeoff for him.

They were nearly at the end of the runway when Tim turned the plane around. In the distance, Jackson stood with his legs wide and held the gun straight out. He had figured out that they would have to come back around, and he was waiting.

Tim ramped up the throttle and headed straight for him. He heard the pop and saw the smoke drift from the end of the barrel. Jackson was shooting at them.

"I wanna get out now," Amy Lynne said. She pawed at the door.

Tim tried to get control of his own breathing as the plane accelerated. He heard more distant pops and saw the smoke. He waited for one of the bullets to shatter the windshield, or penetrate his chest. If a bullet didn't go in, it felt like his heart might burst out. His heartbeat thudded in his ears even over the sound of the engine.

Tim veered the plane just before the wing could hit Jackson. The young man didn't move. He turned with the gun, but there was no more smoke, and no more pops. He must have emptied his ammunition while they were farther away.

Tim's heart began to slow as the wheels left the runway.

Tim fumbled and found headsets in a case behind Amy Lynne's seat. She was pushing with both hands against the door, but it was too late. The air pressure from the wind was holding the door shut now.

Tim got himself hooked up and enjoyed the peace he associated with putting on the headset. It was a powered rig, and when he found the switch, the noise-canceling brought him wonderful silence. Tim sighed and heard his breath key the microphone.

Amy Lynne had slumped against the door. Her exertions had drained the last of her energy. Tim checked her pulse and then checked his gauges. Everything looked good. If Jackson had hit them, he apparently hadn't done any major damage.

Tim circled and eventually spotted the boy at the side of the hangar. With a spray of silent dirt, Jackson accelerated his motorcycle out onto the road. Even at their distance, Tim saw Jackson's face turn up as he tracked the plane. Tim turned out and headed for the open water of Lake Erie.

Tim reached back and scratched Cedric's head. At the touch of the warm fur, he felt his panic subsiding. His heart slowed more and he settled into the seat of his new airplane.

When he got over the water, Tim headed north.

CHAPTER 16: VERMONT

THEIR BIKE PATH ENDED at a street. Stairs led to a pedestrian bridge, which crossed to the other side. Bicycles could follow a crosswalk and continue in a painted bike lane that ran down the side of the road. A wide channel of the pulsing liquid ran right down the double-yellow lines.

They climbed the stairs and used the pedestrian bridge. Brad pointed his light over the railing and looked at the liquid.

"That's the biggest amount of the stuff we've seen," he said.

"It's like an artery," Pete said. They came down the steps carefully on the other side. They used their lights to scope out the pavement before they set foot down on it.

"This way," Romie said. She pointed up the sidewalk.

"I still don't think you've explained it very well," Lisa said.

"Look at the book yourself," Romie said. "You'll understand."

"No!" Pete said. "Nobody is looking at that book until we've found someplace safe. What are we supposed to do, carry her until she wakes up again?"

"I wasn't out that long," Romie said.

"The hell you weren't," Pete said. "You were out for most of the day."

"I don't remember that."

"Can't you just tell us what you saw?" Lisa asked. "What makes you so sure we'll be safe if we head west?"

"That's where the center is," Romie said. "This is ancient

knowledge. God told me."

"You don't even believe in God," Lisa said.

"I *never* said that. You hear what you want to hear sometimes."

"Me?"

"Can we debate this later?" Pete asked. "I believe we need to focus one-hundred percent of our attention to avoiding that damn liquid."

They had moved away from the road with the artery. Pete swung his little beam from side to side, looking for any other trace of the stuff. The whole time they'd walked down the bike path, they hadn't seen it at all.

"Maybe we should figure out where the other end of that bike path is. That seemed like a pretty safe route. Wait a second—when we went north into the snow, didn't you want to take the railroad tracks then, Robby? Are they safe somehow?"

Pete and Romie were up front, followed by Lisa, Robby, and then Brad. When Robby shrugged, only Brad saw it.

Pete looked back.

"I don't remember," Robby said.

Pete turned away and then looked back again, as if he didn't believe Robby. Brad felt the same way—Robby didn't forget anything.

They were walking quickly. Romie chose the direction. When they got to an intersection, she was the one who decided if they would turn or go straight. They kept their general heading, but Romie made a lot of decisions on exactly how to get there. She didn't seem to make mistakes. At least they never got to an impasse and had to turn around. Somewhere in the back of Brad's head, he began to wonder if maybe they were being allowed to make progress west, just so they could be boxed in later.

"This is ancient knowledge?" Lisa asked. "Then how did you get it?"

"God told me," Romie said.

"Did God mention where we could get something to eat, or maybe some water?" Lisa asked.

They walked through the night, and didn't discuss stopping until the sky behind them began to brighten. The road they walked closely followed a brook. Every few turns through the hills, the brook passed under their road through a big culvert, or a bridge spanned the rocky stream bed. Brad glanced over the railing on one of these bridges and he could smell the running water. It smelled fresh, and made him even more thirsty. They'd already exhausted the bottles of water they'd carried from the ranger station.

Brad wondered if this running water was keeping the killer liquid at bay, or if maybe they'd finally passed out of the range of the stuff.

"We can stay here today," Romie said. She pointed up into the dark. Pete and Lisa pointed their flashlights in the direction of her arm, but what she was pointing to wasn't obvious.

"God told you where we should stay?" Lisa asked.

Hardly a mile seemed to pass without Lisa making one of these snide comments. It was a role reversal for the women. Usually Lisa was the calming factor as Romie made the remarks.

"No," Romie said. "I saw the sign."

Brad read it. "BB&B. Fine Dining. Accommodations."

The bridge to the place hardly looked capable of supporting automobiles. It was wood planks, and barely wide enough for two cars to pass each other. On the other side of the brook, the driveway wound up the steep hill on a series of switchbacks. The building was bigger than Brad expected. Four stories of windows looked north at the top of the hill. Pete tried the door and found it open. Brad went in last. He glanced east at the pink sky. It was going to be a cloudy morning, by the look of it. From what he could see, mist covered the lower elevations.

"Oh, god!" Lisa called from inside.

Brad rushed in.

He found the others clustered in the kitchen. They stood around the center island. There, on top of a slate countertop, a serving dish held an appalling display.

The thing was surrounded by candles that had burned down to

their holders. Milky wax pooled around each one. The silver platter was tarnished with a dark gray patina. The turkey looked like it had melted and congealed too. It was surrounded by a black fluid that had dried out and turned to hard enamel. A stack of plates stood at Brad's end of the counter, as well as carving tools. A colony of mushrooms was growing form the crusty remains of the stuffing.

"Who's hungry?" Pete asked.

"That's disturbing," Lisa said. She turned away and began rummaging through the cabinets.

Brad looked over to the stove, where various pots likely held the rest of the Thanksgiving meal. They all turned at the popping sound from the corner. Pete turned with a bottle of sparkling wine foaming in his hands.

"I think it's warm," he said. He sloshed the foam from the top of the bottle and took a swig. He handed the bottle to Romie. She set it down on the counter and Pete moved around her to retrieve it.

"We've got crackers and cans," Lisa said. She pulled out some food and carried it to the adjoining dining room after surveying the cluttered counters in the kitchen. She came back and opened drawers until she found a can opener. Robby went to a tall cabinet next to the refrigerator and immediately found some drinks. He carried those and followed Lisa.

After a second, Lisa appeared in the doorway.

"You guys ready to come in here? We're still waiting on your story, Romie," she said.

✪ ✪ ✪ ✪ ✪

Brad stuck out his hand and waited. Pete got the idea and handed over the can opener. The candle nearly went out when Brad's hand brushed near it, but it wouldn't have mattered too much. There was a decent amount of morning light leaking in through the windows by then.

They sat at a formal dining table, set for seven. They had napkins, silver, and glasses. Everything was set except for the plates. Apparently, dinner was going to be served buffet-style, in the kitchen. Brad's aunt had always served formal dinners this way. It kept the clutter from her small table and almost gave the impression that servants had delivered the food to the waiting feasters. This table was huge though. It could have easily supported the big turkey as the centerpiece. Brad kept glancing at the chandelier. The cut glass seemed to dance in the flickering candlelight.

"We're still waiting for your story," Lisa said.

"Fine," Romie said through a mouthful of canned peaches. "God forbid we actually get to eat something."

"Eat while you talk," Lisa said. "We're not fancy here."

Nonetheless, Romie finished chewing and swallowing before she spoke.

"It was those symbols that Robby showed me," Romie said. "I don't know how to explain the feeling. When we get someplace safer, you're just going to have to try it for yourself. I really think you should."

"But what happened?"

"Relax. I'll tell you," Romie said. She laid her hands down on the table, like she was going to rise. Instead, she took a big breath and began her story. "As I looked at those squiggles, the world felt like it was pulling away. The book became like a dot of light in the center of my vision, and everything else was black. The black parts just grew and grew until the book just looked like a tiny little pinprick of light, right at the edge of what I could see. It was like I was looking at the night sky, but there was only one star.

"And that's what it was, too. I understood as the light began to get bigger and bigger. I was zooming in on that little dot of light. It was like I was a spaceship and I was getting closer and closer to that star."

Brad had an unsettled feeling. He had been just about to spoon a black olive into his mouth when she said this. He paused and waited with his spoon halfway to his mouth. Olive juice dripped from his spoon to the fancy lace tablecloth.

"A dark dot passed between me and the star. I knew it was a planet, and I figured I should be heading for it, but it zoomed by me. As I got closer, and the star got bigger, I realized that the planet was going to return. I was going to reach its orbit just as it came back around. I was right. The star was like the size of a softball and I saw that planet again. It got bigger and bigger as I moved closer. Then, I started to get nervous that I was coming in too fast, and the planet was coming too fast at me."

"Is this important?" Pete asked. "Is it important to your story?"

"Shhh!" Lisa said. "Let her talk."

"I realized from the colors, that the planet was Earth. I even saw the moon come around. It didn't look exactly like Earth though. I knew it even at a distance. The land was too green, and the oceans were too washed-out looking. There were a ton of clouds, but I could see the continents and they were wrong, too. They were all packed together."

Robby was slurping a mouthful of cold soup when he spoke. "Pangea."

"Yeah, I guess so," Romie said.

"What's Pangea?" Pete asked.

"All the continents used to be packed together," Lisa said. "Like back when the dinosaurs were around."

"You went back into time?" Pete asked. He had a big smile on his face, like he was about to make a joke.

"Shhh!" Lisa said. "Keep going, Romie."

"I kept going, fast as ever, and the Earth went around again. I went through the atmosphere and thought I would burn up for a second. I didn't."

"You got all this from that diary?" Pete asked.

Lisa pursed her lips and looked like she was about to shush him again, but Romie answered the question.

"You know how instinct works, Pete?"

"You just feel it," he said.

"No, I mean how it works."

"I guess not. I guess I'm not entirely convinced there is such a thing."

"Neither do I," Romie said. "Understand it, I mean. I do believe there is such a thing as instinct. You put a nipple in front of a baby, and it knows how to suckle. Your house cat still knows how to hunt a mouse, even though nobody taught it. They all wriggle their butts, right before they pounce. It's like they're trying to get their hindquarters settled in before they're about to make a run at something, and they all do it."

"I suppose," Pete said.

"So where do we get the suckling behavior? How do cats know to wiggle?"

"Genetics," Pete said.

"You could call it that. Or you could call it instinct. What's the difference? However we get it, some behaviors seem to come standard with all people. What I realized when I was swooping down to that planet, is that there might be even bigger instincts we have locked away in our consciousness. They might need a trigger to release them, like maybe a set of symbols. You look at those, and suddenly you remember something that's burned right into every human being."

"In the DNA?" Brad asked. He set down his spoon and let the rest of the liquid and the olive slosh back into the can.

"I don't know," Romie said. "It could be in our DNA, or maybe there's some other mechanism that we don't know about. Maybe there is a spirit that's made of energy or something. Maybe there's a soul that gets attached to your body when you're born. Maybe that soul has a collective memory that transcends a single life."

Pete made a derisive buzzing sound with his lips.

"Shhh!" Lisa said, again.

"Or maybe it was God. I think that's what it was. I think God was talking to me. He was letting me know what's going on."

Nobody said a word to that.

"I swooped down low and saw all the wonderful creatures of that old world. It was older than people. Maybe it was older than mammals. I don't know for sure. There's a huge gap in what I was able to see. I was hovering over the ground, like a view you'd see from an airplane, and everything below me started to change. First, the forest began to change. Everything happened in fast motion. The greens became washed out and the new color spread with little veins coming out from the center of a circle. Then, in the very center, a black spot formed. The black turned to bright white and that began to spread. Clouds formed above it, like a hurricane, but I could still see through them. I saw the ground below turning white and I realized that it was snowing under those clouds. In the very center of the circle, a bright light appeared.

"Next thing I knew, I was on the ground, just outside the circle of snow." Romie took a second to collect her thoughts before she continued. "I moved inside the circle. I saw some of the dinosaurs. All the other animals were gone already, but some dinosaurs were still there. They don't look anything like we portray them. Some of them had feathers that were so fine they almost looked like fur. They had bright colors."

"Were you scared?" Lisa asked.

"No," Romie said. "They were all dead. Maybe a few of them had lived through it, but those were smart enough to hide. All the ones I saw out in the open were dead. Some had popped out eyes, like we saw with all those people." Romie looked up at the ceiling for a second. Some memory brought a quick smile to her face. It disappeared as quickly as it had come. She shook her head. "You start to realize that it's the overload of the nervous system that makes their eyes pop out. It's like they've been hooked up to too much voltage."

"But why?" Lisa asked.

"They're going to be puppets later," Romie said. "Their bodies will be marched in to the baby when it gets far along enough to need the meal. They're being prepped for that purpose. Some will stay behind and be processed by the liquid, but most will trek to the center when the blue lightning starts up."

"Wait a second," Pete said. "Didn't you say it's safe towards the center? Are you moving us towards the thing that wants to eat us?"

"We're at a different stage of the process right now," Romie said.

Brad looked over at Robby. He'd been mostly silent since he had woken up from his weird coma, but somehow he seemed particularly silent now. He looked like he definitely had something to contribute to the conversation, but he was holding back for some reason.

"It's like last year," Romie said. "The snatchers come in bulk and it begins snowing. We haven't even gotten to that phase on this go around."

Pete ticked off his objections. "But we already have the killer liquid. We already have the snatchers. The world has already fucking ended, if you hadn't noticed."

Romie shook her head. "It's not the same. You tell him, Robby."

All eyes turned to the boy. He was pressing the sides of the candle, near the top. The wax walls were soft and the hot liquid spilled down the sides.

"Go ahead, Robby," Pete said. "You knew about this stuff before, right? You had us take all those bodies to the light, and a lot of what she's saying seems to fit your theories from back then. What's your opinion?"

Robby didn't look at Pete as he answered. "I think we should hear Romie's whole story before we cloud it up with other ideas."

Pete gave a shrug with a resigned nod. They looked back to Romie.

"There's actually not much more. My vision is incomplete and I knew it was when I was having it. It's like there was a jump in the movie, like a whole reel was missing. Maybe the guy from the ranger station was missing a chunk of his DNA. Maybe that's why he killed himself. Anyway, in my vision, I flew to the center of the circle and time advanced. I watched the ball of light send out its tendrils. It makes a whole network around itself to bring it what it needs to develop. And here's the hardest part to understand: all the times it has been to this planet were the same exact time for it."

She let that sink in.

"You said that like it should mean something," Lisa said.

"It does. Shit, I don't know how to explain it. Imagine you're in a room, and someone takes that room and plugs it into different houses. When the residents of the different houses open the door and see you inside, they think they're looking at someone in their house. But, to you, it's all the same room. You get it?"

"Not at all," Pete said. Lisa shook her head.

"Robby, help me out," Romie said.

They looked at the boy again.

"I don't know if I can," Robby said. He took a breath and let it out slowly. "Take a ribbon, and fold it back and forth. Then stick a pin through the center. You made one hole with one pin. But if you take the pin out, and stretch the ribbon out again, it looks like many holes."

"Time is folded," Brad said.

"In some higher dimension, it doesn't have to be," Robby said.

Pete pushed away the can of chili he had been eating cold. "What else happened in your dream, Romie?"

"That's about all I can remember," she said.

"How about you fill in some more details, Robby. You clearly had another perspective on the same topic."

Robby pushed back from the table and stood. "I think we've had enough talk for now. I suggest we sit on what Romie said for a while."

Robby walked from the room.

Brad watched the flickering candles and then turned to the sunrise coming through the windows. They had lived nocturnally long enough so that the sight of the sunrise made him yawn automatically. He swallowed one back only to see Lisa throw back her head and yawn. That set off a chain reaction amongst them. Pete looked at his watch. Romie pushed back from the table.

"I guess the conversation is over then," she said.

"Wait," Brad said. "What about the taxidermy?"

Romie leaned over the table, holding herself up with her palms on either side of the fancy place setting.

"What?"

"The bear? The wolves? We saw taxidermy come back to life and attack us. Those things were just fur on top of foam and metal skeletons. How did they come back to life? If this thing has the power to reanimate animal skins, why would it need to go to all the trouble to manipulate dead bodies like puppets?"

"I don't have the whole picture," Romie said. She walked out.

They watched her leave and heard her climbing the stairs. They hadn't explored the rest of the inn. Brad wondered if the room doors would be locked. He figured they wouldn't, but he hadn't stayed in a Bed & Breakfast before.

"Now we've got two of them," Pete said.

"You said that already," Lisa said. She stood and began collecting the cans they'd eaten from.

CHAPTER 17: NEW YORK

JUDY HAD TWO PAIRS of jeans. She was scrubbing the cuffs of her good jeans when Ron walked by. He slowed as he passed.

"Hey," Ron said.

"Hey."

"Meet me on the porch," he said. He kept walking.

Judy paused for a fraction of a second to watch him walk away and then returned her focus to her jeans.

✪ ✪ ✪ ✪ ✪

She didn't see him at first. Judy walked up and reviewed the chore list. She was still excused from chores, apparently. Her name didn't appear on any of the lists.

"Hey," she heard from the side of the building.

She glanced around. She was still being tracked. Two bearded men sat on a bench outside one of the barns and kept an eye on her. Judy moved to the end of the porch and sat down with her back against the wall of the house. She cupped her chin in her hand to disguise her whisper.

"Hey," she whispered.

"What did they do to you?" Ron asked, from around the corner.

"Nothing," she said. "They've been watching me, but they didn't do anything to me."

"They questioned me for an hour. They wanted to know how I

found that hatch in the bottom of the grain shed."

"Luke asked me about that, but I didn't tell him anything."

"Yeah," Ron said, with a long pause. "Me neither. I think we have to do something. Like maybe we should tell everyone else. Luke and his men are trying to cover something up."

"Yeah?"

"Don't you think? Why would they be so secretive? I think they knew about that hatch the whole time. Or, maybe they knew about it, but didn't know where it was or something."

"Really?"

"I don't know," Ron said. "I'm just trying to make sense of what's going on."

"They're coming," Judy said.

She heard the bushes rustle as Ron moved away from his side of the house. Judy stayed where she was and watched the men approach. Three of them approached. The pair on the bench held their position, but watched carefully.

Judy recognized the bearded man they all called Hampton. He walked between two other bearded men. She'd seen them before, but didn't know their names. Hampton had joined their group near the end of the journey. He said he had been living alone and saw their convoy when they stopped to refuel. He had joined up with Luke's little army right away, but his beard was still scraggly compared to the men who had been growing them for weeks.

"Judy," Hampton said. He made a motion to the other two and they backed up and turned around.

"Hello," she said.

"They call me Hampton. My name is Sam. You can call me either."

"Okay."

"Where's Luke?"

Judy shrugged and raised her eyebrows. "Haven't seen him."

"He didn't come to visit you?" Hampton waited for an answer, even though the question implied that he already knew the answer.

"Yesterday," Judy said. "He came to my tent yesterday."

"Not in the woods today, beyond the manure pit?"

"I hope not," Judy said. "I was peeing in the woods."

"Two men saw him go into the woods after you. He wanted to talk with you about something and asked the men to hold back. They say that fifteen minutes later, you came back alone."

"That doesn't sound right. It doesn't take me fifteen minutes to pee. Are they sure?"

"You didn't see Luke?"

Judy shook her head. "Maybe he ran away?"

"We found his sidearm," Hampton said.

"Careless," Judy said, shaking her head. "It's careless to lose your gun like that. What if a kid found it?"

Hampton regarded her for a second before he spoke again. His tone changed. "I think you did see him. I want to know what happened in those woods."

"Can I be honest, Sam?"

"Of course."

"You guys scare me. You bearded guys are like the pigs in *Animal Farm*. Or maybe you're the dobermans. Either way, you scare me. I don't know why you're following me around. We went on a supply run, I got attacked, and then I screwed up when I followed Ron down into that crazy silo. We thought it was just a bomb shelter or something and we got lost. I told Luke the same thing yesterday and I haven't seen him since."

Hampton nodded. He made eye contact with Judy and then nodded again.

"Can I be honest with you, Judy?"

"Sure, Sam."

"I have to use a testosterone cream to grow this beard. I rub the cream on my arm, but it gives me the hormones I need to grow the beard." He scratched his face and then smiled again. "I don't even like wearing it. It itches like hell. But I would use the testosterone cream anyway. It helps me maintain my muscle mass. I've had to use it since I was twenty-four. That's when I volunteered to have my testicles removed."

Judy flinched and scrunched up her mouth, like she'd just taken a bite out of a lemon.

"Some people thought that it would be enough to give us

vasectomies, but I'm glad they neutered us. I'd rather be alive with no balls, then to vanish like everyone else. You're looking at me like I'm crazy, but Luke told me what you said yesterday. You said that there wasn't a fertile person in the whole group, and I believe you're right. They wouldn't have left any breeders amongst us. That wouldn't fit their plan. I assume that most of the survivors, like yourself, just happen to be sterile. Others, like me, made a conscious decision. Now that you know what I've sacrificed to be here, would you like to reconsider the lies you've been trying to feed me?"

"Hampton... Sam... I don't know what you mean."

He blinked. "People have studied this phenomenon since the beginning of science, Judy. There are little clues everywhere, if you know how to look. You're not the first person that has gotten caught up in this story."

"Phenomenon?"

"The oral history of humans is clouded by mysticism, but legends of cataclysms exist in every culture. Before all this happened, people were obsessed with the idea of an apocalypse. You saw it in movies, and books, and even songs. As a race, we all had a sense of what was coming."

"You think that people knew about all this?" Judy threw up her hands with her palms towards the sky.

"They had a sense of it. Some organizations, like the one I work for, planned for it."

"Well, good fucking job. You did a stellar job with this whole thing."

"There were circumstances beyond our control, but our operation wasn't a total failure. We're still here, aren't we?"

"Just by dumb luck." Judy laughed.

"It's not luck that I had myself sterilized. That was planning, and sacrifice. It's not luck that this farm is here. It *was* luck that the initial landing didn't happen where we had hoped, but it was bad luck. If everything had gone to plan, our casualties would have been much fewer."

"Why did you bring people here?" Judy asked. "If this is all some kind of plan, why did you round up all these people and bring them to the farm? You're suggesting that everyone is sterile, so I know you're not intending to repopulate the Earth from this group."

"I think you know the answer to that, Judy. Let's dispense with questions that we already know the answers to. Why did you come here, and what did you do with Luke?"

"Honestly? I have no idea. I'm not some mastermind, regardless of what you think. I'm the victim of wrong place, wrong time. That's all."

"I don't know what your role is supposed to be in all this, but you know much more than you're telling me. We're watching you, Judy. We're always watching."

Hampton stood and walked away. When he reached the other two men, they fell in behind him.

✪ ✪ ✪ ✪ ✪

Judy left the porch and headed for the latrine. On her way back to the tents, she saw Ron hanging out near one of the barns. She walked right up to him, despite the two men who watched her from the fence.

"Are you okay? I saw those guys asking you questions," Ron said.

"Everything is fine. Listen, don't tell anyone, but that guy Hampton is the new Luke."

"What happened to Luke?"

"Nobody knows. Maybe he had something to do with it, because now he's making a move for control. I think it's going to be fine, but a lot of people say that he will do anything to get his way. I don't know if he and Luke had a disagreement, or what."

"What was he asking you about?"

"He knows that Luke and I are close, and he wanted to find out what I know, I guess."

"That's weird," Ron said.

"Listen—just don't mention it to anyone. I don't want it to become a big thing."

"No problem."

Judy walked away, satisfied that she knew what Ron would do.

CHAPTER 18: ROCHESTER, NEW YORK

"LISTEN. LISTEN!" TIM SHOUTED. In the back seat of the plane, Cedric barked.

The girl flinched for a second and then resumed her feeble attempts to grab at the controls for the airplane. Tim held her back with one arm, and corrected their course with his other.

"Do you see that down there?" Tim asked. He tipped the plane and pointed out her window. They were fairly low. She still didn't seem to see what he was pointing at. Tim suspected that either her vision wasn't very good, or maybe the drugs were affecting her eyesight. "That's a helipad. I think it's a hospital."

She mumbled something. She didn't comprehend that he couldn't hear her over the noise of the engine unless she shouted.

"I'll put us down," he said. "Easier said than done."

Tim looked for a good place. The highway near the hospital was wide enough, but he would have to go right down the center to avoid the light poles that projected out from the sides of the road. It would have been much easier if he'd still had his old plane. This one seemed fine until you tried to actually maneuver it. Then, it bobbed and weaved for no apparent reason. Tim didn't like the idea of trying to bring it down between the light poles and before an abandoned car got in their way. He didn't have much choice. He'd bypassed Buffalo—there was no obvious hospital near a good place to land—but by Rochester, she was starting to come out from her drug stupor. She was getting feisty.

She had another outburst just as Tim brought the plane down. This time, she went for Tim's eyes.

Tim slapped her with the back of his hand.

"Amy Lynne! You will kill us both if you don't settle down RIGHT NOW!"

She lowered her head and folded her hands in her lap. Her good behavior didn't last long. As soon as the wheels touched down, she was out of her seatbelt and pawing at the door. Tim got the plane stopped and got his fingers on the back of her dress before she could fall through the open door. She screamed and cursed as she banged her bad ankle on the door.

"Just give me a second," Tim said.

He exited through his door and Cedric bounded over the seat right behind him. The dog didn't like being in there with Amy Lynne any more than Tim did.

"I'll go get you a wheelchair if you'd just stay put," he yelled at the plane. She was already trying to get out again. Tim ran across the road to the parking lot with Cedric at his side. "Maybe she'll disappear before we get back."

The doors to the hospital were wide open. They were glass—the kind that slid to the sides like Star Trek doors—but someone had pried them apart and left them that way. Tim found what he was looking for. There was a heavy, clunky wheelchair in triage, right next to the nurse's window. Tim pushed it through the door and got it going faster as he crossed through the lot. It had a very subtle pull to the left. It reminded Tim of a bad shopping cart. He strained to keep it headed for the plane and increased his speed.

Amy Lynne was already sitting on the wing. She was trying to find a way to slide to the ground.

"Here," he said, breathing hard. He held out his arm and waited for her assault.

"Where have you been?" she asked. "I need help, for fuck's sake."

Tim helped her slide a little farther and then let her wrap her arm around his neck as he grabbed her around her shoulders and under her knees. He put her in the chair and propped her bad foot up on the rest.

"Ow," she moaned. She kicked him with her good foot.

Tim got behind the chair and pushed. He aimed her for the Star Trek doors and tried to form a plan. His knowledge of first aid was limited, and this was not a simple case. He didn't even want to look at her ankle, let alone try to treat it.

He spun her around to back up the ramp to the door. The lobby had plenty of light from the glass wall, but as he banged through the double doors to the treatment area, Tim blinked until he could see just enough to navigate. The hospital had little glass rooms for each patient. A few windows across the hall gave him a dim view of his surroundings.

"I'm going to look for supplies," he said. What would he need? Tim figured he would want antiseptic, some bandages, and maybe one of those inflatable casts. Perhaps he could find a drug cabinet and get her some more painkillers for when her current batch ran out. He didn't know where to start. There were machines here and there, but he didn't see any kind of medical supplies.

"Shit," he whispered to himself.

He remembered Cedric. They'd been separated at some point while he wheeled Amy in. Tim ran for the double doors. Cedric was waiting there.

"Come in here," Tim said.

He turned around as the oxygen tank swung through the air. Amy Lynne had turned on him again. She was balanced on her good foot and had managed to limp within a couple feet of Tim without him noticing. Now, she was trying to bash his brains in with an oxygen tank.

She missed. The weight of the thing pulled her to the side and she came down on her bad foot. Amy Lynne screamed collapsed to the floor.

"Stay there," Tim said. He stepped over her and went back to searching.

He found a cart with gauze, tape, bandages, and antiseptic. The casts and splints ended up being in a tall cabinet behind the nurse's station. He dumped an armload of stuff next to Amy and looked around. It would be easier to work on her on one of the tables, but the light was better in the hall. It was even better out in the lobby.

"What are you doing?" Amy asked.

"I'm trying to figure out how to help you," Tim said. "We have to clean up your leg and maybe figure if we can get the bone going in the right direction before we put the cast on you. I don't think you want it knitting back together at an angle."

"Not you," she said. "Him."

Tim turned and saw the man.

✪ ✪ ✪ ✪ ✪

Tim had never thought of himself as tall or short. He was just normal height. Some people were taller, some shorter, but Tim was average. He reassessed this idea as he looked up at the hulking figure. With men like this around, Tim was an elf.

In the low light, Tim couldn't see the man's features very well. His face was all shadow. He saw the crooked smile, though. The man's lips were parted on the side, revealing a triangle of white teeth.

Tim took a step back. Cedric held his ground and gave his tail a half-wag. It was the dog's way of saying, "I don't know you. Are you a friend?"

Tim saw a dark hand move forward towards Cedric as the man bent his knees to lower himself.

"Dog," the voice said. It was deep and rumbling.

"What are you doing?" Amy Lynne asked again.

"Hello?" Tim asked. The word started with a pop. Tim's mouth was so dry that his tongue was glued to the roof of his mouth.

"I haven't seen a dog in a long time," the man said. His words came out slow and careful, like he was relearning to speak as the sentence formed.

Tim finally noticed the man's clothes. He was dressed in hospital garb. They were like light-colored pajamas. Probably blue, but it was difficult to tell in the minimal light.

"Are you a doctor?" Tim asked. "She needs help. Her leg is badly broken."

The crooked smile pointed towards Tim as the man considered

the question and statements. His smile turned down as he considered himself. Finally, the man replied. "No. These clothes were here." He pointed vaguely, off into the darkness.

"Can you help?" Tim asked. He moved to behind Amy Lynne's shoulders and grabbed her under her armpits. Her eyes were still locked on the giant man.

"What are you doing?" she asked him. This time the question sounded more amused and thoughtful, than accusatory.

The big man lowered himself to one knee. Cedric sniffed at him as the man moved his hands carefully under Amy Lynne's legs.

"Cedric, get out of the way," Tim said.

They lifted the girl and moved her to the wheelchair. The man set her feet down on the footrests. He must have done it better than Tim had. Amy Lynne didn't scream at all.

Tim crouched and picked up all the supplies he had collected. He pressed them to his chest as he stood. The big man had already moved behind the wheelchair. He stooped to grasp the handles.

"I figure there's more light in the lobby," Tim said. He backed towards the doors and pushed them open. He held one to the side with his foot as the man wheeled Amy Lynne out into the lobby. "I'm Tim and this is Cedric and Amy Lynne. What's your name?"

"Call me Ty," the man said. He rolled the chair right over to the window, next to a set of chairs.

The man looked even bigger in the light. He arranged the chair parallel to the glass and glanced frequently out at the sky. When Ty crouched in front of the wheelchair, he moved with a fluid ease.

"What's she on?" Ty asked Tim.

"I don't know. Some kind of pills? She was on them when I met up with her. I haven't seen her take any since."

"I can't give her anything unless I know what she's on," Ty said.

Tim shrugged.

"Darling? Can you tell me what you're on?"

"What are you doing?" Amy Lynne asked. She had a curious smile on her face now, like she was waiting for the punchline of a joke.

Ty's fingers moved gently over her ankle. He pushed back the dirty hem of her dress and revealed her ankle. Tim had seen glimpses of it, but he forced himself to really look at it now. He saw bruising, torn skin, and a jagged piece of bone before he looked away.

"Okay, darling," Ty said. "Let me get some supplies." He stood with that same fluid ease and laid a giant hand on Amy Lynne's shoulder as he walked by. The hand moved to Tim's shoulder and he led Tim away from the girl before he spoke in his low, rumbling voice. "She's in tough shape."

Tim nodded. "I know."

"We might be able to get the bone lined up, and we might be able to get that cast on. Then she'll likely die of a terrible infection."

"I understand. We have to do what we can."

"It's going to be bad. Maybe not even humane."

"What are you saying?" Tim asked. He glanced around the mountainous man and saw that Cedric had put his head on the girl's lap. She was stroking the long fur around his ears.

"I've got some pills," Ty said with a big exhale. "It would be easier than suffering for a week while a fever makes her crazy and the pain steals her sanity."

"Easier for who? Her or us?"

"Us? I'm not adopting her."

"I don't even know her. I'm just trying to help."

"If it's up to me, she's going to eat a big handful of pills. If you're going to take care of her, then I'll do my best to set her leg and close up that wound."

Tim thought about it and glanced at the girl again. He figured it was likely that the girl wouldn't make it. If she died in a week, he wouldn't have to worry about her anymore, and he would have a clear conscience. If she lived, then so much the better.

"Yeah, okay. I'll take care of her."

Ty nodded and turned to walk back over to Amy Lynne.

"Wait. What are the odds that she makes it?"

"Probably none."

Ty worked on Amy Lynne's leg for an hour. Tim's job was to distract her, and when that didn't work, hold her down. She screamed, cried, cursed, and bit Tim's arm before Ty inflated the cast and called the job done.

"She can't put any weight on it for a while. The cast will help keep everything in line, but it won't be able to bear weight."

Amy Lynne had been moaning for several minutes.

"What about the pain? You said there were pills?"

"Yes, but you'd better wait another hour or two before you give her anything. Let her sober up a bit." Ty reached into the pockets of his scrubs and produced a couple of bottles of pills. "These you have to give her every eight hours for the next twelve days. Don't miss a dose. The last thing this world needs is a super bug."

"I can't believe they make scrubs in your size," Tim said. He couldn't help himself.

"We had to order them."

"Wait. I thought you didn't work here."

"You didn't ask that. You asked if I am a doctor."

"Oh," Tim said. "Listen... Is there any way we can just stay here with you for a few days? I won't ask you to do anything. It would make me a lot more comfortable if I knew you were around."

Cedric approached and sat at Ty's side, pressing against his leg. It was as if he was helping to make the plea. Ty had to bend his knees and lower himself towards the ground to pet the dog. The crooked triangle of a smile appeared again on Ty's face as the dog smiled up at him.

"It's going to be hard, watching her suffer."

"But the pills will help, right?"

"If they don't, nothing will."

"You're living here at the hospital?"

Ty nodded in response. He lowered his massive frame down to one knee, so he could pet the dog with both hands. Cedric loved the attention.

"It's a big place. I'll take her to some corner so we won't bother you. We'll stay until her antibiotics are done."

"Then what?"

"What do you mean?"

"When her course of pills is done, how do I know you'll move along?"

"Oh. I'm headed east of here, but I'll be dropping her off a little south. She has a boyfriend or something down there."

"Where are you going?"

"It's a long story," Tim said. He tried to think if there was a reason he might regret revealing his plans to Ty. He couldn't think of one, but still, he wanted to be cautious. "There seems to be a circle of these murals. Actually, the murals are everywhere, but the farther out from the center, the bigger they get. I used to have a map of the whole thing. Anyway, I'm going towards the center of the circle to see what's there."

Ty considered this for a minute while Cedric lowered to the ground. The dog rolled over, inviting Ty to rub his chest.

"Why on Earth would you be curious about what's at the center? Don't you think it might be something dangerous?"

"Maybe," Tim said. "Everything is dangerous though. Have you seen the tornadoes? Have you seen the burned zone? The danger is everywhere."

That crooked smile took over Ty's face again. Tim didn't know if it was a response to something he'd said, or maybe the way Cedric's leg bounced as Ty scratched him.

"I like your dog," Ty said.

"Maybe you should come with us."

"I saw that little airplane you left out on the highway. I don't think I would fit inside that thing. And I have everything I need right here. I'm not a curious man."

Tim nodded. Amy Lynne began to moan louder and she squirmed in the wheelchair. Tim moved to her side and considered the bottles of pills that Ty had given him.

"Remember to let her sober up for a bit before you give her anything more."

"I will."

"Follow this hall down through the dark and you'll find your way to the patient wing. There are no stairs, and each room has a sofa that converts to a small bed."

"Thanks."

"I'll bring you some food in a bit."

"That's very generous. Thank you."

✪ ✪ ✪ ✪ ✪

By the time night began to fall, Tim was eyeing the pills. Amy Lynne still seemed dopey, so he didn't want to dose her with more painkillers, but he was beginning to wonder if he should take one himself. Perhaps he would be able to get some sleep. Her moaning and squirming were unbearable. Even when he moved to the adjacent room, the sounds from her room kept him awake.

Cedric didn't like it either. He whined in sympathy with Amy Lynne until Tim yelled at him to stop.

At first, the minutes ticked by slowly. Then, as Tim's patience evaporated, the passage of time seemed to come to a complete halt. He began to wonder about what Ty had said. The big man had talked about what was humane, and then said, "I have some pills." Did he mean euthanasia? That must have been what he meant. Maybe he was right. It took a certain amount of heartlessness to listen to the girl suffer and not do anything about it. Tim was beginning to wonder what the more compassionate solution would be. Should he care for her the best he could, or put an end to her pain?

The thumping of Cedric's tail against the floor alerted Tim to Ty's presence in the hall.

"You awake?" the low voice asked.

"Can't sleep. Her eyes are still slow to dilate, so I don't think it makes sense to give her any drugs yet."

"I think you mean they're slow to constrict, and that's not a great indicator of sobriety."

"Oh."

"I'll go check her."

Cedric followed the giant man as he left to go to the next room, where Amy Lynne was groaning. Tim felt jealous of the dog's instant kinship with Ty. He knew Cedric would come back. In a few seconds, he was right.

Ty came in after a minute. Miraculously, Amy Lynne's moaning didn't start up again.

"I gave her two. You can give her two more in four hours."

"Thank you."

Tim studied the man's face to see if the crooked smile would appear. He couldn't see anything except the whites of his eyes. Ty was scratching Cedric's chest again. Tim heard the dog's leg thump against the floor and hoped it wouldn't elicit a response from Amy Lynne.

"You have dreams, Tim?"

"Sure. Sometimes."

"Recurring dreams?"

"No."

Ty was silent for a few minutes. Tim wondered if he should probe to find out what the man clearly wanted to tell him.

"I do," Ty said, eventually. "I have the same dream almost every night."

Tim thought carefully. He could remember a few dreams. It was only the scary ones—the ones that woke him up—that he really remembered. They were different each time though. In one dream, he was being chased by an alligator, or some other kind of lizard. The thing kept hiding in the grass. In another, his teeth fell out all at once. He couldn't find anything to eat and he began to waste away rapidly. The dreams were scary right when he woke up, but almost comical by morning. It helped having Cedric there.

"What's your dream?"

"It's stupid, but it scares the living shit out of me," Ty said. The giant man sounded like a frightened child.

Tim's throat went dry again. He wasn't sure he wanted to know what would make such a powerful man feel that afraid.

"Right after everyone disappeared, I came to work, expecting to find patients. There wasn't a soul. No matter what happens—blizzard, power outage, hail storm—it always brings in a flood of patients. We even had a tornado one time. Nobody was hurt. The thing touched down in a potato field and it didn't do any more than turn over a couple of tractors, but we still had patients. People came in with all manner of injury, even though the tornado didn't hit any of them. But on Thanksgiving, this place was empty. That night I had the first dream."

Ty stopped talking. For a second, they both listened for Amy Lynne. She muttered something to herself and then she was quiet again.

"I was here in the hospital, alone. This was the first night that everyone disappeared, but I knew in the dream that I'd been here for weeks, maybe even months. I climbed the stairs to look out at the city and there was a blue lightning running down the highway. In the distance, I saw something moving. It was coming towards the hospital, and for a second, I was glad. A hospital needs patients. The building is like a living thing, and the patients are like the blood cells that keep everything oxygenated. As they got closer, I realized that the people who were headed my way weren't going to stop at the hospital. They weren't moving under their own control. The worst part was that I knew that I was going to be one of them before long."

"What were they?"

"I don't know. I never get that far into the dream. I always wake up screaming."

"Every night?"

"Every single night."

"That doesn't sound so bad," Tim said. He tried on a smile.

Ty shook his head at the memory. "There should be a peace in death. The dead shouldn't have to march."

"What does the blue lightning represent to you? Maybe if you can figure out the symbolism of the dream, you can make it go away."

"Wait."

"What?"

Ty reached out through the darkness and put his hand on Tim's knee. Tim understood and shut his mouth. A fraction of a second later, he understood why. There was something coming down the hall. It clicked on the tile floors as it walked, as if it were wearing metal shoes. It had the slow, uneven pace of a gentleman on a stroll. Tim looked down at Cedric. The dog had been sitting at Ty's feet. Now, Cedric silently crawled towards Tim. The dog stopped when his head reached Tim's foot. Tim put his hand down on Cedric's head and felt as it turned towards the door. All three were focused on the sound.

The only light in Tim's hospital room was the starlight coming through the windows. The door to the hall was like a rectangle of black construction paper. Tim could imagine anything moving across that canvas. He wondered what he would see first. Would a naked white skeleton move by the door with its boney feet tapping out the rhythm on the floor? Would a well-dressed aristocrat pass by with metal taps nailed to the soles of his shoes?

The clicking reached a crescendo. Each footstep was louder than the last. Tim knew the thing would have to reveal itself at any second.

The sound stopped.

After a minute, Tim's muscles vibrated with anticipation. Where was the source of the clicking footsteps? Where had the thing gone?

He heard Ty release a deep breath.

"That's the closest it has ever come," Ty said.

"What has come? What was it?" he asked. As soon as Ty's hand lifted from his knee, Tim couldn't help himself. He rose and moved towards the door, aware that Cedric was right next to him. He stuck his head out into the black hallway and waited for his eyes to adjust. He still couldn't see much. He pulled out his flashlight and stabbed the beam of light into the dark. He cut it back and forth, finding nothing.

He shut off his light before returning to Ty. Tim took his place on the sofa near the window.

"What was it?"

He saw the man's head shake back and forth in the dark.

"I don't know. No matter where you go in this hospital, it will eventually track you down."

"That's terrible! Why would you stay here? I'd be out of here the next morning."

"What makes you think the walls of this place will confine it? Besides, it has never hurt me."

Cedric hopped up beside him and pressed his furry body

against Tim's side.

"No wonder you're having nightmares. You need to get out of here. I've stayed in several places and I've never heard any phantoms wandering around. You've never seen what makes the noise?"

"There's never anything there," Ty said.

"I don't think that makes me feel better about it. So you've been here since Thanksgiving?"

"Yeah. I knew people would come here, looking for help."

"Forgive me for saying, but when we came, it didn't seem like you were very willing to help."

"I was willing, but I wasn't convinced that treating her was the same as helping her. You understand?"

"Yes, you made that point clear earlier. Has anyone else come?"

"A few. I do what I can. Most of the problems I've seen aren't physical though. Too much stress will break more than bones. I can set the bones, but I'm not qualified to do much about the other things."

"Where did the people go?"

"They moved on. Everyone's headed somewhere. A pair from Ohio thought they needed to get to the CDC in Connecticut. They read about it in some book. I met a guy from the Finger Lakes who thought that the Gulf of Mexico was where he'd find salvation. He was diabetic. He came in to find insulin."

"What was wrong with the people from Ohio? I mean why did they come to the hospital?"

"Nothing wrong with them. I used to run a generator up on the fifth floor. It was hooked up to a light. They saw the light and came to see what it was for. The man was a bit unstable, but there was nothing really wrong with either of them"

"I wonder if they made it to the CDC. You didn't have any desire to go with them?"

"No."

"I'd go crazy if I were on my own."

"I've always preferred it," Ty said.

They sat in silence for several minutes. Cedric seemed to relax a bit. He moved away from Tim's side and curled into a tight circle on the sofa.

"Will the thing in the hallway come back again tonight?" Tim asked.

"Maybe. If it does, it will be right before dawn."

"Great."

Eventually, Tim slept.

CHAPTER 19: VERMONT

ROMIE SEEMED TO CHOOSE her turns randomly. Pete flipped through his maps, trying to figure out their location. It seemed that as soon as he found a clue, she would turn again and he would lose their place. She utilized a lot of gravel and dirt roads with few markings.

The car smelled stale. Brad couldn't quite put a name on the smell, but he kept picturing french fries that had been fried in rancid oil. His stomach flipped as he imagined shrimp left out in the sun. Even opening the windows didn't seem to help much.

"Are we going the right way?" Lisa asked Robby, in a whisper. They were packed into the back seat. Robby was in the middle, and Brad was on the far left. Brad's neck hurt from leaning forward to try to see where they were going.

To Lisa's question, Robby only shrugged.

"Would you just slow down a bit?" Pete asked. "Some of these roads don't go anywhere, you know. They just come to a dead end on the side of a mountain."

"I'm sure they'll be marked," Romie said. She barely slowed as she steered around a sharp curve and lined the car up with a narrow bridge.

As far as he could tell, Brad was the only one looking out to make sure they didn't cross any of the killer liquid. He hadn't seen any yet.

"Wait," Pete said, looking up from his map. "Did that say Woodford Road? Shit! Go back and take a right."

Brad was surprised when the vehicle slowed. He couldn't believe that Romie was actually taking a suggestion on their route. She turned around and stopped with the headlights pointed down the intersecting road.

"I think you're right," she said. "That road follows the creek."

She pulled down Woodford Road and brought the vehicle back up to speed. This was a much better stretch of asphalt. The center line was clear, and the potholes could be avoided. Brad noticed Lisa relax, now that they weren't being jarred upright by the bumpy road.

"Deer," Robby said.

Brad was thrown forward against his seatbelt as Romie screeched to a stop. She must have seen the animal at the same time as Robby.

"Where? I don't..." Lisa said. She angled her head to see around Romie.

They all watched the doe. She stepped carefully from the brush to the side of the road, keeping an eye on the car. She bent down and nibbled at the vegetation. The light inside the glove compartment came on when Pete opened it and took out the gun stashed there.

"Don't you dare," Lisa said. "She could be a mother."

"No," Robby said. "She's not."

"You don't know," Lisa said. "You're not going to shoot the first living thing we've seen in a month."

"How long has it been since you've had fresh meat?" Pete whispered.

"I don't care," Lisa said.

"It would go to waste," Romie said. "We couldn't eat all of her, and we don't have a refrigerator."

"I could salt it," Pete said. The desire in his voice was already turning to melancholy. He sensed he was outnumbered. The gun clunked on to the dashboard.

The deer turned and looked off at some sound none of them heard. It chewed a couple of times. Instead of returning to its browsing, she crossed the road in front of them. To Brad, it looked like she was placing her hooves delicately, trying to stay quiet. As far as he knew, that was how they always walked.

Halfway across the road, the deer paused again. It faced away from their vehicle, looking into the night. Something spooked her. The deer ran off into the woods.

"Nice to know that things might get back to normal someday," Lisa said.

"What makes you say that? One deer can't exactly repopulate anything," Pete said.

"There could be more," Lisa said.

Romie began to roll the car slowly forward. She looked back and forth, checking the sides of the road.

"Deer move in herds," Pete said. "Especially the females. If that one was alone, that suggests to me that she's the only one around here."

Romie brought the car back up to a reasonable speed. The cool night air took away some of the stale smell. Brad leaned his face out the window to take a deeper breath.

"Don't be such a pessimist," Lisa said.

"What is that sound?" Romie asked. She began to slow the vehicle. Her idle question was all the warning they got. Their feet pounded like distant thunder as they sprang over the little hill at the side of the road. The deer poured out of the forest, streaking across the road in front and behind the car. Brad shrank back from his window as a deer charged straight for him. At the last second, the buck jumped and Brad saw the animal's feet pass within inches of the car.

"Holy shit," Pete said. He fumbled for the gun on the dashboard and then dropped it as he thrust it out his window. It hit the pavement as the deer scattered into the woods on the other side of the road. The interior lights came on as Pete opened his door and scooped up the gun. He threw it back in the glove compartment.

"Get out of here," Lisa said.

Robby was nodding in agreement.

"Yeah, no shit," Romie muttered. She put the car in gear and revved the engine. They started fast and then everything went out. The headlights, the engine, and even the gauges on the dashboard went out. Brad heard the rumble of the retreating herd and the low crackle of the tires still rolling on the pavement. Romie grunted as she tried the ignition. It didn't make a sound. "Shit, shit, shit," Romie whispered.

"Push it!" Robby said. His voice had an urgency that Brad hadn't heard in a while.

Brad threw open his door while they were still rolling.

"Put it in neutral," Pete said. He opened his own door.

Brad took the left side and Pete took the right. They seemed to be on the same page. The car was on a flat stretch of road, but ahead the road went down a gentle slope. With a push, they could get some momentum that would take them a decent distance.

"She's not going to be able to steer," Brad said. "You know, without power steering."

"She can handle it," Pete said. "She has more upper body strength than most people."

Brad was putting all his effort into pushing on the back of the vehicle, but it was barely moving. He began to wonder if maybe they were on a slight uphill. One of the doors opened and closed and Robby came around to take a position between the two men. With three of them, they finally began to gather speed.

"Oh shit," Pete said.

Brad didn't ask what he was referring to, he just followed Pete's eyes. It was a dark night, but the mist behind them almost gave off a glow of its own. It was rolling out of the woods and beginning to lap over the edge of the road behind them.

"What the fuck is that mist? We haven't seen any goddamn mist," Pete said.

"I have," Robby said.

"Great," Pete said.

They were beginning to gather speed. Brad almost fell over when he turned to see the progress of the mist. Behind them, where the deer had crossed the road, the mist had almost reached the centerline of the asphalt.

"Get in, Robby," Pete said. "We're starting to move."

Brad craned his neck to see over the top of the vehicle. The downhill section was just ahead. The car was starting to feel lighter.

"You ready?" Pete asked.

"You go," Brad said. "I can catch up." He saw that Robby had climbed in and was holding open the door for him.

Brad had to bear down to against the weight of the vehicle when Pete ran ahead. He heard Pete's door close and glanced back at the mist one more time. It was across the road and was defying physics to roll up into the forest on the other side. Even more frightening, fingers of mist were now rolling in Brad's direction, following the progress of the car. He gave one last burst of effort and felt the car beginning to pull away as it gathered speed down the hill.

Brad tripped as he ran. He stumbled and looked down to see the mist rolling up on his feet. Somehow he kept his balance and quickened his pace. He caught the open door and used it to pull himself forward. He flopped into his seat and pulled the door shut. The stale smell almost seemed welcoming now. Brad turned in his seat and joined Robby and Lisa as they looked out the back window. The hill was accelerating the car away from the mist. When they pulled far enough away, it seemed to give up its chase. They saw it up on the hill, glowing in the dark, until Romie guided the car around a slight turn.

BONG! BONG! BONG!

The car's electronics came back to life. Romie's hands moved fast. The ignition was already on, so she put it in gear and popped the clutch. The car jerked and then the engine roared back to life. Romie shifted quickly and they sped away.

Within a few seconds, she was jamming on the brakes again.

"What now?" Pete asked, with a sigh.

Brad spun back around to face forward again. At the bottom of the little hill, a short bridge spanned across the stream. These bridges had been a common sight for them in Vermont. The roads Romie preferred followed little streams, and often crossed back and forth from side to side.

This one had a sentinel. A column of dancing flame burned orange and red as it patrolled back and forth across the bridge. It looked to be as tall as a person, and at least a couple of feet in diameter. With the car still running, Romie jerked back the parking brake.

"I guess we're on foot again," she said.

"No," Pete said. He was out of the car before anyone replied. At the back of the car, Pete popped open the trunk.

Brad jumped out and came around the back. Pete was pulling things from the trunk—some rags, and a red plastic gas can.

"What are you doing?" Brad asked.

"The liquid things hate running water. Maybe the fire things hate fire. I'm sick of being sidetracked," Pete said.

"You have to keep it together, Pete. Stay calm. We just have to stay calm and we can get through this."

"I'm sick of it," Pete said. He slammed the trunk shut and filled his hands with his supplies. Romie shut off the lights and Pete walked down the hill in the dark.

"Pete, come on." Brad chased after him. The man wouldn't listen. "Pete!"

Brad stopped about twenty yards from the end of the bridge. Pete got much closer. The column of flame was at the far end of the bridge. It turned and started back in their direction. Brad looked nervously back up the hill. He saw the car and imagined the faces of Romie, Lisa, and Robby, waiting for him to save Pete from his own anger. Brad didn't know what to do. Farther up the hill, he didn't see any sign of the mist, but he didn't doubt that it might still be coming for them.

"Come on, man," Brad said. "We'll go through the woods. We'll find another trail or something. This stream is shallow enough to cross on foot if we have to."

Pete had the cap off the tank and he was soaking gas into one of the rags. Brad didn't see any way for this to turn out well. Even if Pete didn't get killed by the column of fire, he was likely to burn himself to death with the gasoline.

✪ ✪ ✪ ✪ ✪

Pete handed Brad a lighter. Before Brad knew what was happening, Pete was off with the gas can. Pete ran towards the bridge. About halfway between Brad and the bridge, Pete started dumping a line of gasoline. Meanwhile, the column of flame was marching in his direction. It didn't speed up or change course. It still seemed to be locked into its own patrol.

Brad bent and picked up one of the rags. Pete had tied a knot in the end and soaked the knot with gas. Brad held the rag by the dry tail, and held the lighter in his other hand.

Pete laid a trail of gas. The column of fire was almost to their side. Pete and the fire were on a collision course. Just before he reached the bridge, Pete veered to the side. He sloshed gas towards the column of fire and Brad cringed. He expected the marching column to ignite the gasoline. He expected fire to race back to Pete and explode the can in the man's hands. The gas Pete sloshed might as well have been water. Pete circled the column, and splashed gas everywhere. Even when it hit the column of fire, it didn't ignite.

Brad looked down at the rag in his hand. He could smell the fumes. He looked back up at the column and wondered what it was actually made of, if not fire.

Pete was finishing the can. He tossed the red can right in the path of the column.

"Do it," Pete yelled. He jumped over the railing of the bridge where the ground sloped away.

Brad realized it was time to act. His numb fingers fumbled with the lighter. He only got the lighter halfway to the rag before the fire leapt out and the rag burst into flames. Fire licked up at Brad's hand. The hair on the back of his hand went up with a flash. Brad nearly dropped the tail of the rag. He swung it in a circle and launched it at the trail of gas. The rag rolled towards the trail, but its flight had put out the flame.

Brad took half a step forward before he remembered the other rag. He had one more chance to get it right. A burst of flames sent a wave of heat towards him. The rag had remained lit after all. Fire shot down the trail and then lit up a big circle around the column of flame. Brad saw Pete's face peek up over the side of the bridge and then flinch back down as the flames lit up the night.

When the gas fire hit it, the column of flame flashed and flared.

The column turned from orange and red to a deep blue and it moved towards the break in the circle. Pete's trail of gas didn't encompass the column perfectly, and it was moving towards the gap.

The column reached the gas can and this time it did have an effect on the gasoline. The fumes inside the can heated and the exploded. Brad thought he heard the thing screech when the can exploded, but it might have been air escaping the plastic can. Fire shot every direction. The orange flames of the gas were mixed with the hot blue fire of the column. As little clumps of fire shot every direction, Brad had a terrible premonition. He imagined all the little bursts of blue flame moving independently. He imagined a nightmare of little sentient flames chasing them through the night.

His fear was short lived. As the little blue flames hit the ground, they turned orange with the gas fire and then burned out. The last bit of blue flame burned on a chunk of the gas can before it flared and turned into harmless orange flame. The gas flames looked different than the sentient column.

Pete was hunched low as he ran up the side of the road and then joined Brad.

"You okay?" Pete asked.

"Yeah, I'm fine," Brad said. He watched the gas burn out, waiting to make sure that no columns came back.

"Your hand was on fire for a second," Pete said.

The car rolled up behind them. Romie's window rolled down.

"Is it safe?"

"I guess," Pete said.

"Good," she said. "We have company." She hooked a thumb over her shoulder. Brad looked up the hill. It took a second for his eyes to adjust after the fire, but then he saw it. The mist was beginning to roll down the hill. "Robby says if it gets any closer it will shut off the car again."

Brad and Pete nodded and then headed to opposite doors.

"I understand why you're choosing roads that follow streams, but I don't know how you're picking the overall route," Pete said. He traced his finger along his map and flapped the paper for the hundredth time. Brad leaned his head against his window and rolled his eyes. Romie and Pete had been having this discussion for an hour.

"I can't explain it," Romie said.

"The sun will be up soon," Pete said. "We should be looking for a place to sleep."

"We just have to go a little farther," Romie said.

"Do you remember when I used to get so mad at Robby? Remember how I said it was so maddening that he could be so confident without any empirical evidence?"

"You never got mad at Robby," Romie said.

"Oh, right, *that was you*," Pete said, triumphantly. He rattled his map again.

"Could you two stop?" Lisa asked.

They both started to argue again when Robby finally spoke. He had been quiet the whole time, so when he talked, everyone's ears turned to him.

"It's like the pyramids," he said. "Or Stonehenge."

"What?" Pete asked. He turned to Robby.

Romie kept her eyes forward, on the road, but Brad could see the annoyance in her shoulders. She hated it when Robby said cryptic things.

"There are areas which hold power. Some people believe that they hold power because of the objects that are there, like the pyramids, or sculptures, or other manmade things. But what if those things are built there because the area itself holds power?"

"That's some really new age bull," Pete said. He snapped a fold into his map. Brad knew he would just unfold it again in a few seconds.

"Romie is taking us to a place of power," Robby said. "She's allowing herself to feel her instincts. If you allow yourself, you'll feel them too."

"My instinct says we should get indoors before daylight. We've been lucky that we haven't run into any killer liquid, and we got really lucky with the mist and the flame. I don't want to take any chances on being snatched up into the sky."

"We're past that now," Romie said. "There's no danger of that."

"See, you *say* that, but you have no evidence. Do you understand why that's so damn annoying? You're risking our lives on a hunch. When we stop, I'm going to take the keys and I'm going to drive next time. The person driving has to understand that this is a democracy and we all get a say in whether we keep going or we stop for the..."

His sentence trailed off as Romie slowed. They saw a few abandoned vehicles, parked next to the road. The doors were open and they were empty.

"Hey," Lisa said. "Aren't those the Land Rovers that..."

"Luke's group," Brad said. He pressed his hands on the window, like he wanted to reach out and touch the empty Land Rovers.

"Why would they leave them here?" Lisa asked.

"Don't stop," Pete said. He put his hand on Romie's shoulder. "Go slow, but keep moving."

Brad turned to watch the Land Rovers as Romie kept rolling. He turned around to see that they were moving slowly down another hill. Romie had her eyes on the rearview mirror and only Pete's yell turned her attention back forward.

"Wait, wait!" Pete said. He pointed through the windshield. As they drew closer, everyone saw what he was pointing at. The way the road sloped down, it was difficult to see. A washout had taken a chunk of the road away, leaving a miniature canyon at the bottom of the hill.

"Hold on," Pete said. "I think I saw something back a ways. Can you turn around?"

"Sure," Romie said. She swung the front end of the car over to the left side. She spun in her seat as she put it in reverse.

"Romie?" Lisa said.

Pete had his head in the map and everyone else seemed to be focused on what Romie was backing towards. Only Lisa was looking out the front.

"Romie, I think you should stop," Lisa said.

"Why?" Romie asked.

"Them."

✪ ✪ ✪ ✪ ✪

Lisa pointed out through the windshield. They all turned to see the men coming from the woods at the side of the road. Everyone jerked as Romie stomped on the brake. First there were two, then three, and then five, as more appeared from the brush. A couple held handguns. The rest had rifles.

Robby tapped Pete on the shoulder, who lowered the map and then saw what the rest of them saw. The bearded men approached quickly, and with their weapons at the ready.

"Hey!" Pete said. "I think I recognize that guy." He pushed open his door and jumped out of the car.

"Get down!" one of the men shouted. They all raised their guns higher. "On the ground!"

"Show us your hands!" another man yelled.

"Hey, hey," Brad heard Pete say.

Another bearded man reached the front of the car and brought the butt of his rifle down on the hood. He tapped twice and then raised his weapon again. "Get out," he ordered.

"What do we do?" Lisa asked.

"We get out," Romie said. "Don't be stupid."

They opened their doors.

CHAPTER 20: NEW YORK

"COULD EVERYONE PLEASE HOLD on for a second? You're all talking at once and nobody can hear a thing," Hampton said. He was standing atop a hay bale and addressing the crowd. The discussion at breakfast had gathered momentum naturally and slowly morphed into a mob. Judy stood along the side, about three-quarters of the way to the back. She could barely see Hampton over the angry heads. People were shifting on their feet. They were agitated and couldn't hold still.

"Where's Luke?" a woman asked.

"As I was saying—Luke is on a supply mission. We expect him back at any time," Hampton said. He held up both of his hands as he spoke. It wasn't a "I surrender" gesture, it was more like he was trying to tamp down their aggression.

"Who elected you the leader?" a man yelled.

"Nobody elected me anything. I happen to know that Luke is on a mission, so I'm addressing everyone to make sure you're informed."

Judy heard an older man turn to a younger one in front of her. "Who is this guy?" he asked.

"We should have an election," a woman yelled. "Why don't we have a say in the decisions?"

Judy looked across to Ron, who stood on the opposite side of the group. He had his arms crossed and looked pleased with himself. Judy hadn't expected the people to get that riled up so quickly. In fact, she hadn't realized how big their group had become until they all gathered there behind the big barn. She guessed that there were at least sixty people, and more walked up every minute. A heated discussion between two picnic tables had turned into a group debate. That debate ended with a call to action. That's when the mob had formed and gone to find answers. What they'd found was Hampton, and he had tried to assuage their concerns. Everything Hampton said just seemed to make the mob more angry.

Murmurs were breaking out all through the group. Little side conversations were turning into shouted debates here and there.

"If you want to have elections, then please feel free," Hampton said. "But don't accuse me of usurping power that I neither have nor want."

A man, mid-twenties if Judy had to guess, stepped up on another hay bale near Hampton. He hardly needed to stand on anything to be seen—he was already pretty tall. He didn't need to speak to draw everyone's attention. People turned to him and quieted down.

"Who here wants to have an election?" the tall man asked the group.

About half the group voiced their agreement with the idea. The tall man didn't ask how many disagreed.

"Let's just do it then. I nominate Ed Allen to be our leader," the tall man said. The name was only halfway out of his mouth when the boos began. Only a handful of people had a positive opinion of Ed. The rest seemed to hate him. "Hold on. Hold on. I know some of you are still sore at Ed because of what you think happened at the creek. I was there. Ed did everything he could. It's in a time of crisis that we see the true character of a person."

The boos grew so loud that Judy could barely hear the tall man trying to defend Ed. She knew his argument was lost as soon as the tall man began to address individual complaints that were yelled at him. People around the edges of the group began to disperse. She didn't notice Hampton until he was right next to her.

"Can we talk, Judy?" he asked.

She walked with him. A faction of the group had begun

chanting. Judy couldn't quite make it out as she and Hampton walked down the path that led to the pond.

"That was clever," Judy said.

"What was?"

"I've seen your guys talking to that tall man. I'm pretty sure he nominated the most hated person of this whole little community. That's a good way to break up the election."

"That does sound clever, but I didn't do it," Hampton said. "I want an election. If you people would install a system of government, it would give me the freedom to get away with a lot more."

"What did you want to talk to me about?" Judy asked.

"We found the patch of vines behind the manure pit," Hampton said. "I have a pretty good idea of what happened to Luke. You lured him off to the vines and let them take him away."

"I have no idea what you're talking about," Judy said.

"Right. Of course you don't. Listen, Judy, it's not arrogance or ignorance that makes us want to keep you around. We know a lot more than you give us credit for."

"Does this conversation have a point?"

Hampton nodded and paused. He looked out over the pond to the woods on the other side. When he looked back at Judy, he was smiling. "I know you're just one nerve ending in an enormous network. What are the odds that a signal from you would reach the brain? Still, I hope you understand. We've got the solution here. We understand all the variables and we are moving forward with the protocol. You're going to lose. And, on some level, I think that loss will hurt you. At the very least, it's going to leave a bad taste in your mouth. There are plenty of examples of times when you've pulled out in the face of overwhelming odds. Our fossil record shows us those times. Pull out now and save us both some effort. What happens next has only one conclusion if you persist, and it's not a conclusion that you'll find satisfactory."

"That's quite a speech," Judy said. "But I'm afraid you've confused me with someone else. I'm just a survivor, living amongst the wreckage of a destroyed world. I don't have the power to do anything."

"Judy, don't play dumb. You saw what we did to the last envoy. Is that how you want to end up? You think you'll feel rewarded with a bullet in your head? Do you think that..."

He was cut off when a bearded man ran up. The man looked at Judy and then cupped a hand to Hampton's ear and whispered something.

"Think about what I said," Hampton said to Judy. He ran off with the bearded man.

✪ ✪ ✪ ✪ ✪

Brad had a blank spot in his memory. As he thought through the timeline, he found a ridge where a memory was locked. One minute, he had been in the back of the stale-smelling car, hoping that Romie wouldn't tumble the vehicle down into the washout as she tried to turn around. The next minute, he was being hustled from the car by armed men. Now, he was in a gray, windowless room, looking at his own breath as it misted every time he exhaled.

The door opened.

A man walked in.

"Mr. Jenkins," the man said with a big smile. He held a sheath of papers under his arm and he pressed them to his side as he reached up to remove his reading glasses. He let them fall to dangle at the end of the tether that held them around his neck. "I'm so happy to see you."

Brad stood up from his chair and bumped his thigh on the metal table.

"Don't get up. Let's have a chat for a second." The smiling man sat down opposite and waited for Brad to sit. They were alone in the room, but Brad imagined that there were probably more compatriots of this man, just outside the door.

The man opened his folder and began flipping through the contents. It looked like a diary—dates, followed by a paragraph of what happened on that day. The man flipped through to a picture and then slipped that out of the folder.

"We've been training our people on your photo for weeks. I'm so pleased that they spotted you. We were very embarrassed that nobody recognized you back in Portland. You can imagine."

"No," Brad said. "I can't."

"You look remarkably different," the man said. When he flipped the picture around, Brad finally recognized himself. It was a picture of him out in the yard of his Kingston house. The soft lines of that face seemed like they belonged to someone else.

"After the embarrassment of Portland, you can imagine how pleased I am that you were spotted and identified. It was one of the volunteers that made the identification, too. I'll make sure he gets an extra piece of cake."

The man retrieved his glasses from where they hung against his chest. He flipped back through his papers.

After several seconds, Brad asked a question. "Where did you get that picture of me?"

"One of Herm's guys took it," the man said. "You know, before the dispersion, I would say that the majority of us didn't believe in collusion. Herm made a strong case for why you should be evacuated and set free somewhere else in the world."

"Collusion?"

"I believed that you were a facilitator. I still believe it, actually. You were there at ground zero once, and now you're here for round two. That seems like a tad more than coincidence."

"Maybe you could back up and explain things so I can understand," Brad said. He failed to keep the frustration out of his voice, but he stopped short of yelling at the man.

"Okay, fine," the man said. He let go of a weary sigh. "It's probably not your fault anyway. Here's the last report from Herm." The man read over the passage and then paraphrased it for Brad. "They achieved ninety-three percent containment. That exceeded his goal by seventeen percent. They only needed seventy-six to prevent dispersion."

"I have no context for what you're saying," Brad said. "I don't understand any of it." Brad stood up and moved towards the door.

"Sit down, Brad," the man said. His tone had an edge that stopped Brad's feet. Brad turned to regard him.

"The *only* way that ninety-three percent containment would fail, is if the effort were sabotaged. Do you know what my former position was? I was in risk assessment. There is *nobody* better in the world to issue that judgement, before or after the dispersion."

"And what..." Brad didn't get far into his question before the man interrupted him.

"And who would survive after that sabotage? Possibly only the saboteur himself."

"Are you suggesting that somehow I had a hand in killing off the vast majority of the world's population?" Brad asked. He wavered on his feet. His head felt light. Brad reached back and steadied himself on the wall. From its cold feel, he deduced that it was some sort of painted metal.

"Depressed. Lonely. Mourning a wife who divorced you and then died while you were engaged in efforts to reconcile with her. Reaching out to old friends in desperation. Hallucinating. You were not the picture of mental health, Brad."

"How exactly do you suppose I facilitated the apocalypse?" Brad asked. "With whom did I collude?"

"That's what I've brought you here to answer," the man said.

✪ ✪ ✪ ✪ ✪

Robby's feet seemed to fall automatically in rhythm with the others. He blinked a few times and glanced left and right. They were all shuffling up the gentle slope through the leaves. Their glassy eyes barely seemed to register the trees as they moved between them. Robby almost called out to Pete, who was on his right, but he decided to keep his mouth shut.

The sky was brighter ahead. It looked like the woods opened up to a clearing. Lisa extended a hand as they walked forward. Robby saw someone jogging along the edge of the woods. The person's head bobbed as they ran.

"Hello?" someone called from up ahead. Pete shook his head and stopped. Robby, Romie, and Lisa, kept shuffling.

More faces appeared at the edge of the woods. Some were bearded, like the men who had forced them from the car. But these bearded men looked different. Their eyes didn't have the same cold intensity. They looked slightly frightened.

"Hello? Who's there?" someone else asked.

"Don't be an ass. It's just people. Go greet them," another voice said.

Soon, one of the bearded men slung his gun over his shoulder and pushed his way through the brush. He stood at the edge of the woods and waved a welcoming arm to the shufflers. Robby watched as Lisa and Romie seemed to regain their senses. Pete trotted up behind them as they moved towards the waving man.

A smile broke across Lisa's face.

"Hello?" she called.

✪ ✪ ✪ ✪ ✪

Robby sat at the end of the picnic table and thanked the man who brought over the plates of food.

"You guys look half-starved," the server said with a smile.

Another bearded man—this one looked soft, like an insurance salesman, or an accountant—came over and sat next to Lisa. She smiled at him as she used her fingers to raise a tiny potato to her mouth.

"Where did you get potatoes?" she asked.

"We grew them," the man said. "My name is Hampton."

They made their introductions. Pete spoke through a mouthful of canned beans. Romie went last.

"There aren't enough pollinators. You know—bugs. You have to use a tiny paintbrush to move the pollen from one flower to the next. It's a pain," Hampton said.

"It's delicious," Lisa said.

"Where's Brad?" Pete asked.

"I thought you might be able to answer that," Hampton said. Concern furrowed his brow. "The men who found you in the car said that there were five of you. Then, when you came up the hill, only four. A couple of people are looking in the woods. I'll make sure more people join the search."

"Wait," Romie said. "What happened?"

"It's that little valley down there," Hampton said. "It's a geographic oddity. Gas collects down there in that little valley and it crowds out the oxygen. That's why we sent those men down to get you out as soon as we spotted your car approaching. Any longer down there, and you might have suffocated."

"Brad!" Romie said. She stood up and tried to untangle her legs from the picnic table.

"He's not in the dangerous part. We've got a watch on that. If you didn't see where he went, then he probably just got confused and wandered off," Hampton said. "They should have escorted you up here, I'm sorry. I think that people get sensitive. They don't want you to think that you're being arrested or something, so they usually just point people at the hill and let them make their way up to the camp on their own. Don't worry. We'll find your friend."

Romie settled back down to the bench, but she didn't look like she was going to make herself comfortable.

"I'll leave you guys to your food," Hampton said. "We've made up some rooms in the house for you. We like to welcome our new arrivals with a little luxury. After that, you'll be assigned duties and tents if you decide to stay. We encourage you to stay, of course."

They picked through their food as they listened. Hampton excused himself and moved away from the table. They were one group amongst many. People moved between the picnic tables with their plates. The four of them received a few glances, but their presence didn't seem to surprise anyone.

"What happened?" Pete asked. He had been moving like he was hypnotized. Now he blinked and glanced around.

"Welcome back, Pete," Romie said.

"How did we get here?"

Robby lifted his napkin to his face before he spoke. "Drugged. We were drugged."

"What?" Pete asked. It was his turn to try to climb out from the picnic table. He banged a knee but got one leg out. He swung it around to the other side of the bench before he fell back to a seat.

"They seem friendly enough," Lisa said. "They've found a bunch of new people."

"Who has?" Romie asked.

"Luke's group," Lisa said.

"These are the people that went with Luke? I don't recognize anyone," Romie said.

"You wouldn't," Lisa said. "You have a terrible memory for faces. Look—there's that guy, Frank."

"Where?"

"The one with the beard."

"Tons of them have beards," Romie said. "Pete has half a beard."

"I have a headache," Pete said. "Where are you going?"

He seemed to know that Robby was getting up to leave before Robby had even swung his legs out from under the table. Robby understood why Romie and Pete had experienced so much trouble trying to stand. Since he had been sitting there, his legs had gone to sleep.

"Just going to take my plate up," Robby said. He pointed to a place where people took their plates. There was a can for compost right next to a tub with soapy water. Robby followed a woman up and waited his turn to rinse his plate.

She smiled at him as she finished and it was his turn. Robby took the opportunity. "Hey, do you know a woman named Judy? Judy Densmore?"

The woman pushed her hair back and glanced up as she thought. "Judy... I think so. Twenties? Brown hair?"

Robby nodded.

"I think her tent is..." The woman turned and glanced a couple of directions before she settled on one. "I would try the little camp between that garden and the barn."

"Thanks," Robby said. He glanced back at the table before he followed the direction she had pointed out. His compatriots were back to their stupor—smiling and lifting food to their mouths. Robby stuffed his hands into his pockets and followed the fence that ran next to a line of trees. The sun was just beginning to heat up the morning. Robby wondered what time it was, and how much time they had lost. Someone had stolen hours from them. It wasn't quite daylight when they'd found the washout in the road, and now the sun was up.

Movement caught his eye and Robby saw the horses grazing in

the pasture. In the driveway, several Land Rovers were parked. The paint under the gas caps was stained pink. The roofs were scraped and dented from hauling gear. On a couple of the vehicles, the headlamps had been painted black except for a thin strip in the middle. Robby took all this in as he watched people making visits to the porch of the big house. Regardless of where their paths began or ended, people veered up to the porch, consulted the clipboards hanging from the clapboards, and then continued on their way.

Robby decided to mimic their pattern.

He slowed his pace so he would arrive after the couple in front of him had checked the clipboard and left. He found lists of chores for the day. Each list began with the name of the person in charge and then listed out who was assigned that chore. Robby scanned three clipboards until he found Judy's name.

He put the clipboard back on its hook and looked back and forth across the little settlement. They had three areas of tents, plus the house. Tractors and vehicles were stored in the driveway next to the house. He knew where they took their meals, and he could see stacks of wood over near where they had an outdoor kitchen set up. He blinked at the sky and wondered how this camp would change if they experienced any heavy rain. Or snow. What would they do if it began to snow and didn't stop?

He returned his attention back to the lawn. He was looking for the most-traveled path, and he found it. It ran down a set of ruts that looked like it used to be a road. In the woods, he saw what must be the latrine area. That was Judy's assignment for the day. Robby followed the path.

Robby passed a group of seven people coming the other direction. They seemed reasonably clean. Everyone's clothes were beginning to look a bit worn, especially at the ankles and the cuffs. They didn't smell as bad as he expected. When a breeze carried their odor to Robby, it wasn't offensive. He suspected that his own stink might have something to do with that. When everyone's hygiene suffered the same consequence, would anyone notice? Only one or two of the people even seemed to register Robby's passing. They must be accustomed to seeing new faces, he thought.

As he walked by a barn, Robby saw a boy hauling a bucket to one of the stalls. The boy was probably is own age. Robby nodded, but the boy barely seemed to notice him. He was focused on not slopping the contents of the bucket before he could lift it into the stall.

He drew closer to the woods and realized his assumption had been correct. They'd erected a simple latrine at the edge of the woods. It was a long shack with a few improvised doors down the face. It might have been a chicken coop, or some other utility building before being conscripted into latrine duty. The doors of the empty stalls had little towels over the handle. When someone went inside, they took the towel with them, indicating their occupancy. Robby slowed and glanced up and down the tree line. There had been too many names on the list for the duty to simply be maintenance or cleaning. He was looking for a whole crew of latrine workers, which meant they might be digging a new facility. He spotted it before too long.

The lucky ones were clearing brush. The hard work was going on underground.

Robby approached. The new latrine site was a good fifty yards from the old one, and it was going to be twice the size. Robby slowed and backed up to let a pair of men carry a large log up the path a bit. They added it to a pile.

Robby went forward until he could see over the lip of the new hole. It was already seven or eight feet deep, but people were busy digging. He spotted her hair first. She flipped it back and then brushed dirt off her face with the back of her hand.

"Judy?" he asked.

She froze. Before she turned around, she set her shovel down carefully. Her eyes were blank for a second before they lit up.

"Robby!"

They sat on the fence. Robby looked out over the pasture to where one of the horses was rolling in a brown patch of dusty dirt. Judy was picking much darker dirt out from under her fingernails. She moved one towards her mouth, like she was going to chew on it, but she stopped and intertwined her fingers.

"You guys didn't call me on the radio," Judy said.

"We tried that first night and didn't get you. After that, I guess you were too far away to pick up the signal," Robby said.

"What happened?" she straightened up and waited for his reply.

Robby took his time, like he was organizing his thoughts. "A lot of stuff happened. We collected the bodies and took them up north, into the light. It was very much like that dream I had. You remember that dream?"

She nodded and looked back down at her feet.

"I'm sorry I didn't believe you," she said.

"You believed," Robby said.

She met his eyes for a second, and then looked away.

"You believed, but you didn't want to be a part of it. It's okay. I understand," Robby said.

"Just because you were right about what happened, doesn't mean it was the thing we were supposed to do," she said.

"I know. You're right."

"Maybe we should have just stayed out of it. Maybe it was just nature's way of moving forward, you know?"

Robby shook his head, but didn't say anything. They had lived together for a while, like foster kids who become as close as siblings when placed under the same roof. All that time, they had only really disagreed about two things—her smoking, and whether they should fight back against the force that threatened humanity.

"You quit smoking?" he asked.

"How did you know?"

"For one, you would have had one by now. Second, your color looks much better. Third, your fingernails look like you've been digging most of that latrine with your hands. Fourth..."

"Okay, stop!" she said, laughing.

Over near the latrine site, one of the men looked up. He wore a thick beard. Robby was starting to get the impression that he was the one in charge of the digging. When Robby looked back to Judy, the clouds had returned to her brow.

"Luke's gone," she said. "It's not common knowledge."

"Oh," Robby said. "I never really had a problem with Luke. He and I just had a difference of opinion about what to do."

"You didn't know him," Judy said.

"I met him twice. I think I had a pretty good idea of what kind of man he was."

"No," Judy said. "You were wrong. You thought he was reckless, and dangerous. You were wrong. He was controlled, and calculating. He had an agenda the whole time."

"What are you saying, Judy?"

"Nothing," she said, shaking her head. "Nothing."

"Do you like it here?"

"Yes," she said, answering quickly. "It's safe here. We're all safe."

"Are you sure about that?"

"Why?" Judy asked. She turned on the fence so she could really look at him.

Robby liked it when Judy listened. Lots of people listened to Robby—at least they had, during the initial crisis—but when Judy really focused on him, Robby knew that she sincerely cared about what he had to say. Her attention was unwavering.

"Maybe it seems safe because they want it to," Robby said.

She tilted her head and bit her lip.

Robby nodded at the bearded man who was in charge of the latrine digging.

"They're just a self-appointed police squad. They don't have any real authority," Judy said. "We're having an election soon. The people are going to pick their own leader."

"When that happens, I'm sure it will all be closely monitored to make sure it aligns with their plan," Robby said. "If it doesn't, then adjustments will be made."

An easy smile spread across her face. "I missed your cynicism. You have to meet my friend Ron. He's just as cynical, but he's not nearly as smart as you. It's fun to watch him get spun up about things he doesn't understand."

"No thanks," Robby said. After a moment, they both laughed.

"I should get back to my work," she said. "We all pitch in together to make stuff happen. Even if you don't like what you're doing, you still want to do a good job because everyone's in it together, you know?"

Robby nodded.

"I'll see you at dinner though. Do you know where you're staying?"

"We're in the house tonight," Robby said.

"Fancy. Come find me at dinner. I usually eat over near where they're trying to grow squash."

"I'll do that," Robby said. Judy was about to slide down from the fence when he put out a hand to stop her. "Jude, there's nothing else going on, is there?"

"What do you mean?"

"Something here feels off."

She shook her head and frowned. "Nope. Not that I know of."

"Okay," Robby said. His voice sounded completely untroubled. The tone was a lie.

CHAPTER 21: ROCHESTER, NEW YORK

IN THE MORNING, TY was gone. Tim checked on Amy Lynne. She was asleep. There was a note on her table under a travel clock. It told Tim the last time she'd had pills and how long until she was due. He had a couple of hours, so he took Cedric outside.

They walked the perimeter of the hospital. The wind caught on the corners of the building and made whistling sounds. Sometimes it sounded like breathing, sometimes it sounded like a distant church organ. Tim didn't like any of the sounds. He checked on the plane. It was just where he'd left it.

Up the street, Tim found a convenience store that was untouched. He foraged for food and packed a few bags to take back. They even had a small bag of Cedric's favorite dog food. The dog would eat nearly anything, but he went crazy for Bowman's.

Tim paused as he left the store. While the door swung shut behind him, he thought he heard the sound of a faraway motorcycle. It disappeared with the wind and Tim hurried back.

Amy Lynne's room was empty, but Ty wheeled her back up the hall before long.

Her eyes were glassy and she looked very concerned.

"How are you feeling?" Tim asked.

"Like shit," she said.

"I washed everything again with hot water. It wasn't her favorite thing in the world," Ty said.

"I brought you chips and candy," Tim said. He held up the bag.

"That smells like shit," she said. She was pointing up the hall, where Cedric was eating his food out of a pink plastic tray. The dog looked up at them for a second and then went back to eating. "I want to go home."

"We'll open the window for you," Ty said, wheeling her back into her room. Ty did slide the window open, but he quickly moved away from it when he was done.

"Do you have the flying things here?" Tim asked. "I notice you stay away from windows."

"I haven't seen any lately, but if you're taking about the things that snatch people and make them disappear, then yes. I've seen them before."

"How long is lately?"

"Weeks? Maybe two months. I don't know exactly. But it has been some time. I stay cautious during the day though," Ty said.

"I want to go home," Amy Lynne said again.

"Let's get you back in bed," Ty said.

"I want to go home," she repeated. She let him lift her from the chair and didn't object as he swung her legs into the bed.

"I'll take you back to Jackson as soon as you're healed," Tim said. "For the moment, I think you're better off here, don't you?"

"Where is Jackson?" she asked.

Tim calculated. She was much more alert today, but her voice was still slurred and her eyes glassy. If she remembered more, a lie now might prevent her from ever trusting him. However, the truth might do the same thing.

"He's waiting for you back on Sunset Point. I'll take you back there when you're healed."

She nodded and looked through the window.

"I want more pills," she said.

"I just gave her the eight," Ty said to Tim. "You'll do the noon?"

"Of course."

✪ ✪ ✪ ✪ ✪

Amy Lynne was a terrible conversationalist. She either couldn't remember, or didn't want to tell Tim any stories about how she'd wound up with Jackson at Sunset Point. When he tried to ask any questions about her life before Thanksgiving, she closed her eyes and wouldn't say a word.

She ate, but she would only eat candy that tasted like fruit. The only thing she would drink was grape soda. By ten, she was beginning to twist and change position every few seconds. By eleven, she was groaning and pressing her hands to the side of the cast. Tim didn't think he'd make it to noon. She threatened him and tore at the sheets. The only thing that kept her in the bed was the throbbing pain she complained about whenever her ankle dropped below her torso. With her leg raised, there was only so far she could go.

Tim approached to give her the noon pills and she lunged at him, trying to grab the whole bottle. He wondered if he should give them to her. In the daylight, it was harder to imagine letting her eat pills until she slipped away, but the thought did cross his mind. Tim put the dose in a small cup and set it down on her table before sliding it over to her.

She ate the pills and closed her eyes.

Ty showed up in the afternoon with hot food. He made his delivery and then positioned himself in a chair near the door to the hall. Cedric sat next to him and the giant man stroked the dog's head as he and Tim talked.

"Her pain is going to get worse before it gets better. There's a peculiar sensation when the bones start to knit, especially with a break that bad."

"She was only really bad for an hour. The rest of the time was okay."

"She'll have a hard time quitting the pills when this is all done, too. Those things are very addictive."

"Fortunately, that part won't be my problem to deal with," Tim said. He lowered his voice and told Tim about Jackson and the motorcycle.

"What makes you think he'll go back to Sunset Point without her? If he followed you to the airport, then maybe he's still out searching."

"If he's out searching, then I guess I hope he'll hear the plane as I go south. I can fly around a bit before I land. Maybe I'll draw him down that way before I drop her off."

"You know how to fly a helicopter, too?"

"No," Tim said. "The idea crossed my mind, but that's difficult stuff from what I understand."

Ty nodded.

"Did you make this bread?"

"Yes. I have a whole bin of flour down in the pantry, and enough gas to make the oven go for a year."

"It must have been cold in here a few months ago."

"It's not so bad. You get used to it. I fixed up one of the offices to..." Ty stopped in the middle of his sentence. Tim automatically strained his ears to hear what the big man was listening to. He couldn't hear a thing.

"What is it?"

"What? Oh nothing. I just remembered something."

Tim waited to see if Ty would reveal the memory that had caused him to stop speaking so suddenly. Nothing was forthcoming. Amy Lynne whimpered in her sleep and rolled halfway over.

"What are we going to do?" Tim asked.

"About what?"

"In general, I guess. You know—as a people," Tim said. "Are we supposed to repopulate the Earth? Is it even fair to think about children when the world is such an inhospitable place?"

"Not my concern," Ty said. "I can't have kids. That's why my wife divorced me."

Tim nodded and frowned. He couldn't help it.

"You have kids?" Ty asked.

"No. Not me."

"How about you? You have any pups?" Ty mussed the fur between Cedric's ears and his mouth fell open in a dog smile.

"You're the first person I've really talked to since this whole thing happened. I had a couple of very brief conversations with Jackson and Amy Lynne. You should meet Jackson. He's charming. Cedric and I saw a couple of people down in Virginia, I think. It might have been West Virginia. They ran away. I keep thinking that I'll run into a small community. People like to group together, you know? Humans are a very social bunch."

"Maybe when people come together, it draws the attention of the birds. Or maybe only the loners survived."

"I suppose."

Amy Lynne opened her eyes and turned her head to look out the window. Every few breaths, she inhaled deep and then sighed.

"Do you want something to eat?" Tim asked.

"Candy," she said without looking over. Her hand came out and the palm opened in his direction.

"No, darling," Ty said. His deep voice commanded her attention and she turned her head to look at him as he stood. "You need something substantial. Your body requires proper nutrition in order to heal."

He rolled the tray closer to her and then helped her straighten up in the bed. Tim knew he would never be able to exert this much authority over Amy Lynne, but he paid close attention.

"You're running hot. I'm going to add a couple more pills, and you're going to have to drink a lot of water. I want you to have this much every hour, okay?" Ty looked back to Tim to make sure he was getting the instructions as well. The giant man hovered over the girl until she'd eaten a sufficient amount. He pulled back the tray and she immediately closed her eyes again.

"How is she doing?" Tim asked in a low voice as Ty lowered himself into the chair again.

"She's young and strong, but that ankle is serious. There's your boy."

Tim looked over and Ty had his head cocked to the side. Before he could ask what Ty was talking about, Tim heard it too. Cedric stood up. In the distance, so low it could have been an insect, he heard the whine of a motorcycle.

"I hope he doesn't find us before she's healed," Tim said.

"He will."

Tim studied the man's face before Ty answered the unasked question.

"Some of the people who stopped in put up signs on the highway. They point towards the hospital. If Jackson has any sense, he'll come here."

Tim shook his head. "We could have stopped in any town. We could have gone to any hospital."

"He probably checked in Buffalo and then came east."

"I should go hide the plane," Tim said. He got up.

Ty waved him back down. "Let him come. His girl is doing okay."

Tim's voice was barely a whisper as he spoke. "You don't know this kid. He's a nut. He almost shot Cedric, and I don't think he's very smart."

The whine of the motorcycle wavered as the wind shifted outside. Tim heard it downshift and then accelerate again.

"You want to go stay in my room for a while?" Ty asked Cedric. The dog's ears were perked to the motorcycle, but he wagged his tail.

"Yes, that's a good idea. Do you have any guns or anything?"

Ty stood and gave the dog a wave with his fingers. Cedric followed him. Tim followed as well. He was curious about where Ty lived in the hospital, but he mostly just didn't want to be alone.

✪ ✪ ✪ ✪ ✪

Ty settled Cedric on top of his bed and tucked a teddy bear between the dog's paws. Cedric rested his head down on the bear. Tim looked around the room. It had once been the office of a doctor, or an administrator. The photos on the wall showed a middle aged woman who always wore a big smile, and had big bags under her eyes. The room had no windows to the outside, and the window that looked out to the hallway was taped up with newspaper. Ty lit a candle when they entered, and its glow made the room cozy.

One of the desk drawers was open, and Tim saw that it served as Ty's bureau. The bookshelf was a pantry. The floor was covered in an area rug that showed cartoon kids playing on giant alphabet letters. He wondered how the giant man could fit on the bed. It was just bigger than a cot—even smaller than the hospital beds that were in almost every room.

"He's here," Ty said.

"How do you know?" Tim asked. Ty was already through the door. Tim followed. He shut the door most of the way and motioned to Cedric. "Stay right there." He couldn't bear the idea of shutting the door all the way. What if something happened and nobody was around to let the dog out?

Tim rushed to catch up with Ty.

They snaked through corridors. The big man moved with ease, even when there was barely enough light to see their own feet. He knew every obstacle. When Ty pushed open the last door, Tim didn't realize that they'd reached the emergency room from the other side. Ty glanced around and then moved into the lobby. He headed for the hall.

"Wait. What if he's..." Tim started.

Ty whirled and pressed his finger to his lips. He pointed through the glass and Tim saw the motorcycle sitting there.

Ty continued towards the hall. He pushed open the swinging door and glanced down the length before he committed. Tim slipped behind him before the door closed and they walked. Light came in through the rooms every few paces, dividing the hall into bands of light and shadow. Amy Lynne's room was around the corner, in the wing. Ty moved silently as he approached the corner.

Tim waited a few paces back. He didn't want his own clumsy footfalls to give the man away.

Ty didn't make it to the corner. Jackson stepped around before he got there. His gun was extended and there was a bright madness shining in the boy's eyes. Ty's hands went up immediately, but he kept to his low stance. He either wanted to keep the option of springing forward, or he didn't want to scare the boy with his size. Tim held his ground. He resisted the strong urge to run.

"Where is she?" Jackson asked.

They all heard Amy Lynne moan her response. She was only a few rooms away.

"She's doing better, but she's too sick to move," Ty said. He lowered his arms when Jackson's attention was drawn down the hall by the moans. Jackson kept the gun pointed at Ty and he backed up towards the sound.

Jackson disappeared through the door, leaving Ty and Tim out in the hall.

"Maybe we should fade away," Tim said. "He can catch up with Amy Lynne and maybe cool down."

"He might try to move her," Ty said. "That could kill her."

Tim nodded. He wasn't sure he agreed completely, but when Ty moved towards the room, Tim followed.

They found Jackson hovering over Amy Lynne's bed. The gun was sitting on the rolling table next to her pitcher of water and the plastic cup. Amy Lynne was mumbling something to Jackson. Her hands were gripping his shirt.

The boy whipped around. "You wouldn't give her candy? She loves her damn candy."

"Wait a second, son," Ty said. "Sick people need healthy, balanced diets so they can get better."

Ty moved forward and Jackson jerked back. He put his hand on the gun. "You're not touching her."

"Jackson," Ty said. His voice was slow syrup. It was low and soothing. "The longer she takes to heal, the more likely she's going to get some infection."

"You might try to kill her."

"Why would I do that?" Ty asked.

"Why would we fix her up and move her to this room just to kill her?" Tim asked. He realized that speaking was a mistake as soon as the words left his mouth. The kid had been focusing on the giant man in blue scrubs and wasn't at all concerned with him until he spoke. Once he turned his attention to Tim, Jackson's fear took over.

"You stole her away. You're pissed because I shot at your stupid dog."

Tim backed up. Jackson's hand was closing tighter on the gun. Tim didn't want to look down that barrel ever again.

"You guys get out of here," Jackson said. He didn't exactly point the gun at them, but he waved it in their direction.

Tim didn't need any more invitation than that. He backed up.

Ty pulled the door shut behind him. They moved down to the next room, where Tim had spent the night.

"I'm not sure he's terribly bright," Tim said.

"They're still alive," Ty said. "They must have some sense."

CHAPTER 22: FARM

ROBBY SAT IN BACK, on top of the big rear tire of one of the tractors. Romie and Pete leaned against the side of the machine. They looked across the back of everyone's heads. Apparently, this was the first real assembly of everyone at the farm. Even the horses, who stayed well back from their fence, seemed to be paying attention. Pete rose up on his toes and moved his head back and forth, like he was counting. Robby had a pretty good idea that Pete wasn't looking at all the normal citizens, he was focused on what he called the "Beardo Brigade." He'd been obsessed with them ever since he'd come out of his stupor.

Members of the Brigade usually moved around in pairs. Today, they were spread out. They stood alone, evenly spaced through the crowd.

A nervous-looking man stepped onto the porch of the house, which was at the front of the group. He waited while the murmuring died down and he had everyone's attention. It only took a second.

"My name is Travis, if anyone out there doesn't um..." He looked down for a second, like the rest of his sentence might be written on the boards. "I've only been here a week. I was asking who was in charge, and it turns out that um..." He looked down again. "It turns out that nobody is. I thought maybe we should have an election."

Pete turned to Romie and kept his voice low for an aside. "He could have said, 'Let's vote,' and been done in two words."

Romie barked out a short laugh and a few faces turned back to see who had broken the silence. The man's stammering style might have inflamed Pete's impatience, but it had also endeared Travis to a lot of people in the crowd. He had their ear and their sympathy.

"Anyway, I thought we should publicly nominate people to run, let them say something, and then we can do an anonymous ballot. I don't know how exactly to do it. I heard someone say we could make a list of everyone and let them go into a room. I'm not sure how that would..."

Travis trailed off and several people took the opportunity to shout out their opinions on possible voting mechanisms. A few debates around the group broke out. Finally, in a move that clearly made Travis uncomfortable, he raised his arms, asking the group to be quiet.

"If we could just tackle the nominations first," Travis said. "Then I suggest the nominees could settle on the voting scheme."

The group was silenced by this. As soon as Travis had asked for input, it had all stopped.

"Does anyone have a nominee?" Travis asked. He turned left and right, looking for anyone to bail him out.

There was a man on the right side of the group who wore fairly clean clothes and had a well-maintained head of hair. Compared to the rest of the people, he looked very dapper. He raised his arm and held his palm straight forward as he spoke. "I nominate Tanya."

With the exception of Travis, the people seemed to be sorted from front to back. The people near the front of the group had been together the longest, and the ones near the back were the most recent arrivals. Robby noticed that some of the people near the back, himself included, looked back and forth, looking for the woman who would respond to the name Tanya.

At the urging of those around her, Tanya made her way to the front. Hands guided her up the porch steps and she turned to address everyone.

The first thing Robby noticed about Tanya was her hair. His eyes moved back and forth from the nominator to the nominee and quickly decided that one or both of them was a stylist, and they cared for each other's hair.

"I'm flattered, but I would like to withdraw my name. I care for you all deeply, but I don't know a thing about politics."

There was some dissension from the group, but also a few nods of agreement. Tanya made her way towards the stairs again, but paused before she descended.

"Oh, but I would like to go ahead and nominate Judy. She's a smart cookie."

Heads swiveled until people found Judy. She was standing very near a bearded man over by the pump house. She was almost hidden in his shadow. Someone reached out and touched her on the shoulder. It took a lot of urging from the crowd to get her up on the porch.

"Hi," Judy said. She folded her arms awkwardly and blushed. She looked down at the porch and then cleared her throat. "I can be a real pessimist. Sometimes people take that pessimism for superiority, and sometimes they assume it's wisdom. It's neither one. I'm just pessimistic, you know? I'm not going to withdraw my name, but I think you guys know that there's someone better here. I haven't seen Luke in a few days, but I think maybe we should just elect him. He's the real leader, you know?"

Robby couldn't hear what Travis asked, but he gathered the question from Judy's response.

"Yes, I guess I am. I nominate Luke in his absence. Let him come back to find that we've all elected him our leader, you know?"

A light applause followed Judy as she made her way down from the porch.

"How about Burlington?" a voice shouted.

Travis took the porch again. "Is that a nomination?"

"Sure," the voice called.

This seemed to open the floodgates. Suddenly waves of names were shouted towards the front and Travis had to call for someone to get him paper. He borrowed one of the chore clipboards to use as a writing surface. The meeting began to break up while names were still being added to the list. Robby climbed down from the tractor's tire.

"That was a goddamn travesty," Pete said. "It was just the damn Beardos naming their friends at the end. Did you see that?"

"Wait, I thought they were the Beardo Brigade," Romie said.

"Whatever," Pete said. The three of them turned towards the tent area they had been assigned. They were finally kicked out of the house, and they had to set up tents for themselves. Based on the condition of the tents they'd been given, the group would run out soon.

Lisa joined them. She had a six pack of beer and held it out as she approached. They were walking slowly. None of them were too eager to get back to the task of setting up the tents.

"Hey, look what Ollie gave me," she said.

"It looks warm," Pete said.

"Of course it's warm."

Robby reached for one and she pulled it away.

"Just kidding," Robby said.

Pete kept turning his head to look back at the group of people who still surrounded Travis and the porch.

"You know those Beardos are going to take over the voting process and set it up so one of them is going to win," Pete said.

"Always with the conspiracies, Pete," Romie said.

"Well? What happened to your master plan?" Pete asked her. "You were so intent on getting us here, and then you just clammed up. What are we supposed to be doing now? What happened to your certainty?"

Romie shook her head and looked down at her feet as she walked. "I never said I knew what to do when we got here. I just said that this place would be safe from all the snatchers, and liquid, and fire. And it seems like it is."

"Maybe safe isn't the right word for it," Pete said. "Seems like the dangers here are maybe not as obvious, but they're still around. Whatever happened to you filling in the gaps from Romie's premonition?" Pete asked Robby.

"We should talk about it when the time is right," Robby said.

A pair of Beardos passed just as he said it. Pete turned down one side of his mouth and nodded.

"I've just about had it with being told what I can't do or can't talk about," Pete said. "In fact, I'm going out to look for Brad today. They say we're not supposed to go into the woods because it's too dangerous? Well isn't it dangerous for him then? I'm going."

Robby turned to Pete and put a hand on his arm. Robby worked hard to not let his stature affect him. He knew he was small, and young, and it was difficult to get people to take him seriously. But if anyone should respect his ability to figure things out, it should be Pete. Still, he felt small standing in front of the man.

"He's not out in the woods, Pete. If you want to rescue Brad, that's not where you should be looking," Robby said, keeping his voice low.

"What the hell are you talking about?" Pete asked in a hoarse whisper. "Do you know where he is?"

"I have a theory, yes," Robby said. "Let's look at the horses."

They walked a short distance over to a bench that was set up under a pretty maple tree. It was positioned so they could sit and look out over the pasture. Robby sat on one end and Pete waved for Romie and Lisa to take the rest of the bench. After they did, Pete squatted down next to Robby.

"Spill it," Pete said.

Robby paused before he spoke. When he did, he spoke with confidence and authority. He wasn't persuading them—he was informing them.

"Brad was at the center of the first event. His house was the nexus of all the activity. He told us that the government sent in a team to study the vines that he found behind his house. All those guys disappeared like everyone else on the day it started snowing."

"Thanksgiving," Romie said.

Robby nodded.

"They didn't expect the arrival to be at Brad's house. They expected it to be here. They knew about this place the same way that Romie sensed this place. It's the same way that people have determined special places throughout history. There are unique spots on this globe that are burned into our DNA. We evolved to revere those places so that we would know where to go when everything went bad."

"So how come nobody went to Brad's house?" Lisa asked.

"Maybe they focused everything here. Or, it's possible that the presence of their forces managed to change the event."

"The government knew that the whole world was going to end and they sent people to Brad's house in order to stop it? You know I don't like to be this guy, Robby, but you're giving me no choice. You're turning me into a naysayer by starting up your crazy ideas again," Pete said.

"I'm only giving you enough background so you'll know how I've determined where Brad is," Robby said.

"Okay?" Pete asked.

"If you needed to create a permanent installation of people in a powerful spot, but keep it out of the public eye so you wouldn't cause panic, where would you hide it?"

"In plain sight," Lisa suggested.

"Or underground," Robby said with a shrug.

"You think they're keeping Brad underground?" Pete asked.

Robby nodded. "You remember that guy with the scraggly beard who talked to us when we first got here?"

"The guy who looked like a kindergarten teacher?" Lisa asked.

"Yes," Robby said. "That guy and the two guys with the long hair in the back. All three were missing from the nomination meeting we just had."

"So what? I'm sure there were plenty of people who didn't go."

"Nope," Robby shook his head. "Everyone was there except for those three, and all the vehicles are here. Unless they went somewhere on foot, I think they were down in their headquarters."

"Does this speculation help us?" Pete asked.

"I'm sure there are at least two entrances and a couple of vents for air exchange. One of these buildings will hold an entrance, and there will be one hidden in the woods. There may be a third that's either at the end of a long tunnel, or buried under a thin layer of turf. That's how these places are typically designed. The main entrance is sometimes hidden in an outhouse, but here it would be one of these little buildings. It would be somewhere people wouldn't gather, but would have a reason to visit once or twice a day."

"Could be any one of several buildings, if you're right," Pete said.

"It's in that area," Robby said. He pointed by nodding his head towards one of the smaller barns.

"Why?"

Lisa was the one who answered. "Because that kindergarten teacher just appeared over there."

✪ ✪ ✪ ✪ ✪

Robby dragged the spreader and carried the shovel. Pete pushed the wheelbarrow. They hauled four forty-pound bags of lime and Pete was not very careful with the load. Every time they came to a turn in their path, he jerked the cart to an abrupt halt, spilling a bit of the lime.

Pete had talked his way into getting assigned this duty. Amongst the gardeners, none professed to be an expert on maintaining a horse pasture, so they didn't question when Pete suggested that the paddock soil was too acidic. Unfortunately, to make the lie convincing, Pete and Robby had to spend the day spreading lime and working it into the dirt of the paddock while the horses were sequestered in another field.

"What if this doesn't work?" Pete asked as he tossed another shovel of the powder in front of Robby's rake.

"We can set up rotating surveillance on one of the Beardos," Robby said. "We'll do someone with medium-high rank. The top guys might be too careful about their movements."

"How do we find out their rank? I thought you said that most of the Beardos weren't aware of what's going on."

"You can see it in their grooming," Robby said.

Pete stopped and leaned on his shovel. "Say what?"

"You'll see it. Focus on the beard length. The ones with very thin beards that aren't well filled in are the highest rank."

"Sure," Pete said. "Why wouldn't they use facial hair to signify rank?" He smiled.

"It's useful to have a scheme for identification. Military organizations always signify rank somehow."

"I think I'll just trim myself into a general then," Pete said, rubbing his chin.

"Keep working," Robby said. "Amongst the regular people here, rank seems to be determined by how hard you work."

✪ ✪ ✪ ✪ ✪

Dinner was a very social time. People moved between tables, breaking up the cliques before they could solidify. Robby sat with other teenagers. When Judy showed up, Robby moved to her table and she introduced him around. Pete aligned himself with some Beardos and laughed as loud as they did over whispered, off-color jokes. When the plates were cleared, the Beardos broke up and spread out to various tables. Romie and Lisa sat together and were visited by a few factions. The people seemed intent on strengthening their bonds through many social interactions. Most everyone had lived alone for some amount of time before finding the group. Some joined together the day after Thanksgiving, and some had only found their way to the farm weeks or days earlier.

Sharing their stories was their primary form of entertainment. Lisa and Romie talked mostly of their life before, and left out descriptions of their travels into the snow.

After dinner, they were finally able to find a quiet place to talk.

People headed to the west side of the hill, to sit on the mowed slope and wait for the sunset. Pete, Robby, Lisa, and Romie sat in a tight diamond.

"There are two possible spots," Lisa said. "There's a garden shed next to the barn where three tractors are parked. We found footprints that led up to the tractor in the middle. Maybe you have to move the tractor to find a door or something. We couldn't figure out how they would have moved that tractor without moving the one in front or in back though."

Romie took over the report. "The other one is that little grain shed. The bins look like they were re-lined with metal sometime recently, and there was half of a footprint under one of the bins."

"White?"

"Yes, someone stepped right in one of your lime piles and tracked it into the shed," Lisa said.

Robby nodded. "That's the one. Are you talking about the shed that has the old painted milk cans next to the door?"

"Yes," Lisa said.

"You guys head to the latrine after dark. After ten minutes, we'll meet you at the shed," Robby said.

"What about Judy?" Pete asked. "Don't you think she could help us search for Brad? She knows these people a lot better than we do."

"No," Robby said. He shook his head. "We can't trust her."

"You think she's working with the Beardos?"

"No," Robby said. "I'm not sure who she's working with, but I think it's safest to assume she's not on our side."

CHAPTER 23: ROCHESTER, NEW YORK

THEY TOOK TURNS DELIVERING food and medicine to the room. Jackson stopped threatening them with his gun, but he kept the dangerous hunk of metal within his reach. When Amy Lynne was conscious, she seemed to have a calming effect on the young man. He wasn't exactly polite, but he was nearly civil. When she was out, he was short-tempered and mean. Unfortunately, as the days passed, she was unconscious more and more of the time.

Ty, Cedric, and Tim shared the little room that Ty had made his home. Ty returned one morning with a deep frown.

"I think she took a turn in the night," Ty said.

"Worse than before?"

"Much worse. Her breathing is shallow, she's showing signs of dehydration, and Jackson won't let me start her on fluids."

"Why?"

"He thinks there's something in them. He only trusts the drugs that she identified before she went out," Ty said, shaking his head. "Why does he think we would want to hurt her?"

"Not too bright," Tim said.

Cedric stood up halfway and turned his nose towards the closed door. The dog didn't make a sound, but the fur between his shoulder blades was standing straight up. After a few seconds, the dog worked his tongue in his mouth and settled back down.

"He's doing that more and more," Tim said. "You think it's your hallway walker?"

Ty shook his head. "That thing only comes at night. I don't know what he's hearing."

"When Cedric is frightened by something, it's a good idea to pay attention," Tim said.

Ty wiped his face with one giant hand. "I always thought her odds were pretty grim, but now that Jackson is involved, I don't think there's any way to save her."

"If he were just smarter, I'm sure we could reason with him. Why don't we spike his food? We can knock him out and leave him here. Or maybe we could lock him up somewhere. Hell, if we just get that gun away from him, he wouldn't be able to stop us from helping Amy Lynne."

"It's too dangerous. What if she's awake and she eats the food? It's a delicate thing to sedate someone. You have to get the dose just right for their weight or it's too easy for something to go wrong."

"So then we have to leave," Tim said. "As sad as it is, we have to admit that there's nothing we can do because he has a gun and he's too dumb to listen to reason."

"I don't want to leave this place," Ty said.

"I know you don't, but I'm not sure you have a choice. If she dies, and it sounds likely that she will, then he might become even more unstable. You don't want to be around when that happens."

"I won't be frightened off by him," Ty said.

"I believe you, but maybe you should," Tim said. "The world is a dangerous place, but those threats are unpredictable. The danger of Jackson is certain. You wouldn't have to leave forever. Just go away for long enough so he takes his rage elsewhere. Then, you could come back."

"I could hide here," Ty said. "He doesn't know about this room. He always stays on the perimeter of the hospital, where all the windows are."

"When he got angry with me, he burned my plane. If Amy Lynne dies, there's a good chance that he'll try to burn this place down."

Ty sighed. He rubbed his face again and then moved to the floor, so he could stroke Cedric's back. The dog glanced at him and then returned his attention to the door.

"This world," Ty said.

Tim let the silence grow before he spoke again.

"Come with me and Cedric. If you want, I can drop you off a few miles north and you can make your way back here. If you take your time, the boy will probably be gone by then."

Ty considered the offer for a while before he finally gave an answer.

It surprised Tim.

"Okay."

✪ ✪ ✪ ✪ ✪

Ty rolled the cart to a stop just outside the doors to the hallway. On it, he had placed all the meds Amy Lynne would need and instructions on how to administer them. He didn't have faith that Jackson would execute the instructions correctly, but he refused to leave without trying to help.

They met at the glass doors of the lobby. Ty hunched down so he could look up at the sky.

"Are you sure they aren't out there?" Ty asked.

"No, but I've been okay moving around in the daylight," Tim said.

Cedric whipped his head around and looked in the direction of the wing where Jackson and Amy Lynne were taking a morning nap.

"Should we disable his motorcycle so he doesn't try to follow us?" Tim asked.

The bike was parked on the sidewalk, just outside the door.

"No," Ty said. "He might need it."

Tim nodded.

They left the hospital at a jog. Ty wasn't very fast, but he was silent. Tim heard the jingling of Cedric's collar, but didn't hear Ty's feet hitting the pavement. When they left the cover of the building, all Tim heard was the wind. It had picked up. He tried to get a sense of it, so he would know what to expect when he got the plane in the air, but it was swirling between the buildings. It was too random.

When they reached the plane, Tim threw the bag up on the wing and climbed up behind it. Ty stood on the pavement and looked around nervously. The sun wasn't quite at the top of the sky yet, but it would be soon.

"I have to check a few things first," Tim said.

"This thing is safe, right?" Ty asked.

"Safer than a car," Tim said. He was pleased to see that Ty was helping Cedric up onto the wing and trying to figure the best way to climb up there himself. The plane had little stickers where you were supposed to put your feet.

Tim didn't make it far down his checklist.

On the other side of the plane, the cowling was lying on the ground. Someone had taken a hammer to the engine. Clean spots on the dented metal showed where it had been hit. Tim ran around to where Ty was loading the bags in the plane.

"We need a new plan," Tim said.

Ty didn't wait for an explanation. He turned and immediately began unloading the plane. Tim called Cedric, and the dog hopped out of the compartment.

"There's an ambulance that I start every few weeks, just to keep it fresh. It's down in the garage," Ty said.

Cedric barked and they turned.

Jackson stood there. He looked tired and leaned to one side.

"I knew you'd leave," the young man said.

"We were just going to look for supplies. You know, food and stuff," Tim said. He put his hands up and shifted to the side. The gun was poking from Jackson's pocket.

"That's bull," Jackson said. "I saw the note."

"Listen, kid," Ty said. His voice was so deep and soft that Tim could barely tell what he was saying. "You don't need us. You won't let us near her, and I understand that. You're protective of her. You take care of her."

"Nobody else will," Jackson said.

"That's right. And nobody else can take care of Amy Lynne as good as you can. We're going to give you two some space. You've got everything you need." Ty's voice was almost hypnotic. It was so persuasive, that for a second Tim thought it might actually work.

It didn't.

Jackson began fumbling to get the gun out of his pocket. Cedric, who'd never shown any aggression that Tim could remember, ran straight for Jackson. Tim wouldn't have made an attempt to wrestle the gun from Jackson. But he couldn't allow the dog to go against the young man on his own. Tim rushed forward.

Cedric jumped up and put his paws on Jackson's chest. In his attempt to pull the gun from the front pocket of his jeans, Jackson had bent over. The stance put him off balance, and the dog's push sent him backwards. As Tim arrived, Jackson was falling back on his ass and the gun pulled free from his pocket. Tim went for the hand. He pushed it up and away as Jackson pulled the trigger.

The shot was deafening at such a close range. Tim fell forward, pushing all of his weight against Jackson's hand and coming down on the young man's chest. He pressed Jackson's hand to the pavement, but didn't have any defense for the blows that Jackson threw with his other hand. The boy caught him with a wild punch to his ear and Tim saw stars. His balance evaporated and he felt like he was falling.

Ty reached them just in time. Tim lost his grip on Jackson's gun hand and Jackson had just begun to raise it again when Ty's foot came down on his wrist.

Tim hit the pavement. He saw Ty kneel, putting a knee on Jackson's chest. The kid kicked, but instead of hitting Ty, he managed to drive the toe of his shoe into the back of Tim's thigh. The muscle cramped immediately and Tim rolled onto his back.

Cedric's head filled Tim's vision as the dog hovered over him. Blood dripped on Tim's face. He tried to pull himself backwards.

"Let go or I'll break your wrist," Ty said. His voice was soft and menacing.

Tim heard the kid whimper and then heard the gun clatter to the pavement. Tim managed to push himself upright. He swayed, trying to fight against the rolling inside his own head. He blinked and managed to focus. Ty pulled Jackson up under his armpits, like he was lifting a toddler. He set Jackson on his feet and towered over him.

"You go back to Amy Lynne. You don't need us anymore, but she needs you. Run," Ty said.

Jackson did just that. He ran towards the hospital, stumbling at first but then picking up speed. Ty picked up the gun between two fingers. He threw it towards an alley.

Tim's hands found Cedric's head. Sticky blood matted the hair on the side of the dog's face.

"What happened to you?" Tim asked. He couldn't find the wound.

"The bullet grazed him," Ty said, looming over Tim and Cedric. Ty knelt and examined the dog. The giant man pulled his lips back into a grimace as he looked at Cedric's ear. "Here it is. He needs a couple of stitches. I'll do it in the ambulance."

✪ ✪ ✪ ✪ ✪

With the engine idling, Ty performed the procedure. He injected a local anesthetic and shaved a patch of fur while he waited for it to work. Ty talked to the dog while he treated him. Cedric looked very serious and watched with keen eyes as Ty's hands moved.

"It's just a nick," Ty said. "We might get away with gluing it, but I'll feel better with a couple of sutures in there. Can you feel this?" he asked. The dog didn't react when Ty poked him with the needle, so Ty began.

"Hello?" Jackson called. His voice echoed in the parking structure.

"Shit," Tim whispered. He looked around for something to use as a weapon. The only thing he found was a fire extinguisher. He fought the clasp and pulled it from its bracket.

Jackson appeared around the side of the back door. Ty was right in the middle of a stitch and didn't look up.

"Go away," Tim said. "You've got what you need and we're leaving."

"I just wanted to say I'm sorry for what happened," Jackson said. "I know your dog got hurt."

Tim heard whispering and saw Jackson turn towards it.

Jackson continued. "And I hope you will accept my apology."

"Fine," Tim said. He glanced at Ty. The man's giant fingers were tying a delicate knot in the nearly invisible thread. Cedric was holding still, but his eyes were locked on Jackson. "Apology accepted. If you don't mind moving, we're going to be backing..."

"Can we come?" Jackson asked, interrupting Tim.

Tim shook his head before be began to answer. "No. You need to stay here to take care of Amy Lynne."

"She's right here," Jackson said. He wrestled with something around the other side of the door and the wheeled Amy Lynne backwards into view. She was in the wheelchair from the lobby. Tim wondered how Jackson had gotten it down the stairs, but then he saw Amy Lynne. She looked alert and perfectly capable of limping down a flight of stairs on her own. Her color was good and her eyes were bright. "She wants to come with you. It was her idea. I told her you wouldn't take us because I shot your dog."

"Listen, Jackson, no offense, but I think it might be best if we just go our separate ways," Tim said.

"Amy Lynne says you know things. She says you're smart and it would be smart if we came with you."

"I understand," Tim said.

"Kid," Ty interrupted. "Give us a second to talk things over, would you?" He snipped the thread with a tiny pair of scissors. He didn't wait for Jackson to answer, but pulled the big doors on the back shut with his gloved hands.

"Good," Tim said. "Keep Cedric steady and I'll back out." Tim began to move for the driver's seat. The ambulance was still idling, so all he had to do was put the heavy vehicle in gear and Jackson would have to move out of the way.

"No," Ty said. "I think we should bring them."

"What? That kid is half insane, and dangerous."

"They might need help," Ty said. "She's looking better, but that could change."

"That's a shame, but why would we risk our lives for hers? Like you said, if she takes a turn, who knows what he will do."

"I think he's all bluff."

"Like when he tried to shoot me?"

"The gun went off accidentally."

"Sure, this time. Last time he pointed it a foot away from Cedric and pulled the trigger. That bullet could have bounced and killed me or Cedric. You weren't there."

"He's scared, and he's just trying to take care of his girlfriend."

Tim shook his head. "You're crazy. This is crazy."

"You brought her here, looking to save her life. Don't give up on her now."

"She looks good. You just said so yourself. Maybe he is capable of caring for her. Or maybe she's a lot stronger than we give her credit for. I don't see why we need to be involved."

"She might need more help as she heals."

"We're going to die. This is going to end really badly, and then we're going to die," Tim said. But, as he spoke he moved to the doors. He opened them up to find Jackson and Amy Lynne still there. "Get in," Tim said.

"I've got one more stitch to do," Ty said.

CHAPTER 24: BUNKER

BRAD LOST TRACK OF time. It was even more disturbing when he lost track of space. In the dark, with every sound reverberating in the metal cylinder, he could imagine that the walls were a hundred yards away. The air was so still that it seemed to heat up around his skin. Only when he moved did he sense the real temperature of the place. It was cool and damp until he held still. When he didn't move, the heat built up around him and he began to sweat.

The worst part was when condensation on the metal grate, or even sweat from his own forehead, would fall. Between his breaths he heard the liquid as it pulled away from the surface that it clung to. The liquid snapped as it formed into a falling sphere and began gravity's descent. Brad thought he could almost hear the falling drops of liquid. He cringed while he waited for each one to hit the bottom. When they did, he would hold his breath.

Somewhere down there was a pool of water. At one point—it could have been hours, or even days before—he had climbed carefully down the spiral stairs. The treads were a diamond pattern of bands of steel. The lower he climbed, the more rusty the treads were under his hands. He wondered how long the silo had been flooded. Had it been decades? Centuries? He would have believed either. He imagined the concrete in the walls transitioning to stone, and then blocks of granite, as he descended into the past.

Brad had never made it down to the pool at the bottom. What

he heard down there was too terrifying. He imagined a waterlogged arm of flimsy flesh reaching out of the water. It clawed at the metal stairs, trying to gain enough purchase to climb up to him.

A blinding light opened above him and Brad climbed towards it.

A shape blocked the center of the light. Brad knew not to get too close. If he got too close, they would send the electric darts down, to shock him back into the dark.

"Tell us again," the voice said.

Brad's voice croaked when he tried to speak. He hadn't used his voice since the last time they had asked him the same thing, and by the end of that session, he had been screaming.

"It's the same," Brad said. He gained control of his weak voice and continued. "It will always be the same."

"You say that, but it changes every time, Brad. Tell us again."

"I need water."

"There's all the water you can drink at the bottom of the stairs," the voice said. He heard a smile behind that voice. The smile mocked him.

"Fresh water."

Something clanged on the steps and Brad threw his hands out. He couldn't see well enough to know what he was reaching for, but he could guess. He caught the bottle of water just before it rolled off the back of the step in front of him. He pulled it to his chest as the door above him slammed shut, leaving him in the dark again. For several minutes, he couldn't bring himself to open the water. In his imagination, he kept dropping the bottle, losing it to whatever lurked below.

The next time the door opened, Brad's fingers were cramped from gripping the stair treads. He was convinced that gravity had been rendered meaningless, and he wasn't certain which direction was up and which was down. He couldn't hold a thought for more than a second. His ears constantly strained for the sound of whatever was waiting for him in the water below.

The circle of light finally drew his blinking eyes. The shape of a man's head blocked the center of the light.

"Tell us again, Brad."

He didn't object this time. He simply blurted out his story.

"I was walking out behind my house in the summer and I found a vine," he began. He told his story fast. Using only a sentence to declare each major event from the time he'd found the vines until he reached Portland on the back of his old snowmobile.

"You said the name of the government guy was Herm this time," the voice said. It had that same mocking smile behind the voice. "Last time you said it was Stavros."

"No," Brad said. "Stavros is my old college buddy. I called him to come look at the vine because he works as a game warden." He realized that past tense would be more appropriate. Stavros was certainly dead, along with his job as game warden.

"You said the name of the game warden was Rick," the voice said. Brad thought he heard a laugh at the end of the statement.

"No! Rick was the forest ranger we found in Vermont," Brad said.

"You said you never learned the name of the corpse in Vermont. And you said that you didn't know if he was a ranger, or if he just stumbled onto the ranger station, much like yourself."

"No!" Brad said, but something about the accusation rang true. Hadn't Robby said that the ranger never signed his diary? Where had he gotten the name Rick? Had his brain simply assigned the name because of Ranger Rick, the magazine from his childhood?

"Why are you lying to us, Brad?"

Was he lying? He was troubled to discover that he couldn't remember.

"Listen. Listen. I'll tell you everything. I was walking out behind my house in the summer—I think it was last summer—when I discovered these vines. They..."

The light went dark as the door slammed shut.

This time when the door opened and the light appeared, Brad was at the top stair. They didn't warn him back, like they'd done before. They let him stay up near the light, and he was thankful. He would do anything to stay in the warm glow of the light, and he told them so. Unfortunately, all that came out of his mouth was mumbled nonsense.

"Tell us again, from the beginning," the voice said. This voice was much softer and more kind. It was almost sympathetic.

Brad told them everything.

CHAPTER 25: FARM

THE FOUR OF THEM packed into the little grain shed. Robby wouldn't let them use their flashlights. There were too many ways for the light to escape the tiny building, and they'd been lucky to get in there without being spotted. They stood there, listening to their own panting breaths as Robby knelt.

"Describe what you saw," Robby said.

"There was half of a white footprint going under the left bin," Lisa said.

They heard Robby shuffling and running his hands along the wood. A second later, they heard the catch click and a creak as the bin swung up and out of the way.

"Won't they have guards posted?" Romie asked.

"Maybe. But it would have to be someone we've never seen before. I walked around at sunset and everyone was accounted for except for the guy they call Hampton," Robby said.

The metal hatch made a sound like uncapping a soda as Robby opened it.

A light from below showed them the ladder that descended into the ground.

"Let me go first," Pete said.

"Our hero," Romie said, mocking him.

Robby went last. He pulled the hatch shut behind him and found the lever to return to the bin to its normal position.

When Robby reached the bottom of the ladder, the others had

added their flashlights to the dim bulb that lit up the space.

"I found a door," Pete said.

Romie was investigating the dark control panel and the moldy chair. Lisa stood with her arms crossed. She was looking back towards the ladder.

Robby followed Pete through the door. They found stairs going down. Those ended at a giant metal door. It was open wide enough that they could fit through the gap. Pete led the way with his flashlight and a length of pipe that he'd brought as a club. They moved into a big room.

"How do we find him?" Lisa asked.

"I suggest that two of us stay here in case Hampton tries to escape. The other two can search the place. If we find Hampton, we force him to take us to Brad. If we find Brad, we go."

"Yeah?" Romie asked.

Robby shrugged. He moved into the adjacent room while Pete, Lisa, and Romie debated who would guard the exit. Robby swept his light around the little room. He found a switch on the wall and toggled it up and down—It didn't do anything. The room was lined with desks and had cork boards on rolling stands. Robby used his light to examine the pictures and articles pinned there.

Romie appeared in the door. "Let's go, Robby. We've been elected as the search team."

"I need a minute in here," he said.

"No. Come on."

"It will only take a minute, I swear." He moved to the next set of articles, trying to tune Romie out. He blinked, trying to take them all in. He couldn't memorize everything, but he could at least get a sense of what was there.

"This thing was your idea," she said, moving closer to him.

Robby slid around to the other side. He was trying to just skim, so he could take it all in, but there was fascinating information in the article about binaural beats. The researcher suggested that an audio signal could align a person's neurons to fire in sequence, establishing a pathway to facilitate recognition of...

"Come on!" Romie said, pulling his arm. "This room contains no doors, no Brad, and no Hampton. Let's move on."

✪ ✪ ✪ ✪ ✪

The big room where Lisa and Pete were stationed was the central hub of the network. Doors led off into smaller warrens. Some contained bunks. Some had racks of equipment. A lot of the rooms were empty, but scuff-marks on the floors spoke of heavy things that had been stored and moved by many hands. Rooms led to rooms. Romie lost track of where they'd been, but Robby employed a system with a piece of chalk he found. He put a tiny mark on the door frame after they inspected a room.

Romie was inclined to check everywhere, but Robby stopped her several times. He pointed out the dust on a door handle, or a spiderweb that joined a door to its frame. Some of the passages hadn't been used in years, and didn't warrant the time it would take to inspect them.

Romie shouldered her way through one door and they saw a long hall.

Robby pointed his light towards the ceiling before going through the door. He saw the red and white exit sign and then joined his light with Romie's to point down the hall. It was long. They could just see a door at the far end.

Their pace slowed as they walked down the long hall. Their footsteps echoed. Robby spun around to see if they were being followed. It was an absurd notion. The only thing behind them was the big room with Lisa and Pete, and they would have heard the door open if someone had joined them in the hall.

When Robby turned back around, Romie stopped. Her light was trained on the center of the door and her hand was shaking, making the beam bob slightly.

"What?" Robby asked.

She looked at him with wide eyes. "Don't you feel it?"

Robby did feel it. There was a weight in the center of his chest, making it difficult to breathe. He imagined that it would feel the same if you tried to breathe through a garden hose at the bottom of a swimming pool. The water pressure would try to keep you from sucking in air through that little passage.

The door in front of them looked the same as the other doors in the place, but the latch was different. The latch was thicker, and tougher looking. And there was a bulge in the bottom panel of the door, like something behind it had been desperate to get out and had taken out its frustration on the metal.

Robby moved by Romie and approached the door. She put out a hand and grabbed his shoulder. Robby barely swallowed back a scream at the contact.

"Don't open it," Romie whispered. "There's something terrible behind there."

As if to prove her right, they heard a noise from behind the door. It was a thump followed by a slow scrape. Romie's grip tightened on Robby's shoulder. Her fingers dug into his flesh. Her pressure stayed constant as Robby raised his own hand to the door. He closed his fingers around the thick latch and he felt the vibration as the scraping sound continued.

"Don't," she whispered.

Robby pushed down on the latch. It screeched as it turned. When it reached the bottom of its travel, a serious THUNK rang out when some mechanism clanked into place. Robby pulled.

The door was heavy. Once it got moving, it kept swinging on its own. Robby let go of the handle and he and Romie backed up as their lights penetrated the darkness on the other side. They saw a landing and then metal stairs that spiraled down into the black. Whatever had rubbed against the door a second before was nowhere to be seen.

Romie's hand was still clamped to Robby's shoulder. He tried to move forward, but she held him back. He ducked out from under her grip and slipped forward, angling his light down the stairs. The landing and treads were made of vertical fins of metal, wide enough apart that fingers might slip through from underneath. Robby placed his foot on the landing carefully, waiting for the fingers.

He saw something down there move away from his light.

Robby moved farther in. If Romie were to swing the door shut, he would be locked in this little silo. Water dripped and hit some kind of pool below. Robby heard something splash in the water. It sounded like a fish breaching the surface as it jumped after a bug.

"Come back," Romie said, in a hoarse whisper.

Robby inched closer to the spiraling stairs.

A voice croaked from out of the darkness.

"Romie?"

✪ ✪ ✪ ✪ ✪

Robby backed up at the sound of the voice and then ran forward again when his brain processed it. It was Brad's voice. Even knowing the man was down there in the dark, Robby couldn't find the courage to go down the stairs. Romie stayed back at the door. She kept one hand against the metal frame. It was her lifeline.

"Brad? Come up here. We'll get you out of here," Robby said.

"Robby?" Brad asked. He sobbed somewhere down in the dark.

"Come up. We know the way out," Robby said.

"It's terrible down here, Robby," Brad said. He sounded terrified.

Robby put out his hand. He struggled to keep it still as Brad's hand reached out of the darkness towards him. As Brad got closer, Robby finally saw his face. His eyes were rimmed in red, puffy flesh. His lips were cracked and bleeding. He seemed too weak to pull himself up the stairs. Robby gripped the railing as if his life depended on it and took a step down. He stretched the flashlight down, and Brad shrank back.

"Come up," Robby said.

"Too bright," Brad whispered. Robby turned out his light.

Robby's shadow blocked most of Romie's light from the doorway. He held his position. He didn't see Brad until he felt the hand clamp down around his wrist. For the second time in a few short minutes, Robby almost screamed.

He pulled back against Brad's tug. It felt like his friend wanted to pull Robby down into the darkness, instead of pull himself towards the light. Fortunately, Brad was weak, and Robby could compel him up the stairs with gentle pressure.

Romie emitted a startled cry when she saw Brad. He held up an arm to protect his eyes from the flashlight. She turned the flashlight away from his face.

As soon as Robby pulled the man across the threshold, Romie slammed the door shut and lifted the handle. They heard the mechanism THUNK back into place. Brad tried to shrink to the floor of the hall.

“No, no,” Robby said. “Let’s keep moving.”

He and Romie took opposite shoulders. They lifted Brad and helped him down the long hall. He stunk of fear—a mixture of sweat and urine. He swayed from side to side as he walked.

Brad spun in their hands and looked back at the closed door. He whimpered and went limp.

“Come on, Brad,” Robby said.

“Don’t you hear it? It’s coming,” Brad said.

“I don’t hear anything,” Romie said. “Now, come on.”

They practically dragged him back to the big room.

✪ ✪ ✪ ✪ ✪

“Straight up and out,” Pete said. “We get him some rest, and maybe some first aid in the morning.”

“Once they know we have him, they’ll take us all,” Romie said. “We’ll all be locked up down here.” She stood with her back to the door. They had closed themselves in the room with the desks and cork boards so they could figure out their strategy.

“What did they do to you?” Lisa asked Brad. She was crouched in front of him, holding his hand. Brad didn’t answer. He stared straight forward and didn’t say a word.

Robby was back at the cork board, studying the information and pictures.

“Every second we stay down here, we risk that they’ll come down and lock us in. At least if we go topside, we can be seen by everyone. There are a hundred regular people up there, and only a few dozen Beardos. If we make our case to the regulars, they won’t be able to take us all.”

“What makes you think the regular people will be on our side?” Romie said. “We’re newcomers. They’ll say Brad is a threat somehow, and then they’ll lock us all up.”

"Let's vote," Pete said. "Who's for getting the hell out of this dungeon?"

"Wait a second," Romie said. "I'm all for getting out of here. I just think we shouldn't slow down when we get to the surface. We get out of here, steal a car, and get the hell out of this place."

"You were so intent on getting to this farm," Pete said. "Now, you want to leave. There are good people here. They can help us stand up to the Beardos."

"Hush!" Lisa hissed. "Brad wants to say something."

They all turned to Brad.

"They know," Brad said. He swallowed and cleared his throat. Lisa pushed a bottle of water into his hands. They'd found it in one of the supply rooms. It tasted like hot plastic, but it was drinkable. Brad took a tiny sip. "They know about the thing."

"Right," Romie said. "You said you told them everything."

"No," Brad said, shaking his head. "They knew before I told them. They knew from when it has been here before."

"That can't be," Lisa said. "It was tens of thousands of years ago. There's no history that goes back that far."

"They know. That's why they set up this place," Brad said.

"We can debate all this when we're safe," Pete said. "I say we go topside and find support amongst the other regular people in the group. All we have to do is show them this bunker and they'll know that the Beardos are up to no good."

"And I say we hit the road again," Romie said.

"Let's vote," Pete said.

CHAPTER 26: ROAD

TIM WAS BEHIND THE wheel and Cedric was curled up in the seat beside him. The dog was fast asleep. With the shaved patch of fur brighter than the rest of his head, Cedric looked almost like he wore a bow on his ear.

Their progress was slow. The big vehicle was difficult to navigate around places were the cars had piled up. The first time a bottleneck stopped them, Tim got out to roll a car out of the way. Ty came forward from the back as Tim got back in the ambulance.

"Just shove them out of the way," Ty said.

"But I..." Tim started. "Okay."

Ty's way was noisy, but easier. He slowly approached a car until the ambulance's bumper made contact, and then he just shoved. The cars dented and crushed, but they moved. Still, it took time. A smaller vehicle could have navigated around, but they wouldn't all fit in a smaller vehicle.

Tim glanced into his mirror. Amy Lynne was stretched out on the cot. Jackson sat at her side, holding her hand. Ty sat across from them. His head bounced with the movement of the ambulance. He kept his eyes pointed at the floor.

A sign above told him he could veer right for Syracuse. Tim kept going straight. He wanted to avoid the city. There were more stopped cars near the cities.

Tim slowed. He regretted not taking the exit. In front of them, a red Chevy had rolled into the back of a big pickup. The pair of vehicles nearly blocked the whole road. There was nowhere to push the car. A concrete wall separated them from the westbound lanes, and a metal guardrail on the right protected them from a gully. The ambulance beeped as Tim put it in reverse.

"Problem?" Ty asked.

"Yeah. Road's blocked. I'll take us through Syracuse."

"Shit," Ty said.

"It's not that bad," Tim said, putting the ambulance back into drive. "I'll find a road on the outskirts and take us around."

Ty's eyes were wide. His finger came up and pointed through the windshield. Tim finally saw what Ty was looking at. On the horizon, a clump of dark clouds were concentrated over one area. Little needles jabbed down from the clouds, descending to the ground. They were the little funnel clouds of tornadoes.

"What the hell..." Ty said.

"It's the cleanup crew," Tim said. He swallowed, and tried to get spit back into his suddenly dry mouth. On the seat beside him, Cedric whimpered in his sleep. "I've see it before. Those little tornadoes go through and tear apart a whole area."

"I don't understand."

Tim shook his head. "Me neither. This is usually when I start up my airplane and don't stop until I'm a couple of hundred miles away."

"Turn back around," Ty said.

Before Tim could even get the ambulance into reverse again, Ty had disappeared through the back door. It slammed shut as the beeper came on and Tim pulled around. When he got the ambulance straightened out again, he saw Ty. The man was pushing the Chevy out of the way. It was locked up with the pickup truck. Tim saw the truck jolt as Ty pushed on the Chevy. He got the car free and once he got it going, he moved it aside like it was a kid's bike.

Tim navigated through the gap Ty created. He stopped, and a second later, Ty jumped in the back. Jackson and Amy Lynne didn't even seem to register the interruption in their travel plans.

Tim accelerated.

Ty appeared between the seats and watched the tornadoes as

they drove by. There were too many hills and trees to see where the tornadoes were touching down. They could only see them when they lifted back into the air. When they did, the funnel clouds sparkled with debris. Ty didn't take his eyes off the sight until a hill finally blocked their view.

"That could have happened to the hospital," Ty said.

Tim nodded. "Or maybe not. They seemed to skip some cities." He drove on.

Ty leaned close to the windows and kept a constant watch for the tornadoes. Tim didn't notice the gas gauge until a light indicated that it was low. He pulled off at the next exit and turned right. There was a parking lot with several cars.

"Gas or diesel?" he asked Ty.

"What?" The giant man took his eye off the sky for a second to look at Tim.

"Do you have a siphon in here? Does this thing take regular gas or diesel?"

"Oh. Gas. Give me a second."

Ty disappeared between the seats and Tim pulled up to a big Ford. He lined up the side of the ambulance with the gas door of the Ford and shut the engine off.

He heard the back door and then Ty appeared in the mirror with a length of clear tube in his hand. He shoved it into the Ford, sucked on the end until he saw liquid, and then let it run into a plastic bucket he set at his feet. Tim heard the door again and then saw Ty moving with more tubing and another bucket. He went to another car and repeated the process.

"You want to go out?" Tim asked. The dog woke instantly and climbed off the seat.

Tim found Ty leaning against the Ford, waiting as the bucket slowly filled.

Ty looked at the sky again. "I guess I didn't realize things could get worse."

"What, the tornadoes?"

"Yeah," Ty said, sighing. "I can't go back to that hospital now that I know what happens to cities."

"Not all of them," Tim said. "Rochester is pretty small. It might be really low on the list."

"What devils are these, that steal all the people and then tear apart our world?"

Tim shrugged. "I'm not sure it's worth thinking about. What good would it do you if you knew?"

"It's natural to want to know why," Ty said.

He pulled the tube from the Ford and submerged it in the gasoline.

"Hold this up," he said. Tim held the bucket higher than the fill pipe and Ty used the same tube to start moving the gas into the ambulance. Once it was going, Ty walked off to retrieve the other bucket.

When he returned, Tim asked him a question. "Suppose you lost an arm. Would you spend your time wondering why, or would you get on with the business of learning to tie your shoes with one hand?"

"It's not that simple," Ty said. "There are more options than that."

"None worth thinking about."

Tim was grateful when Ty took the bucket away. He was getting tired of holding it up and the fumes were strong. Ty switched the tube to the other bucket and then handed it back to Tim.

"You said there's a circle?" Ty asked.

"Certain activity seems to happen at different distances from what I would call a center," Tim said. "I don't know. It's confusing, but when I put it all on a map, it suggested a circle."

"And we're headed for the center?"

"I think so," Tim said. "Honestly, it may have been more like an ellipse, but I'm not sure. The focus seemed to change several weeks ago. Either that, or I just didn't understand the data well enough to see the real pattern."

They heard a banging from inside the ambulance. Ty set up the Ford bucket and then walked around to the back door. Tim heard part of the conversation on the air.

"You guys bring anything to eat?" Jackson asked.

Ty's response was too low to hear.

"I could eat a horse," Amy Lynne said. It was a tone that Tim had never heard from her before.

Ty appeared again. He got to the Ford bucket just as it was about to overflow. He swapped it out with the one Tim held.

"She looks really good," Ty said. "I think she's on the mend."

"That's good news," Tim said.

"I'll run over to that store and see if I can find something to keep those two quiet. Can you put another few buckets in here?"

"Of course. Get me something salty," Tim said.

Ty nodded. As Ty started to walk away, Cedric appeared from between two rows of cars. He bounded after the huge man. Tim smiled at the funny shaved spot on the dog's head. It really did look like someone had tied a bow there, or maybe tucked a flower behind his ear. Until you got a good look, of course. At close range, all Tim saw was Ty's neat little stitches. He tried to hold a grudge against Jackson, but it wouldn't stick. It would be like holding a grudge against a rock that landed on his foot. The rock was too stupid to blame—it was his fault for being in the way.

From inside the ambulance, he heard Amy Lynne laugh. The sound was bright and bubbly. It didn't sound at all like the drugged slurs she had uttered earlier.

Tim changed the bucket and found the right height to hold the one feeding the ambulance. At just the right height, it would drain as the other one filled. A small puddle of gas formed around him on the pavement from his spills. He imagined an action hero walking away from him, throwing a cigar over his shoulder, and torching Tim alive. He hoped that Jackson didn't smoke.

Tim lowered the bucket when he heard Cedric's bark. He'd read somewhere that parents learn the different cries of their babies. One cry means wet, another means hungry. This bark from Cedric wasn't one that Tim had heard before. It wasn't his playful bark or his afraid bark. This was an alarm call. This bark sounded like the dog was trying to warn Tim that the action hero was about to flick his cigar over his shoulder.

Tim set the bucket down and ran towards the bark.

✪ ✪ ✪ ✪ ✪

He caught up with the dog at the fence. As soon as he did, Cedric tore across the little parking area towards the store. Tim had to contort his body to fit through the hole in the wooden fence. He wondered how Ty had ever squeezed through the gap.

Tim wobbled as he stood up. He was still woozy, either from the gas fumes or from the blow to the head that Jackson had given him much earlier that day. Tim fought to regain his balance as he chased after the dog.

Cedric had disappeared around the corner. His head reappeared and he watched Tim run. Tim reached the brick wall and leaned against it. His strength and stamina had been pretty well tapped. He followed the dog and saw the line of stores connected by an awning. The one on the corner had its door propped open. It was a small grocery store. The characters in the window suggested that most of the food inside would be of Asian origin.

Cedric ran inside and barked again.

"What's wrong?" Tim asked as he pulled himself through the door.

As soon as he saw Ty, Tim's arm went up to protect his vision. He had only seen the look on another human once before, but he recognized it immediately.

Ty had been immobilized by one of the murals.

"Ty!" Tim yelled. Of course the man didn't respond. He stood there, looking towards the left side of the store. The giant man was gently swaying on his feet. "Ty!"

Tim ran up to him and grabbed Ty's hand. He pulled. Some part of Ty's brain was still active. It was the part that kept him upright, and it had no problem balancing Ty's massive weight against Tim's pull. The man didn't budge. Tim lost his grip on Ty's fingers and he fell backwards, landing on the hard floor. Tim looked up and saw the curved mirror mounted near the register.

He saw the writing on the far wall. It was distorted by the mirror and held no power over Tim. The letters were scrawled on the glass doors of the refrigerator cabinets. The glass was opaque with condensation and mold. The bright red letters stood out clearly against the grime.

Tim glanced around for a dolly or a cart. He found nothing but a rack of hand baskets.

Back near the door, Cedric barked again.

Tim looked beyond him and saw the dog's other piece of bad news. The sky to the south was dark. A round cluster of clouds had gathered at the horizon. The little needles of funnel clouds darted down from the perimeter to the ground. The unnatural weather was moving towards their position at a good clip.

"Shit," Tim said. He whipped around to look at Ty one more time and then gathered his feet beneath him. He sprinted for the door.

✪ ✪ ✪ ✪ ✪

"Hang on to something," Tim yelled as he threw open the door to the ambulance.

Jackson and Amy Lynne were laughing in the back. Cedric jumped in through the driver's door and took the passenger's seat. Tim climbed in and leaned towards the back.

"Hang on!" Tim screamed.

The faces of Jackson and Amy Lynne looked like those of frightened children. They were shocked by his scream. Tim pulled himself back to the wheel and cranked the key. The metal dug into his fingers as the engine fired. He saw the tube hanging from the gas tank, but he didn't care. Tim gunned the engine as he shifted into drive. The ambulance lurched forward. Cedric flopped back against his seat and then fought against the acceleration to curl up in the footwell of the passenger's side.

Tim looked back up in time to see the rear end of an old Honda. The owner had either parked carelessly, or had been snatched up by a monster before he got the car to a safe place. The ambulance corrected that. Tim clipped the rear end of the Honda and it flew to the side, bashing into a truck.

Tim dragged the wheel to the right and the suspension resisted the vehicle's momentum as it screeched through the turn. Tim was on a side street. He was headed directly towards the storm clouds.

With another savage turn, he bounced the front tires of the ambulance up over a curb. They dug into the grass and left rubber on the sidewalk. The front end of the ambulance plowed over a decorative tree and Tim made it to the store's little parking lot. As the rear end of the ambulance completed the transition over the curb, Tim heard Jackson and Amy Lynne scream their surprise as they became airborne. Tim didn't have time to worry about their safety. Less than a mile away, a funnel cloud dropped from the sky and tore up trees and chunks of building. Tim saw them swirl up and away as they were torn to shreds. This would happen to him very soon if he didn't move fast.

The brakes buzzed as Tim stomped on the pedal. He threw the ambulance into park and jumped from his door.

"I need help!" he yelled to Jackson as he rounded the back of the ambulance. The rear door banged against its hinges, still swinging from the trip.

Tim found Ty right where he'd left him. He ran to the other side of the man and pushed. It was like trying to push a cement cylinder. There was no give in the giant man whatsoever. He grabbed a paper bag from the counter and whipped it open with one hand. On his tiptoes, he managed to settle the bag over Ty's head.

"Stop!" he yelled to Jackson as the young man came through the door. Tim threw up his hand, palm towards him.

Miraculously, Jackson followed orders. His face was turned towards the refrigerator cabinets. A hanging sign advertising some kind of noodles was the only thing that prevented Jackson from compounding Tim's problem. It blocked out Jackson's view of the mural.

"Don't look at the writing there. Remember what happened to you at the airport."

Jackson squeezed his eyes shut and put up a hand next to his face.

"Good," Tim said. He was surprised that Jackson seemed to grasp the situation so quickly. "Just keep your hand there and you can open your eyes." Tim was leaning into Ty so hard that his body was almost at forty-five degrees to the floor. "That's it. Come forward and pull. We have to get Ty to the ambulance."

Jackson reached him and grabbed Ty's big hand with both of his own. He pulled while Tim pushed. The result was the same. Ty didn't move.

"Get him rocking," Jackson said.

Tim had no idea what he meant until Jackson started doing it. He tugged rhythmically at Ty's arm, giving pressure and then letting up. Sure enough, the giant began to rock. They got him to stumble towards the door. Ty's body compensated, throwing a leg out to rebalance himself. Tim and Jackson started the process again. They coaxed him into another step.

Outside, they heard Cedric barking again. It was the alarm call from before, but it had even more panic behind it now.

"Too late," Tim said.

Jackson turned and let go of Ty's hand. They watched as the funnel cloud came out of the sky and descended right on their position.

CHAPTER 27: HOUSE

JUDY TOOK A DEEP breath and then reached for the handle. It wasn't even locked. She pushed into the kitchen and saw the room dancing in candlelight, just as it had on the night when they'd first arrived. That was the night that Bill had shot Woolly. Judy knew that was part of it. Somehow when she had witnessed that ghastly murder she had begun to mentally distance herself from these people. That distance allowed her to be swayed.

She walked towards the table.

Three men sat there. The one at the head was called Hampton. His real name was Sam.

"I'm ready, Sam," she said.

"I'm sorry?" Hampton asked. He gave the slightest nod to the other men. They folded shut their papers and rose to leave. Judy took the seat opposite Hampton and faced him over the light of a flickering candle. It was burned all the way down to its holder. In another hour, it would be out.

When the other men had left, Judy continued. "I'm ready to tell you about what happened to me when I left the grocery store that night."

"Oh?"

"I told the truth before. I just didn't tell you the entire truth. For instance, I didn't tell you the reason I ran away from the front of the grocery store. I was going to leave the group. I probably could have gotten away, but that's when I ran into the creature."

Hampton tilted his head and scratched at his scraggly beard. "It makes a sound. It's hypnotic, I suppose. The sound makes you fall back into memory. The creature doesn't see time the same way we do. It lives in every time. When you're in its presence, you can't control exactly where your memory will take you."

"And where did it take you?"

"Christmas. When I was a kid. That's not the only thing it did to me though. It altered me. It changed my instincts. Do you know what your own instincts are, Sam?"

He frowned and blinked several times. "Same as everyone, I guess. Even though I'm incapable of reproduction, I suppose we all still have the drive. We want to do that even more than we want to survive, although I think those two are in a pretty close race."

Judy nodded. "Yes, absolutely. Do you know what's underneath though?"

"Underneath?"

"Believe it or not, there are instincts under those. They're from before we were individuals. The first little snippets of DNA evolved before there was such a thing as individual reproduction or survival. Back then, before there were even eyes to see, life was concerned with engendering life itself. There wasn't anything selfish about it. There were no proprietary genes to consider."

"You lost me."

"It's not important. Even if you did understand it intellectually, you wouldn't be able to feel the truth of it. Your instincts would drown out the real message."

"Which is?"

"That our host is the most important thing. Humans are a parasite. We are the worst kind of infection. This genetic experiment is over."

"Why are you telling me this?"

"The chess game is over. The snow will start in six days, but before that, the tornadoes will come and tear this place apart. They'll rip down this house and turn over the soil until they uncover and exhume your underground structures. It's too late. These events can't be stopped."

CHAPTER 28: FARM

"COME ON, ROBBY," LISA said.

"Just give me two more minutes. The information is here. I'm sure of it," Robby said. He swept his light back to the cork board and then back to the desks. He pulled open drawers. Most were empty, or contained scattered office supplies, but in one he found files. Robby's fingers walked through the tabs, trying to make sense of the numbering scheme.

"We have to stay together. It's our best shot at getting out of here," Lisa said.

Robby pulled one of the thicker files. The documents in it were printed on a thick paper that felt almost like plastic. The words there were encoded into a strange alphabet. It was no language that Robby recognized. Lisa grabbed his elbow. Robby tucked the folder under his arm and followed. The others were waiting at the bottom of the stairs.

"Straight up and out," Pete said. "If we meet anyone along the way, just keep moving. No matter what they say, just push on through."

He glanced around at each of them.

They all knew what Pete meant. Robby saw it on their faces. They'd been through a lot together and had developed a communication that seemed to go beyond words. Robby knew that Beardos might try to stop them from leaving. He knew that they might have guns, and they would certainly order the group to halt.

But, as long as one of them made it by, they had a chance. Romie went first, followed by Brad. Robby went next and he wasn't surprised to see Lisa right behind him. Pete would bring up the rear. If they ran into trouble, Pete would find a way to draw the attention to himself, giving the people in front a better chance to sneak by. Robby understood the plan even though nobody had said it aloud.

They climbed the stairs as quietly as they could, but their feet clanged on the metal treads. The stairs spiraled up towards the light from the dim bulb in the room above. They shut of their flashlights and climbed.

Brad seemed unsteady as he climbed the stairs. Robby began to wonder how the man would fare on the ladder. Not that it would matter—the little control room between the stairs and the ladder was the perfect bottleneck to place armed Beardos. Robby had little doubt that they would find resistance there.

Romie slowed as she approached the doorway. Robby saw the silhouette of her head scan the room. She moved forward into the light. As Brad followed, Robby waited to hear one of the Beardos bark an order. None came.

Robby climbed up and through the doorway next. Romie and Brad stood there, glancing around. They'd all expected a welcoming party, but nobody was there. Robby moved to the ladder and looked up into the darkness. The hatch was still closed, as he had left it.

When he came back, they all looked to him.

"Beardos up there?" Pete whispered.

Robby shrugged. "I don't see anyone."

"They've probably locked us in here or something," Brad said. He looked to the dark rectangle of the doorway and clasped his hands together at his stomach.

Robby tucked the folder of papers into the back of his pants and went back to the ladder. He climbed up about halfway and then looped his elbow around a rung so he could dig out his light. He stuck it in his mouth so he could see the latch when he got to the top. He squeezed the mechanism. Something clicked and the hatch opened. Above it, the bin swung up and out of the way.

Robby fumbled at his light, turning it off as fast as he could. What he'd seen of the little shed was burned into the back of his eyes—the room was empty.

He climbed back down. The others were gathered at the bottom of the ladder.

"It opened, and the shed is empty. If there are any guards, they're outside."

"That's good," Pete said, nodding. "We'll gather there and burst out. If they try to stop us, at least we can make enough of a ruckus to draw attention."

"Wait," Romie said. "If they didn't try to trap us down here, they're probably not guarding the outside of the shed. That would just draw attention to it. I say we sneak out. Maybe they haven't discovered that we're down here."

"She's right," Lisa said.

Pete shrugged. "But if you see anyone—ruckus."

They climbed. Pete followed Brad closely, to lend support if Brad's muscles gave out. Brad was sweating and trembling by the time he got to the top, but he made it. They slipped out into the night. They found no guards outside the shack.

"What are they doing?" Pete asked. Over towards the house, lights were bobbing and sweeping across the buildings. A tractor cut across the lawn pulling a trailer filled with white bags.

"Who cares," Romie said. "We voted to get out of here. Let's get out while they're busy doing whatever."

"Hold on," Pete said. "There's something going on."

Pete headed for the moving lights.

CHAPTER 29: ROAD

ADRENALINE COURSED THROUGH HIS veins as Tim pushed Ty. Instead of rocking on his feet, the giant man began to tip. Jackson wasn't paying attention. He was focused on the trees across the side street. They were all leaning to the right, like gravity was playing a weird joke.

Cedric was still barking, but the sound was lost in the freight train of approaching wind as the tornado touched down. One of the trees across the road gave up several limbs and they flew up into the sky.

Ty tipped into Jackson and the young man came back to his senses. He turned in time to catch Ty. Tim hip-checked a candy rack out of the way and got around to the other side of Ty. Together, Jackson and Tim turned Ty's slow fall into forward momentum. They slid Ty on his heels towards the door.

The ambulance door began to swing in and out in the wind. Cedric stopped barking and timed his leap to jump through the door. When he disappeared inside the ambulance, Amy Lynne appeared. She was trying to hold the door open with one hand while she held her hair out of her face with the other.

Across the road, a whole tree was plucked from the ground. It flipped, end over end, as it rose like a helium balloon. There was an abandoned car at the side of the road. Tim saw it slide.

Amy Lynne screamed something. Tim saw her mouth move but all he could hear was the rumble of wind.

They were stuck. Ty's heels caught on the threshold. Tim was exerting all of his energy and barely able to keep the man upright. He glanced at Jackson. The young man clamped his jaw and squeezed his eyes shut. Ty began to slide again. They stumbled forward the last couple of steps and managed to flop Ty's huge torso down into the ambulance. Tim and Jackson moved down to the man's legs and they hoisted him up by his scrubs, pushing him into the back.

Amy Lynne slid out of the way, dragging her bad foot like an anchor. They couldn't shut the door. Ty was too big to fit and his unconscious body wouldn't bend. Jackson crawled over him, looped an arm through Ty's, and yelled something to Tim. The sound was lost.

Behind him, the door to the store slammed shut and the glass shattered. The plate glass at the front of the store bowed with the pressure and Tim suddenly felt light on his feet. He tried to run around the ambulance and felt his traction evaporate as he was lifted into the air by a gust of wind. His ears popped as sharp needles of pain drove into his skull.

The car across the road didn't move slowly, it just jumped up into the air and flew away. A fraction of a second later, two other cars in the lot did the same. The trees went like dominoes. One went and then three more followed it like they were stringed together.

The wind threw Tim back into the side of the ambulance and he managed to grab the driver's door. He pulled himself into the seat and pulled at the door. It ripped itself back out of his grip. Tim looped his elbow through the steering wheel to keep himself inside and dropped the lever into drive. He couldn't tell if the engine was still running or not, but he stomped on the gas and it lurched forward. He was going the wrong way—they were headed right for the funnel cloud. Tim dragged the wheel to the left. The ambulance obeyed, but the top of the heavy vehicle rocked to the right as the wind hit the side.

Tim let up, so he wouldn't tip over. In his mirror, he saw Amy Lynne pressed to the wall, defying gravity. Tim's door slammed shut. A crack shot through the glass. In an instant, the whole side window burst into little tiny diamonds. The glass shattered and was sucked out into the wind. The vehicle banged back down to all four wheels and Tim was able to steer again. The only exit to the parking lot was where the funnel cloud was now tearing up huge chunks of asphalt from the road.

Tim braced himself and aimed for the wooden fence. He couldn't see the rows of cars on the other side and prayed that he would hit the gap between them. The top rail of the fence slapped into the windshield, and fell to the side.

They were headed straight for the Ford. The bucket of gas was somehow still sitting next to the truck, unmoved by the wind that was destroying the world behind them. The rear tires of the ambulance bounced over the remains of the fence and Tim saw Ty float up in the mirror. Jackson was clutching the big man with one arm and the stretcher with the other. They crashed back down and somehow managed to both stay inside.

Tim heard Cedric bark. He realized that although his ears were still ringing, the world had grown much quieter. He clipped the Ford, but didn't lose much speed as he aimed for the exit back to the highway. Tim glanced in the mirror again. Jackson was still holding Ty in the vehicle and the grocery was being dismantled by the tornado. Debris rose up like a swirl of glitter.

Tim took the gentle turn as fast as he could. They began to leave the dark clouds behind them.

When the dipping tornadoes were no more than a dark spot in his mirror, Tim began to slow.

"What are you doing?" Jackson yelled. "Keep going!"

Tim ignored him and brought the vehicle to a stop in the middle of the road. He squeezed between the seats.

"Push him onto his side," Tim said. They got Ty up on his shoulder and managed to pull until the man's feet clear the rear door. Amy Lynn pulled it shut and then Tim climbed back to the driver's seat.

Cedric barked.

Tim accelerated again as Jackson climbed up onto the stretcher next to Amy Lynne.

✪ ✪ ✪ ✪ ✪

Ty woke about ten minutes later.

He pushed up to his feet in one quick motion and slammed his head on the ceiling. Ty dropped into a crouch and whipped his head around. His eyes were wide.

"What happened?" he asked.

Tim could barely hear him over the wind rushing through the broken window.

Jackson yelled something that Tim didn't catch at all. Ty moved closer and Tim glanced in the mirror to see Jackson's arms waving around as he told him the story. Tim looked at the gas gauge. It was barely off of the empty peg, and the light would probably come back on soon. He had no intention of stopping.

Ty squeezed between the seats and came to the front. Cedric vacated the seat and Ty sat down. He had one hand on the dashboard and the other on the back of Tim's seat, as if those two grips were the only thing holding him down.

"Go that way," Ty said.

"Pardon?" Tim asked. He heard nothing but the wind in his ear. Tim reached up, instinctively, for the headphones he would have been wearing in an airplane.

Ty lifted his hand from the dash and pointed.

"That way!" he yelled.

"Okay," Tim said. He guided the ambulance towards the exit.

When they slowed, and the wind died down, Ty offered an explanation of sorts.

"We need to head up into the hills. This might sound crazy, but I have a strong feeling that there's a safe place," Ty said.

Tim nodded. As long as they were headed away from the tornadoes, he didn't have an opinion about their destination.

CHAPTER 30: FARM

PETE CAUGHT A MAN with a wheelbarrow as he pushed it down the center of the path. Robby was right behind him.

"Where are you going?" Pete asked.

The man kept pushing until Pete grabbed his arm. He turned and pointed his headlamp right into Pete's eyes.

"We're all leaving. We're going to the backup site or something. Let me go, almost all the cars are full."

The man tore his arm from Pete's grip and pushed away towards the driveway. Two other people ran by at a full sprint. Headlights swept across the buildings as one of the Land Rovers pulled out with a full load of people.

"Backup site?" Pete asked Robby. "Do you know about a backup site?"

"No," Robby said. He saw the door to the house open and several people came out to the porch in a group. The two in front were Beardos, as were the two in back. The one in the middle was Judy. Robby sprinted towards them just as Romie and Lisa helped Brad to reach Pete's position. As Robby ran, the file fell from where he had tucked it into his belt. The thick documents fell to the ground in his wake.

Robby arrived as they reached the bottom of the steps. The two Beardos in front pulled out handguns and pointed them at Robby.

"Stay back," one man said.

"Judy, what's going on?" Robby asked.

Her hands were pinned behind her back and she had a man at each shoulder, guiding her forward.

"Get out of here, Robby," she said. "Just keep yourself safe and get out of here."

Two men jerked her towards the driveway while the other two kept Robby at bay with their guns.

"Let go of her," Robby said. "She doesn't have to go with you, if she doesn't want to."

"She's coming with us. She's a sympathizer," one of the gunmen said.

Robby charged at him and batted the pointed gun away. He aimed at the space between them, hoping to run into the men holding Judy. If he could break their grip on her, then she could run off and escape amidst the turmoil.

The men with the guns each took a step back and pointed their weapons at Robby.

He shoved the man on the right, who fell backwards, but didn't relinquish his grip on Judy. She yelled as he dragged her back. The man on the other side simply let go. Robby caught Judy's elbow and tried to keep her upright, but she fell on top of the man still holding her. He finally let go when Judy came down on his stomach.

She moved awkwardly because her hands were bound behind her back. Robby helped her up. The men with guns stood back, pointing their weapons. The other Beardo didn't seem to know what to do. He settled on going around Robby and Judy to help the other Beardo up.

"Just run," Robby said. "They won't shoot you."

"No," Judy said. "I'm going with them. This place will be torn apart soon."

She backed away from Robby. She pulled her elbow from his loose grip. The Beardos grabbed her again.

"Judy, what are you doing?" Robby asked.

"Go, Robby," Judy said. She turned away.

"Transport is over there," one of the Beardos pointed. "If you miss this wave, then you stay put. Another wave of vehicles will be back here as soon as possible. And don't try to interfere again with our business."

They moved Judy towards the drive, leaving Robby standing.

Pete arrived first, followed by the rest.

"Everyone likes Judy," Pete said. "When we get to the backup site, we'll start a movement to get them to let her go. What do they think she did, anyway?"

"They said she was a sympathizer," Robby said.

"We're not going with them," Romie said. "We all agreed. We're hitting the road."

Pete threw up his arms and turned his head to the night sky. "Why *not* go with them? Everything has changed. We're in another crisis and we have to stick together."

"I'm not leaving here until I figure this out," Robby said. "Judy said that this place will be torn apart soon. I'm going to figure out what that means."

From the driveway, they heard a bullhorn bark out orders. "Everyone line up here in the driveway. Bring only what you can carry on your lap. Our space is limited. Transport vehicles will be back here in thirty minutes to load up the next group."

"Come on, guys," Romie said. "We'll have to find some other way to get out of here." She started to help Brad move in the direction of the driveway. Lisa stayed on Brad's other side, and helped as well.

"Coming here was your idea," Pete said to Romie. "You were so sure it was safe to come join up with these folks and now you're running away from them." He turned and headed for the tent area.

Robby stood alone, watching what remained of his little group split up. He walked slowly back towards the shed and stooped to pick up the plastic documents. He wiped mud off of them using his pant leg. People were still collecting gear and migrating to the driveway area. Robby found the folder and stuffed everything back in it.

He looked down at the folder. It was too dark to read anything. He pulled out his light, but didn't bother turning it on. He looked in the direction Pete had gone and then looked back at the folder.

Robby dropped the folder. He didn't understand the documents. If they were around, the answers were still underground, in that bunker. He turned and walked slowly towards the shed.

✪ ✪ ✪ ✪ ✪

Brad wasn't injured, he was simply worn out. Climbing the ladder from the gray control room had sapped the last of his energy. He didn't know how long he'd gone without eating, but his head had a constant buzz and little flashes lit up in the corners of his eyes whenever he took a step. Romie and Lisa kept him upright. His only job was to move his feet, and he was barely managing that.

They walked up to the Beardo with the bullhorn. He was standing at the driver's side of a Land Rover. The bullhorn was powered by a cord coming from the interior.

He was about to make another announcement when they approached.

"Are you Denver?" Romie asked.

"Dover," the guy said.

"Close enough. Yeah, that guy Hampton is looking for you. He's in that big barn over there," Romie said.

"Looking for me?"

"You're Dover, right?"

"Yeah," the guy said.

He looked at Romie and Lisa, flinched when he looked at Brad, and then set the bullhorn down on the driver's seat. The Beardo trotted off down the path towards the big barn.

Romie opened up the back door.

"Get in!" she whispered. "I never in a million years thought that would work."

Brad practically fell into the back seat and Lisa climbed in next to him.

Romie threw the bullhorn to the passenger's seat and it squawked when it landed. Another Beardo, who was helping some of the regular citizens understand how much gear they would be allowed to bring, saw Romie as she closed the door.

"Hey!" he yelled. "Get out of there." He began to run towards them. "That vehicle is for the commander."

Romie gunned the engine and took off.

✪ ✪ ✪ ✪ ✪

Pete was surprised at the mess he found in the camping area. Half of the tents were still standing. Some of the others were torn down, but lying on the ground. People had sorted their possessions quickly, taking some and apparently throwing the rest in random directions. He found his tent and stared at it. There wasn't anything inside he particularly cared about—just a sleeping bag and some underwear. Still, it seemed wrong to leave a mess behind.

He pulled up a couple of the stakes and saw a light moving through the field. People were crossing the pasture on the other side of the fence. He saw a few pairs of legs and then the light shut off again. Pete lost track of the people in the dark. Soon, another set of lights started out from the side of the field. These lights were carried by people with a purpose. When they were caught in beams of the pursuers, the runners froze. Soon the two groups came together and marched back towards the camp.

Pete tore down his tent, keeping an eye on the progress.

When they reached the fence, he saw what he had feared. The runners were only regular frightened people. Two men and a woman carried clothes and blankets in their pillowcases. Beardos were the pursuers. They had tracked them down and brought them back to the camp area. Pete glanced around at the night. He wondered how many other pairs of Beardos were wrangling the herd, and keeping anyone from escaping. He wondered why they were so intent on keeping everyone together.

Once the runners were back on the right side of the fence, the Beardos shut off their lights and shrank back into the darkness. There was no telling where they were, or who they were watching. Pete shook out his tent and began rolling it up.

Robby was almost at the bottom of the ladder when he heard the hatch open above him. He dropped to the floor and scurried under the shelf of the control panel. He tucked his light under his shirt and then found the switch as feet began to clomp down the rungs.

The man reached the floor and stopped. He was looking almost directly at Robby and held perfectly still. He rubbed his temples. Robby didn't dare to breathe. The weak light from the overhead bulb didn't project much light around the room, but Robby felt exposed.

The man took a deep breath and looked up as he let it out. He flipped glasses down from the top of his head and opened a small panel in the wall. The controls there looked just as useless as the ones on the panel where Robby was hiding, but the man's fingers moved with purpose. A moment later, a metallic clang erupted and the light from the bulb was augmented by several more lights, shining down from the ceiling.

When he turned, Robby got a better look at the man's face. It was Hampton. Mercifully, he didn't turn back towards Robby, but went straight for the door. Robby heard his feet as they rang down the spiral stairs.

When the sound of Hampton's feet disappeared, Robby slid out from under the panel and ran to the ladder. The shaft to the surface was gone. A big steel plate blocked the ladder.

Robby investigated the panel that Hampton had activated. He didn't see anything but rust and dust. Robby looked to the stairs. Placing each foot as gently as possible, Robby climbed down the stairs. At full power, the place looked completely different. Bright lights chased away the shadows from the big room at the bottom of the stairs. Some of the equipment made more sense now that he could see it. The thing against the far wall had a motor that drove a pump. Next to it, a machine had big steel plates that could be used to compact or crush with hydraulic force. Some of the machines appeared to be for manufacturing. Others, Robby couldn't figure out just by visual inspection.

He wondered where Hampton had disappeared. Robby had a pretty good mental map of the place, after exploring with Romie, but he was only really interested in one room. Robby worked his way over to the doorway. From inside the room, he heard a turning page. Robby froze. Hampton was in there. He was in the room with all the information that Robby wanted to comb through. Robby looked back across the big room. There were plenty of places to hide, but he had no idea how long Hampton would be in there.

"What did you see?" a man's voice asked from inside the room.

Robby was about to run when the voice spoke again.

"Robby? What did you see?"

Hampton rolled back in his chair and appeared from around the corner.

"Don't run. Just tell me what you saw."

"Where?"

"Up north," Hampton said. "I assume you saw the landing site before the being retreated. Did you see a long tunnel of white light, surrounded by all your loved ones? Did you see the face of God?"

"No," Robby said. He moved closer. When the man had first spoken, Robby had assumed that he was talking to someone else in the room. Now, Robby understood that Hampton was alone. The man seemed to be in charge of the Beardos, but he wasn't menacing. Robby wasn't afraid of him.

"Well, what did you see?"

"It was a big ball of light in a depression in the snow."

Hampton moved his glasses higher up on his nose and looked back down at the documents on his desk. He flipped a page. "That's Stage Three. There was a researcher named Higgins. He said that Stage Three would be followed by the final landing within two weeks. I suppose it's a good thing he's dead. He would have been really embarrassed."

"How did he research? How did you know about any of this?" Robby asked. He leaned against the door frame.

Hampton waved him to a chair, but Robby held his ground.

"Part of keeping a population safe means keeping them safe from hysteria. Some information is so toxic that only a small number of..."

"Save it," Robby said, interrupting. Hampton seemed shocked at first, and then a tiny smile touched his lips. "Where did you get your information about this phenomenon? You're part of the same group that went to Brad's house, right?"

Hampton leaned back and raised his glasses to the top of his head. His smile was bigger than ever. "Which question should I answer?"

"Where did you get your information?"

Hampton reached to his side and opened a drawer. He pulled a file from the very back of the cabinet and slapped it down on the table. "Ever heard of Crick and Watson?"

"Yes," Robby said. "They discovered DNA."

"Not exactly, but close enough. They figured out the chemical structure of the stuff. They won the Nobel prize for documenting how nucleic acids are able to *transfer information* in living material. People think their DNA just tells their bodies how tall to grow, or what color their eyes should be. It conveys a lot more than that."

"You extracted information from DNA?"

Hampton seemed to consider this question carefully before he answered. "Given completely unforeseen circumstances, do you know what the smartest soldier in the world would do?"

"What?"

"Whatever he's told," Hampton said.

Robby waited for more explanation.

"It's funny—I had this same conversation with Judy a few hours ago, but she was the one informing me," Hampton said. "At least she thought she was. There's some documentation here, and I've learned as much as I can from it. But I was the guy assigned to carry out the orders, not create them. I'm following a script that was written by people who were long dead before the world even ended."

"So they knew this thing was coming, and you built this place?"

"We did."

"Why didn't they know about Brad's house? Nobody showed up at his house until he found the vines."

Hampton nodded. "Believe me, a lot of people wondered that same thing. Even at my level, plenty of fingers were pointed. In the end, it was Gertz who came up with the most popular explanation. He showed that the pattern of her arrivals is like an interference pattern between two waves. It's like a double-slit experiment, except with time instead of light. Way beyond my understanding. He showed that sometimes the arrival is at one location. Sometimes it's two. It can go up to five. The only prediction we get is the final location. Gertz said that the only way to know about the secondary ones was to wait and watch."

"Why didn't Luke help me fight that thing up north? If that's your mission, why wouldn't he help?"

Hampton shook his head. "That wasn't part of our orders. Our confrontation happens here. We're going to survive this the same way people always have. We wait for the arrival and then we drive it back. The only thing we're missing is a pyramid, and the researchers assured us that it's not critical."

Robby considered that statement. "You're missing the people, too. You just sent them all away."

"Not far," Hampton said, narrowing his eyes. "They're close enough to bring back after the tornadoes have passed. You should get going. You don't want to miss the last transport."

"What about you?"

"I have a few more things to finish up before I go. I'll be fine. I always believed the tornadoes would come through. It was nice of Judy to get us an exact schedule though. Makes everything simpler."

Robby stood. Hampton flipped through a few more documents and the looked up at him with his eyebrows raised.

"I'd like to see that information first hand," Robby said. "I think I've earned it. If we hadn't stopped that thing up in Kingston, you wouldn't be here to make your stand."

Hampton laughed. "You think you stopped anything? That landing had run its course. Whatever theatrics you engaged in didn't do anything to change it."

"I disagree," Robby said. "For one, I'm not sure you know exactly what we did. Two, I'm not sure it's much different than what you have planned here. You're going to let it hatch and then you're going to feed it a human sacrifice, is that right?"

Hampton didn't answer. His face was a blank mask.

"That's what people have done historically, right? They just line up a bunch of people and feed it to the thing to make it go away. Do you even know *why* it's done? Have you even seen the symbols, or did you simply let the researchers tell you they found the clues in our DNA? Why don't you tell those people what you're planning to do, instead of moving them around like cattle?"

"Part of keeping a population safe means keeping them safe from hysteria," Hampton said again.

"What's in the water?" Robby asked.

Hampton shook his head. "What do you mean?"

"Down that hall, where you had Brad, there's something down there. What is it?"

"You're smart, and you've figured out a few things, but this time I believe you've gone too far. We only used that silo to stress your friend. I have the reports from Herm. Brad Jenkins was remarkably quiet when Herm interviewed him, but he gave up the information to me."

"Then he was lying. Brad doesn't know anything."

"On the contrary, Brad was a very rich source of information. If Herm had tried harder, he might have learned enough to keep himself alive."

"You can't blame Brad for what happened."

"No, I don't blame him, but neither do I trust him. There were over one-hundred men stationed at that landing. Your friend was the only one to walk away. Luck only gets you so far." Hampton returned his attention to his documents.

"I'm not leaving until I finish my research," Robby said.

Hampton didn't answer. He turned the page.

CHAPTER 31: FIELD

PETE HAD HIS TENT and bedroll stacked up on his lap. The night slipped by as a series of dark shapes. Whenever the SUV bounced over an obstacle, Pete got the worst of it. He seat was in the back row. When Pete had piled in, he'd seen the short black and white hairs everywhere on the seat. The upholstery smelled like an old sock.

"Where are we going?" a woman asked.

The driver turned his head to answer. Pete couldn't see him. All the lights of the vehicle were disabled. The driver was using some kind of night vision to navigate.

"The athletic field of the high school. We cleared it out," the Beardo said.

Pete imagined him up there with his bug-eyed night vision mask. It was unsettling. It reminded Pete of that guy who had chased them in Vermont.

"I thought it was dangerous there," the woman said.

"We cleared it out," the Beardo repeated.

They made a series of sharp turns, slowing down for the last couple. The brakes whined as the SUV stopped.

"Follow the path. Stay between the red and green lights at all times," the Beardo said. Pete didn't see where the man went. After the driver's door shut, everyone began moving. Pete had to wait for the people in front of him. When they finally opened their doors, the overhead light came on, nearly blinding him.

Everyone spilled out to the parking lot. They were next to a tall brick wall. Pete only read half of the sign on the wall before the light went out again. It read, "...lley High School."

A man's voice came out of the dark.

"No lights beyond this point until you reach the athletic field. Once you do, please only use lights inside the tent," the man said. "Follow these lights to get to the field."

Pete had no idea what the man was talking about until the people in front of him began to move. Once their bodies were out of the way, he saw the lighted path on the ground. They were dim little pinpricks of lights—green on the left, red on the right. They formed a path about three or four feet apart. There was just enough starlight for Pete to make out vague shapes looming on the sides. Pete assumed they were buildings as he walked forward on the concrete path.

The lights led him up a few steps. From the echoes, Pete guessed they were passing between two buildings. The bobbing dark shapes ahead of him were pulling away. Pete sped up to catch them.

The world of darkness opened up around him and the ground underfoot transitioned from concrete to trampled grass. Pete heard murmuring from up ahead.

As he got closer, he realized it was man repeating, "Stay away from the orange lights. Stay away from the orange lights."

The ground underfoot changed again. It was softer and spongier. The lights on either side of his path changed from red and green to white. Pete saw a couple of paths ahead.

When he reached the first intersection, a voice spoke to him. Pete saw only the man's feet, in the glow of the path lights.

"Straight ahead," the voice said.

Pete obeyed.

He sensed an object looming in front of him and then caught a flash of light as he heard fabric rumpling. Pete held his possessions in one hand and reached out with the other. His hand hit the canvas side of a big tent. He found the opening and pushed his way through. It was dark and humid inside. He took another step and realized that there was a second flap. As he began to lift it, he saw the light from inside.

It looked like the big tent his cousin had used for her wedding reception, but it was all black. They had lanterns hanging from the big posts. The roof of the tent was at least eight feet up at the lowest part, and Pete guessed that the thing was at least thirty yards long. At the far end, some tents were set up inside the tent. They were the little, two-person kind, like the one that Pete carried.

A Beardo with a clipboard approached as Pete stood there, taking it all in.

"You alone?" the Beardo asked.

"Yeah."

"Give your tent to Bridgeport," he said, pointing to a Beardo on the right, "and you can set up over there. Go as far down as possible, and all the way to the left."

"Where's the bathroom?"

"Through that side. Close the interior flaps before opening the exterior. Stay between the white lights. Don't go near the orange lights."

"Thanks," Pete said.

He dropped his tent off with the other Beardo and began to walk down the center. Now that he had light, he saw that he was walking across the lines of a football field. It was artificial turf, and it felt like walking on rubber. He crossed the twenty-five yard line before he took a left. Some people hadn't followed orders, and they'd set up closer to the center aisle. That made sense to Pete—it would be easier to make your way to the exit if you didn't have to step around a sea of sleeping bags. The lights were more dim on this side. The lanterns gave off an amber glow. Some people were already asleep. Their bags were only used to soften the turf—people didn't need the warmth. The air inside the big tent was hot and humid. Pete wondered how long the oxygen in there would last.

He picked a nice spot between two sleeping bags that were unrolled, but empty. Pete rolled out his mat and his bag. With his area claimed, he walked back to the aisle and began to head for the side flap. There wasn't much conversation going on inside the tent.

Pete heard a couple whispers. People seemed to be extra courteous of their sleeping neighbors. The smaller tents, set up at back, looked like little bubbles of color. They were lit from the inside and Pete saw shifting shadows inside some.

When Pete tried to lift the flap, a hand on the other side held it down.

"Wait," someone said.

It lifted a second later and a man came in. Pete recognized him from the farm, but didn't know his name. He nodded at the man, but the man didn't notice. He was scanning the tent, perhaps looking for the little area he had claimed.

Pete ducked under the flap. He folded it back and found himself in the dark again. He felt his way for the outer flap. It was a relief to push back out into the night. He took a deep breath of the cool air and saw the landing strip of white lights. They led him a few yards and then veered right into a slant route. The smell guided him the last few yards. He found another double-flap tent there. This one was much smaller. Inside, there was just enough room for a dozen Port-A-Potties and a short line. When one door banged open, the person at the head of the line marched forward and the door slammed shut again. The oppressive atmosphere inside the sleeping tent was like vacation compared to the aggressive stink of the latrine tent. Pete shifted uncomfortably and hoped the smell wouldn't permeate his clothes.

A small woman in front of him looked up when Pete joined the back of the line.

"This is a pretty complicated set up," Pete said. "How long do you think they were working on it?"

She pressed her finger to her lips. "We're supposed to be quiet," she said.

Pete looked around. "Oh," he whispered back. "Nobody told me."

Another door banged and the next person went in.

When Pete left the latrine, the air outside felt twice as good on his face. He stopped and turned his head up to the sky. The stars were out in full force. They made a much more inviting glow than the white lights of the prescribed path on the football field. Pete stepped to the side as someone brushed by him on their way to take care of their emergency in the latrine tent. He smiled in the dark, knowing they would have to wait their turn in line.

Pete stepped off the path. He moved away from the latrine tent to get away from the seeping smell, and busy people. He saw the white lines on the artificial turf, so he knew he wouldn't get too far away from his new home.

He walked farther and thought he saw a spark of flame. A little closer and he recognized a line of orange lights.

"Stay away," he whispered to himself. He got closer anyway. These lights were different than the path lights. The path lights were only really visible if you were walking down the path. They had little blinders on the sides that hid them from side view. These orange lights could be seen from all angles. He sensed a dark shape beyond the lights. When he blocked out the orange lights with his arm, he could see it better. It was a fence and it looked to be covered in cloth. He knelt down to see the fence against the starlight. He saw the top bar and some chain link. Just under that, the cloth began.

He wondered how long the Beardos had been setting this place up.

He wondered if the fence were meant to keep something out, or to keep the people in.

Something clicked and shook in the night. It sounded almost like a rattlesnake. Pete turned his head to try to pinpoint the direction the sound was coming from.

"You lost?" a man's voice asked.

Pete turned. He saw their shapes against the night sky. On their helmets, they had tiny orange lights that looked almost like the lights near the fence.

"Yeah, I guess I am," Pete said. "I'm supposed to stay away from the orange lights." He put a little chuckle at the end of his statement, to let them know that he was good natured.

The man's voice was flat when he responded. "Follow us."

They backed up, so Pete could see their lights and follow them. Before long, he caught sight of the white lights marking the path.

"It's okay," Pete said. "I see the lights now."

He sensed them keeping pace behind him. They stayed with him until he opened the flap of the sleeping tent. Pete went back inside to the stale humidity.

CHAPTER 32: VALLEY

"MAYBE WE SHOULD WAKE him up," Lisa said. She rolled down her window and added her flashlight to the headlights of the vehicle. She panned around the river of green that covered the road.

"It's just plants. No need to wake him up. He's exhausted," Romie said. She dropped the transmission back into drive and took her foot off the brake. She had just begun to accelerate when Brad's voice scared the hell out of her.

"NO!" he yelled. His mouth was practically in her ear.

When she stomped the brakes, he flopped forward and landed on the center console.

"What?" she asked.

Lisa was helping Brad up. Romie reached under him to push the shift lever into reverse. She backed away from the plants.

"Those are the vines," Brad said. His voice was hoarse from the yell. He coughed to clear his throat. "They're dangerous." He pushed himself back upright.

"You could have fooled me," Romie said. "They look like goddamn plants to me. How do we get around them?"

Lisa put up her hands. "How should I know?"

"You're supposed to be navigating."

"With what?"

Before Romie could answer, a loud TOCK rang through the night. Lisa jumped in her seat at the sound. Brad fell forward again. This time it was intentional. He stabbed the button on the dash, turning on the radio. All that came out was static, but he turned up the dial anyway. The next TOCK they heard was partially muted by the white noise.

"Go back," Brad yelled. "Away from the plants."

They went almost half a mile before they didn't hear another TOCK and Brad declared it was safe to stop.

"Now what?" Romie asked.

"It's happening again," Brad said. "We're right back at the center. This is the same thing that happened at my house."

"Great," Romie said.

"What do we do now?" Lisa asked.

Brad flopped back against the rear seat. "Prepare for the snow. It's coming."

Romie turned the radio down to a gentle hiss. "I hate to say it, but Robby was right. We need more information. There has to be some way to stop this thing from coming again."

"Those government guys descended on my house in droves. They didn't manage to prevent anything."

"Yeah, but I bet they didn't see it the way I did. When I saw those symbols in that diary, I went back into time and saw that thing being defeated a million years ago. If I'd seen the whole picture instead of just part of it, maybe I'd know what to do," Romie said.

"Or maybe you would have committed suicide," Lisa said.

"I suppose that would be a solution as well," Romie said. "Tell us about what happened at your house, Brad."

Brad sighed. "I don't know much. I was trapped inside. There were those plants, and the spinning rock. Something dug a hole under my garage. It think the rock was the center of the activity."

"Maybe we should look for the rock and blow it up or something," Lisa said.

"Well, we could," Brad said. "Except the rock is probably in the middle of a bunch of killer vines, and if the thing could have been blown up, then don't you think the government guys would have tried that? Isn't that their first approach to everything?"

"Not everything," Romie said. "They only blow things up when they don't see a way to profit off of them."

"Past tense," Lisa said. "They're all gone now. There's no government to muck things up anymore."

"And that's what they were good at," Romie said. "Mucking things up, I mean. So let's not assume that blowing the thing up isn't a good idea. The government guys who showed up at your house might have been incompetent, and they might have had ulterior motives."

"There's still the problem of getting close enough to the thing. If it's in a patch of vines, you're not going to get very close to it from the ground."

"Maybe we could find an army base or something. Maybe we could get those rocket propelled grenades or whatever," Lisa said.

"You'd need headphones, too," Brad said. "That big ticking noise we heard will hypnotize you until the vines come. I think it's a defense mechanism. It paralyzes you with sound somehow."

"That's easy," Romie said. "We get headphones and heat. If the thing makes it snow, then maybe it hates heat. We just throw some gasoline bombs at it, and maybe that will stop it."

"That sounds like a long shot," Brad said. "I've survived the snow once, I can do it again. We should just concentrate on finding a place we can winterize. Shouldn't be hard around here. We just need to stockpile water, food, and firewood."

"We might as well go back to the farm if we want to do that," Lisa said. "Those people were already making good progress on those fronts."

"No," Romie said. She slammed her hand down on the steering wheel. "We can't sit back and wait. Who knows what would have happened if we hadn't taken all those corpses up and fed them to the light? We might be dead now. How are we going to do that again if the ball of light comes back? We don't have access to that many dead bodies anymore. What are we going to do? Are we going to feed it all the people who were living at the farm? Sacrifice all those people? For what? If we do that, then there's nobody left to save the planet for."

Lisa and Brad were silent as Romie's words faded. The static from the radio once more filled the interior of the vehicle.

"And it might have worked to some extent, but it wasn't exactly a permanent solution, was it? Here we are, facing the same thing," Romie said.

Brad looked out his window into the night. He imagined what was lurking there, behind the back yards of the houses, in the forest that ran up the little hill. Somewhere there might be a trail that led to a patch of vines. Maybe in the center of that patch, he would find a big rock that was out of place. That would be slowly spinning, emitting a rumbling TOCK every few minutes that had the power to hypnotize. It was a crazy thought that made absolutely no sense. He had no business believing in such things, except for the fact that he had seen and heard them himself.

"Gasoline and headphones?" Brad asked. "Shouldn't be too hard to find."

CHAPTER 33: ROAD

Ty wouldn't talk. He wouldn't describe what he had seen, or how it might have influenced his new strong opinions on what direction they took. Ty simply stared out the windows and barked instructions.

"Left here," he said.

Other times, he would just say a single word. "Right."

"Wait, wait, wait," he said. "Slow down a little."

Tim was so startled by the volume of words that he jerked the ambulance to a stop. Ty threw open the door and jumped from the vehicle. Tim watched him in the mirror. The giant man ran back to a landscaping truck and pulled two red gas cans from the trailer. He hoisted them and then returned to the drivers side where he unscrewed the cap on the ambulance's fill pipe.

The needle on the gas gauge stirred for the first time in a while.

When Ty jumped back in, he seemed much more calm.

"We're almost there, but we wouldn't have made it."

The sky was growing dark. Tim flipped on the headlights.

Ty's last instruction took them up a long drive. The driveway was lined with white fences and stately trees. It led up a hill to a pretty white farmhouse, revealed by the ambulance's headlights as they approached.

"What is this place?" Jackson asked from over Tim's shoulder. He was kneeling between the seats. Cedric was in back, curled up on the stretcher with Amy Lynne. Tim heard the dog's tags jingle when Jackson spoke. The dog still didn't trust Jackson.

"It's where we're supposed to be," Ty said. "Don't you feel it?"

"I guess," Jackson said.

Tim didn't feel it. In a world that was empty, this place looked especially abandoned. His eyes began to pick out the details that his subconscious had already processed. The gates to the pastures were open and untethered. They swung loose like the front door of the house. The grass was trampled. A few tractors were left out on the lawn instead of tucked away from the elements. He saw trash and clothes scattered in a patch of yard between two barns.

Tim put the vehicle in park, but he didn't shut off the engine.

"I don't like the looks of this place," Tim said.

"This is where we're supposed to be," Ty said again. He was out the door and walking across the driveway before Tim replied.

Tim got out and left his door open so Cedric could join him. The dog was right behind him.

Ty was walking straight for the front door of the house. Tim walked over to one of wooden fence gates. A patch of mud just outside the gate was dotted with hoof prints. Cedric sniffed around in the mud. In the periphery of the glow from the headlights, Tim saw a pile of fresh horse manure in the pasture. Cedric made his way towards the pile.

"Don't do that, Cedric," Tim said. "Who knows if they're sick or something."

The dog looked over at Tim for a second before he gave in and came towards him.

A sound drew their attention. It was Ty. Even though it was wide open, he was reaching through the doorway and knocking on the front door.

"Come on," Tim said to Cedric. He walked up to the house as Ty was slipping inside. "Ty? Hey, Ty, wait up."

Ty was climbing the staircase to the second floor as Tim reached the door. He was about to go inside when the headlights and engine of the ambulance shut off. Tim waited on the porch. As his eyes adjusted to the starlight, he saw Jackson helping Amy Lynne from the back of the ambulance. They shared a flashlight. Jackson propped her up and helped her walk towards the house.

Ty didn't take long on the second floor. He came back down the steps with his big feet almost sideways on the treads.

"Nobody here," Ty said.

"Where do you think they went?" Jackson asked.

"Who?" Amy Lynne asked. "Who did you think we were going to find here?"

"I don't know," Ty said. "Other people who had the same idea about this place, I suppose."

Ty came out on the front porch.

"So what do we do? Try to find where they all went?" Tim asked.

"This is the right place," Ty said. "I say we stay here and see if anyone comes back."

CHAPTER 34: FARM

"THIS WOULD BE A lot easier if we had the key to this code," Robby said. On the desk in front of him, he had a dozen documents arranged side by side.

"If I had the code, do you think I'd still be here?" Hampton asked. "But I believe that the encoded documents are simply the analysis of the other research. We have the original research in plain text, so you need to draw your own conclusions."

"That may or may not be true," Robby said. He stood up and pointed at the cork board. "Do you see this article? It's quoted here in this encoded document, but so are at least five or six other documents. Where's that research? It's not in any of the relevant files that I can find."

"You're crazy," Hampton said. "If you don't know the code, then how do you know that article is quoted."

"You can tell," Robby said.

Hampton took the document from him and held it up next to the article on the cork board. He shook his head. "No, I can't."

"Trust me, then," Robby said. "It's a quote."

"Then use it as your Rosetta Stone. Use it as your key to unlock the rest of the document."

"I can't. I need more examples. That's why I'm looking for the source articles. Is this all there is? Are there any more cabinets of documents in this place?"

"Not that I know of," Hampton said. "This place is big, but I've been in every inch of it at one time or another. There were other centers in the world though. The primary research was down in Puebla in Mexico."

"Probably take too long to get there," Robby said, slumping back in his chair.

"Ten hours by jet, but I wouldn't go anywhere near the place. The Laguna Verde Nuclear Power Plant would have gone critical, let's see, about five months ago. That whole region will be uninhabitable for the next million years or so. Imagine Chernobyl time a thousand."

"I wondered about the nuclear plants," Robby said.

"We're safe enough here. I'd stay out of Asia and most of Europe though," Hampton said. "Assuming they still exist. You might as well put California on that list. Only a few plants, but if there's an earthquake..."

"Did any of the researchers study the symbols?" Robby asked.

"Symbols?"

"There were some written in blood on the wall of a house near mine. I found a transcription of some in a diary in Vermont. They seem to trigger some kind of memories."

Hampton shook his head. "I've never heard of anything like that."

Robby interlaced his fingers on his chest. After a minute, he sat up and rearranged the documents on the desk. "If this is all the documentation you have, then what steps are you following? You're carrying out the plan that the researchers invented, right? Where's that plan?"

Hampton tapped the side of his head. "It's all up here."

"They've got all these hardcopies of documents, and the most important part is committed to memory?"

"Can't be intercepted if it's not written down."

"Intercepted by whom? Do you think that planet-sized aliens care about the plans of men?"

"They should. Besides, why take the chance?"

"I'd be less worried about that, and more worried that you only have one-hundred and fifty people. That's not nearly enough biomass to turn back the embryo."

Hampton didn't respond. Robby studied his face to try to discern whether his comment had hit home. He thought it did. He thought that if he hadn't been right, Hampton would have come back with a comment of his own.

A buzzer went off. Hampton reached forward and hit a button to silence the alarm.

"I suspect my ride is here," Hampton said. "I suggest that you don't stay here too long. She said that the shit would hit the fan in six days, but she might have been trying to lull us into thinking we had more time to evacuate."

"From the tornadoes."

"Accounts are untrustworthy, but I hear they're quite bad."

"I've seen them," Robby said. "I saw them taking apart towns on the coast."

"You're one of the few then." Hampton stood and began collecting his documents. "There used to be a polished white limestone casing on the Great Pyramid at Giza. It was stolen hundreds of years ago to build other structures. I've heard that it wasn't even the original skin. When the thing was first built, the skin was completely sealed. They say a tornado sat on top of the pyramid for four days, until the whole skin was stripped away."

"Who said that? No historic record of that would exist," Robby said.

"The records at the Ancient Library of Alexandria spoke of it, until all those accounts were burned by the Romans." Hampton began to walk for the door. "You'll need to come at least as far as the landing. When I flip the switch to open the hatch, the lights will go out in here."

Robby stood up. "Can I ask you two more questions?"

"You can ask. I may not answer."

Robby followed the man out into the big room.

"If you sacrifice all those people, what good will it do? All the humans will be dead either way."

"I won't validate your supposition to answer your question."

He began to climb the stairs up to the dusty control room.

"What's at the bottom of the silo where you had Brad locked up?"

"Water. It flooded years ago."

"Is there something in the water?"

Hampton's feet clanged up a few treads before he answered.

"That's something that can never be explained, only experienced. I wouldn't recommend it though. Unless you have about a decade to commit to intense psychotherapy. Do you?"

They reached the room.

Robby stood right at Hampton's side as he reached into the little panel. He ignored the cracked and dusty controls and pushed on a patch of rust. The metal underneath clicked, like it was fatigued and flexing. Everything went out, leaving them in the dark. Robby heard the metal barrier sliding aside to reveal the shaft up to the shed. When the barrier stopped moving, Robby heard the click again and the dim bulb came on.

"That's the courtesy light. You can leave it on when you're done," Hampton said. He slung his bag over his shoulder and began to move towards the ladder.

"Wait, what's the point of evacuating everyone and then bringing them back here? Why didn't you take them to the backup place initially, if you knew this place was going to be leveled by a tornado? Why bring them back here if you're going to feed them to the entity?"

"That's way more than two questions."

"But you didn't answer the first one."

Robby heard Hampton laugh as he climbed towards the surface.

When he heard the hatch lift at the top of the shaft, Robby looked back towards the black square that was the doorway leading to the stairs. He looked back at the rusty spot on the panel. If he pressed that, the lights would make the place more bearable, but he would also be sealed inside. He wasn't ready for that. He wanted to see the sky again, just to be sure there were no storms on the horizon. He'd seen one of the tornadoes tear apart a town. If one sat on top of the bunker for four straight days, it would no doubt be able to unearth the bunker. Robby ran for the ladder.

As he climbed, he reassured himself. "I've learned everything I could from those documents. I'm not going to decode them just by staring at them hour after hour." The bin was latched above him. It must have clicked back into place after Hampton left.

Robby struggled with the catch. All he could think about was the thing in the water. Whatever it was, it scared Hampton. Robby had heard the fear in the man's voice. His grip on the rung slipped as his other hand struggled with the latch. Robby took a deep breath and closed his eyes. He heard something move below.

✪ ✪ ✪ ✪ ✪

Robby kept his eyes shut and counted. When they had rescued Brad, they had closed and latched the door that led down to the water. And there was a door at the end of that hall, and rooms, and stairs, and a ladder. Nothing was coming for him. His brain knew that. He took another deep breath and willed his pounding heart to understand as well.

Robby imagined the latch and moved his fingers in the dark. He manipulated the lever and heard a snap. The door above him opened. In the little shed above, he saw cautious dawn light seeping between the gaps of the boards.

Robby climbed.

When he opened the shed door, he heard the grain bin closing automatically over the hatch.

Hampton was crossing the back yard, headed for the driveway. Robby scanned the sky. It was clear and dark. The sunrise was just beginning to breach the eastern horizon, and that's the only place he saw even a trace of clouds. Robby walked towards the house. He found the folder he'd dropped, and picked it up. His stomach rumbled. He tried to think how many hours he'd been underground, depriving himself of food and water.

The grounds were a mess. Clothes and gear were scattered—left behind in the hasty evacuation. Hampton was walking towards an ambulance that sat in the center of the drive. Robby watched as the man slowed and then stopped. Hampton tilted his head and stared for a second. He broke for the house at a run.

The screen door on the back porch banged open and a man emerged who was so tall and muscular that he filled the entire doorway. Hampton stopped in his tracks. The enormous man was dressed like a surgeon. Robby's eyes shot to his right. The man had probably seen him, but he could easily run for the barn. The man would get Hampton, but Robby could escape through the barn and then down the path between the pastures to the woods. A dog emerged between the man's legs and came to the edge of the porch with a wagging tail. Robby smiled and thoughts of running away faded. A much smaller man came through the door. Robby and Hampton both approached.

CHAPTER 35: FIELD

EVERYONE SEEMED TO STIR at once. Pete tried to sleep through the noises, but the general rustling of sleeping bags shifted into coughs and whispers. People stood and walked between the rows of sleepers. Pete gave up and moved outside. The flaps of the tent were tied open and people moved outside in a steady stream. The morning air was clean and delicious after the recycled air of the tent.

It was going to be a beautiful day. Pete surveyed their encampment.

Nearly the entire football field was taken over by the tents. He saw a first aid tent and the latrine tent that he had already visited. At the perimeter, the chain link fence was lined with black tarps. Over the top of the tall fence, he could just see the highest railing of the bleachers. They were covered with a blanket of vines.

Pete tried to look casual as he strolled towards the fence. He glanced towards the Beardos who drank coffee near the first aid tent. They seemed unconcerned by his movements, so he kept walking to a place where he saw a gap in the black tarps. Pete stayed back from the fence until he spotted movement outside the perimeter. As he puzzled out what he saw, and felt the heat, he moved forward.

He pulled apart the edges of two tarps and saw what was on the other side of the fence.

In the sideline area of the football field, a Beardo walked. He wore a backpack with canisters and tubes that ran to the weapon he held. The Beardo pulled the trigger and Pete shrank back as a jet of hot flame shot from the end of the weapon. He directed the flamethrower at the bleachers and torched the vines that were creeping between the tiers of metal seats. The man walked methodically towards the end zone, burning up the creeping vines. In the wake of his flames, the vines burned only for a second and then left behind black husks.

Pete looked beyond the Beardo. This wasn't his first pass. There were already charred remains of vines in the direction the Beardo was walking, but the vines had advanced over their burned siblings. Pete wondered how often they had to drive them back to keep the vines at bay. He let the tarps fall shut again.

Pete walked in the direction of the other end zone. That was where the gate sat. It was where he had come in the night before. They had been led on a concrete walkway between buildings. Atop the brick school buildings, more Beardos stood. Pete saw that one of those men was also carrying a flamethrower.

"Can I help you?"

Pete looked back down. "I guess not. Just stretching my legs."

"Please stay on the marked paths," the Beardo said.

"Yeah. Sure." Pete nodded. "I'm curious. Why bring us here, when it's clearly surrounded by danger?"

"Where else?" the Beardo asked. "Danger is everywhere. At least this is a defendable position."

"Ah," Pete said. He smiled and nodded before turning back towards the tents. He caught the smell of breakfast cooking from the main tent. It was briefly overpowered as the breeze brought him aromas of burning leaves and then chemicals from the bathroom tent. The field was beginning to feel a bit claustrophobic for Pete. They had more than a hundred and fifty people crammed into the space, and their sounds and smells overlapped to crowd Pete's senses.

He rubbed his chin and wondered if he could simply join the Beardos just to get a turn on top of one of the school buildings. He would still be trapped with these people, but at least he would be able to see beyond the enclosing fences.

Pete heard a scream and turned to see several Beardos running out through the gate and disappearing around the other side of the fence. Pete quickened his pace and walked around the first aid tent before dashing for the fence. He reached the fence as another scream called out from the other side.

There was a gap between sections of the bleachers there. The vines had come up over the railings of the bleachers, but had respected the walkway between them, leaving the concrete path bare. It looked like a trap. Pete wondered why the man hadn't recognized it as such.

He was pinned there, lashed to the vertical support of the bleacher and held by ropes of green vine. One vine spiraled over the man's ear, ran down behind his sideburn and looped under his chin before disappearing down his shirt. The man was panting quickly. Trickles of blood seeped through his beard.

Pete was about to speak to him—tell him to hold still and that help would be there soon. He didn't get the chance. Beardos appeared from both directions. One had a flamethrower. The others held machetes.

"Burn it back. I want this whole section cleared," one man shouted at the flamethrower man. The others moved with their machetes and approached slowly. Pink and purple flowers erupted on the vines. The flowers were beautiful, but chilling, the way they suddenly budded and opened. The machetes swung, hacking off sections of reaching vines. As they hit the ground, the vines twisted on the concrete. One flopped and rolled towards a Beardo. He stomped at it, and the vine rewarded him by curling up his leg. He slid his machete between his pants and the vine and began methodically dicing the vine into little sections. The other men hacked at the roots of the vines that held their friend.

The pinned man continued to pant and emitted a low moan and people encouraged him to keep calm. They had to speak up to be heard over the low roar of the flamethrower. The man shooting fire worked his way up the bleachers, burning the vines and paying extra attention to flowers. Those glowed like miniature torches as they burned.

Pete gripped the fence. A few other people had joined him.

They were all looking through the fence at the battle playing out on the other side. The Beardos were too involved to order them back.

One of the observers shouted a warning and Pete saw the danger just before it was too late. A vine had sent out a runner from the other set of bleachers. It reached the foot of one of the machete Beardos as he was engrossed in cutting the vines from the pinned man.

It circled the Beardo's ankle before he heard the shouted warnings. When the vine looped around his ankle, it suddenly recoiled, pulling his foot out from underneath him. The man slammed down to the concrete, throwing his arms out to catch himself. His machete clanged away from his hand and the other Beardos turned at the sound. They hacked at the vine, severing it before it could drag the man under the bleachers. More vines began to descend from over the side of the bleachers while the flamethrower Beardo was occupied.

More people yelled, and this time the Beardos heard the warnings. They ducked and backed out of there, dragging the man with the section of vine still looped around his ankle. Meanwhile, more vines had slipped under the bleachers to ensnare the other man once more to the support pole. He screamed again as the new vines dug into his flesh. The other Beardos had learned their lesson. The area was too dangerous to attempt a rescue. They pulled back to within a couple of paces of Pete as he watched.

The flamethrower Beardo finished clearing the seats and backed down from the top, taking giant steps to move from row to row. New tendrils of vine came up from underneath, but he saw the threat and cooked the vine before stepping on the bench.

The man trapped underneath called out again.

"It's a trap," Pete said.

"No shit," one of the Beardos said over his shoulder. He said something in the ear of one of the other men, who ran back along the fence towards the gate.

"If you've got more machetes, we can get a whole bunch of volunteers to clear the back side of the bleachers," Pete said. "It will be easier to keep clear that way—take away the high ground from them."

"Back away from the fence," the Beardo said. "We've got this under control."

"It doesn't seem like it," Pete said.

"Back away," the man shouted. He rapped the flat side of his machete against the chain link fence, making Pete flinch back. Pete unwound his fingers from the fence and took a step back. The gap in the tarps gave him a narrow window on what was going on. He glanced over his shoulder and saw more people coming from the sleeping tent. Everyone wanted to see what was happening. Down the fence a ways, one young man had actually climbed up the chain link so his head and shoulders were above the top. He was scanning the bleachers from his perch. Pete began to walk down towards him.

More people were arriving every second. Pete saw a dozen or more looking through gaps in the tarps and several others joining the young man in climbing.

Suddenly Beardos began to swarm towards them from the gate area.

"Everybody back. Everyone back. It's not safe to be near the fence," they said. They were unarmed and held their hands up to motion people away from the fence.

"What's going on?"

"We deserve to know what's happening out there."

"Is that man going to be okay? Why is nobody helping him?"

The Beardos were peppered with questions and comments. They didn't answer any of them.

✪ ✪ ✪ ✪ ✪

A new sound came from the other side of the fence. It was the grinding, moaning squeal of bending metal. To Pete, it sounded like a toothache. He moved with everyone else as they pressed forward to the fence to see what was happening. The Beardos didn't try to stop them. They were right alongside the civilians, running to the fence to see what was happening.

Pete got to a section of chain link that was covered securely by a tarp. He had no option to see beyond the fence except to climb. He looped his fingers through the links and pulled. When he got his head over the top bar, his eyes widened.

The bleachers were being ripped from their supports. The benches were being pulled back and they were tearing apart the metal scaffolding. The agent of the destruction had to be the thick ropes of vines looped around the metal benches.

The Beardo with the flamethrower opened up his weapon. It shot a long line of fire. The flames didn't slow the destruction. Entire sections of benches were liberated from the supports and flew away from the field, dragging lumps of concrete meant to secure them to the ground.

Another Beardo with a flamethrower arrived. He picked a new angle and added his flame to the cause. New vines slipped under the destruction and slithered towards the flamethrowers. With quick dips, the flames lit up the fresh runners and cooked them black. People on the fence cheered as the flamethrowers managed to easily control the approaching vines. Still, the bleachers were dismantled.

Pete pushed away from the fence and dropped back to the ground. His ankle objected to the rough treatment, but held together. It didn't make sense to Pete. With the bleachers intact, the vines had good cover from which to attack. They had already demonstrated that they could slip underneath or come over the top. Under the cover of the benches, they could approach with stealth. Maybe the vines weren't smart and didn't understand how to use their environment to the maximum benefit.

Another idea occurred to Pete. Perhaps the vines were smart enough to use the benches as a distraction. Pete ran for the other side of the field. He slammed into the fence at the other side and the chain link rattled against the posts. Pete pulled apart two tarps and peeked between them. There was no Beardo patrol on this side. Everyone was either focused on vine control or population control.

Pete let out a relieved breath. Everything was quiet on this side of the field. He saw no vines coming over the top of the bleachers to threaten the field. He pushed back from the fence, reevaluating the intelligence of the vines. Maybe they just knew to tear things apart. Maybe the flamethrowers would be enough to hold them back.

Pete stopped. There hadn't been vines coming over the top of the bleachers, but something had been different. He went back to the fence. On his second look, it was obvious. The shadows under the seats were more filled in. There was something down there.

They all came at once. Little green runners erupted from the shadows, coming over the lower seats. Pete stumbled back and then ran. He screamed, "Hey! Help!"

Nobody was paying attention. Another triumphant yell rose up from the people watching the Beardos with the flamethrowers.

"HELP!" Pete screamed. One woman turned around and saw him running. She poked someone standing next to her and Pete pointed over his shoulder. "HELP!"

Finally, people began to turn around and Pete saw that he had the attention of the Beardos over at the gate.

"They're coming!" Pete screamed. He pointed at the fence. He didn't need to scream anymore. Vines were breaching the tarps and reaching their green fingers over the top of the fence. The invasion was apparent. Everyone began to scream and point.

The rest of the group streamed from the big tent. Some still rubbed sleep from their eyes and some carried plates with breakfast. Food was forgotten as the group became a mob. People swelled towards the gate. Pete had a jump on them. He reached the gate before the rest. A couple of Beardos from the gate were headed towards the new threat. They had machetes drawn. The rest turned and seemed to be heading for high ground. Pete joined them. He fell in behind a small contingent of men who began climbing a ladder to get on top of a low porch roof.

Pete hung back enough to avoid being kicked in the face by the boots of the man ahead of him. As soon as he was off the ladder, he turned to evaluate the situation. From his height, he could see the flamethrowers fighting off the vines on one side and the machete men slicing and dicing on the other side. Nobody was focused on the vines coming over the opposite end zone. Those vines were curling up the goalposts and flowing over the fence towards the main tent.

A swell of people reached the ladder. The first few climbed in an orderly line, and then people became impatient. A man tried to climb the back of the ladder, and a young woman tried to go up the side. Pete gripped the rails, trying to steady the ladder.

One person spilled over the side to the roof and ran over the porch roof to the next ladder. The Beardos had set up another ladder on the flat porch roof to get up to the higher roof of the school building. When the guy pushed off to run for even higher ground, he kicked the ladder and it shook in Pete's hands. Someone fell off the side and then it ripped from Pete's hands. He watched as the ladder slid and then tumbled to the side. Frantic hands of people below tried to set it back up. Others gave up and ran for the parking lot. Pete heard screams from that direction and guessed that the vines might have cut off that retreat as well.

✪ ✪ ✪ ✪ ✪

Pete climbed the second ladder to the flat roof of the school. The top of this ladder was lashed to metal rings at the top of the wall. The Beardos up there were organized and efficient. They had a flame guy on each wall. They had backup tanks at the ready. Their supplies were piled near the air conditioner stacks in the center of the roof.

Pete walked over to the wall that faced the parking lot.

The asphalt was a battlefield. A narrow line of vines didn't envelop the vehicles, but it cut off access to them. People who ran down the concrete path between the buildings had to take a sharp right to avoid the thick stream of vines. Someone broke open the front doors of the building on the right. They ran inside, but Pete guessed it wasn't any safer in there. Farther down the face of the building, he saw that the vines had smashed in a window and sent their runners inside.

Other people decided to make their stand between the buildings on the concrete path. Surrounded by brick buildings and completely paved, the place looked to be devoid of plant life. But, as Pete watched, vines began to come over the top of the other building. There were only a few Beardos over there, and they only had machetes to defend themselves. The vines overtook them easily.

Pete watched with nauseous fascination as the vines captured the Beardos on the other roof. Once their ankles were ensnared, it was only a matter of time before the men were immobilized. The Beardos on Pete's roof didn't pay any heed to the fate of their comrades. They were busy fighting off the vines encroaching on their roof. Pete didn't see where they came from, but the Beardos mobilized more flamethrowers. Soon, each side had two flamethrowers and multiple machete slingers.

The sun crested the trees. As the rays hit the vines, they seemed to gather speed, but the men were on top of them. Smoke from the burning vines filled the morning. Pete looked down at the people trapped between the buildings. Vines had taken the football field, which cut off the group's retreat. The vines in the parking lot cut off their escape.

Some stragglers got the ladder back up and climbed to the roof. Pete turned when one man near the air conditioning units barked a short scream.

A single thin vine curled from the exhaust of the air conditioner.

Pete ran to it and picked up a machete from the stockpile. He cut the vine back to the metal grate and the trunk disappeared back inside.

"Pick up weapons," Pete said. "Circle any openings."

The group was scared, but obedient. The Beardos stayed focused on the walls, and Pete rallied the little group of non-Beardos to patrol the center of the roof.

There was no notice when the battle began to turn. Pete felt good that his little group was managing to hold back any vines that crept through the vents and exhaust pipes. Every time he checked the perimeter, he saw the Beardos efficiently holding the edges. People down on the ground occasionally screamed for help as each pocket of people was overrun, but there was nothing the roof people could do to help them. The Beardos had plenty of fuel stockpiled up there for the flamethrowers, but only enough units to cover their walls. The ladder disappeared as vines took it from the bottom. Pete wasn't too concerned. The drop to the porch roof wasn't too far, and from there they could climb down the support poles.

Everything was going fine until he checked over his shoulder and saw that there was only one flamethrower covering the west wall. Somehow, they'd lost a man. Perhaps he had slipped, or maybe a vine had snaked up the wall faster than he could burn it back.

That was all it took. The next time Pete looked, one of the flamethrowers from the north wall was trying to cover his own post and help out the machete men on the west wall too. As soon as the vines came up over the edge of the roof, Pete knew the battle was lost. They hit the sunlight and doubled their speed. Pete yelled to his little group and they turned to fight alongside the Beardos. They swung their machetes down at the advancing carpet of vines, but they were driven back. One man discovered that if he reached forward to cut back the vine that carried the flowers, a section would draw back and regroup before swelling again. It was good information, but it came too late. Pete found himself amongst a small group defending one corner of the roof. Below them, the concrete path was a sea of green vines, dotted with pink and purple flowers. Vines came up the wall and across the roof. They moved with striking speed.

Pete's arms burned as he swung a blade in each. His own pants were dotted with nicks and cuts from clumsy machete work. He spun to cut a vine that was curling up his calf from behind. Pete saw that he was alone. All around, screaming men had been immobilized by the vines. Their wrists and ankles, thighs and biceps, were wrapped. One Beardo had a vine disappearing into his mouth. Pete screamed when he saw the little tendril of vine coming out of the man's nostril.

He gauged the jump. He might make it with only a broken ankle or a popped knee, but he would land in the sea of vines.

Across the alley between the buildings, he saw a window about half a story above the ground. On the other side of the glass, he saw the landing of a stairway. The glass would be too thick for him to crash through, but he didn't have any other choice. Pete didn't allow himself to think about the consequences. He gathered all the momentum he could in a few steps and launched himself off the side of the building. As soon as his foot left the ledge, Pete threw his twin machetes to his sides. His landing would be dangerous enough without carrying the steel blades.

Pete brought his knees to his chest in a cannonball and wrapped his arms around his head. He was halfway across the gap when he realized he had misjudged the distance. His leap wasn't going to carry him to the window.

CHAPTER 36: ROAD

"I HAVE TO REST," Brad said.

"What?" Romie asked. She pulled the headphones away from her ear and leaned in.

"Rest," Brad said.

"I don't think that's an option," Romie said.

They stood in the middle of a suburban street—right in the center. On either side, the homes were lovely, although the lawns and bushes could use trimming. People in this neighborhood favored brick and stone, and muted earth-tones for their trim. They also cultivated big trees, that stretched their protective limbs over the slate roofs. They probably wouldn't have thought much of the latest green infestation. On top of most of the roofs, and even spilling from some of the windows and front doors, the killer vines had taken over the neighborhood. The vines held their ground at the houses, not venturing out into the yards. That's why Brad, Lisa, and Romie kept to the center of the street. They wanted plenty of notice if the vines decided to close on their path.

"Let him rest," Lisa shouted. "We should get these ready anyway."

Lisa gestured to her backpack. They'd stuffed it with empty plastic bottles and rags. Romie carried the gasoline. They crouched in the street to bring their ingredients together. Brad rested as Romie and Lisa poured the gas into bottles and stuffed the top with rags. None of them were fully confident that the bombs would work. They agreed that glass would have been better, but they didn't find any glass bottles. The store they raided had already been visited before, and someone had taken all the bottled beer. They were left with a selection of diet drinks in plastic bottles and had settled for those.

As they finished, they packed the bottles carefully into the backpack again. Lisa balanced it on her back like she was carrying dynamite.

They did all this without talking. The music blaring in their ears made casual communication impossible.

"I'm slowing you down," Brad shouted as they huddled together. "You go on without me."

"You know what it looks like," Romie said.

"It's a big rock. If you find it, it will be hard to miss," Brad said.

"Come on," Romie said. "Who cares how slow you are. They're just plants."

Another block up, their street ended with a cul-de-sac. They were roughly following the river of vines—moving to where it seemed the vines were thicker and the clump was wider across. They were hoping to find the source of the infestation. Brad suspected that the source of the vines might be where the rock was located. He cautioned them, of course, that all his thoughts were complete and utter speculation.

Lisa pointed to a path between the two houses. Cutting through the tall grass and weeds, they saw a dirt path stomped into the lawn. Brad scanned the ground as they walked. His eyes locked in on every leaf. He was looking for the leaves—they looked almost like shiny grape leaves—of the killer vines.

They walked in a line. Lisa went first and Romie brought up the rear.

Lisa paused after she ducked under the tree branches. She pointed again. The river of vines was a dozen paces away. It dipped into a creek bed and then ran uphill. They walked parallel to the vines until they saw another set on their other side. The farther they walked, the more the paths of the vines came together. Somewhere up ahead they might join, leaving the trio nowhere to go. Lisa stopped and motioned for them to listen.

Brad could just hear her yell over the top of *Soundgarden* blasting from his headphones.

"Maybe we should try to burn our way through," Lisa said.

Brad shook his head. Romie shrugged. They kept walking.

After a bit, Lisa held up her hand, signaling everyone to slow. They spread out so they could all see what she was looking at. The source of the vines on the right was a creek that cut diagonally across their path. This branch of vines came from the much larger group on their left, and it followed the creek a short distance before emerging to traverse through the woods.

Lisa was looking straight ahead, where a log spanned the depression that held the creek. She approached slowly, ignoring Romie's hand as Romie tried to hold her back.

Lisa waved them forward.

The tree connected the two banks of the creek about three feet above the vines.

Lisa motioned to them. "We could make it."

It wasn't very far from one side to the other, and the tree did look plenty thick enough to be safe to cross. All Brad could think about was slipping on the bark and falling down into the hungry vines. He remembered having one of those things wrapped around his leg, and the pain was excruciating. And that was just one vine. What would happen if a dozen or more suddenly curled around his whole body?

There had been a rumor back at the farm that a man had been torn in two by vines.

Brad shook his head at Lisa's idea.

He mouthed a single-syllable response. "No."

She pursed her lips and turned away. Without warning, Romie walked confidently across the tree. She did it in four easy steps and then turned to wave them across. Lisa looked down at the vines below. She held out a hand for Brad to take, so he could steady himself. On the other side, Romie held out her hand. He would only have a step, maybe two, of walking on his own between the grips of the two women. Brad stepped forward. Music screamed into his ears.

The footing was good and Brad leaned heavily on Lisa's grip as he started. He shuffled fast across the gap and nearly fell into Romie's hand on the other side. He turned, sucking in frantic breaths, to watch Lisa. She had her arms straight out and was walking too carefully. It was too late to say anything. She would just be distracted if Brad tried to offer her advice. But he wanted to tell her that it was like pouring water from a pitcher. You had to move with sure ease, or disaster would result. Romie held out her hand and Lisa took another step. Her hands tilted back and forth as she tried to regain her balance. Her eyes were pointed straight down.

Movement below drew all their eyes. Flowers erupted down the vines. They saw pink, purple, and orange blossoms pop out from brand new buds. They looked like the hungry mouths of baby birds, awaiting a worm.

Lisa's knees were bent now and she swayed wildly. Romie leaned forward even more, trying to offer her hand. Brad leaned out too, but didn't trust his own balance. He was just as likely to take both of them down into the vines.

Lisa took one more step before she slipped. Her foot went right out from under her and she fell. Her hip hit squarely on the log. Romie threw one hand out as far as she could. Brad fell on Romie's legs, steadying her so she wouldn't fall too.

Lisa threw out a hand. Blind luck connected Lisa and Romie's hands and they gripped tight. It wasn't enough to keep Lisa atop the log. When she screamed, Brad heard it over the music in his ears. Romie pulled and Lisa kicked. Her other hand found a branch of the fallen log. Her foot dipped into the river of vines. Romie pulled and Lisa flailed. Brad pulled on Romie. When Lisa's other hand grabbed at a bush, Brad caught her wrist. Together, Romie and Brad pulled Lisa to the bank.

A vine was cinched around her leg. Flowers opened up in a spiral, from her ankle to her thigh. The flexible tip of the vine probed at the tail of Lisa's shirt.

Lisa's screaming mouth was turned up towards the sky. Brad saw blossoms of blood appear on her pants. Romie had her knife out. She was reaching it towards the base of the vine near Lisa's foot.

"NO!" Brad screamed. He wasn't loud enough. Romie couldn't hear him through her own music. Brad shot his hand out and caught Romie's wrist. Her knife dug into his forearm before she could stop the momentum of her swing.

Brad pushed off his headphones in time to hear Romie. "What are you doing?"

He barely heard the question. This time, it wasn't because of the ringing music, it was because of Lisa's screams.

Brad pulled the long lighter from his back pocket. It was for the bombs, but now needed it for something else. Romie stopped his hand as he had stopped hers a second earlier. She took the backpack from Lisa and tossed it several feet away. The thing was full of bottles of gas, capped only with rags.

With the explosive backpack away, Brad triggered the lighter. At the end of its shaft, the flame looked tiny in the morning light. He held it under the base of the vine, near Lisa's foot. She screamed louder as the vine tightened its grip. The moist plant began to smoke and turn black under the flame. It would take forever to burn through, but he didn't think that was entirely necessary. He only wanted to drive it off—to convince it to move on.

The first response of the vine after it tightened was the disappearance of the flowers. They folded up like umbrellas and receded into the vine. Then, so fast it seemed like an illusion, the vine unwound. In a second, it slipped back into the creek bed, leaving Lisa moaning and gripping her own thigh.

Brad's body pulsed with adrenaline. When Romie grabbed Lisa's arm, Brad found he had no problem grabbing her other arm and helping her up. They ran at a slow shuffle away from the vines. Romie stooped to pick up the backpack.

Something snapped in the woods and Brad fumbled his headphones back into place. After a few more steps, Lisa was able to limp along on her own. Through the woods, they saw the backs of some buildings up ahead. They slipped through the hole in a fence and found themselves on the edge of another overgrown yard.

They put their heads together for a conference. Each lifted a headphone partially away from an ear so they could hear.

"The vines are even thicker over there, but they take up the whole space between those buildings. We'll have to go through that building and see if we can pick them up on the other side," Romie said. She pointed at the back of a building that might have been a bar, or maybe even a small garage. It was hard to tell from the back, especially with the overgrown bushes.

"We don't need to," Brad said.

They looked at him.

"I think that's our goal," he said. He pointed and waited for them to line up to see what he saw. Between two buildings and across the street, he'd spotted a big pile of new dirt. It looked like some giant burrowing creature had made a den under the big brick building on the other side of the street. Mud was slung up the side and sprayed across the columns. On one side of the mound, they could just see the corner of a black hole that led underground.

"What is it?" Lisa asked.

"I don't know," Brad said. "But there was one at my house. The government guy said it was a breeding hole, but I don't think he knew any more than we do."

"Let's burn it," Romie said.

CHAPTER 37: FARM

THEY SAT AT THE kitchen table. Hampton sat in the chair next to the window and kept an eye on the driveway. Cedric had his head in Robby's lap, and the boy scratched ceaselessly behind the dog's ears. Tim and Ty told quick versions of their stories.

Jackson wasn't as forthcoming. "Nothing happened. Everyone disappeared, so me and Amy Lynne took the house on the point. That's all."

Hampton looked down at Amy Lynne's ankle, wrapped up in its air cast. His look seemed to challenge Jackson's assertion, but Jackson offered no more explanation.

Amy Lynne broke the silence. "How did you get here?"

Robby looked at Hampton. The man was quiet. Robby told a quick version of his own story. He only touched on the big movements—leaving the island, settling in Portland, seeing the ball of light, and traveling to the farm.

When he finished, the table was silent again.

"I've never been much of a conspiracy person," Tim said, "but I guess I assumed that this whole thing was an attack by a foreign government. Some new weapons from China or something."

"Really?" Ty asked. He looked at Tim like he was seeing him for the first time.

"I guess I didn't think about it too hard. Stuff happened and I reacted," Tim said. He blushed.

Ty turned to Robby. "Is that what's going to happen here? The snow and the ball of light are going to happen again here?"

"I think so," Robby said. "Let me ask you something—how did you happen to come exactly here? Did you happen to see anything? Did you see some kind of symbols or anything that led you here?"

Ty and Tim glanced at each other, but neither man responded.

Jackson looked confused. "Didn't you see something in that Chinese store?"

Tim looked off towards a corner.

"Yeah," Ty said.

"We weren't going to mention it," Tim said. "It seemed like something maybe we shouldn't discuss. I don't know why, exactly." Tim leaned back and dug his hand into his pocket. He slapped a USB drive down on the table. "You have a computer?"

✪ ✪ ✪ ✪ ✪

"I've logged you in as a guest, but you should be able to view your photos," Hampton said.

They all crowded around a rugged laptop that Hampton set on the edge of the table.

"Will this automatically preview the pictures?" Tim asked. "Because if it does, we have to turn that off."

"No need," Robby said. He took control of the laptop and plugged in Tim's USB drive. Before he opened the folder, he turned to address the group. "Everyone cover one eye. Like this." He demonstrated, holding one hand up in front of his left eye. "You all have use of both eyes, correct?"

"Yes," they all answered eventually.

"Good. Then you just need to cover one eye to be safe."

Robby opened the images. He flipped through a couple. Tim had taken pictures of the sides of buildings, rock walls, hallways, and even one parking lot as seen from above. The one thing they all had in common was the symbols. Most were dark maroon, or red, like they'd been written in blood. Some images also contained a corpse lying nearby. In one, an eviscerated deer was visible in the corner.

Amy Lynne gasped and Jackson helped her limp away from the laptop.

Cedric wouldn't look at the screen. He curled up under the table.

"Why can we look at them if we cover one eye?" Tim asked.

"I don't know," Robby said. He turned to Hampton. "We're going to need a printer."

Robby worked for an hour, sending the images out to the printer in the little room. It smelled slightly of ammonia and other chemicals that Robby couldn't identify. The printer sucked in giant paper, three-feet wide, from a thick spool and the output piled on the floor. Tim came in for the next piece. Like everyone, he had a piece of tape over one eye. He bumped into a table on his way to the printer and cursed under his breath.

"How many more?" Tim asked.

"Maybe a dozen. How does it look?" Robby asked.

"I think we're almost done."

Robby helped Tim collect the rest of the posters and they walked them out to the main room. Ty could reach the ceiling without the ladder, so he was taping up the images to the top of the wall. Hampton was working on a couple near the center.

Amy Lynne, Jackson, and Cedric were still up above. The girl and the dog couldn't handle the ladder, and Jackson stayed with them in case there was trouble.

Tim consulted the laptop. "It looks pretty good, I think."

Robby handed his latest printouts to Hampton and then he returned to the center of the room. The printouts of the symbols were pasted on the walls of the big room. A couple of the symbols were too small. He directed Ty to rotate one of the symbols near the ceiling. It was only off by a few degrees, but it was enough for Robby to notice.

"We're missing a couple over here," Robby said. He pointed to a spot beside one of the machines. "It was just beyond the corner of one of your pictures."

"Sorry," Tim said.

Robby shrugged. "I saw it too. It was at the edge of a mural I saw in a basement near my house. I could only memorize so much, so I missed that one piece. Bad coincidence that we missed the same thing."

Hampton finished his work and came towards the center of the room. "Is that it? Did we recreate your vision?" he asked Robby.

Robby had been the first to see it, but everyone had agreed quickly—the symbols shown in Tim's photos formed a chain. If you lined up the edges, they were like little snapshots of the inside of a cylinder. Arranged properly, they would form a circle. Now that they'd printed them all out, Robby stood at the center of that circle.

Ty finished his adjustment and he joined the others at the laptop. Tim flipped through the images. He rubbed his taped-up eye and used his other eye to compare the images on the screen to what they'd hung. Everyone looked between the laptop and the walls and nodded their agreement.

"If just one of these images put me out for several minutes, what's the whole bunch of them going to do to a person?" Ty asked.

"We'll see," Robby said. "But I have an idea that it will be okay."

"How can you say that?" Tim asked with a little laugh. "I avoided looking at those things like the plague, at least until you showed us the one-eye trick. I'm with Ty—I'm kinda nervous just being in the room with all these things."

"We should be cautious," Robby said. "You guys leave the room and I'll look. If I don't come out in five minutes, then come in after me. But be careful."

"Why?" Ty asked.

"Who knows what the sight will do to me," Robby said.

"This man outweighs you by about a buck-fifty, Robby. I think we'll be okay," Tim said.

Robby didn't get a chance to respond.

"You're not looking at it alone," Hampton said. "I'm going to look too. You guys get out of here and give us a minute, will you?"

Tim and Ty glanced at each other and then looked back to Hampton and Robby. After a second, they acquiesced and turned for the door. When they were safely in the side room, Hampton turned to Robby.

"I'm taking your word that these symbols do anything at all. They only reason I even half believe you is that you mentioned them before these guys showed up, and then they had the same story."

Robby shrugged.

"I recommend you close both eyes, take the tape off, and then open them both to let it hit you all at once," Robby said. Robby already had the tape off his eye and his eyes firmly shut as he finished his instructions. With his head pointed down and his eyes shut, he climbed up onto the chair and stood, putting his arms out to his sides for balance.

Robby opened his eyes and took in the mural.

He saw nothing but the symbols. He'd printed them in red, just in case it made a difference. It wasn't the dark maroon of the originals—that color seemed hard for the massive printer to reproduce. This red was brighter, like a barn instead of dried blood. The images surrounded him, so less than half were in his field of view. Still, it felt like he could sense the symbols behind him. The whole thing, the entire three-sixty mural of symbols, was like a hologram, forming a giant picture for him.

The hologram formed a living history that was too big to fit inside his head. He felt like he'd been dropped into a giant tank of water, and he was trying to drink his way to the bottom. The information filled him. Like Romie, he saw back to one of the early arrivals when the world was filled with enormous reptiles. Like in the cellar of Irwin Dyer, he saw a vision of an egg, filled with light. He hadn't told anyone about that vision, but it came back to him in a flood of sensation.

He saw the lifecycle of the alien that had impregnated the Earth. First, it cleared away its nest. Next, it set a snare to collect its deutoplasm, the food it would use to sustain early development. Then, the temperature would be regulated for the incoming embryo. Robby saw it all, including the mistakes he had made when he had hauled the corpses north through the snow.

Robby lost his balance and tumbled from the chair. He realized when he broke his eyes away from the mural that he had been spinning. As he fell he was facing the opposite side of the room. Hampton landed on his knees next to him.

A big smile spread over Hampton's face.

"What are you so happy about?" Robby asked.

"We were right," Hampton said.

The lights went dim and a klaxon sounded.

"What's happening?" Tim yelled from the doorway.

"It's beginning," Hampton said.

CHAPTER 38: BOX

JUDY RUBBED HER WRISTS. The red mark from the cuffs was almost gone. She lifted a hand and pressed it against the thick glass. The flowers were beautiful. The purple almost seemed to glow. She suspected that it was one of those flowers that showed up really well in a spectrum that the human eye couldn't quite see. The center of the blossom didn't contain the little pollen-delivering structures of a normal flower. There was a bundle of red and blue veins there.

Everything was so still on the other side of the glass. It could have been a painting. Then, all at once, the vines shifted and swam. She almost lost her balance looking at them. Judy smiled. She couldn't hear it, but she could feel the thunk as they called to her with their strange, hypnotic song.

"I saw two vines only half that big tear a man into several discrete pieces," one of the bearded men said over her shoulder. At one time, she had thought that all the bearded men were the same. The differences were so obvious. Ones like Frank, who had simply joined up because they'd fallen under the spell of a charismatic leader, were soft and reasonable. The man behind her barely had a beard at all. The hair on his face was sparse and patchy. But, despite the patchy facial hair, this man was hard. She could see it in his eyes and hear it in his voice.

"I think they're pretty," Judy said.

"It takes three generators to supply enough power to keep

those things out of this box. If any one of those generators goes down, you're going to find out how dangerous those vines are."

"I'll take your word for it."

"A researcher in Guatemala found fossilized specimens of those vines. They were coiled so tight around skeletons that they were fused to the bones. Their thorns had pierced into the marrow."

"Why are you telling me this?" Judy asked.

"I thought you should understand what you've chosen to align yourself with."

"Why do you people have to turn everything into a war? I'm not out fighting on the side of these vines," she said, gesturing towards the window. "I've simply chosen not to fight the inevitable. All our history lives in that thing. Did you realize that? Every good memory you've ever had is waiting for you. The time in your life that you felt the most secure—you could be right back in that moment. I've seen it."

"It's an illusion," the man said. "It feeds on our consciousness. What you saw was the digested remains of your memories. I prefer not to be food for some alien."

Judy laughed. "You really have no idea what you're talking about. Who came up with that? It's just absurd. You can't trust an organization which favors loyalty over critical thinking."

"I know one thing for sure—in the history of life on this planet, one threat keeps returning. It's a ruthless, emotionless, monster that doesn't even comprehend that we are living, sentient beings. This thing is so big and so powerful that it can stomp us from existence without even breaking a sweat. The fight is so important, that the instructions on how to defeat it are encoded in our very DNA. We know ninety-nine percent of what we need to do here, Judy. We will win. You've experienced something that very few people survive. You may have knowledge that will help us finalize that final one percent. If you accept our victory as inevitable, and share what you know, you might help us win this battle with a little less loss of life."

Judy turned away from the man and pressed her hand against the window again. "You talk about this thing like it's evil."

"It is."

"What's more evil—to simply want to live and grow, or to sacrifice your own friends in order to fight some imagined battle?"

"This thing has no regard for us."

"That's right. It's like a tree that's growing in the center of a termite hill. If you hadn't noticed, the termites were poisoning the soil anyway. Maybe the tree will have better luck."

He didn't reply. He walked through the door and disappeared for several minutes. When he came back, he was even less friendly.

"You're going to be part of the solution, one way or another," he said.

The man hit a button on the wall next to the door. The door slid up and out of sight. Judy heard the gentle hiss coming from speakers and felt hot air float through the door. The man stepped out and gestured to someone Judy couldn't see. A second later, two more bearded men came through the door and motioned for her to step out. Judy rubbed her wrists again. She learned her lesson earlier—when she didn't comply, they got rough. Judy walked between the men.

They led her outside. The sun was up over the trees. The walkway was made of metal and felt warm under her shoes. The vines were piled on either side of the walk, but they didn't trespass on the metal. Judy didn't see where the other man had gone. She could run, but where would she go? The walkway was the only place safe from the vines and the two men walked directly behind her. The walkway took a left and led towards a cluster of buildings. She could just see the brick walls under the carpet of vines draped over the structures. The vines were everywhere.

The walkway ended at a circular pad. It was just big enough for Judy to stand on alone. She turned back to her escorts.

"Stand on the pad," one man said.

"What if I refuse?" Judy asked.

"Then we'll pitch you into the vines. They don't discriminate."

Judy sighed. When she stepped onto the pad and turned around, she saw where the other man had gone. On top of the metal box where she had spoken with him, there was another room. He must have climbed up there after leaving her. She saw his face through a window.

One of her escorts held a box that looked like a remote control. He pointed it at her feet and pressed a button. When he did, the hot metal under her shoes went cold. She looked down. The vines responded immediately. They began to creep over the edges of the pad.

One vine curled around her left ankle. It tickled at first. Judy heard a moan from somewhere in the still morning. She looked up. A sharp pain lit up her left foot like a bee sting.

"Ow!" Judy said.

She tried to shake the vine from her foot and felt it curl up her calf. It wasn't moving up her leg, it was growing. With each inch the thing curled, it sunk another thorn through her pants. All at once, like they were simultaneously releasing venom, the pricks of the thorns burned with hot fire into her flesh. Judy screamed and the strength poured from her legs. She fell backwards.

✪ ✪ ✪ ✪ ✪

Judy was caught by a soft bed of vines. Her next scream was cut off by vines that encircled her chest and tightened around her neck. All she could manage was a gurgle. Breathing became difficult as the vines constricted. She was reduced to tiny puffs of air. Her head swam.

Judy felt herself carried backwards. She saw her escorts growing smaller and smaller. They weren't moving–*she* was. The vines were transporting her on their leafy fingers.

Judy's face was turned up towards the sky. She could only move her eyes, and saw little but blue sky, the side of a vine-covered building, and passing limbs of vine-choked trees. The thorns immobilized her in a cocoon of pain. The fire pulsing through her nerve endings overloaded her brain and she felt reality slipping away.

She didn't know how much time had passed. It could have been a minute or an eternity. The only thing that was real was the pain. She felt herself turn.

She saw an arm. The vines rotated her and she saw the torso

that the arm was connected to. It took her a second to recognize the face. It was twisted by a pain that must have been equal to what she felt. The man was Bill Cody. Judy hadn't spoken to him since they had sat in Woolly's kitchen. They didn't speak now. Neither one of them had the capacity.

Judy turned and saw other people she recognized. All the people she remembered from the camp were twisted up in the sea of vines. She even saw some of the bearded men in the vines. They were set up like an audience, but the thing they were pointed to was just a low spot in the carpet of green.

She struggled to make a noise, but all that came out was a choked gurgle.

Judy blinked and felt a fresh vine curl over her forehead. No matter how she strained her muscles, she couldn't move an inch.

Something reddish brown caught her eye. Judy realized that a few yards away, one set of eyes looking towards the clearing didn't belong to a human. One of the horses from the farm was ensnared and was held with its legs tucked under itself. White foam leaked from the horse's nostrils as it panted shallow breaths.

A single tear leaked from Judy's eye and she felt another tendril of vine curl across her cheek to intercept its path.

CHAPTER 39: HOLE

ROMIE HELD THE BOTTLE. She nodded to Brad.

His music was still blaring in his ears, and he couldn't hear the lighter as he clicked the trigger. The rag burst into orange flames and Brad worried the bottle might explode right in Romie's hand. She cocked it back and threw it towards the hole.

Romie threw like a quarterback. She tossed the bottle in a tight spiral with the burning rag in the lead. Before it reached the hole, the bottle started to tumble. The rag popped out and fell to the ground. The gas sprayed from the tumbling bottle. The bottle continued its trajectory towards the hole, but the gas wasn't on fire. The only thing burning was the rag, which lay in the dirt.

Romie looked to Lisa.

Lisa nodded and stuffed the rag tighter into the next bottle. She handed it to Romie and they repeated the process. The rag stayed in this one, and it hit the dirt right next to the big hole. Lisa handed another bottle as the second bottle rolled down into the darkness.

They were on their fourth bottle before smoke began to pour from the hole.

As Romie threw the sixth bottle, they saw the tops of flames dancing at the edge of the darkness.

They lit and threw bottles until they exhausted their supply.

Romie removed her headphones. Brad and Lisa did the same.

"I don't think it's working," Romie said.

They heard a low whooshing sound and a big puff of smoke erupted from the hole. It was followed by even higher flames.

"What do we do now?" Lisa asked.

Romie's eyes grew wider. She was looking between Brad and Lisa—over their shoulders. They turned to see what she was looking at.

Brad's mouth dropped open, and he remembered something from a time before the world had ended. It was only a day or two after he'd discovered the vines in his back yard, and it was the first time he'd met one of the casually-dressed government guys. The man's name was Herm—it was an absurd name for a very serious man. Standing in Brad's driveway, he had asked, "Did you see any out of place puddles, patches of fog, boulders, piles of sand, or lava flows?"

The last item was crazy. That's exactly what Brad was seeing now. Across the path they'd taken on their approach to the hole, their retreat was now blocked by a flow of molten lava. The liquid rock flowed and churned. It glowed with heat. The heat was just reaching their faces as they watched it roll.

"Where did it come from?" Lisa asked. Her voice was just a whisper. It was barely as loud as the music that still leaked from the headphones around Brad's neck.

Romie pointed. They looked upstream and saw the source of the lava. It was flowing from a crack in the pavement. Bubbling up from the ground, it set off in three directions. Each arm of lava was at least three feet across, and they seemed to be getting wider with each passing second.

Brad spun. They had the burning hole in one direction, vines on their sides, and the glow of the lava behind them. The lava flowed right into the thicket of vines.

"Can we jump it?" Lisa asked.

"Do we have a choice?" Romie asked.

"We could try to climb around the hole," Brad said, pointing.

"What's on the other side of that pile of dirt? More vines?" Romie asked.

An explosion erupted from the hole. The blast of air knocked the three of them to the ground. Brad gripped the ground, which was still shaking. Dirt and mud began to rain down from the sky. Lying on the pavement, they covered their heads with their hands as sand and dirt came down for several seconds.

"What is it?" Lisa yelled.

Brad lifted his head and looked towards the hole.

The falling dirt ended and was replaced with a much gentler precipitation. Light snow began to fall from the sky and a cold wind blew over them.

CHAPTER 40: FARM

ROBBY WAS THE FIRST up the ladder. They had left the klaxon behind in the big room, but he could still hear the alarm reverberating up from below. Mixed with that sound, he heard Hampton, who was giggling to himself. Robby wondered if the man might have gone a little crazy when he'd witnessed the vision in the symbols. It had nearly overpowered Robby, with all the sights and colors of an ancient world, but Hampton seemed like he was pretty well unhinged. Robby hurried. He didn't like the idea of Hampton being close enough to grab him.

As Robby pulled himself through the hatch, he knew that something big was coming. There was almost a hollow feeling in the little shed, like someone was letting the air out of the world. He swallowed to pop his ears and heard a brisk wind picking up outside.

Hampton's giggles turned into a laugh as he came out of the hatch. His eyes were wild with excitement.

"I told you it would come early," Hampton said to Robby. He had a big smile on his face. "The tornadoes are already here."

Robby studied the man's face. Whatever he had experienced from the vision, he hadn't gotten the whole thing. If he had, he would know why the tornadoes were here early.

"It's because we recreated the mural," Robby said.

Tim came up out of the ground and they had too many people in the little shed, especially with Ty on his way up. Robby opened the door and the wind took the handle out of his grip.

"The tornadoes come to try to erase the murals," Robby said.

Tim agreed immediately, even though he was just joining the conversation. "I've seen that happen."

They spilled out into yard as Ty began to climb from the hatch. The morning sky had a weird glow from the gathering clouds above. The low clouds seemed to be materializing from nothing. To Robby, the pink clouds looked like cotton candy being spun out of the air. The tendrils swirled and gathered above.

"Where are the kids?" Ty asked. He said something else, but the wind picked up and swept away his words.

"There," Tim said. He pointed towards the driveway. The lights of the ambulance flashed and began to roll backwards, away from them.

Tim broke into a run. The rest followed him to the place where the ambulance had been. He pulled up to a stop. Robby reached his side and saw why. The ambulance was sitting in the front yard of the house. Its wheels were cranked to the side. Jackson was behind the wheel, but he was looking behind himself instead of where the ambulance was beginning to roll.

Ty took a step backwards.

The ambulance bucked and then lurched forward.

They scattered to get out of the way and the ambulance ground to a halt. Ty ran to the door and whipped it open.

"Get in back," he said.

Tim opened the rear door and they piled in.

Robby turned to look out the open door as he stepped up inside. The funnel clouds were gathering on the horizon. The nearest one was at the other side of the pasture. It was dipping towards trees. Limbs thrashed back and forth. Tim stepped in and closed the door behind him.

Ty turned around from the driver's seat.

"Where are we going?"

Robby looked at Hampton. "Where did you take everyone?"

Hampton gave him another chilling smile. "High school."

"Point the way," Robby said.

✪ ✪ ✪ ✪ ✪

As Ty drove away from the farm, Robby pressed his face to the little window in the back of the ambulance door so he could see the destruction. His view was quickly blocked by hills and trees, but he could see the funnel clouds when they rose back up to the clouds overhead. The sky flashed with debris carried by the wind. As the clouds thickened overhead, a light snow began to fall. It didn't stick to the warm pavement.

There was nowhere to sit, even if Robby wanted to. Tim, Amy Lynne, and Cedric sat on the stretcher. Hampton sat in the paramedic's seat. Hampton looked crazy, but he fed directions to Ty. They passed more houses and buildings as they approached the town.

Ty drove aggressively. Robby steadied himself against the side of the ambulance as it swayed through turns.

Through his rear window, Robby saw a patch of brown and withered-looking vines stretching across the road. Ty had driven right through them.

"Here. Up here," Hampton said. "That's the spot."

When the ambulance came to a stop, Robby figured out the latch and opened the rear door. He stepped down on the bumper and stopped. They were in a clear spot of pavement, but the rest of the parking lot was overrun with the withered vines. A few feet away from the side of the ambulance, he saw wilted flowers on the vines. They looked dead.

Robby dropped to the pavement. The asphalt was wet from the falling snow. The leaves on a vine-choked tree were curling in the frigid air.

"What is all this?" Tim asked. He stepped out and was quickly followed by Cedric. The dog approached the plants cautiously and sniffed at the brown vines.

"This is the place it prepared for itself. It was never going to be at the farm, was it?" Robby asked.

Hampton laughed as he climbed out. He didn't waste any time. He strode through the withered vines towards a small metal building which sat in the middle of the parking lot. It looked like it had been constructed by stacking one shipping container on top of another one.

The driver's door closed and Ty joined them. He put out his giant hand and let a few flakes of snow land on his palm. They melted quickly.

"What is this place?" Ty asked.

"Stage Two," Robby said. "Almost Stage Three. Somewhere around here, the final portal is opening and the egg will be fertilized."

"What do we do?" Tim asked.

"Nothing!" Hampton yelled back at them. He climbed rungs built into the side of the metal building. Robby saw movement behind the window on the second level of the shipping container building. Hampton climbed to the top and then disappeared into a hole up there. His shape reappeared at the window.

"Nothing?" Ty asked.

"They believe that the process can't be stopped until the Stage Four, so they're waiting it out."

"I should have looked at that damn mural myself," Tim said. "No offense, kid, but I would feel a lot better about this if I'd seen the information firsthand." He and Ty exchanged a glance.

"No offense," Robby said, "but you might have gone insane, like Hampton."

Jackson and Amy Lynne were just getting out of the ambulance. He handed her crutches and helped support her until she got her balance.

"It's snowing? What are we doing here?" she asked. "It's freezing out."

Robby stepped into the vines. At first he stayed in the trampled path that Hampton had left behind. The vines crunched under his shoes. It felt like walking through leaves in the fall. As he got closer to the metal building, Robby veered right. He saw the metal walkway leading away from the makeshift headquarters and he followed that. After a turn, the walkway ended and Robby struck out through the vines again. He saw where they looked greener and fresher up ahead. He walked towards that spot.

He heard Ty and Tim debating behind them, but he couldn't

hear what they were saying. He didn't wait to find out.

Robby stopped. To his left, under the bed of wilted vines, he saw an orange glow. He followed it farther and got a better look. It looked like molten rock flowing over the pavement, or maybe even in a channel cut in the pavement. The vein of lava appeared to be getting wider.

Robby held out his palm and got closer. He felt only a little heat coming from the flow.

The snow was falling harder and making it more difficult to see. The flakes were melting as they hit him. He wanted to run, but forced himself to walk so he could watch carefully where he stepped. Although the vines he was walking through were dead, he suspected that the same might not be true up ahead.

The school buildings were off to his right. They were brick, and covered in wilted vines.

He kept moving towards where the vines looked greener. He turned to look behind himself. He saw Ty and Tim starting out across the brown vines. Tim was turned, trying to coax Cedric to follow him. The dog wouldn't leave the bare pavement.

Robby looked down to be sure he was still following the glowing rock. It was hard to see under all the vines, but he spotted a line of it a few paces away. His course took him to the left of the school buildings. Across the vine-covered street, he saw an automotive repair shop. The vines creeping up the face looked more lively. Robby headed that direction. As he grew closer, he noticed that the heat coming from the lava was hotter. The snow was replaced with a light fog, like the flakes were sublimating because of the heat.

Robby turned one more time and saw Tim and Ty back at the ambulance. He saw no movement at all from the metal bunker where Hampton had disappeared. If he was still in there, he was hiding behind the thick glass of the second-story window.

Robby slowed as he walked towards the greener vines. He remembered Brad's story about their thorns and how they constricted. He knew from his journey into the visions from the mural that the vines would ensnare animals to use as fuel for the embryo.

He reached out a foot and tapped his toe on a vine that was wilted, but still green. The thing twitched when Robby's foot hit it, but then the life seemed to drain from the plant. With the twitch, its green color ebbed away, leaving it as brown and lifeless as the ones underfoot.

Robby took a tentative step. One time, Robby had stepped on a snake. The vines felt like that. They squirmed under his shoe, but quickly came to a stop. A circle of brown death spread from the spot where his foot had landed. He took another step and waited for the vines to die down before he brought his feet together.

Robby looked up. He could almost see around the corner of the next building, where the vines were even more green and the undersides of the leaves glowed orange from the pulsing lava.

"Robby?" someone shouted. Robby turned to see who had called to him. The first thing he saw was the dirt. He'd been so focused on the vines, that he'd missed the pile behind the garage.

CHAPTER 41: SITE

IT WASN'T BLACK IN there anymore. The hole was glowing with red fire, like it led down into hell itself. They were still several paces from the mouth of the hole. It seemed to be as close as they could force themselves to get to the pit.

"I'd rather take my chances with the vines," Romie said.

"You'll take certain death over the risk of death?" Brad asked.

"If the risk looks like that, then yes," Romie said.

"We can stay here," Lisa said. "The snow has stopped." She looked up at the sky.

"It hasn't stopped, it's just melting before it gets to the ground," Brad said. He looked off to the adjacent building, where they could see that snow was falling by the wall even though at their location, it wasn't reaching the ground.

"Is that?" Lisa asked. She yelled, "Robby?"

Brad and Romie turned to follow her line of sight.

Brad waved his arms over his head and yelled too. "Robby! Over here."

They stood, unbelieving, as Robby walked across the vines that hemmed them in. His face showed a trace of relief.

"I was hoping you were still okay," Robby said. "Have you seen Pete or Judy?"

"No," Brad said. "Weren't they evacuated?"

"Wait a second," Romie said. "Before we get into a big family reunion, did anyone notice that Robby just walked straight across the vines that were trying to kill us?"

"These are dead," Robby said. "Or dying. They're concentrating their energy around the site."

"Let's get the hell out of here then," Romie said. "We tried our best to burn the thing, now let's go."

Robby nodded at Romie's statement, but seemed to ignore it. "They weren't evacuated. That was a lie from the guys that Pete calls the Beardos. They were collecting enough people here for Stage Three. They don't think that the thing can be stopped until it reaches Stage Four, so they're helping it along."

"They're *helping* it?" Lisa asked.

Robby took a few steps closer to the hole. Except for the size of the thing, it looked like a hole a rodent might make. Dirt was piled around it and splattered up the side of the auto shop.

"Don't get too close," Brad said. "There's lava in there."

"I have to go inside," Robby said.

"What?" Romie asked.

Their attention was suddenly drawn to the alley between the buildings, where Robby had come from. They heard the roar of an engine bouncing off the brick walls and they all took a cautious step backwards as the ambulance skidded to a stop in the vines.

The driver's door opened. Ty was behind the wheel.

Tim leaned over him and spoke. "That crazy guy, Hampton, is getting ready to do something."

✪ ✪ ✪ ✪ ✪

They didn't bother with introductions. Ty and Tim stepped out of the vehicle and Cedric appeared next in the doorway. The dog looked carefully at the ground before he lightly jumped down.

"They're gearing up," Tim said. "They've got these big suits they're strapping on, and some kind of guns or something."

"Good," Romie said. "Maybe they know how to kill the thing."

"No," Robby said. "They won't touch it until it's impregnated."

They heard the back door of the ambulance bang open. After a few seconds, Jackson appeared, propping up Amy Lynne.

"I'm going to need some help," Robby said. He looked to Brad.

"Doing what?" Brad asked.

"We have to go in the hole," Robby said.

"Wait a second," Romie said. "Those guys think they know what they're doing. Why don't we give them a chance and see if they're right?"

"Because their approach involves sacrificing everyone who was at the farm. Somewhere around here, they're all being held prisoner. There are one-hundred and fifty people who will die if we don't stop the process. Pete is probably among them. And Judy."

"Why would they sacrifice everyone left?" Lisa asked. "What's the point of saving the world if everyone is gone?"

"They only want to beat it," Robby said. "They're not concerned with the cost. They believe that the organism can't be destroyed until it has been fertilized. The fertilization requires the sacrifice."

"You think you can save those people if you go in the hole?" Brad asked.

"Yes," Robby said. "According to the mural, there's another way. It's not easy, but there is one way to drive it off before it takes those people."

Brad rubbed the back of his neck.

"I'll go with you," Tim said. "Is it safe?"

Robby shook his head no.

Ty glanced at Tim and then the two moved as one towards the lip of the hole. The orange glow from the hole lit up their faces. They began to lower themselves to the dirt so they could climb down. Cedric walked slowly up next to them and followed.

Robby glanced back at Brad.

"I can't move very fast," Brad said.

Lisa still favored her one leg, but she moved up and took one of Brad's arms as Romie took the other. The three of them followed Robby as he approached the hole.

"I have to stay here with Amy Lynne," Jackson said. It didn't sound like an excuse, it sounded like a complaint. He genuinely seemed upset that he couldn't go with everyone else. Amy Lynne took his hand.

"Find a rope if you can," Ty said to Jackson. "Lower it down so we'll have a way back up. This is steep."

✪ ✪ ✪ ✪ ✪

They slid down the dirt. The glowing lava swirled its patterns up the side of the hole, somehow sticking to the underside of the tube that the group descended. Ty was right—they would need a rope if they ever had designs of getting out of the place. The angle the tube cut into the loose dirt was so steep that they couldn't hope to climb it.

Ty reached the bottom first. He attempted to brush the dark dirt from his scrubs and then gave up. Cedric, who had skidded down most of the slope, bounded down the last few feet and shook himself. Tim arrived next. He turned and looked up. The sky was opaque and gray at the top of the hole. He figured they were at least thirty feet down.

If he were to stretch to the extent of his height, Ty might be able to reach the ceiling of the tube, but Tim would have to jump. Neither were likely to try it. The iridescent metal flowing there wasn't putting off a tremendous amount of heat, but it looked like it would burn to touch.

"What if that stuff drips on us?" Lisa asked as she reached the floor.

Robby was just getting up. He glanced at the lava above and ignored the question.

The cross section of the tunnel was roughly circular. It was lit in orange from the glow of the lava flow running along the ceiling. The walls and floor were nearly smooth, like they had been cut instead of dug.

It dipped and curved up ahead. Robby led the way.

"The rock digs this tunnel," Robby said. "It connects the portal down to the water table."

"How does a rock dig a tunnel?" Tim asked.

They walked quickly.

"It's a moving rock," Brad said. He was back with Romie and Lisa.

"It moves over the surface until it finds a high concentration of gametes," Robby said. "Then it digs these tunnels to allow them to access the egg. We have to stop them from reaching the egg."

"How exactly do we do that?" Tim asked.

"The same way that people and animals have always done it," Robby said. "We'll drive them back with our hands until there are no more."

"And that will save the others?" Lisa asked.

"We'll save as many as we can," Robby said.

"What does that mean?" Lisa asked.

"Each one binds to an animal and uses that animal as its vehicle to reach the portal and the egg," Robby said. "We won't be able to save them all. But, with luck, we should be able to save most of them."

Up ahead, the tunnel was joined by two others. They came together at a spot where a vertical tunnel came up from below. A column of lava flowed up through the center of the vertical shaft and hit the ceiling, where it split into three streams. The column of lava was completely unsupported. It moved, a cylinder of molten rock, up through the center of the shaft until it hit the dirt above and spread out. Robby leaned over the side of the shaft and Lisa sucked in a breath.

"Careful," she said.

Robby inspected the other two tunnels.

"This way," he said, pointing. It was no easy task to follow the path he chose. There was only a thin lip of loose dirt to traverse around the circumference of the shaft. Robby pressed his chest to the side of the wall and moved pretty quick. Dirt tumbled down from the lip and slipped down the shaft, disappearing below. Brad inched forward and looked down. The lava illuminated the depths, and reflected off of liquid far below. He couldn't tell if it was a puddle or a pool, but there was water down there.

Ty went next. He practically ran, using the curve of the wall to catch him. He reached Robby's side on the balls of his feet. Cedric followed fast and Tim took a more cautious approach.

"I can't do that," Romie said.

"Of course you can," Lisa said. She left Romie there. She pressed her back to wall and held Brad's hand until she couldn't reach him anymore. With one shuffling step she could reach Ty's outstretched hand on the other side. She took it slow and somehow made it across.

"You go next," Brad said. "That way you can hold my hand."

"Huh," Romie barked out a short laugh. "If I fell, I'd drag us both down. You go and I'll bring up the rear."

"We'll go together," Brad said. He held out his hand. He went first, but they moved across the lip together. Romie was solid. Brad was the one who slipped. The dirt crumbled beneath his foot and his balance disappeared immediately. Brad's fingers dug into the soft wall, but didn't slow his fall. Romie held him up for a moment, but then she began to slip as well.

Ty's hand caught Brad's wrist and the giant man hauled them up to the passage with ease. Romie's legs spilled over the edge, but Lisa and Tim were there to grab her and haul her up.

Robby was already moving down the tunnel.

It sloped up from the union, and curved to the right. They were spread out as they climbed the tight spiral. The tunnel looped back around until another tunnel split off at a tangent to its direction. There was no lava flowing down the smaller tunnel that split off. Robby inspected the branch, but stayed with the spiral.

Cedric flanked Robby and they climbed together. They came to a spot where another tunnel intersected their path. The lava flow above split, and followed the tunnels to the left and right. Ahead, their tunnel kept going, but it had no lava on the ceiling to light their way.

Robby dug around in his pockets, looking for a light. He always kept a light with him, even if it was just one of those tiny lights. He couldn't find one.

He turned and waited for the others to catch up. They were lagging behind. Above the sound of them climbing and breathing, Robby heard something else. It was a low rumble from Cedric. The hair between the dog's shoulder blades was standing up, and Cedric was beginning to growl. Robby looked in the direction the dog was facing and then he heard it. He heard a snort from the darkness. Something stamped and then pawed at the ground. Robby had a sense what it would be, even before he saw the eyes approaching from the darkness. The big eyes caught the glow of the lava and seemed to burn with orange fire. Next, Robby saw the moisture gathered at the nostrils of the beast. It stamped again and let out a challenging chuff of air.

CHAPTER 42: PORTAL

PETE TRIED TO FOCUS his eyes and realized he had no sense of his own limbs. Everything was numb. He blinked and got the world to resolve itself back into some kind of order again. His body was wrapped in vines. Around his legs and arms, the vines were graced with deep-throated flowers, turned up towards the gray sky.

He wasn't injured. He remembered jumping from the roof to avoid being captured. It took him several minutes to recall how the vines had caught him—swelling beneath him to provide a soft landing that turned into a thorny prison.

About thirty feet away, directly in front of him, his eyes were drawn to a tiny sparkling pinpoint of light. It was dazzling, and too bright to stare at, but he couldn't seem to look away. The light grew to the size of a pea and then a marble. Pete's brain made the connection, although he had tried not to look at the thing the last time he had been in the presence of it. He knew this was the same type of thing he'd traveled north to witness before. It was the thing they'd fed a thousand corpses into. Or, at least, it was the much smaller version at the moment.

He tried to pull his eyes from it. He heard Robby's voice echo in his head. It was a memory from another day. "Don't look at it."

The light made his eyes itch and burn, and somehow prevented him from blinking. Pete tried to raise his hands so he could rub his eyes. He remembered the vines. He couldn't move his arms, or legs, or even his head for that matter. With his eyes still locked on the light, unable to move, he managed to investigate his peripheral vision. The light was hovering a few feet over the ground, above a bed of thick vines. Trapped in the vines, in a semicircle around the light, were other people. They were arranged like an audience for the hovering light.

It grew bigger.

Something thrashed to the right of the light and he heard a low, insect-like crackle and hiss as the vines dragged something forward. He saw it as it came into the sparkling glow. It was a horse. The thing was stretched out on its back. Its nostrils were flared and its mouth was open. The lips were peeled back from the horse's white teeth.

Pete expected the animal to be absorbed into the light, but he was wrong. Instead, the ball of light rose up. Pete's eyes helplessly followed it upwards as the horse moved forward. The vines wrapped the animal's body and it disappeared in a wave of green foliage. Its head tipped up and was the last to be absorbed down into the vines.

The light flared as the horse made a strangled cry from somewhere below.

Pete felt the vines under him began to move.

He tried to yell, but the vine around his throat barely allowed him enough air to breathe. The most he could managed was a croak. He was being conveyed by his bed of vines towards the light. The closer he got to the light, the more it filled his head. He couldn't see the other people and horses trapped in the vines. He could barely see the bubble of snow that surrounded the light's area of influence. All he could see was its dazzling brilliance.

He'd heard the stories from Robby. Inside that light, he might see all his deceased friends and relatives. The draw of the light had been powerful enough to attract Christine, and Brynn, and Nate. Maybe he would see them too. He remembered as the vines drew him even closer—the horse hadn't been allowed to join the light, and it seemed that it wasn't his fate either. The vines thickened at his feet and ankles, and then blanketed his legs. He felt them creeping over his whole body, until only his head was exposed. At this point, he was close enough to the light so that his head was tilted back so he could still see it. Still, he moved forward and down. His legs were numb, but he could feel them moving down.

Finally, his head descended too, until he was wrapped in a cocoon of vines and he descended under the ground. He sensed the dirt walls on his sides, just beyond the grip of the vines. He smelled the damp earth and felt its coolness as he went lower. He was being consumed by the ground.

Pete was able to blink now that the light wasn't capturing his attention. He squeezed his eyes shut against the tickle of the leaves. The itch wouldn't go away. He knew that the itch was burned into his retinas, and would have to heal like a sunburn. He didn't dare to hope that he would live that long.

As the light from the sky was blocked by the vines and the walls of earth around him, Pete saw an orange glow through the vines. There was a column of lava that he caught glimpses of. It seemed to be running up the wall as he descended.

The walls opened up. Pete wondered if the horse was below him. He wondered if the horse had fit down this same tunnel.

As he moved, the only sound he heard was the terrible rustle of the leaves. To Pete, it sounded like the wings of a thousand black beetles rubbing together. It was the dry-mouthed sound from a nightmare. Not more than a few seconds later, he heard something much more horrible. From somewhere deep in the shaft, he heard the slosh of a thick liquid. It was followed by dripping and then another splash.

He didn't want to know what the liquid was, or what could possibly be living down there to make that sound.

Pete realized that his head was free. The vines weren't gripping his skull anymore and he could turn and look where he wanted to. He looked up, hoping to see a round circle of sky up there. If it was still there, it was blocked by all the vines. Below him, the vines seemed to end just beyond his feet. But maybe they went lower—that's as far as he could see. The orange glow of lava didn't penetrate much beyond his current position.

The vines carried him deeper.

He heard the sloshing again and his blood ran cold. He couldn't tell if it was the progressing numbness in his legs, or if his feet were being slowly dipped into whatever liquid was down there.

A new light drew his eyes downward. He saw it. The tunnel was like a well, but this one had only dirt walls instead of stacked rocks or bricks. Only an insane person would drink from this foul well. The dirt walls were visible by the green glow. The light looked fuzzy around the edges, like it was from a foreign spectrum that his eyes couldn't quite decode. It lit up the rippling water.

Pete couldn't see whatever it was that reached up from the dark and closed around his leg. He was surprised to feel any sensation from his numb leg at all, but he felt the cold, slimy grip of whatever it was. He heard water dripping from it as it curled up and around his leg, replacing the grip of the vines. He imagined a giant octopus down there, bleached white from never having seen the sun. It must be the thing giving off the troubling green light.

Like a million tiny needles, he felt the thing penetrating his clothes and then his skin. It seemed that whatever gripped him was working its way between the cells of his legs. Still, the slimy grip advanced higher up his body. It entwined around his waist, and then torso. He saw that he was very near the water now. Pete realized that his head was close enough to the water's surface that his feet must actually be in the water. He slipped farther down and felt his consciousness fading away.

✪ ✪ ✪ ✪ ✪

The pain flooded every cell of Judy's body. She wanted to retreat into her memories, but the light kept her present. She couldn't turn away from the light. It was still growing. What had started out as a pinprick, like a hole in the tapestry of reality, was now the size of a basketball. She felt it burning into her eyes, but she couldn't look away or even blink.

When the vines started carrying the man towards the light, Judy recognized Pete. She had known him vaguely from Portland, but more as Robby's friend. He was one of the optimistic followers who had gone along with Robby's plan to save the world. Now, he was being carried off towards probable death.

The light swelled as Pete disappeared into the vines under it.

Judy felt herself moving forward. There was no sense in struggling. The vines were clamped tight around every part of her body, and the effort only brought more pain.

She wished for the hypnotic ticking noise again, but of course it didn't come. The memories it brought had come with sadness and regret, but also comfort. There was comfort in knowing that she hadn't wasted her life. The memories had convinced her that there was no grand scheme to things. It was a feeling that she suspected many times before, but somehow seeing her childhood again through her adult eyes had been the final nail in the coffin.

Even what should have been the happiest moments of her life were scorched at the edges by disappointment. The upper limit of her joy had been locked in place by that reference point.

Why shouldn't the world end? Why shouldn't the world be rid of the last remaining survivors of the disappointing human experiment?

She felt rage bubble up inside her and then she remembered the face of Robby. He had saved her once, and had never asked for anything in return. In fact, when he had needed help, she left him. He never once complained, and didn't retract his friendship for her.

The vines pulled her closer and closer to the light. They showed no regard for her safety or well being. She had delivered Luke to the vines, but they didn't offer her special treatment. She was stuck in their thorns just like everyone else.

Regret came late. As her feet disappeared under the carpet of vines and she felt herself descending under the light, Judy finally felt regret. She had played a part in the end of humanity, even though the people who had hurt her were already gone. She tried to take a deep breath, but the vines constricted around her chest.

CHAPTER 43: TUNNEL

THE ANIMAL CHARGED FORWARD, until it stood at the crossing of the tunnels. The group shrank back as it screamed and bared its teeth.

Robby took a step closer and the animal gave a snort before stepping closer to him. The reflection of the lava made its eyes glow. Robby saw the front leg rise up and then stamp down at the dirt floor of the tunnel. It tossed its mane with another stamp.

With the next toss of its head, the beast clacked its teeth together and flared its nostrils.

Robby felt Ty's giant arm press him to the side, as Ty brushed by him.

The horse reared up at the giant man and Ty wasted no time. He slid forward with amazing speed and grace. He dodged between the striking feet and drove his shoulder into the horse's chest. It seemed like he was lifting the horse up, but that was impossible. The horse must have been rearing higher to get away from Ty's bear hug. Whatever the reason, the horse's head lifted higher and it crashed into the flow of orange lava on the ceiling.

The glowing fluid splashed out from the confines of its flow and rained down. Ty was protected—blocked from the splashing lava by the body of the horse, but glowing globs of the stuff burned into the horse's head and mane.

Ty slipped to the side and let the animal crash to the ground. He danced out of the way as the horse's thrashing feet pawed sideways. It looked like it couldn't decide if it should run or roll in the dirt, and it was doing a combination of both. Suddenly it sprung up, and Robby saw that the lava had burned away big patches of flesh from the horse's head. Everyone pressed themselves to the side of the tunnel as the horse sprinted between them, running to where the tunnel ended at the vertical shaft. The horse didn't seem to notice. It ran straight for the gap and never slowed or turned.

The horse ran straight and flew through the air until it hit the column of vertical lava. The lava cut through the horse like a bandsaw. Cauterized halves of the horse thrashed and flopped as they disappeared down into the darkness.

They continued on, climbing as the tunnel pitched upward and spiraled around.

Robby explained as they walked. "I saw this in the vision I had from the mural. The thing creates its gamete carriers from local animals. We're lucky that the only thing it had at its disposal was horses and people. It could have been bears or lions."

"Or dinosaurs," Romie said.

"What do these gametes do?" Tim asked.

"They're the things that will fertilize the egg. They've been here forever. That's what makes a place special—the seeds of the thing have been underground the whole time. They're here, and under Stonehenge, and the Pyramids at Giza. Anywhere the thing has landed before. It chooses the site based on the presence of those seeds."

"Even my house?" Brad asked. "There was nothing special about my house."

"Must have been," Robby said. "If the gamete carriers are being created, then it won't be long before the portal opens for the egg. I was hoping we had more time."

"To do what?" Lisa asked.

"We have to destroy the rest of the gamete carriers and stop whatever is creating them before it takes them all."

"Takes all of what?" Brad asked. "The horses?"

"No," Robby said. "The gamete carriers will just as likely be people. That's one of the things it needs the people and animals for. Everyone from back at the farm could be taken over, just like that horse."

There was only a little light in their part of the tunnel and it was difficult to even see where they stepped. Robby was in the lead and he tread carefully, knowing that he could encounter another vertical shaft and slip before he even realized it was there.

He was almost relieved to see little tendrils of lava overhead once again. It gave him enough light to see better and he could climb more confidently.

He stopped when he saw the dark shape ahead of them. Whatever it was, it was in their way and they would need to get beyond it if they wanted to ascend farther.

Robby took another step.

"What is it?" Lisa asked.

"*Who* is it?" Brad corrected her.

"Pete?" Robby asked.

✪ ✪ ✪ ✪ ✪

Cedric growled again as the dark shape lurched forward.

With another step, there was no doubt. The man approaching was Pete. At least it was Pete's body. The movement showed none of Pete's personality. As the face came into the light of the lava, Robby saw nothing of his friend in the features.

Robby realized that the orange glow he had seen in the eyes of the horse wasn't all reflections of lava. Pete's eyes had the same glow, and the orange burned like tiny embers inside his skull. Pete's lips pulled back to show his teeth.

"Pete? Are you okay?" Lisa asked. "Where have you been?"

The shape took another lurching step forward.

Robby watched Pete's legs. When he stepped, the leg would jerk up from the dirt, like a string was attached to his knee. But the second step was more coordinated than the first, and he suspected that the next would be even better.

"That's not Pete," Brad said. "It's Pete's body, but it's not Pete."

"Is this one of the gametes?" Tim asked. "You said we had to destroy the gametes, right?"

"No!" Lisa shouted. "That's Pete. Get the thing out of him."

Pete took another step. Robby watched the leg. It didn't jerk as much this time. The motion was almost natural.

"Stop right there, Pete," Romie said.

The Pete-thing turned to look at her. His next step was in her general direction.

"We'll just move around him," Lisa said. "He moves pretty slow. I'm sure after we kill the embryo or whatever, we can figure out how to..."

The Pete-thing's glowing eyes shifted from Romie to Lisa as she talked. Before she could finish her thought, the Pete-thing charged. None of its earlier movements would have suggested the easy speed with which it now moved. The Pete-thing shot between Robby and Ty before they could even react. Even Cedric barely had time to turn as the Pete-thing ran by.

Brad, who stood right next to Lisa, had the best opportunity to intervene. As Lisa's hands came up defensively, Brad moved into the space directly in front of her. He was the one who took the bulk of Pete's impact. The Pete-thing hit Brad in the chest and Romie tried to interject herself in between them. Brad screamed, and the tunnel was a confusion of limbs and bodies.

Robby got to the fight at the same time as Ty, and they pulled at shoulders and arms, trying to separate Pete from Brad. Robby caught an elbow in the forehead. Blood sprayed out from the pile as people hit the ground. Brad screamed.

With everyone pulling at the Pete-thing's clothes and limbs, Romie and Lisa were the ones to drag him away. They pulled at his feet. His arms thrashed as they pulled him away from Brad. When the Pete-thing lifted its head, Robby saw blood smeared across its face.

Lisa shouted. "Pete! If you're in there, you have to help us fight it."

The women held onto his feet, despite the kicking. The Pete-thing clawed at the dirt, trying to get back to where the others stood. It didn't seem to notice the women behind it, holding it back by the legs.

Brad had a hand clamped to his other forearm. Robby saw the bite as Brad pulled his hand away to inspect it. Blood welled in deep punctures. A patch of skin had been torn away, and the muscle glowed in the orange light.

Brad pressed his hand back over the wound.

"We have to get that disinfected," Ty said. Brad shot him an irritated look.

"No!" Lisa screamed.

Robby turned to see Tim launch a brutal kick right at Pete's head. The Pete-thing got its hands up enough to soften the blow a little, but its head was rocked back by the hit. The Pete-thing gagged, and its head hung to the side, like a hinge in its neck was bent.

Lisa dropped the foot she was holding and ran to stop Tim before he could kick again.

Robby thought the Pete-thing had been incapacitated by the first kick, but he had to revise his assessment. The Pete-thing shot out a hand and caught Lisa's ankle as she ran to its defense.

Her cry was shocked as the Pete-thing pulled her off her feet with one quick jerk.

Lisa landed on the ground and Tim kicked again. With this kick, his toe landed squarely in the back of the Pete-thing's head. Tim jerked his foot back and hopped away. Lisa pulled her ankle from the Pete-thing's grip.

"Is Pete dead?" Romie asked. She dropped a lifeless foot.

"It's not Pete," Brad said.

Robby helped Lisa back to her feet. Ty moved to Tim, who couldn't seem to put much weight on his kicking foot.

Lisa was the last to move on. She stood there, looking down at Pete's body. She didn't dare get too close, even though he looked dead. She joined the rest of the group before they got too far away.

✪ ✪ ✪ ✪ ✪

Ty took care of the next two people they encountered. He moved with deadly speed, as soon as their lurching forms came into focus in the dim light. They saw a woman emerging from the darkness with that same uncoordinated, lurching stride. Before she got full control of her legs, Ty moved forward and swung a massive fist at the side of her neck. She went down in a heap and Ty knelt to check her pulse while the others caught up.

"She's gone," Ty said. His voice sounded sad, but Robby didn't hear any guilt or remorse there.

The next one went in almost the same way. Tim's limp had nearly disappeared and he was walking alongside Ty when they saw the bearded man in their path. Tim and Ty both jumped at him, to catch him while he was still jerking around. But Ty's speed couldn't be matched. He fell on the bearded man in an instant and the body was slumped to the dirt by the time Tim was within striking distance.

Once again, Ty knelt to check the pulse.

If he hadn't, the next few moments might have gone differently. Ty was kneeling next to the body, verifying that he was dead. Tim was looking down, while the others were still catching up. Only Cedric saw the next body coming out of the dark. Robby looked up when the dog barked.

This one was younger—maybe just a teenager—and seemed to have complete control of its limbs. When it began to lunge for Ty, Cedric leapt at it.

The teenager-thing shot out a hand and caught Cedric right under the chin. It held Cedric in mid-air as the dog's legs flopped and clawed at the air.

Ty looked up and was on his feet in an instant. He took a giant step and swung his fist, but the teenager-thing moved Cedric's body into the path of the blow and Ty had to check his swing. The teenager-thing caught Ty's wrist in its other hand. With Ty in his grip, the teenager-thing dropped Cedric and joined both its hands on Ty's arm.

Tim went for the thing's throat and caught him as the teenager-thing bared its teeth.

Ty tried to swing his other fist, but Tim was in the way and his punch had no power. He turned his head towards the lava on the ceiling as the teenager-thing twisted its hands and snapped Ty's arm bones. The spiral fractures of Ty's radius and ulna bones cracked through the tunnel. Robby heard the breaks over the sound of Ty's scream, and then Ty went silent.

Tim had the teenager-thing by the neck. He clamped the thing's neck in the crook of his elbow, and squeezed as he pressed his body to the thing's back.

Robby saw the teenager-thing's eyes widen and then almost pop from their sockets as Tim exerted more and more pressure. The thing let go of Ty's ruined arm and it reached back to claw at Tim. Its nails left bloody red gouges in Tim's flesh, but Tim held tight. He didn't let go as the strength ran out of the thing. He didn't let go as he lowered the thing to the ground. When he finally did let go, Tim stood and kicked the thing in the head. It didn't move.

"Pull it," Ty said. Sweat glistened on his brow. "Pull it and twist it back."

Robby grabbed Ty's lifeless hand and tried to do what the man said. He didn't have the strength to untwist the fractured bones. Romie and Lisa joined him and they managed to hold Ty's hand and wrist still as the giant man twisted his own arm. The bones realigned and Ty cried out again. The man clamped his hand around his broken forearm and settled to the dirt.

Cedric hacked and coughed back to life. He moved a little and then whined.

Ty's voice was deep and quiet. He had to repeat himself to be heard. "I'm going to need a minute."

"We have to push on," Robby said. "If we don't stop it, it will keep making more of these things."

"I understand," Ty said. "But I'm going to be here for a minute."

"Stay here with him," Tim said to Cedric. He cupped the dog's chin in his hand and pointed with the other. Blood ran from the gouges on his arm down to the tip of his finger as he pointed at Ty. "Stay with him."

Cedric stood and walked with his head hung low. The dog moved carefully, like he was in pain. He lowered himself to the ground next to Ty.

"Can you go on?" Romie asked Brad.

Brad kept his hand clamped over the bite on his arm, but he nodded.

They left Ty and Cedric next to the body of the teenager-thing, and continued up the dirt tunnel.

✪ ✪ ✪ ✪ ✪

Robby slowed as he saw the orange light glowing through green leaves up ahead. The others caught up to him. Tim flexed his sore foot. Brad peeled his fingers from the wound on his arm. The bleeding had nearly stopped and only seeped from the bite.

"Vines?" Brad asked.

"Vines," Robby said. "There will be a vertical shaft up ahead. The shaft is where the thing takes people to be converted."

"So what do we do?" Lisa asked.

"We have to destroy the shaft," Robby said. "We have to cut off access to the pool where they're doing the conversion."

"Great," Romie said. "Sounds easy. Who brought the explosives?"

"What exactly is the plan here?" Tim asked. He took a couple of steps forward.

Their spiraling tunnel met another vertical shaft, but this one was behind a veil of green vines. The glow of the lava lit up the leaves enough so they could see the gentle movement. From higher up in the shaft, it seemed like some amount of sunlight was actually making it through the leaves.

Through the curtain of leaves, they saw something big moving. Robby moved closer and ducked down to see. When it passed by a gap in the leaves, he saw the wild eyes of a trapped horse. The vines were lowering the animal down the shaft. The movement made a clattering sound as the leaves brushed together. Robby hated the sound, but he dropped to his knees and crawled closer.

When the dark shape passed the opening and dropped below his view, Robby began to push at the loose dirt at the bottom of their tunnel. He heard the dirt shower down on the leaves as it fell down the shaft. His hands uncovered a potato-sized rock. He threw it in and heard it bounce off the walls of the shaft before splashing down. The more he pushed the dirt, the looser it became. He pushed his way into a sandy pocket of earth that was mixed with round rocks. He pushed it all, and heard the bigger chunks splashing down.

Lisa joined him, and then Romie appeared at his other side.

As they pushed dirt into the shaft, some of the dirt and rocks battered the vines and they lost some of their grip on the wall of the shaft. A little hole opened in the curtain of vines and they could see the shaft.

Thick vines were clustered into cables. They descended through the center of the shaft, presumably lowering the horse slowly towards the bottom. Along the walls, a couple of lines of lava pulsed upwards, flowing against gravity towards the surface.

Robby was digging a hole at the edge of the tunnel, and it was getting harder to push dirt down without slipping towards the shaft. He rolled a big rock towards the lip and gave it a push.

As the rock tumbled over the edge, the tip of a vine curled towards Robby's hand and then wrapped a quick coil around his wrist. Robby screamed and pulled back, but the vine only tightened.

Romie grabbed him around the waist, so he wouldn't be pulled forward into the shaft.

Lisa grabbed his arm. She pulled him towards the edge of the tunnel—towards the curtain of vines.

"What are you doing?" Romie yelled.

"Just another few inches," Lisa said.

Romie didn't fight, but Robby did. He struggled against the grip of the vine and against Lisa's pull. She won. She pulled Robby's wrist towards the left edge of the tunnel. When he saw the orange glow reflected off his skin and felt the gentle heat, he understood. The vines seemed to keep their distance from the lava, but Lisa was pushing his wrist right towards one of the flows that ran up the wall of the shaft.

His wrist got closer and he felt his skin tightening as it seared under the heat. The vine gave up and uncurled from his wrist. As soon as it let go, Lisa and Romie pulled Robby back to safety.

Tim and Brad had pulled a giant rock from the wall of the tunnel. The two men swung the rock and then launched it. It pulled a couple of weaker vines from the wall as it fell. There was a hollow thump from below. The rock must have hit the horse because it gave a low squeal after the thump. They heard a splash and then heard something thrashing in the water.

All five began to push more dirt down into the shaft. They were encouraged by the sound of a struggle below. The sandy pocket of dirt extended to the right of their shaft and a small avalanche began to tumble down as the sand lost its support. The group accelerated it by digging away even more of the dirt below it.

Romie liberated another big rock and it tumbled down. When this one hit, it made a cracking sound, like it had hit bone. They all pushed big handfuls and chunks of dirt over the edge, down into the hole. As the tunnel collapsed, it drove them back. Despite their efforts, they could see the vines rising. The taut vines were raising the horse from the depths.

Brad abandoned pushing the dirt and pulled his utility knife from his pocket. He leaned out and slashed at a vine. The vine was under tension, so when he cut it, it recoiled upwards and disappeared from view. He leaned out more and tried to cut another.

Tim was trying to get another rock loose from the wall. As he pulled away chunks of dirt, he weakened the arch of the tunnel. A clump fell from the ceiling and hit Brad's shoulder as he leaned. Brad tumbled. Lisa caught the back of his shoe, but it pulled right off. Robby caught him around the ankle as Brad's good arm flailed into the curtain of vines. One of the loose vines immediately curled around his arm and began to wind its way towards his neck.

Lisa plucked the utility knife from Brad's grip as Romie and Robby pulled him in. Lisa cut the vine, but the severed end only clamped tighter around Brad. He screamed. Another big piece of the ceiling fell, dusting everyone with loose sand as it tumbled down into the shaft.

Lava dripped from a newly exposed stream on the ceiling. Tim pulled Lisa away before the lava could fall on her.

Brad screamed with fresh pain as the severed vine tightened again.

"Get his arm in it," Romie shouted. They flipped Brad over and drove his arm towards the small pool of glowing liquid. More rocks tumbled from the ceiling. They sounded like distant explosions as they tumbled into the shaft and hit bottom. They touched the vine to the lava and it uncoiled quickly. Brad screamed once more as the thorns backed out of his flesh. Tim kicked the vine towards the hole.

The collapse of the ceiling gained momentum. Huge clumps of dirt and rocks were falling on their own. The group backed away, dragging Brad. Dust filled the air, making it difficult to even see the edge of their tunnel. The ground rumbled as the shaft began to collapse.

The group backed away slowly from the advancing dust.

Then, something different appeared from the end of the tunnel.

The vines began curling out from the cloud. They advanced along the floor, walls, and ceiling. The group turned to flee.

CHAPTER 44: TUNNEL

THE VINES MOVED FAST. The group had to move at a good pace to stay out of their reach. With Tim's foot, Lisa's leg, and the injuries suffered by Robby and Brad, only Romie was fully healthy. The ground rumbled again and the speed of the vines increased.

Cedric barked as they approached.

They split wide around the teenager-thing, still on the floor where they'd left it. In the dim glow of the lava, they saw Ty leaning against the curve of the wall. His head was slumped to the side and his eyes were closed. His good hand was on the dog's back.

Cedric wagged his tail when he spotted Tim, but he kept his position under Ty's hand.

"Is he?" Lisa began a question.

"Ty," Tim said. "Time to go. Vines are coming."

The giant man opened his eyes. He raised his hand and Cedric jumped up. Tim took Ty's hand and pulled the man to his feet. Ty's bad arm was wrapped in a sling that he'd made out of his shirt.

Romie ushered everyone forward, but Brad turned his head and then stopped.

"Keep moving," Romie said. "They're right around that turn."

"No," Brad said. "They've stopped."

Robby turned to see what he meant and then he stopped moving too. One by one, they all turned.

A woman emerged from the darkness. Behind her, the vines

had stopped advancing. They piled on themselves and formed a wall. Judy's face came into view as she walked. The vines resumed their approach, matching her speed.

Robby couldn't decide if she was moving like Judy or not. It looked like his friend approaching, but he knew that couldn't be true.

A hand grabbed the back of his collar and dragged him backwards. Robby's feet caught up and kept him upright. He backed away with the rest.

Judy kept coming forward as they descended on the spiraling tunnel.

They left her behind, moving faster than her. When they reached the spot where they'd seen the horse, the tunnel with Judy was nearly dark. Brighter lava illuminated the path behind them.

"Which way?" Lisa asked. "This way has the ledge, but at least we know which way to go."

"Yeah," Brad said. "This way."

They kept moving, retreating the way they had come in.

Robby moved as slow as he could. He wanted to see Judy again. He wanted to see which direction she would go. Romie wouldn't let him fall behind. She grabbed his seared wrist and clamped tight. She pulled him back with the rest of the group.

They kept backing until they reached the vertical shaft with the tight ledge. Part of the dirt ledge had collapsed when they'd used it earlier. Ty pressed his back to the earthen wall and took a big step across the gap. He moved carefully around the shaft until he reached the other side. Lisa went next.

Romie and Robby stood side by side and watched the vines. Judy stopped several paces away. The vines built a new wall behind her.

"Why aren't they coming after us?" Romie whispered he question to Robby.

"I think the other tunnel to the surface has collapsed. She's wants to get aboveground as much as we do," Robby said.

It was Robby's turn to go. Lisa stretched out her hand on the other side, beckoning him to traverse the ledge. Romie pushed him towards the shaft.

"I'm going," Robby said.

As Romie backed up, Judy finally began to advance again.

"We have to stop it, right?" Romie asked.

"Yes," Robby said. "But we'll figure it out when we get out of here. We just need to stop her from getting to the egg."

"I can stop it right now. I'll throw it into the column of lava, like the horse," Romie said.

"No!" Lisa shouted. "Romie, you come with us."

"I can do it," Romie said. She was on the other side of the shaft and was backing towards the edge. As she backed up, they saw Judy and the vines advancing. Romie flexed her knees and looked like she was getting ready to pounce.

"No, Romie," Brad said.

"No," Lisa said again.

"Come with us," Robby said. "We'll figure out a way."

Romie judged the distance to Judy and then glanced back at the vertical shaft and the column of lava that ran up the middle. Judy stopped, just beyond Romie's reach. Romie swiped at her with one arm and Judy didn't move. The vines swirled behind Judy and sent a couple of tendrils out beyond Judy. They seemed ready for the next attack.

Romie gave up and darted for the ledge. She made the first few steps just on momentum, but then her foot slipped and she lost the edge. She swung her arms towards Lisa, and they caught hands. Tim and Robby helped steady Lisa and they dragged the two women to safety.

As the group backed farther away from her, the vines swept forward and lifted Judy. They transported her over the shaft and then gently set her down on the other side. Robby glanced over his shoulder and saw the daylight at the end of their tunnel.

Tim picked up his pace and ran ahead with the dog.

As Robby got closer, he saw that Tim was tugging on the end of a firehose, testing his weight against it. Tim sent Cedric up the slope and the dog bunched his legs up and began a bounding climb.

"Come on," Tim said, waving Lisa forward.

Tim held the end of the firehose steady while Lisa found the right angle to climb. She walked up the slope and used her arms to assist with her traction. Romie went up close behind her.

"You'll have to go last," Tim said to Ty. "You can wrap the hose around your good arm and we'll pull from up top."

"I can make it," Ty said. "Just don't follow too close." He looped the hose around his arm and slid his grip up the hose in between steps. Even with one arm, he climbed steadily.

Robby stayed deepest in the tunnel. He watched as Judy came to within a few paces and then stopped again. The vines filled the passage behind her. Robby glanced up. The stream of lava that lit up the tunnel looked like it was cooling. It gave off less light. Judy's vines reached the ceiling, but still maintained a margin around the lava.

"Come on, Robby," Brad said.

✪ ✪ ✪ ✪ ✪

Robby held the end of the firehose. Brad and Tim were climbing slowly. Robby couldn't tell if they were moving carefully because of the danger, or if they were exhausted from the constant panic. Robby listened to Brad panting as he climbed.

Judy held her ground. Her eyes stared forward. Robby looked for the orange glow that he'd seen in the eyes of the others. There was just a twinkle.

"Judy?" Robby asked. He glanced back over this shoulder to make sure that Brad didn't hear him. "Judy? Can you hear me?"

A jolt of electricity ran through Robby when her eyes locked on his.

"I keep thinking, but I can't figure out a way to save you, Judy," Robby said. "Even if we let you go to the egg, the thing will swallow you. I'm not even sure you're still really Judy."

She blinked several times. He knew it must be a trick of the light, but it seemed like the orange glow in her eyes faded.

"Robby!" a voice called from above.

Robby glanced back. Tim and Brad had climbed almost all the way up. The hose shook in his hand.

"Tie yourself on. We'll haul you up," a voice called. It was a man's voice. He supposed it could be that guy, Jackson.

"Judy?" Robby asked.

She blinked.

Robby waited another second and then began to climb. He kept his head turned as much as he could, so he could watch her. He wanted to know if the vines were coming after him. When he had just passed the rounded bend of the shaft, and he could no longer see Judy, he heard the voice.

"Robby?" she asked.

"Judy?" Robby called. He stopped climbing and tried to focus everything on sounds from the tunnel. He heard the distant chatter of leaves from the moving vines.

"Robby you have to get up here right now," a voice called from above. He looked up. Brad and Tim were over the top edge. He saw Ty's back at the lip of the hole. He was doing something with his good hand behind his back.

"Robby?"

Robby couldn't tell if it was her or not.

He let the firehose slip between his hands and slid back down to the floor of the tunnel. The vines stopped. They were gathered all around Judy, almost enclosing her.

"Judy?"

Her lips were parted and her eyes were on him, but she didn't speak. He began to think that her voice had been some sort of elaborate trick. The thing didn't want to kill him, but it wanted to break his spirit for some reason. It was working.

"Robby," she said.

"Judy!" Robby exclaimed with a relieved smile. He took a step forward. "Hold still. We'll get you out of there."

"No, Robby, don't!" she yelled. Her body was perfectly still. "It's in me, Robby. I can feel it."

"We'll figure a way to get it out," Robby said. He took another step forward. He was only two paces from her when he paused. Tendrils of vines, his mom would have called them suckers, came out towards him, like he was a magnet and they were threads of steel wool.

"You can't get it out. It's in the empty space between my atoms.

I can't describe it, but I can feel it," she said. The corners of her mouth were turned down into a frown and it looked like she would cry. She didn't take her eyes from his. Robby wanted to reach out, but the vines were slowly closing the gap. He fought to keep his arms at his sides.

"There has to be something we can do," Robby said.

"Just say goodbye," Judy said. "And get out of here. I can't hold them back any longer. I don't want to."

"Judy, no," Robby said. "I'll go with you. I've seen the inside of the ball. It's not so bad."

"No, Robby. Finish what you started," Judy said. A tear escaped the corner of her eye.

Her eyes slowly closed. As her eyelids slipped down, the vines picked up speed. They were halfway to Robby, then only a foot away. They were like a thousand green fingers, reaching forward around Judy's still body.

They had two types of leaves. The bigger leaves almost looked like grape leaves. Smaller, oval leaves ran down each stem. As they moved, the little oval leaves undulated in little waves, almost like it was that motion that propelled the things through the air.

Robby turned and ran.

✪ ✪ ✪ ✪ ✪

He heard the vines clattering behind him. Robby grabbed the firehose and turned his face up towards the sky. He pumped his legs at the loose dirt of the slope and pulled on the firehose. He could heard the things right behind him. Robby knew that any second one would loop around his neck or close around his ankle.

His foot slipped and he fell. With his hands clamped around the firehose, he crashed into the dirt slope. He scrambled, trying to get his feet back underneath him and felt the hose pull through his grip. Robby tightened his fingers as the friction from the hose began burn his skin.

Robby found his feet again and the hose jerked upwards, nearly toppling him again. He looped his arm around the hose and held it tight as he ran to keep pace.

As he got higher, he saw what Ty was doing with his hand. Behind his back, Ty was motioning for Robby to stop, or go back. Robby glanced over his shoulder. He was barely staying ahead of the vines. Robby crested the lip of the hole and saw the rest of his group. The snow was falling harder. It dusted everything except the lava.

A handful of Beardos encircled them. They held guns. These were serious guns, not the odd collection of rifles and shotguns like at the farm. These guns gleamed with military deadliness.

"They're coming," Robby said, panting. "He pointed over his shoulder."

One Beardo motioned to the rest and the circle closed in. Robby found himself herded together with Tim, Brad, Romie, Lisa, and Ty. Cedric was over with Jackson and Amy Lynne, near the ambulance. Another small set of Beardos guarded them.

Hampton appeared from the back of the group as Robby was directed away from the mouth of the hole. Hampton stood just a few inches from the lip. Robby watched as the fresh vines appeared from underground. Their green vitality stood in stark contrast to the brown, snow-dusted vines on the asphalt.

Judy rose from the ground with her face pointing up towards the falling snow. She was lifted on a thick bed of vines. The vines tilted her up until she was vertical again.

Hampton held his ground and laughed. The vines turned Judy around and began to move away from Hampton. The man laughed harder.

"Stop her!" Robby shouted. "There's still time. All you have to do is stop her, and you can end this now."

Hampton wore a big smile as he turned towards Robby. "We let it fertilize, and then kill it before it gestates. That's the plan."

Robby shook his head and took a step forward. One of the Beardos stopped him with the barrel of a rifle. "No. Just do it now. What do you have to lose?"

"*This* is the plan, Robby," Hampton said. "We're going to blow the damn thing up. People smarter than all of us put together came up with this plan."

Robby turned to the Beardo who was closest to him—the one

who was currently jamming the barrel of a gun in his chest. "Why are you listening to him? Can't you tell he has lost it? Look at him." Robby pointed and gestured at Hampton.

The Beardo kept his composure and didn't look.

"Did you ever think that maybe he's the one who is helping this thing?" Robby asked.

One of the other Beardos glanced over towards Hampton.

"Do you even know what happened to Luke? You think Judy was responsible for that, or was it more likely Hampton?" Robby asked. Another of the Beardos took a look at Hampton as the man laughed again. There was more than a hint of madness in his laughter. "Who took over when Luke disappeared? Have you guys ever seen the original orders? Are you certain that Hampton hasn't been making all this up?"

The man with his gun pointed at Robby held his concentration on the boy. He didn't react at all to Robby's accusations until Hampton laughed again. The sound was a crazy cackle. The Beardo turned his head to look over his shoulder.

Robby slapped the barrel of the gun away from his chest and pushed the man. The Beardo's gun swung up towards the sky as he fell over backwards.

✪ ✪ ✪ ✪ ✪

"Stop!" another Beardo yelled as Robby ran. He turned his gun towards the boy. That's when Ty lashed out with his good arm. The giant man grunted with pain as he drove his fist into the side of the weapon. The gun discharged, sending a spray of bullets off to the side.

Suddenly, their guards were backing away and crouching into defensive postures.

Robby ran through the falling snow and darted around Hampton. He heard the gunshots behind him and kept his body low.

The others scattered, dividing the attention of the guards. One of the Beardos yelled for them to stop and fired his weapon into the air, but they kept moving. The Beardo whom Robby had knocked down rolled to his belly and trained his weapon on the boy. He squeezed off a shot and then his view of Robby was blocked by Hampton.

Robby ran parallel to the river of vines that were transporting Judy's body. He sprinted faster to beat the vines to the corner of the building. Once they reached there, they could cut him off. Robby crunched through the withered brown carpet of vines and swung around the corner just in time. He looked back to see the fresh vines sweep Judy along.

He saw the depression up ahead and the reflection of the light on the windows of a neighboring house. There was a park area behind the school. Robby ran towards drop-off that led down into the park.

He saw the people and horses first. They were arranged in circles. At their center, blocked by Robby's hand, the ball of light sparkled. The people seemed entranced by the ball of light. They were pinned to the ground by vines that looked no more healthy than the ones Robby was running across. The vines didn't need to hold these people anymore. The hypnotic power of the light was enough to hold them.

Robby knew what was supposed to happen next. He had seen it in his vision. The gamete—in the form of Judy—would move into the light to complete the fertilization. The remaining animals—the people and horses in the circles—would become the initial investment of energy. After that, the thing would need to grow as the snow deepened around it. Hampton was waiting for that time, when the thing would be vulnerable, so he could destroy it. In Hampton's plan, all the people surrounding the thing would be absorbed. There were at least a hundred of them.

Robby stopped.

He scanned the area. Amongst the ensnared people, he saw that a number of them were men with beards. They looked softer than the Beardos who carried guns. These were the volunteers who had joined up with the Luke's posse after coming to the group. Robby saw that most of the volunteer Beardos still wore black backpacks. He took a couple of steps closer to the nearest.

The vines holding the man were still alive. They rattled under

Robby's feet as he got closer to the man. Robby saw wires poking out from the flap of the pack. He started to put it together. Hampton wouldn't have known exactly where the egg would land, but he would need a way to deliver explosives to the location. What better way than to sabotage the biomass the entity needed?

Robby turned away from the park. He saw it, over the top of a neighboring building. The second-story window of the metal building Hampton had been in earlier. Hampton's men would watch from there and then trigger their bombers when the time was right.

Robby looked at the closest man again. The bomb wouldn't do Robby any good. It might not even have a way to detonate it except for the remote control, and Robby wouldn't be able to figure it out if it did.

He saw a knife in a sheath strapped to the man's belt.

Robby stepped across the writhing vines and reached down. He unsnapped the strap and pulled the knife from the sheath. The man's face twitched, but he didn't take his eyes from the light. Robby saw the reflection of the white ball sparkling in the man's eyes.

Vines made weak attempts to grab his feet and ankles. They didn't have any power. Only the vines holding the people in place seemed to have any vitality. And, of course, the ones transporting Judy. Robby looked back to her. She was making steady progress and still headed on a collision course with the light.

He ran to intercept her.

✪ ✪ ✪ ✪ ✪

Her eyes were still mostly closed and the vines hovered her feet about an inch off the ground. They floated her forward, supporting her on a thousand delicate little fingers. Judy's mouth was a flat line. Robby lifted the knife in one hand and pressed his other palm flat against the back of the shaft. He lifted it to shoulder-height.

"I'm sorry, Judy," he said.

He swung the knife before he could talk himself out of it.

His blade moved towards her and the vines carried her

towards it. Robby closed his eyes when the knife hit her. He expected stiff resistance, but dumb luck carried the blade right between her ribs and deep into her chest. Her mouth flew open as she gasped in a startled breath. Robby squeezed his eyes shut tighter. He didn't want to know if she opened her own eyes in her final moments.

He heard the vines begin to clatter around them.

He felt them pressing her body into his hands.

Robby finally opened his eyes, stumbled backwards, and pulled the knife with him. The blood—Judy's precious blood—was spilled down her shirt in sloppy splotches. Her body had stopped advancing, but the vines had not. They were above him and on all sides. Robby moved away, backing towards the light.

The vines didn't seem to care that Judy's body was convulsing. Her muscles were contracting as they ran out of oxygenated blood. He swiped at the nearest vines with the bloody knife. The ends he cut fell to the ground and Judy's deep-red blood splattered on the leaves. Still, the vines continued to move.

She had said, "It's in the empty space between my atoms."

Doubt crept into Robby's brain. He had assumed that the gamete needed a living host to transport it. What if it only needed flesh? If the gamete was still viable, he had only seconds to figure out how to prevent it from reaching the ball of light.

Robby ran back to Judy's lifeless form and slashed at the vines that supported her. With every little tendril he severed, two more grew from the thicket behind her. A couple made half-hearted attempts to grab at him, but he cut them away. They seemed more focused on moving Judy than attacking him.

Robby kept swinging the knife. He didn't hold hope that he was having an effect, but he couldn't think of what else to do. He cut away all the vines that were supporting her arm and shoulder. The vines simply bolstered their grip on her other side and turned her slightly to deny him access to the real support. Robby's hand strayed too far into the leaves with his next slash. The thorns tore at the back of his hand and his arm. He pulled his arm away, but with deep scratches and blood welling up from the wounds.

He heard a thrashing noise behind him. Robby turned and saw

a horse. It was in one of the outer circles and it was flopping on its side, trying to free itself from the vines. Robby saw much more subtle movement amongst some of the humans trapped in the vines. One woman was wriggling her arm. A man was trying to bend his leg.

Robby turned back to Judy and then down to the brown vines at his feet.

He saw the whole thing as a balanced equation. In order to add vines here, they had to subtract them from over there.

He slashed and tried to formulate a solution. He was only able to cut so many vines. Given their current pace at moving Judy towards the light, he wasn't going to be able to do enough.

✪ ✪ ✪ ✪ ✪

"Wake up!" he yelled over his shoulder. "You have to struggle. You can get free if you try."

He heard more thrashing, but glanced back and saw it was the same horse. The animal was foamed with sweat, trying to get to its feet.

Robby saw other movement, back towards the alley. Ty was impossible to miss. His shirt, tied into a sling, was a diagonal stripe across his naked torso. Two people were at his sides—Romie and Tim had also escaped the Beardos. Snow swirled and fell around them.

"Help me!" Robby yelled. "Find something to cut these vines."

They ran towards him.

Tim arrived first. He had a utility knife and he used it on the thicker trunks a few feet back from the leading edge of the vines. Ty had a big piece of metal. He swung it in savage arcs, beating back the vines and grunting with each blow. He twisted his whole body and kept his bad arm tight to his chest. Robby focused on cutting the vines that were supporting Judy. Soon, Romie appeared at his side. She had a knife like the one he'd stolen.

Robby sucked in a breath when Romie was ensnared. A clump of vines grabbed her arm and then her leg as she stepped forward to try to free herself. Robby moved to help her.

Brad appeared at his other side. He beat the vines with a length of pipe.

They were still backing up as they cut. The vines continued to make progress. Fear rose in Robby's throat as he realized that the bed of vines they were treading across was wriggling under his feet. That meant they were getting closer to the light. He looked to his side and saw that they'd crossed the outer circle of ensnared people.

Hope returned as he realized that one of the ensnared people was attempting to stand. It was an older woman. She had climbed to her knees and was picking thorny vines from her shoulder. She seemed unaware of everyone else, but Robby was encouraged that the vines had lost their grip on her.

Someone else was working next to Ty. Robby realized it was one of the Beardos. He sliced the vines with a long blade. Judy's body began to rise as the vines lifted her away from the ground. Robby noticed that he could see his shadow against the green leaves. They were being backed right towards the light.

"Wake up!" Robby yelled again to the people around him. Some people were moving, but others were still entranced by the light. At the sound of his yell, a horse screamed. It grunted and screamed again as it found its feet. It sprinted from the circle, trailing streamers of dead vines.

As Judy's feet rose, Robby moved under her body, trying to cut the vines supporting her. He ducked, and barely missed being sliced in two by the long blade of a Beardo.

More people had joined the cutting. Robby saw a couple more Beardos. Back along the river of vines, Robby saw someone dumping gasoline from a red can. They lit the gas and a big patch of vines burst into orange flame. Black smoke began to curl up through the falling snow.

A man screamed and Robby saw a man lifted from the ground by a thick group of vines. The cables looped around his waist and squeezed. The man's body was bent over backwards as he writhed in pain. People moved to the base of the vines and hacked at its support.

Judy's feet dipped several inches as the vines redistributed their effort. Robby and the people around him redoubled their effort.

The vines began to consolidate into one thick trunk, supporting Judy's body.

Robby moved in closer to attack the base. A few other people had the same idea, but there was only so much room to move. Judy's blood dripped down and stained the leaves and blowing snow.

Robby heard a yell from his right. He looked down to see Romie on the ground. She had her hands clamped to the side of her head. Blood seeped between her fingers and began to run down her wrist.

Ty, Brad, and one burly Beardo were all concentrating their efforts on one side of the trunk. They timed their blows and were making good progress at chopping through. The trunk was like a tree. The vines were almost braided together, and began to twist every time they were hit. They turned the strongest vines to the outside of the trunk and pulled the severed ones inside.

Robby looked up. In his peripheral vision, he saw the ball of light. It had swelled to several times the size from when he'd first arrived. It looked like it was growing towards Judy's body as the vines lifted her to meet it. The vines raised her higher as the people hacked at the column. Her feet were now out of Robby's reach. Another person was snatched by the river of vines. Someone else escaped.

Between the timed swings of the three men, Robby jumped and grabbed at the trunk. The vines were thick and didn't have as many leaves or thorns. Still, it was like grabbing a double-handful of glass. Robby pulled and reached for a higher grip. He kicked his legs for momentum and Ty gave one of his feet and giant shove. With the push, Robby swung his legs up around the thick trunk. He clawed and climbed, ignoring the pain from the vines shredding his skin.

Robby climbed higher. The vines sagged under his added weight. He got his foot lodged in between two twisted vines and used the footing to propel himself upwards. He grabbed Judy's body around her waist and pushed himself free. All his weight pulled down on her, and the vines struggled to compensate. His face was pressed to her. The smell of her blood filled his senses, and Robby squeezed his eyes shut.

He felt the tug from below and his spine was stretched as hands pulled at his feet. He gripped his hand around his other wrist and struggled to hang on. One of his shoes pulled off and he jerked back up until the hands returned to grab his foot. He heard a triumphant yell and the stretching abated for a second. Robby adjusted his grip just in time. Even more hands grabbed at him and pulled him down. Soon they were grabbing as high as his knees.

Robby opened his eyes again to discover that he was almost back to the ground. People were pulling Judy's body from the vines and slicing them as they stretched to hold her. Robby released her and helped with the cutting. He pulled the severed ends from her neck. The skin tented as he removed the thorns.

Nearby, a young woman stood, staring at the light. Robby saw Romie approach the woman. Romie still had one hand clamped to the side of her head, but the bleeding looked under control. Romie turned the woman away from the light until she regained her senses.

Brad and Tim were carrying Judy's body away from vines. Lisa appeared and ran up to lift Judy's feet so they wouldn't drag on the ground. Ty led the group still working on the vines.

They hacked back another part of the trunk and another cheer rose amongst the people. Robby saw more than a dozen people working on the vines now. Several still had scraps of brown vines clinging to their flesh. They must have been liberated from the circles. Others were still trapped, staring up at the light, but their numbers were decreasing every second. People seemed to snap out of their hypnosis and some turned to help their neighbors.

One of the military-looking Beardos shouted instructions to the people around him.

"Get all the guys with backpacks!" he yelled. "We have to get them out of here."

Robby ran to that man.

"There are bombs in the packs, right?" Robby asked him.

The Beardo was dragging one of the men with a pack away from the circle. The man with the pack was still in a trance. His mouth hung open and he stared at the light.

"Yeah, but don't try to take them off. They'll explode if you try to take off the pack."

Robby nodded. He found the nearest man with a pack and ran towards him. He was already struggling to free himself, so Robby just helped. He cut at the vines. As soon as his legs were free, the man tried to run.

"Wait!" Robby shouted. "You can't take off the pack."

Either the man didn't hear him, or he was too frightened to listen. He tore the last vine from his arm as he turned and ran. He sprinted up the hill and across the snow-covered vines. Robby started after him until the man began to approach the corner of a building. He was about thirty yards away when the man slipped his arm through one of the straps of the pack. Robby ducked just as the man rounded the corner and exploded.

CHAPTER 45: TOWN

THE EXPLOSION SHOOK THE ground and tore through the corner of the building. Chunks of brick flew every direction. Robby got his arm up in time to shield his face and turned away from the shower of debris. The explosion killed his hearing. As it came back, Robby heard the chaos breaking out. People screamed and ran. The Beardos who had joined the fight against the vines were now spreading through the circles of ensnared people, trying to secure everyone with a backpack.

Robby saw Tim, Brad, and Lisa, dragging Judy's body away from the light.

A new thought occurred to him, and he ran for them.

"Faster!" Robby shouted at them. It was all he had time to get out. He saw a red cloud blossom from Brad's knee. A fraction of a second later, Robby heard the distant pop of the rifle's report.

Brad cried out and dropped Judy's shoulder. He collapsed in a heap, holding his leg.

Lisa turned with a frustrated look that turned to horror as she saw the fresh blood staining the snow. She put down Judy's legs and crouched to help Brad.

Robby was at full speed as Tim realized that he was the only one still carrying Judy's corpse. Tim turned and began to set Judy down.

"No!" Robby yelled. "Run!"

Lisa saw him coming and flinched away. Robby jumped over

her as another bullet ricocheted off the pavement next to Lisa. Tim and Lisa realized what was happening at the same time.

Robby grabbed Judy's body by her arm. Tim turned in the same direction and they ran, dragging Judy's body along with them.

Tim ducked as another bullet tore through his pant leg.

Robby looked in the direction of Hampton's temporary metal building. He saw the flash as the sniper shot again. He and Tim reached the cover of the auto repair shop. Tim kept pulling.

"We're okay," Robby said. "The sniper is over there." He pointed towards the corner that blocked the view of the sniper's location.

Tim nodded. He was panting with the exertion.

They looked back to Lisa and Brad. She was trying to get his hands away from his leg so she could help to stop the bleeding.

"Ty!" Tim shouted. He turned to Robby. "Ty can help him."

"We have to get her body out of here," Robby said. "They'll be coming for her."

Tim looked down at Judy's body and then back up to Robby.

He cupped his hands around his mouth and shouted again. "Ty!"

Ty was still hacking at the vines with one arm. He led a small group that was intent on cutting apart all the vines that were still green. They were making good progress. The living vines were pulling back from the edge of the circle, retreating back the way they had come.

Ty heard Tim shout and he began to stride in their direction. Tim waved his arms and pointed to Brad. Ty approached Brad and Lisa and then slowed when he saw Brad's injury. His eyes went to the rooflines of the buildings.

"Hey!" Ty shouted at Lisa and Brad. He got their attention and got them moving towards the hillside. The place where the ground dropped away from the street would give them cover.

Tim, satisfied that Ty was helping Brad, turned back to Robby.

"Where are we taking her?" he asked.

A phalanx of armed Beardos appeared around the back corner of the auto repair shop. They pointed their weapons at Robby and

Tim. Hampton strode from their midst and spoke low orders as he passed. A dozen Beardos walked off towards the light. Three stayed with Hampton.

"Shoot them if they move," Hampton said to one man.

The other two Beardos shouldered their weapons and came forward. The man with the weapon gestured with his gun for Robby and Tim to step aside. They complied, raising their arms as they moved.

"Don't do it," Robby said. "Don't fertilize it and you wont have to kill these people."

"Does it look like it's going away?" Hampton asked. He waved an arm towards the ball of light. Robby didn't look at it. He didn't have to look to know that it was getting bigger. He could tell by his own shadow. His shadow was both more defined, and smaller. "Soon enough, that thing is going to be so big that you won't be able to hide from it. Once we fertilize it, we can blow it up and put an end to it."

The two Beardos began to drag Judy back towards the light.

"What good will that do?" Robby asked. "If you kill everyone in the process, who are you saving the Earth for?"

"We're defeating that thing," Hampton said. He pointed one arm up at the ball of light. "The rest will work itself out."

Robby saw some of the other Beardos rounding up anyone who was trying to free the men with backpacks. It was confusing. The Beardos with guns were still with Hampton. Another set had turned and were trying to save people. The third group—the volunteers—had been enlisted to sacrifice themselves with the explosive backpacks.

When the two men had dragged Judy away, Hampton gave another order to the man guarding Tim and Robby. "Take them over to the circle and you can secure them there. Point them at the light. If either one of them says a word, just shoot them both."

Hampton walked off, following the men who dragged Judy's body.

Robby and Tim were quiet as the Beardo marched them through the snow towards the light. They kept their eyes down. Robby walked right by the bloody patch where Brad had been shot in the leg. He glanced up to see Ty still working on the wound. Lisa was running away, back towards where the ambulance was parked on the other side of the buildings. Robby hoped that she would find the right supplies to help Ty save Brad's life. Robby wanted to go help, but he didn't have a choice in the matter.

"Eyes front," their guard ordered.

Despite the command, Robby stole a glance back towards where the men were dragging Judy's body. What he saw made him stop in his tracks.

Armed with knives, machetes, and other improvised weapons, a group of people stood in a line between Hampton and the ball of light. Chunks of vine still hung from some of their weapons. They had turned their attention from beating back the vines, to stopping the men who intended to drag Judy into the ball of light.

"Keep moving," Robby's guard said.

Robby walked again, but slowly. He kept his eyes on the line of people. The whole scene looked like it was happening in a snow globe. The flakes were falling even faster now, and they decreased the visibility even more with each passing second.

The men dragging Judy's corpse set her down and raised their guns. Around the circle, Robby saw little skirmishes of Beardos fighting Beardos. It was difficult to tell who was who. Some were trying to help the men with backpacks, and others were trying to keep them in place. Most of the armed Beardos seemed to be on Hampton's side. Nobody was shooting yet.

That seemed about to change.

Hampton gave an order and one of his Beardos put his gun to his shoulder and pointed it at a young woman. Robby's stomach flopped when he saw that Romie was standing right next to the woman. There was no warning before the shot rang out. Robby stopped again. His blood ran cold.

The young woman spun as the bullet crashed into her shoulder. She fell backwards and a man behind her tried to catch her. Both fell down.

Romie and the man on the other side of the gap came together. They filled the space the young woman had occupied. Romie lifted her chin, either in defiance, or in expectation of the next bullet.

The shooter tensed, ready to fire again.

Robby was about to scream. He was about to yell at the people to disperse. He knew that Hampton wouldn't hesitate to shoot them all if that's what it took. The man was intent on carrying out his orders, no matter who got in the way, or whatever the cost in human life. Before the sound left his mouth, Robby realized it didn't matter. No matter if they held their ground and were shot, or if they let the Beardos carry the gamete to the egg, they would all die.

Robby turned to the man who held a gun on him and Tim.

The man had been watching the drama as well. When Robby turned, he raised his gun.

"Keep moving," he said again.

The man's beard wasn't thick. His hair was stringy and uncombed. Robby wondered how old he was. His tired eyes made him seem pretty mature.

"You can shoot me here, or you can realize what's at stake. Can't you see what's happening here? A lot of other people who used to believe in your mission have already converted. Do you really want to be on the wrong side of this?" Robby asked.

The man's eyes darted over to where Hampton and his two guards were facing down the line of people. Another shot rang out and the man winced. Robby didn't. He kept his eyes locked on the Beardo who was pointing a gun at his face.

"In the past twelve months, we lost nearly everyone," Robby said. "That man wants to blow up everyone left."

"Put the gun down," Tim said.

Robby caught sight of Lisa. She was running back, carrying a big white box that looked like a cooler.

Another shot rang out from one of Hampton's guards.

"Romie!" Lisa shouted.

Robby turned. Romie was on the ground. He ran to her.

The battle ended with little blood, and Robby missed most of it. He ran by the guards as they were lowering their weapons. Robby found Romie curled up on the ground. Her breath had already melted a patch of snow.

"He wasn't even pointing at me," she said.

Robby pulled her hands away from her side and lifted her shirt. A thin line of blood pulsed from a triangular hole there. He slapped his hand against the wound to contain the bleeding. He felt on her back to see if he could locate an exit wound.

"You're going to be okay," Robby said.

Hampton was screaming. Robby wasn't listening. He was leaning in close to hear what Romie was trying to tell him.

"He was on his knees," Romie said. "There was no reason to shoot him. He just wouldn't get back up when they told him to."

Robby glanced in the direction she was looking. A cluster of people blocked his view of the injured man. Over in the circle, he saw two Beardos fighting over a third. They were both careful with the entranced man. They knew what would happen if his backpack should accidentally fall off.

When the guards turned on Hampton, they forced him to the ground. That seemed to take the fight out of the other armed Beardos. Without their leader, they were no longer willing to point weapons at their peers.

"It's not bleeding too badly," Robby said. "Press your hand here and I'll see if I can find something to use as a stretcher."

"I can stand up," Romie said.

"Are you sure? I don't think that's a good idea."

"When I pass out, you can go find your stretcher."

Romie stood up with some help. People were moving away from the light. One of the Beardos had set down his gun and was working to disable the backpack of one of the bombers. He finished his work and moved on to the next backpack. Robby directed Romie towards where Lisa and Ty were still working on Brad.

"How is he," Robby asked.

Brad had his eyes closed and he looked pale.

"The bleeding is under control. The bullet didn't hit any major blood vessels, but he's going to take a long time to heal."

Romie began to sway. Robby caught her and helped her to the ground. Robby showed Ty the injury. The big man worked his fingers delicately as he examined her.

"Let's get her back to the ambulance. She's got something in there."

"Is it okay?" Lisa asked. She looked up towards the circle. "Is the fight over?"

"Almost," Robby said. "Take care of Romie and Brad and I'll stay here."

✪ ✪ ✪ ✪ ✪

The snow was still falling as Robby struggled to get Judy up over his shoulder. It was difficult for him to lift her up and get his balance. Once he did, walking forward was just a matter of keeping his momentum. His feet shuffled through the dead vines and snow. He walked between buildings, carrying her body away from the light.

His hands and feet were cold. He was dressed for summer, and only the exertion was keeping him warm. He left the sounds of the people behind him. Some were diffusing the backpack bombs, and some people were simply fleeing. Here and there, people were reconnecting and helping each other with the injuries left behind by the vines. Robby exited quietly, with Judy on his shoulder.

He passed by a convenience store that sat in a repurposed old house. He walked by a coffee shop with a big hole in its front window.

Robby saw a storefront called Village Hardware. He turned and crossed through the tiny parking lot. He lowered himself down to his knees before slipping Judy's body from his shoulder. He sat her up against the side of the building and arranged her so she wouldn't fall over.

Her eyes were closed. Robby brushed a wisp of hair from her eyes and turned away. He looked for a rock to use on the glass of the store's door.

✪ ✪ ✪ ✪ ✪

When Robby emerged from the hardware store, he wore a new sweatshirt that read, “Belgrade Raspberry Festival.” It had a smiling raspberry beneath the sweeping words. He had a set of gardening gloves, and he struggled to get a blue wheelbarrow through the little door. Robby pulled the wheelbarrow up next to Judy and set a shovel aside.

He kept apologizing to her as he loaded her body in. It was more difficult than he had imagined. He almost dumped her out a couple of times. Once she was in, he wheeled her out to the sidewalk. Robby walked right past a park and pushed Judy’s body uphill until he found a neighborhood. The snow was a few inches deep, but when he turned his face up towards the sky, it looked like maybe it was tapering off.

He rolled Judy across the lawn of a house with a big front porch and kept going until he reached the back. There was a swing set in the middle of the yard. Robby headed for that.

A walnut tree had branches that hung low to the ground. The snow was piled on the leaves, but hadn’t reached the lawn underneath. Robby took the shovel and stabbed at the grass. There was a skin of frozen dirt on top, but under that it was still soft enough to dig through. Robby began to make progress.

He lost track of time as he dug.

The hole was long enough, and he stood about waist-deep in the ground. Roots from the tree stuck through the edges of his hole, but it was good enough. He looked at Judy’s body. Her legs were hanging over the sides of the wheelbarrow and her head was tilted back like she was looking up at the canopy of the walnut tree. The blood on her shirt had dried to a dark brown stain. Robby glanced at the house and headed that direction.

He wrapped her body in a sheet and used it to lower Judy’s body into the ground. Before he threw the first clump of dirt down, he sat to remember his friend.

It was the smell of her cigarette that had drawn Robby. He'd seen the footprints headed up the sidewalk, but at first he'd kept moving. People could be trouble. But with the cigarette smoke, he had remembered his grandmother, and that had drawn him to investigate.

The footprints continued up the sidewalk of the bridge. The railing on the left held back the growing drop down to the river. On the other side, a concrete barrier separated the sidewalk from the roadbed. There wasn't much snow here—just enough to see the outline of small sneakers.

Robby glanced up and saw the woman. She was standing at the railing, but not leaning against it. Her arms were crossed and her attention was focused on the horizon. In the distance, the ocean met the clouds. Both the water and the sky seemed to dissolve into the same gray color.

"Hi," Robby said.

She looked over. Her head turned quickly, but she looked more annoyed than startled.

Electricity shot through Robby's body as she leaned forward and looked over the railing. He didn't like heights. He stopped and put a hand down on the concrete barrier, to steady himself.

She fumbled inside her coat and her hand came out with a pack of cigarettes. She flung them over the edge and then leaned forward again to watch them tumble down towards the water.

"I quit," she said.

"That's good," Robby said. "Those things are deadly."

The comment seemed to catch her by surprise, and then she smiled. They both laughed for a second at the absurdity of the thought. With all the threats that seemed to be lurking, any type of cancer was a distant concern.

"Are you okay?" Robby asked.

She grabbed the railing with both hands and pulled herself back and forth. It almost looked like she was trying to get momentum for a jump. She finally released the railing with an expulsion of air that turned into a sigh.

"Yeah," she said. "I'm fine."

She backed up until she reached the concrete barrier and she sat down on it.

"My name is Rob," he said.

"Rob," she repeated. She turned down the corners of her mouth as she said it. "You don't look like a Rob. What's your name, really?"

"Robby," he said. He looked down and blushed.

"I'll call you Rob if you want," she said. "My name is Judy."

When Robby looked back up, she had a cigarette in the corner of her mouth and a different pack was disappearing inside her jacket. She lit it and then held it delicately between her fingers.

"I thought you quit."

"A dozen times a day."

They didn't speak for a few minutes. Judy puffed and Robby moved closer before sitting on the wall too. They looked out towards the place where the clouds met the ocean.

"I'm not like this," Judy said. "I have my own apartment, and a job. I'm a legitimate adult."

"Okay."

"I don't live there anymore." She laughed at herself and then threw away the cigarette. "I haven't been back since Thanksgiving. I guess I'm homeless. Where do you live?"

Robby was very careful about his living arrangements. He never approached the building from the same direction, and he left footprints and tire tracks all over the neighborhood, to throw off anyone who might try to track him through the snow. Robby had rigged up a security system and slept with a bureau pushed against the door to his bedroom. A rope ladder sat next to the window, in case he had to escape into the night.

Still, he didn't hesitate when she asked the question. "A little house over near the marsh. I've got it fixed up. I have power, and water, and hot showers. You want to see?"

"Yeah," Judy said. She stood up.

Robby stood too. He brushed the snow off the back of his pants and started walking down the sidewalk. It only took a couple of steps for him to realize that he was the only one walking. He turned back around.

Judy was gripping the railing again and leaning out over the drop.

"You coming?" Robby asked.

She looked at him for a second. She really seemed to study him, like there was something important to be learned just by looking.

"Sure," she said. Judy pushed herself back and began to walk towards Robby. "You have a guest room in this house?"

"There's a master bedroom I'm not using. You can have that."

"Can I smoke there?"

"Out on the back bench, sure."

Robby began to cover Judy with dirt.

CHAPTER 46: CLINIC

ROBBY WALKED BACK TOWARDS the school. The snow had tapered down to light flurries. He pulled up the hood on his sweatshirt and stuffed his hands into the pouch. When he looked over the buildings, he still saw the flickering glow of the light back there somewhere. He turned and took another route back. He put a block between himself and the site of the battle.

In the alley, he found the remnants of the vines. Under a thin blanket of snow, they looked wilted and impotent. He walked over them and found the hole that he'd gone into. The firehose was still draped over the edge. It was black down there. The stream of lava on the edge of the hole had gone cold. Its ripples were hardened into black rock.

He followed footprints until he found the tire tracks of the ambulance. They led down to the street and took a turn. Robby followed them on foot.

It wasn't too much of a walk, but it was far enough that Robby lost track of time.

The snow stopped somewhere along the way. He glanced up and saw the ambulance parked outside of a long building with a flat roof. Robby walked towards it and saw the dog, Cedric, run forward. The dog stopped a few paces from Robby, and then came forward with his tail low and wagging. Robby patted him on the head and then entered.

They had wheeled the beds into the lobby and shoved all the

chairs to one side. Robby saw two people hooked up to plastic IV bags that hung from metal stands. To one side of the room, he spotted Tim and Ty working on a person. They wore masks and blue gloves. Robby stood several paces away, in deference to their work. Ty was impossible to mistake because of his size. Robby recognized Tim mostly because of the way that Cedric ran to his side and pressed against him.

"Outside, Cedric," Tim said. He glanced up and saw Robby. He gave him a nod.

Robby looked around the room. Facing away from him, one of the people hooked up to an IV was Brad.

The man stirred as Robby took his hand. His eyes opened about halfway.

"Hey, Robby," he said. "Is she okay?"

Robby took a second to figure out who he was talking about. He glanced over his shoulder. "I'll find out." He patted Brad's hand and then moved on. He checked the other beds. A woman came out of a side room with a pink tub. Her eyes scanned up and down Robby. He looked down and noticed the blood on his own pants. It wasn't his own.

"Are you okay?" she asked.

"Yeah, I'm fine. Have you seen a woman named Romie? She had a wound on her side. Maybe shrapnel?"

"They're working on her now," the woman said.

Robby followed her glance over towards Ty and Tim. He rushed back over to them.

"Is that Romie? Is she going to be okay?"

Ty looked up. Robby saw the sweat on his forehead and the mask puffing in and out as he breathed.

"We got the shrapnel out of her kidney and stitched it up as good as I know how," Ty said. She needs time to heal. Robby barely heard the words. He only caught the sentiment, and all the hedging that was implied.

He approached around the back of Tim and found Romie's hand under the sheet. She was out. He wondered if they'd given her something to sleep.

"We've got food!" someone shouted from the other side of the lobby. Robby turned and saw Jackson pushing Amy Lynne in a wheelchair. Piled on her lap were bags of snacks, liberated from some machine. Ty put a gloved finger up to his mask to quiet them down.

Amy Lynne giggled.

"What do you think?" Robby asked. "What are her odds?" He looked down and saw the stitching. What had been a small triangular hole had been excavated and then closed back up. Romie now had a line of puckered skin running down her side.

"Give her a few hours," Ty said. He turned to Tim. "Ask Hannah to get some fluids into her, would you?"

Tim nodded.

✪ ✪ ✪ ✪ ✪

By the time the sun started to go down, it was noticeably warmer outside. Robby shed his sweatshirt and stood out in the parking lot. He was looking in the direction of the school. Some patches of snow had melted. Robby's eyes were towards the sky. He was looking for any glow from the ball of light. The sun was still too high for him to tell.

Robby glanced behind him. Tim and Ty were sitting on the floor with the dog between them. Robby set off again.

He walked back to the school along the main road and came up to the front of the buildings. Both the main building and the smaller one to the side were covered with dead vines. Robby walked between them and then back towards the athletic fields out back. He paused at the gate to the little stadium and looked over the destruction. The tents were toppled, and the fences were torn from their supports. Even the bleachers had been ripped down on one side.

Robby followed the dead vines that led in a river over towards the lawn.

He slowed as he approached, keeping a dumpster between himself and the view of the ball. He moved to the side until he could just see the corona of the ball. It was much smaller than it had been—smaller and closer to the ground. It pulsed. The light it gave off made the shadow of the dumpster swell and fade.

Robby saw a man walking along the hill. The man looked in the direction of the light and then continued on his way. After seeing that, Robby decided to take a chance.

He came around the side of the dumpster and looked at the thing.

It was maybe the size of a car, and it hovered over a brown patch of vines that wilted down into a hole. The snow was mostly melted. A couple of people milled around the site. The light was still bright, but Robby found he could look at it without hurting his eyes. As he watched, a couple of brown spots moved over the surface. They looked like the spots on an overripe banana.

Robby walked forward and caught one of the men.

"Where did everyone go?" Robby asked.

"Most of them went back that way. They're headed back to the farm. I'm waiting to see if my friend Denise comes back out. You haven't seen her, have you? She's about this tall and has short, curly hair?"

Robby shook his head.

"A couple of people went in the thing, and someone said they saw Denise go in."

"Go into the light?" Robby asked.

"Yes. They just walked right in. That's when it was still pretty big though. Hours ago, when you couldn't look at it. I guess she's not coming back. If you see her, tell her I went back to the farm. I heard they're going to send a car back for the rest of us."

"Okay," Robby said.

The man headed back around the side of the school, where the parking lot was.

Robby stared at the ball of light for several minutes. He sat down on the bank in a spot where the dead vines had been cleared away. The light appeared to shrink, even as he watched it. He considered going in. It might not be too late. Inside, he might see some of the people he had lost, or maybe even his family.

He heard a horn honk and saw the remaining people headed towards the side of the school—their pickup point.

Robby sat. The sun was going down. He looked back at the ball again. It was obviously smaller. He made up his mind to do it. He would go into the light and look for his mom and dad.

"Robby! Oh, thank heavens."

Robby turned and saw Lisa approaching. She put a hand on his shoulder and lowered herself to the ground next to him.

"I didn't see where you went and then I heard that you had gone off alone. Are you okay?"

"I'm fine. I had to bury Judy," he said. He felt the emotion welling up in his throat and he willed it back down. He didn't want his grief to come here, in front of Lisa and the ball of light. He wanted to save it for later, when he was alone and could honor the grief.

"Oh," Lisa said. "I'm sorry."

Robby looked around. "I don't even know what happened. It seemed like Hampton had control. I didn't see the rest."

"He's gone," Lisa said. "They took him off on one of the first trucks. Everyone was so angry and I think they were directing that anger at him. I'd be surprised if he's still alive."

"But what made them turn. Why did his guards turn on him?"

"It was that man next to Romie. He got down on his knees. They said he recited some quote. I wasn't close enough to hear what he said, but I saw the shot. Hampton made one of the guards shoot the man in the head. That's when they turned. They say the guards just turned on him and told him that they wouldn't murder for him anymore."

"Who was the guy?"

"I don't know. I saw him around at the farm, but I didn't know his name. I think he knew Judy."

Robby nodded. Lisa was staring at the light.

"Do you think it's going away again?"

"Yeah," Robby said.

"Will it just come back again in a couple of months or whatever? I mean, we thought it was gone before."

"What would you do differently?" Robby asked.

Lisa didn't answer. She narrowed her eyes and tried to figure out what he meant.

"If it's coming back, would you change your plans?"

"I don't know. I'd like to be prepared."

"There's no way to prepare," Robby said. "But if it makes you feel better, I'm certain that it's not coming back. Not for thousands of years."

Lisa sat for another minute and then began to make her way to her feet.

"I'm going back over to the clinic to see if they need help. I couldn't stand to sit around there while they worked on Romie. She'll be fine. She'll be fine," Lisa said.

Robby glanced after her as she left, but he stayed in his spot, watching the ball of light as it grew dim. A warm breeze took away the chill of the melting snow. Robby stayed there until it grew dark and the world became very quiet.

Robby saw a couple of other people standing vigil. The rest had wandered away. The back of Robby's pants were wet from the melted snow, but he didn't move. He sat and watched as the ball of light shrank to the size of a baseball. It hovered only a few inches above the ground and was no brighter than the rising moon.

Robby heard a small pop when the thing finally disappeared.

CHAPTER 47: FARM

WITHIN A COUPLE OF days, Romie was the last patient in the little clinic.

Robby and Lisa stayed there with her. Ty came back a few times a day to check on her progress. When he was satisfied that she was safe to move, he had Tim drive the ambulance back over.

"I don't know why we can't just go out on our own. We could find a house and Robby could set it up for us," Romie said.

Lisa guided her up from the bed and helped her to the wheelchair. Robby stood to the side.

"We will," Lisa said. "There's no rush. We're going to stay at the house for a while, just to make sure everything is okay. Brad's there. When you're both ready, we'll decide what to do."

"What about Pete?" Romie asked.

Lisa stopped and looked at Robby. Romie had asked that same question several times after her surgery. She'd been on a lot of pills then, and had asked a lot of strange questions. The one about Pete came up the most, and was always the most difficult to answer.

"What about him?" Lisa asked her.

"I mean what about his body? Is someone going to bury him? Isn't he still down there somewhere?" Romie asked.

"Oh," Lisa said.

Robby answered. "Some of the Beardos are going to demolish the tunnels. They're waiting on everyone to clear the area first. They've got explosives."

"Oh," Romie said. "Good. Did you say a few words?"

"I did," Lisa said. "You were still out, but before Brad left we had a remembrance. After everything is demolished, they're talking about having a ceremony back here with everyone. A lot of people lost someone."

Romie nodded and looked satisfied with the response.

Robby sat in the front seat of the ambulance. Cedric sat at his feet. He'd heard stories about the farm, but he wasn't prepared for what he saw. As they turned down the long driveway, everything looked pretty normal. The white fence still swept up between green pastures. He even saw one or two rescued horses grazing in the field. They bolted at the sound of the ambulance and grouped over near the far fence.

The house still stood, but the skyline behind the main building had changed. The big barn was gone, as well as several of the other outbuildings. In one of the side paddocks, a big tent had been set up.

Tim saw the direction Robby was looking. "They pulled that tent from the football field. Apparently, a lot of people want to sleep in one big space now," Tim said.

They pulled up next to the house and Robby got a look at the area where the barns used to be. There was still a big pit carved out of the earth, but a backhoe and a plow truck were working to push dirt into the hole.

"Did they find anything of the underground base?" Robby asked.

"Not a trace," Tim said. "But I heard someone say they spotted some scrap metal on the roof of a house a couple miles away. I'll find it as soon as I can get up in the air. It should be easy to spot the path of the tornadoes from up there."

When Tim shut off the ambulance, Lisa began to get Romie ready to move. They had a bedroom set up for her in the house. Robby jumped out and held the door for Cedric.

Ty came out through the front door wearing a fresh set of surgical scrubs. His broken arm was secured with a tight cast and strapped to his torso. He examined Romie quickly and then gave instructions to Tim and Lisa on how best to move her into the house. Robby wandered through the dooryard, towards the sounds of construction.

It was a beautiful day, and the air was filled with noise. Everywhere Robby looked, people were working. From the pit, the engine of the plow truck either roared, or the little alarm rang to alert everyone that it was backing up. Near where one of the barns had stood, a generator rumbled. There was a steady rhythm of power saws and thumping hammers. A small group was building new housing for the remaining horses.

Robby walked towards the big tent.

All the flaps were open to allow a breeze, but it was warm inside. One end of the tent was set up with beds. The other end was the kitchen. Robby walked through the tent and found the garden on the other side. Robby was amazed to see that some of the plants had survived the tornadoes and the snow. They were interspersed with the new plants.

He stood at the edge of the garden and watched as dedicated hands worked the soil. A girl, younger than Robby, was moving between the plants and picking weeds. Robby knelt in the grass beside the rows and started picking weeds too.

CHAPTER 48: AIR

"RIGHT THERE," ROBBY SAID.

He shifted in his seat and directed the vent towards his face. It was hot in the little cabin. They'd been flying for a while.

Tim brought the plane lower and turned to do another pass.

"That's where Lane Cottage used to be, and Mr. Dyer's place was right there," Robby said, pointing. Tim glanced, but Robby figured it was just to be polite. He'd taken a few people up to go survey their old homes. People always came back depressed. It didn't seem to stop the next person from asking to go up.

Most of the roads had survived on the island. The runoff of melting snow had cut through a few chunks of pavement. Robby guessed that a tornado had taken out the houses on his road. On the hill, his old school still stood. The airplane spooked a couple of deer and they ran between houses towards the woods. Robby looked back at Cedric. The dog was sitting in the back seat of the plane and wearing headphones over his ears. With his panting mouth open and his tongue hanging to the side, the dog looked like he was smiling. Robby smiled back at him.

After a couple more passes, Tim's voice came over Robby's headphones.

"Seen enough?"

"Yeah," Robby said. "I guess. Can we go back over the land?"

"I've got to stick to the coast. There aren't many good landmarks left in Maine. It's all just mud and weeds."

Robby nodded.

The erosion from the melting snow had taken out most of Maine. North of Portland, almost everything was gone. Some of the people from the farm were putting together a big map of the region. A lot of Maine was simply shaded yellow to indicate that it was impassible.

Tim steered the plane towards land. He flew south and west, following the coast. Robby got a good view out his window of the land. Between the tornadoes and the floods, the land had been stripped. There was a carpet of green vegetation on the fertile soil, but little else to look at. Robby felt himself drifting off in the warm cabin. The drone of the engine was almost hypnotic.

He woke when Tim banked the plane to line up his approach. Robby watched carefully until he started to feel queasy. Sweat popped out on his brow and he wished they were back on the ground. He'd made it the whole trip without being sick. The last thing he wanted to do was throw up right as they landed.

Everything was fine once they were back on the ground. Robby's stomach settled immediately, although he felt weary and dehydrated.

"Do you mind if I head back without you?" Robby asked.

Tim had come in a car, and Robby on a motorcycle.

"No, you go ahead," Tim said. "I'm going to refuel."

"Thanks for the ride."

"Any time." Tim smiled.

Robby suspected that Tim would have gone up anyway. He seemed to always find an excuse to go up in the airplane.

Robby threw his leg over the motorcycle and decided to try kick-starting it. Jackson could do it every time, but Robby's success rate was dismal. He usually resorted to the electric start after the lever bit him in the calf. This time, he managed the trick on the third try.

CHAPTER 49: FARM

ROBBY PULLED HIS MOTORCYCLE up next to the van and shut it off.

"I thought we had one more day?" he asked Lisa. She was standing in the doorway and lifting a bag up onto the top of the van.

"Tell it to the boss," Lisa said. She turned and smiled.

Robby saw Brad coming down the steps. He had a cane in one hand and a bag in the other. Robby ran to help him.

"I can manage," Brad said.

"Nonsense," Robby said. He took the bag and walked alongside Brad. The man's limp was better, but he was still terrible on stairs. He still didn't have much strength in his leg. "You're okay leaving today?"

"Why not?" Brad asked.

"I just thought we'd have another day to say goodbye," Robby said.

Brad stopped.

"Do you want to stay here, Robby?"

Robby shook his head immediately. "No."

"We wouldn't blame you if you did. As soon as we get settled, we'll come back and tell you exactly where we are. You could come visit any time."

"No," Robby said. He shook his head again. "I want to go too. I want to do some more exploration, and a lot of people around here..."

"They're superstitious," Brad said, finishing Robby's thought. "I've noticed."

Robby nodded in agreement.

The screen door of the house banged open and they heard Romie's voice.

"I'll do it. Leave me alone," she said.

"Let's go," Brad said quietly to Robby. "Don't get in her way."

Robby smiled and ran ahead with Brad's bag. After grabbing his own things, he made a quick tour of the farm to say his final goodbyes. Word had already spread that they were leaving early. Nan—the woman who ran the garden—gave Robby a box of vegetables they'd saved for him. Wesley, who worked with Bethany, baking in the kitchen's brick oven, gave him a loaf of bread. Robby waited by the end of the driveway, hoping that Tim would get back before they left.

The van rolled up behind him. He heard the brakes whine as it came to a stop.

"Time to go," Lisa said. She was leaning out of her window.

"I wanted to say goodbye to Tim and Cedric," Robby said. He saw Brad's look through the windshield. He knew what Brad was thinking. Robby quickly reversed his position. "It's okay. I said goodbye earlier."

Robby walked to the rear door.

CHAPTER 50: CONNECTICUT

THEY TRAVELED SOUTH AND then turned east before they encountered too many buildings. Sometimes, they would travel halfway through a town and need to turn back. At some point in the past, tornadoes had ripped through, leaving the roads impassible.

Their trip only lasted a few days, but it was enough to break some of their old paranoia. They drove during the day and slept in hotels at night. Each room was already equipped with clean sheets and a minibar. The rooms were ideal.

Romie and Lisa split the driving. Brad's leg ached too much if he didn't keep it elevated.

They didn't intend to go far, but once they started, they wanted to head for the coast. Romie was driving when they crossed under 95 and found themselves in a town called Gladstone. The center of town was almost quaint. All the big box stores were on the other side of the highway. Just east of the public beach, the coast rose up in a rock wall and a gated road led to the fancy houses. Lisa picked a place and Robby ratified the decision. The house was big and had solar panels, a generator, and a rock garden built to disguise the access to the drilled well.

Robby had the generator going and the water running before they finished unpacking the van.

The four spent the early fall preparing for winter. They collected food and fuel. Before long, the house was an efficient machine, but they couldn't stop preparing. They filled the extra rooms with cans and boxes and spent many evenings discussing potential disasters and how they would react.

Romie's injury needed only time to finish healing. Brad's leg took a lot of effort. He split wood, ran, lifted weights, and practiced yoga. Still, as the mornings grew colder, Brad walked with a limp until he managed to stretch through the pain.

Lisa became the explorer of the group. She visited the neighboring houses, and spent long afternoons investigating local buildings. She formed a clear picture of the people who used to live in Gladstone, and talked about her findings at the dinner table like she was disclosing the latest gossip.

Some nights, they fired up the generator or tapped the batteries, so they could watch a movie. It became difficult to find things to watch. It was interesting to see movies with big populations moving through vibrant cities, but it was also depressing. Life didn't look like those movies anymore.

The leaves were starting to turn color when Robby made his announcement.

"I'm going to go back to the farm tomorrow," he said.

The sound of utensils scraping on plates continued, but the conversation stopped. Brad and Romie exchanged a glance and then looked back to their food.

"Do you want us to go with you?" Lisa asked.

"I'm not opposed to it," Robby said. "But I understand that I'm the only one who wants to go."

Everyone took a second to think about what he had said. They ate in the kitchen because it had big windows looking out towards the ocean, and they could see the moon rising over the water.

"We'll go if you want," Lisa said.

"I'm fine on my own," Robby said.

"Why do you want to go?" Brad asked.

"I don't know. I guess I want to make sure that everything is still okay there. I want to check on it one more time before winter."

CHAPTER 51: NEW YORK

IT DIDN'T TAKE ROBBY as long to get back. They'd marked their map on the way to the coast, so he didn't have to explore for good roads. He stayed one night in a hotel, with the couch pushed up against the door while he slept.

The hills leading to the farm were beautiful. The leaves flashed orange and gold in the soft light. Fall was on a faster schedule this far north, and Robby loved the crisp air. It was something they never got much of on his island. It felt like a rare treat.

Robby parked his motorcycle on the other side of the washout and walked up the drive. The horses had eaten the pasture down to a fine fuzz of tan and green. They walked along the fence, tracking his progress, but shied back when he tried to pet them.

There were no sounds from the hill as he walked up. Robby had a terrible premonition that he would find everyone gone—mysteriously vanished, like before. Or, worse, he'd find their corpses littered around the yard with their eyes popped out.

He glanced back towards the road, wishing for his motorcycle. Robby pressed on.

Robby sighed with relief when he saw the people working in the garden. The operation had expanded. There were corn stalks growing in one of the pastures, and the arched poles of a greenhouse where one of the barns had sat. The gash left by the tornadoes had been filled and replaced with fresh grass. The new barn wasn't pretty compared to the old one, but it looked solid.

Robby walked up to the garden.

"Robby?" a woman asked. She stood up from her weeding. She wore a bandana over the lower part of her face. Robby didn't recognize her voice. "It's Elizabeth," she said, anticipating his confusion.

"Hi," Robby said.

She came forward and extended a gloved hand. Robby shook it and then wiped the dirt off on the back of his jeans. She kept her bandana up. Robby noticed that the other gardeners had their mouths covered as well.

"When did you get back?"

"Just now."

"I heard the motorcycle, but I figured it was Jax. He's always zipping around on that thing. Are you guys back in town? Someone was just asking about you. I think it was Frank."

Robby noticed that some of the other people had stood from their work to listen to the conversation, but none approached very close. They kept their distance—a semicircle of masked gardeners.

Elizabeth followed his eyes and Robby saw her eyes smile.

"Forgive us," she said. "We've all become a little germ-phobic."

"Oh?"

"Something spread through here, and a bunch of people got sick. Some said it was the food, but Ty said it was a virus. I forget what he called it. Everyone split up after that. There were just too many people living in one tent. Now, everyone lives alone or in pairs. We're all spread out everywhere now." She swept her arms around to illustrate her point. "We just come back here to keep up the garden." She laughed. "This is the only place people exchange information. Here, and at the clinic."

Robby nodded. He forced himself to not take a step back. He suddenly wondered if the bandana was for her protection, or for his. Another part of his brain spoke up and he wondered if maybe the bandana was hiding some terrible symptom of the virus she talked about.

"You should go see Ty," she said. "He's at the clinic. He's got a vaccination that he swears will work on anyone who's not sick yet."

"Yeah, okay."

"I'd give you some veggies to take, but they might not be safe for you. Better safe than sorry, right?"

"Yeah," Robby said. He gave a laugh, but he couldn't make it sound real.

"You know where the clinic is?" she asked. "In town?"

"Sure," Robby said. He wasn't sure, but he had the urge to go back to his motorcycle. In one of the panniers attached to either side of the seat, he had a bottle of disinfectant. He wanted to soak his hands in it. "I'll go see him."

"Good to see you," she said. She waved and he saw the smile in her eyes again.

Robby waved to everyone and left.

✪ ✪ ✪ ✪ ✪

Ty didn't wear a mask. Neither did Tim.

Robby found them outside the little clinic in lawn chairs. They were sipping drinks and basking in the autumn sun when Robby rolled up.

"You need to wear a helmet," Ty said.

When Robby swung his leg over the motorcycle, Cedric ran up to him with his tail wagging. Robby knelt and pet the dog for a minute before he approached. He found a third chair and pulled it up next to Tim's.

"There's a virus?" Robby asked.

Tim laughed. Ty shook his head.

"It's nothing," Ty said. His voice rumbled low in his chest when he spoke. Robby couldn't tell if he sounded tired, or angry. "We had a little influenza run through the group. Everyone panicked."

"Did you know that guy everyone called Truck?" Tim asked.

Robby shook his head.

"Older guy," Tim said. "Killed himself."

"Oh," Robby said. He shook his head.

"He was depressed. It just caught up with him," Ty said.

"Everyone said it was the sickness that killed him. Even people who saw the body would swear that the sickness took him. Next thing you know, everyone ran for the hills," Tim said. "Ty even gave them all a vaccine, but it didn't help."

"People still got sick?" Robby asked.

"No," Ty said. "They still panicked."

"They all spread out. It's not such a bad thing, I guess," Tim said.

"I suspect they'll come back together over time," Ty said.

Robby thought about his own little group, down in Connecticut. There were only four of them, but sometimes they all seemed to find different corners of the town to disappear to. If it wasn't for their dinners together, they might not see each other at all for a whole day. After each trauma, their bonds were weaker. They were slightly less inclined to rely on each other, knowing how easily they could lose a close friend.

"Where did you guys end up, anyway?" Tim asked. "I've looked for you from the air, but it's a big world."

"I brought you this," Robby said. He took out a folded map from his back pocket and handed it to Tim. It showed the location of their house. He'd also marked the nearest airport. "We left a car there with the keys in it. It's a five-minute drive to our house."

Tim nodded and traced his finger over the map.

"Why do you think that people will come back together?" Robby asked Ty.

"Kids," Ty said. "Families will bring people together. You remember how they used to say, 'It takes a village to raise a child'? The corollary to that expression is that a child will bring together a village. People bond over offspring."

Robby shook his head. "We can't have kids. One reason we were all spared is because we're all sterile for one reason or another."

Ty laughed. "I've heard other people say that too. You know what else I heard? This isn't the first time the humans have nearly been wiped out. Well, guess what?"

"What?" Robby asked.

"We came back from those times, and we'll come back from this."

Robby furrowed his brow as he tried to think of logic that could fit Ty's optimism.

Ty turned to Tim and nodded. Tim smiled back and pushed up from his chair. He didn't say a word, but went through the door to the inside of the clinic.

Robby started to ask what they were up to, but Ty held up a hand, beckoning him to wait. Robby heard Cedric's tail thump against the concrete porch as the door swung open again. Tim held a tiny amber puppy to his chest.

Cedric pulled his ears back and approached with his tail wagging furiously. He sniffed at the little puppy.

"You want to hold him?" Tim asked. He held out the puppy. The little pup looked up at Robby and then closed his eyes. He fell asleep against Robby's chest.

"They're almost weaned," Tim said.

"Where did he come from?" Robby asked.

Ty laughed. "Didn't they teach you anything in school?"

"No, I mean, where's the mother?"

"She's inside. Nursing is tiring. She's taking a nap," Tim said. "I was flying over Massachusetts when I saw a guy out walking a dog. I couldn't land fast enough. I thought Cedric would lose his mind as soon as I shut off the engine. He was so happy to see another dog, it looked like his tail would wag right off. I started talking to Matthew, and it turned out he was a veterinarian. The dog wasn't even his, it was one of his patients. She was a champion show dog who turned out to be infertile. Just by dumb luck, they both survived and they were just living out in the wilds of western Mass."

"But she was infertile?"

"She was," Ty said. "She's not anymore."

Tim laughed and continued the story. "Well... She's fertile with some help from the doctor. Turns out Cedric here has a very low sperm count. But, with Dr. Matthew's magic process, he managed to knock little Wickett up."

"Wickett?" Robby asked.

"The mom," Ty said.

"They're staying here now," Tim said. "He's up at the farm, looking at the horses. We're going to breed another litter next year."

Robby was already thinking about the implications. "So he thinks..."

"He's willing to try it on people, but we'll let nature take its course for a while before we try. It could be that people won't need any help," Ty said. "The body can change based on environmental pressure. You never know what will spark fertility. It could be that some of us were only infertile because we lacked the right environment to be fertile."

Robby chewed his lip. He looked down at the little puppy and smiled.

"You can't take him on a motorcycle," Ty said. "You're going to have to find a car."

"What?" Robby asked. He looked between Ty and Tim. They were both smiling.

"One of the pups is promised to me, and I'm offering him to you," Ty said. "He'll be weaned in a few days, but I'm not letting you ride him around on the back of a motorcycle."

"Are you serious?" Robby asked. "Thank you so much. I can't believe it! Can I take him back to Connecticut?"

"Can you promise me something in return?" Ty asked.

"Anything," Robby said.

"Try to find us another dog, but be careful," Ty said. "There have to be more. Somebody must have a dog around there somewhere. Stay safe, but see if you can find us another dog."

Robby nodded.

"I'll try," Robby said.

"Come on," Tim said. "Let's get him back to his brothers and sisters. You'll have to stay here for a few days until they're weaned."

"And you'll have to learn how to give him the shots he'll need when he's older," Ty said.

The puppy opened his eyes again when Robby stood up. His eyes were dark and concerned when he first looked at Robby, but then his tiny mouth opened into a panting smile. Robby smiled back and scratched his head.

"Do you have a name picked out?" Ty asked.

Robby didn't hesitate. "My dad's middle name was Gordon. I'll call him Gordie."

Ike Hamill
Topsham, Maine
June, 2014

ABOUT *INSTINCT*

THANK YOU for reading *Instinct*. I hope you enjoyed the story as much as I did when I was writing it. Many people have expressed that they really felt a connection with Robby and Brad, and they wanted to know more about their fate. I hope this book gave you a clear picture of where they stand. Their world is in transition, but our friends have found a home.

I think I mentioned the inspiration for these characters at the end of *Extinct*, but here's a quick summary if you're interested. I wanted to write a book about a person isolated in a snow storm, and I wanted to write about kid who's both charismatic and Sherlock Holmes smart. When I combined those two ideas, these books popped out. This book was fun because I got to share more of my ideas about the strange phenomenon we encountered in *Extinct*, and some of those unexplained things finally had some light shed on them.

This is the second sequel I've written (*Blood Ghost* followed *Hunting Tree*), and I find the process very different than writing a new book. There were lots of personalities and relationships that I needed to reacquaint myself with. Characters who grew in *Extinct* continued their journey. Some new characters gave me a fresh perspective on their world. As always, I had a pretty clear idea where everyone would begin, but no idea at all where they would end up.

Please let me know what you think of this book. I'm happy to answer any questions, comments, and complaints, at ikehamill@gmail.com, or Facebook, or Twitter. As always, I'll be thrilled if you leave a review on Amazon, and even more excited if you recommend this book to a friend. Both *Extinct* and *Instinct* are available in both paperback and eBook, and both formats are easy to share.

Read on for blurbs about my other books, and sign up for my mailing list on ikehamill.com if you want to receive a note when I release a new title. I'm in the habit of sending new subscribers my next book for free. So, please, leave a review, tell a friend, and let me know. Check back soon and I'll have another book for you. I'm very excited about the coming titles.

-Ike Hamill

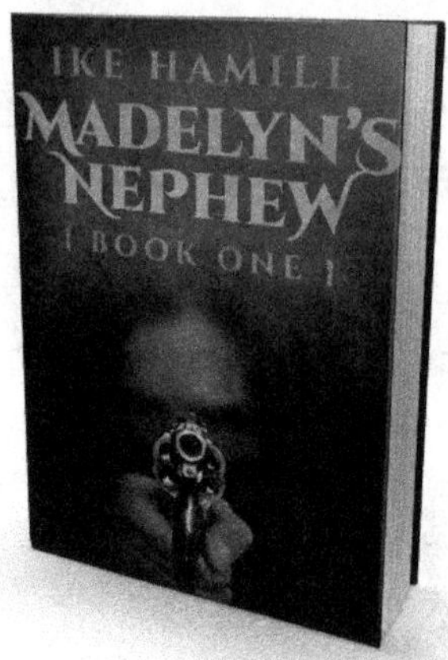

Madelyn's Nephew

After the sun turned, Madelyn fled north to escape the riots and the encroaching glaciers. As long as the world was ending, she wanted to live her final days in the one place she had always been happy—her grandmother's cabin. She survived the Roamers, the scavengers, and the wildlife, but she can't escape her fear of dying alone.

She left behind this note:
"Gather my bones, if you find them. If a bear hasn't dragged them off, or a wolf cracked them for my marrow. My skull goes on the wall with the others. Any other remains can be planted near Sacrifice Rock. That's where my grandfather is buried, and where I dug up the skull of my beloved grandmother.
Her sweet eyes were still wise and kind, even when I only imagined them from their hollow sockets. She taught us so many things—how to hunt, trap, and fish. She should have taught me how to live alone. I never learned the trick of scaring away the ghosts. They won't shut up and leave me in peace. I guess it's time to join them."

—Madelyn

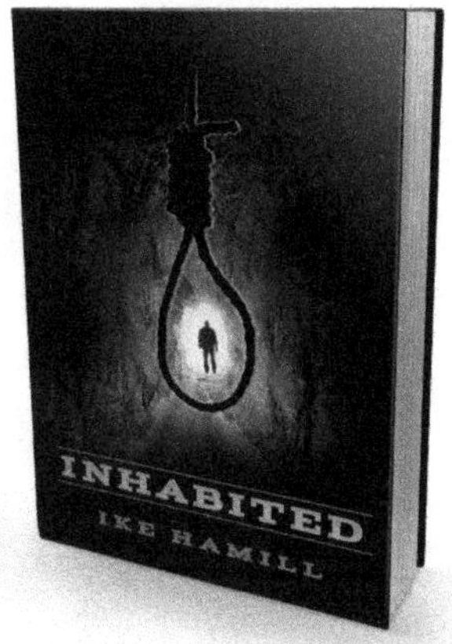

Inhabited

They were looking for an adventure—a night of harmless fun. Miguel has a map. Kristin's friend has the equipment. The mine leads to the cave, and the cave is where they'll find their fortune.

But down in the darkness, something waits.

It needs them.

The caves hold a secret. They're Inhabited.

The Claiming

It wasn't her fault.

It wasn't Lizzy's fault that she saw the cloaked people out in the yard. It wasn't her fault that she was drawn by the moonlight to watch them as they advanced on the house. And it definitely wasn't her fault when people began to die. Lizzy didn't want the strange dreams where she saw how they were killed. Even her sister was starting to suspect her.

It wasn't fair because it wasn't her fault.

Lizzy was claimed.

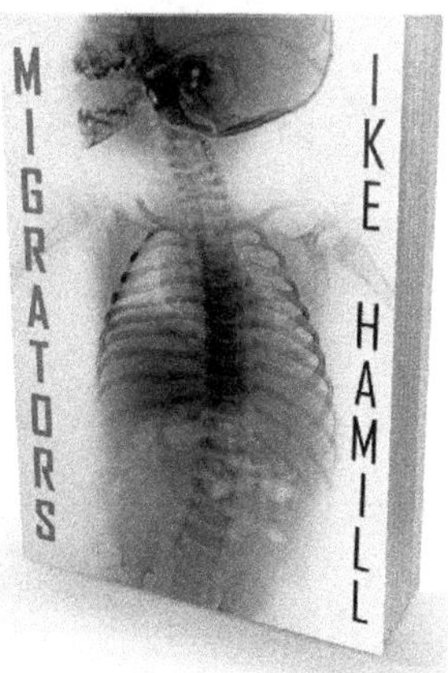

Migrators

Do not speak of them. Your words leave a scent. They will come. Somewhere in the middle of Maine, one of the world's darkest secrets has been called to the surface. Alan and Liz just wanted a better life for themselves and their son. They decided to move to the country to rescue the home of Liz's grandfather, so it would stay in the family. Now, they find themselves directly in the path of a dangerous ritual. No one can help them. Nothing can stop the danger they face. To save themselves and their home, they have to learn the secrets of the MIGRATORS.

CPSIA information can be obtained
at www.ICGtesting.com
Printed in the USA
BVHW041803040421
604172BV00024B/488

9 780692 283837